Praise for **THE D**

"*The Dark Corner* is one of the most riveting and beautifully written novels that I have ever read. Trouble drives the story, as it does in all great fiction, but grace, that feeling of mercy that all men hunger for, is the ultimate subject, and that's just part of the reason that Mark Powell is one of America's most brilliant writers."

> —Donald Ray Pollock,
> author of *The Devil All the Time* and *Knockemstiff*

"Mark Powell's third novel powerfully tackles the ongoing curses of drugs, real estate development, veterans' plights, and other regional cultural banes that plague an Appalachia still very much alive and with us as its own chameleon-like animal. Brimming with fury and beauty, *The Dark Corner* is a thing wrought to be feared and admired."

> —Casey Clabough, author of *Confederado*

"Powell's work is so clearly sourced to the wellspring of all spiritual understanding—this physical world. . . . He is heir to the literary lineage of Melville, Conrad, Flannery O'Connor, Denis Johnson, and Robert Stone."

> —Pete Duval, author of *Rear View*

THE DARK CORNER

A NOVEL

MARK POWELL

THE UNIVERSITY OF TENNESSEE PRESS / KNOXVILLE

The paper in this book meets the requirements of American National Standards Institute / National Information Standards Organization specification Z39.48-1992 (Permanence of Paper). It contains 30 percent post-consumer waste and is certified by the Forest Stewardship Council.

Library of Congress Cataloging-in-Publication Data

Powell, Mark, 1976–
The dark corner: a novel / Mark Powell. — 1st ed.
        p. cm.
ISBN 978-1-57233-918-7 (pbk.) — ISBN 1-57233-918-7 (pbk.)
   1. Mountain life—Fiction.
   2. Environmentalism—Fiction.
   3. Right-wing extremists—Fiction.
   4. Drug abuse—Fiction.
   5. North Carolina—Fiction.
   6. South Carolina—Fiction.
   I. Title.

PS3616.O88D37 2012
813'.6—dc23

2012017305

FOR RON RASH

Most people fear God, & at bottom dislike Him . . . because they rather distrust His heart, & fancy Him all brain like a watch.

—Herman Melville, in a letter to Nathaniel Hawthorne

The parish elders approached him on a Friday in early December, just as he knew they eventually would. Malcolm Walker had woken early that day, climbed from bed, and left the parsonage, spreading salt like birdseed, the sun barely over the treetops and the roads sheeted in ice. Tuesday's snow was still banked along the glittered sidewalks, and when they were properly salted he walked to his office and opened a bottle of white wine, a good Riesling he'd been holding onto since the spring. He drank from a coffee mug and a little after nine stepped into the bathroom, locked the door, and vomited over a shattered urinal cake, the flat cylinder the color of frosting. When he got back to his office the child was waiting for him. Malcolm was not surprised. The child, like the wine, had appeared in the spring, and his presence had been easily understood: here is the incarnation of your failure; here is the consequence of your apathy. Malcolm opened a second bottle, a jug this time, a cheap red pulled from the shelves of the Stop-N-Shop in Lenox. In his pocket he carried a small folded print of Grunewald's *Crucifixion* but did not take it out, not yet. A little after ten, the elders arrived.

He had known, of course, that they would come for him—he had considered even the composition of the group that would confront him—and knew what he would do in response. The only surprise was the suddenness of their arrival. Mr. Darton, Mr. Smiley, and Dr. Zukav let into the church by the widow Delalic, the dour and disapproving Lithuanian who had kept the parish books for thirty years. They entered solemnly, arrayed before his desk and conveying a respect, he realized, that was merited neither by his age nor his actions.

Then he realized it was not so much respect as propriety, the very thing he had violated—sought to violate—in the preceding months.

His church was constructed from slate, a gabled roof and dormers, a two-hundred-year-old fortress folded among the walls of fieldstone that snake through the Berkshires. The men were equities traders and retired diplomats; the women did Pilates and talked of their kids at Williams or Middlebury. Which is to say there were expectations involved, rules of decorum, sumptuary practices he had failed to engage. And now was the reckoning. Mr. Smiley spoke first—kindly, Malcolm thought—of a vacation, three weeks at a clinic outside Boston. Three weeks to dry out. Then maybe some time alone. Mr. Smiley had a house on the Cape, nothing special, more a bungalow than anything else, but lovely really, pushed back as it was behind the dunes. Come back a new man, come back your old self. Malcolm's agreement seemed to please them a great deal and he shook hands and saw them out. It was only when they were gone that he realized not one of the three had referred to him as father and for that he was grateful. He thought it a genuine kindness.

"Well," he told the child when they were gone, "I suppose it's time then."

The child said nothing. The child said: it is time.

That evening he drove Highway 7 north through the falling snow all the way to Pittsfield where he bought two bottles of Wild Turkey, a Diehard car battery, jumper cables, and three yards of black wool cloth. The road was nearly empty driving back and snow weighed the fir trees or sat plowed and browning in drifts along the shoulder. It was a lonely night and knowing what was to come made him lonelier still. He found the public radio station out of Amherst and turned up the volume. Chopin's Nocturne One in B-flat major. The child rode beside him, silent as ever, but had disappeared by the time he got back to Lenox.

Mary Ann lived on a secondary road that wrapped the gray bulk of October Mountain, a summer cabin winterized with an extra bedroom built on cinder blocks and overlooking a meadow. She was on the couch drinking a glass of chardonnay, her son Will in the floor staring at the television, when Malcolm opened the door and stood for a moment to knock the ice from his Doc Martens. She looked at him with glassed eyes and for a moment he thought she might have been crying.

"Where'd you go?" she asked.

"Pittsfield."

"I got worried. All the snow."

"Look here." He held up the Wild Turkey. "Let me get two cups."

She gulped the last of her wine and offered her glass. "Just pour mine right here."

She cleaned buildings, offices or homes, and had been cleaning the parish when he had met her, hands in latex gloves, sponging Murphy's Oil onto the pews. She would push her hair back with her forearm, smile. Crooked teeth and red hair. Pale milk-white skin. He convinced her to attend services and there seemed something welcome in her presence, no matter her employment; Malcolm was thirty years old then and finishing his probationary year at the church. He was patient and soft spoken, steady if nothing else, and it was felt it was time for him marry.

The next year—now the parish priest—he formed a committee on social justice, but within months the group had dissolved: only he and Mary Ann were left. Together, they drank and plotted, and then they just drank. While Will watched television, they would gravitate wordlessly toward her bedroom, black out and wake sweating in her bed, sheets tangled from whatever love they had conspired to make.

The child had appeared the following spring. He did not speak, simply occupied whatever peripheral space he might find, a chair in the far corner, a pew along the back row. He was an Iraqi boy, perhaps six or seven, and judging from his pallor Malcolm guessed he had been dead months before his arrival. His right arm disappeared just above the elbow, though he was always careful to cover the upper humerus with his torn sleeve. His nose was obliterated and a flap of skin covered the socket of the eye he had lost, but it was the textured skin that drew Malcolm. Pockmarked with bits of shrapnel and soft as overripe fruit, it was a pattern of square bulges, perfectly symmetrical, as if he had spent the better part of his childhood pressed against a window screen. When he had failed to speak Malcolm had done some research and found his injuries consistent with those of a cluster bomb. The bomblets were yellow and shiny. Children often picked them up, thinking them toys.

Malcolm carried Will to his bed. He was a lanky child, blond headed with a receding hairline, as seemingly fragile as his mother, and Malcolm moved slowly up the dim hall, the sleeping child piled over his shoulder, the warm weight of his chest, the pipe-cleaner construction of his arms and legs. He pulled the sheets over him and staggered back to the living room.

"He didn't wake up?"

"He's fine," Malcolm said. "Fast asleep."

"I should tuck him in." Mary Ann stood, caught the end table for balance, barefoot and unsteady as a newborn foal. "Bring that," she said.

He took what was left of the Wild Turkey to the bedroom—a little more than a slosh in the bottom—sat on the bed, and took a long pull, heard the door catch shut in the hall. Listened to the snow pile, the steady contraction of the boards.

She came up the hall and stood in the door and then above him and when she kissed him he felt her bared teeth, her hands on his chest and then working out of the shirt she wore. Topless in gray New England Patriots sweatpants, enough light falling through the part in the curtains to show her small breasts, blue and upturned. He put one hand in the small of her back and with the other fished out for the Wild Turkey, caught the neck, kissed her, drank, passed her the bottle. When there was none left she crawled beneath him, her narrow frame impressed in the mattress, the sound of her quiet panting roared against his ear so that she sounded less like a woman than the sea.

He showered in the morning, drank coffee while Will ate Fruit Loops from a punch bowl, Mary Ann still asleep when he left. The day sparkled with snow-melt, prismatic and dripping, cakes of white sliding from roofs in great whispered shushes. He parked downtown and walked to the coffee shop on Natick Avenue. In better weather, in better days, he would ride his bicycle to a main street of boutiques and patisseries, a dozen blocks of ocher brick and delicate filigreed balconies. There were gaslights and secondhand bookshops and good hand-churned ice cream. Neighbors buying newspapers or expensive handbags. The streets were busy this morning, folks anxious to be out, but in their greetings he detected some unspoken fear, the contagion of what he had become.

And what was that? he asked himself.

Above all things a patient man, and then not. Week by week his sermons had presided over the steady entombment of hope. He became violent for everlasting peace, moving past the liberal tolerance of his congregation toward some region tenanted by the maniacal. But that was what they could not understand: that to be a Christian was a radical repudiation of the world and its order; to be a Christian was the inversion of all received wisdom. The Kingdom was to be ushered in by the uncompromising. That was what the child had taught him.

He bought a large coffee and bagel, smiled excessively, and drove to his parsonage. For the next two hours he studied the photographs, image after image of snarled bodies, dog collars and leashes, corpses cushioned in ice. The child sat quietly in the corner. The child had led him here: the great online cache of the Abu Ghraib photographs, a single website composed wholly of suffering.

At ten he tore the cap off the second bottle of Wild Turkey and dialed Mr. Smiley.

"You've been so kind to me," Malcolm said, "all of you have, and I feel selfish asking this, but I'd like to ask one last favor." The line bore a heavy silence and he pictured Mr. Smiley across town in his study, fire billowing in the hearth, Labrador sleeping at his feet, nervously anticipating what obscenity this man would ask. "Allow me," Malcolm said, "to tell the congregation myself."

"Of course," Mr. Smiley said, and Malcolm could hear his relief. "Of course."

"I thought Sunday—"

"Of course. Take whatever time you need."

"I thought Sunday and then I could go quietly the following week." Malcolm poured three fingers of whiskey. "If everything goes well I could be back for Easter."

"Of course," Mr. Smiley almost exclaimed, they were rid of him! free of him! the wrath of God would never again be summoned against their good community! "Take whatever time you need, Malcolm. And there's no need to rush things, none whatsoever. This will always be your home."

It took the rest of the morning and on into the early afternoon to fashion the hood. Though he had no experience sewing he had not expected this. It was a simple triangular point, a flowing cape that would spread like wings when he lifted his arms. In his bedroom he stood atop a footstool and studied himself through the eye slits. He was sweating and the cloth was coarse. He had not expected that, either, and pulled off the hood. When he saw the child staring at him he was ashamed of himself, and abruptly put it back on.

He put the battery in the trunk of his car and drove back to Mary Ann's. She was working but he knew Will would be home and he found the boy in the backyard, nocking an arrow into his compound bow. Several malformed snowmen sat at the base of an abandoned shed, an arrow caught in the abdomen of one, two more arrows embedded in the shed wall. Malcolm led the boy back to the car, showed him the battery, and explained to him to what he needed him to do.

"But why?" His only question.

Malcolm knelt in front of him. "Because of what I told you before, because the Kingdom of God is all around us. Already."

Will shook his head, cheeks flushed. "But that doesn't explain why." He leaned closer. "Mom's afraid you might be getting sick. Really sick."

"I'm fine."

"Mom said—"

"I'm fine, Will. Honestly, right now I'm better than I've ever been." He could tell the boy was on the edge of tears though and put his hands on his shoulders. "Do you remember what I read to you that day? If someone were to prove to me that Christ were outside the truth—do you remember this?—and the truth outside of Christ—do you remember the rest?"

Will nodded.

"Tell me," Malcolm said.

The boy dropped his head as if in penance.

"It's all right. Tell me."

"I would prefer," Will said finally, quietly, reluctantly, "to remain with Christ than with the truth."

Malcolm didn't sleep that night but lay in bed with Mary Ann, handing the Wild Turkey between them until she blacked out and he finished what was left alone. Sunday arrived, as he knew it must, and around daylight he curled behind her, his mouth in the bend of her neck, and whispered into her hair.

She had the right to know, but did not, and he might have lingered longer had the child not beckoned him up. He kissed her a last time. Then he dressed and woke Will.

Just after seven, they entered the sanctuary and locked the doors. Malcolm had neither eaten nor slept in the last twenty-four hours but had managed to drink all the Wild Turkey so that balancing along the tightrope of the pulpit was an act of faith. They arranged the battery cables and around seven thirty heard the organist knock. Malcolm tipped on one foot and then the other, but the moment Will attached the clips to his fingers his senses became acute, his balance restored. Just before eight he heard more knocking, felt the metal crimps compress his index fingers, the polished boards beneath his bare feet. Will arranged the hood and unlocked the door, and when the congregation entered—just as Malcolm had asked him—Will fixed the cables to the battery.

He was two weeks in the psych ward when the child led him to the open supply closet, the gallon of antifreeze eye-level on a shelf, impossible to miss. He stared at the Grunewald print and removed the cap, and in that faint heartbeat before the diethylene glycol touched his lips realized—because he had never realized it before—what a terrible thing it was to fall into the hands of the living God.

PART ONE

I.

He woke miles from the sun, at sea, again, and chasing a dawn that cut along the horizon like light beneath a door. Woke early because this was the time one might be alone with the dark, for—he realized this as he rose from the musty recliner and walked toward the front windows that opened over the porch—for there was no sun, no dawn, and he was not at sea but alone, hours from light.

He collapsed back into his chair.

It was starting. It was starting and now they were back in the big Chinook, chasing its jagged shadow across the paddies while a plume of water towered and spread in a fishnet of dull light. *I am with you,* Christ said, but the old man knew that in a few minutes Christ would be dead, decapitated by a .30-caliber round, headless and bleeding in a ripple of dark water, and when the old man shut his eyes tonight Christ would die again, and tomorrow the same still, his dreams a billion acts of needless resurrection.

He needed to get up.

He needed to get up before it made him any crazier. He reached for the TV remote but stopped. He knew all he would find was another war—three Marines dead in Fallujah, a car bomb in Baghdad—and kicked off his blanket and stood, stiff as a rake, to make his way to the kitchen and put on the coffee.

Someone was up at the homeplace. From the window, he could just see the roofline raked against the flint of the morning sky. He stood over the sink with a Styrofoam cup of orange juice and watched the lights diffuse through the distant trees. Dallas, he supposed, though the old man had no idea why his oldest boy would be out at this hour. When the lights disappeared, he rinsed the cup and placed it in the drying rack. His dead wife, Evelyn, sat at the table and spooned cornbread out of a glass of buttermilk.

"You hungry they leftovers in the Frigidaire," she said.

"I ain't hungry."

"Let me fix you something."

He shook his head as if this might settle things. "I gotta get moving."

He stopped in the hall to stare for a moment at a portrait of his sons—Dallas and Malcolm, smiling—then limped on to the bathroom where he washed his face. His boys. There was no use thinking about them. He tried to pray but couldn't find them, whatever words he sought, standing so still he could hear clouds pass overhead. He dried his cheeks and stared at his reflection.

"Say something." He shook his head. "You old fool."

When the coffee dripped he fixed a cup, took his mug onto the porch and settled into a rocking chair. Evelyn was still near. He couldn't see her, but she was near. Her fragrance today was White Shoulders and baby powder. Other days it was wood smoke and the cool dirt in the crawlspace beneath the house. That was the smell the night before she died, the night he had brought her a glass of buttermilk only to find her mounted up in her four-poster bed as if already gone to that place across the river, as if she knew what awaited her. He sniffed the cold air. The smell always came first, sometimes hours before she arrived.

But he was a patient man.

There were days he would wait out the steady unclocking night only to watch the blue figures rise from the dust to walk again. The yard full of ammo crates and the LZ lined with dead children dressed in fatigues. When he closed his eyes this time he was back in the dim troop hold, sweating machine oil and sitting still enough to feel the submarine groan of the ship's engines. East, aboard the USS *Hermitage*. Pulling dawn from the horizon and watching it falter and fail in the convoy's green wash. Seven thousand Marines two days out of San Diego on the way to Subic Bay. The old man two weeks shy of his twenty-first birthday and sleeping on the third-tier bunk beneath a tangle of metal pipes.

Oh, Christ.

But Christ is not with him.

Christ comes later, wading through the saw grass south of Qui Nhon, the Son of God headshot and caught by the turning rotorwash. For years the old man drank his Early Times and thought of Jesus spinning in the pink surf. He watched his wife and sons toss in their beds while he slept in the cool insect mud, then woke to shoulder his rifle across another flooded field. The dead paratroopers wearing the blush of three-day beards. The VC curled fetally, burnt out of tunnels by demo teams, charred until they were nothing but zippers and the melted eyelets of boots. Their hands clawed inward like dead spiders.

He had come to understand death on a cellular level, and put one hand on his abdomen to feel it circulate. He was dying. That much was clear to him. When he stood in front of the bathroom mirror and probed his stomach he felt a ridgeline of tender bulges. It felt like the last thing that bound him to this world. He had pretty much ceased eating, and when he slept he was back in the dark water, crawling over the stone borders that shredded his hands and knees, so he was pretty much done with sleep, too.

Another old son of a bitch, he thought, gone and outlived his usefulness. The gutter clogged with leaves and not a damn thing he could do about it. Besides his land, he didn't even own anything worth fighting over. In the shed were a few tools no one would ever touch. In the deep freeze, a box of corndogs no one would ever eat. But it wasn't the obsolescence that bothered him. It was the diapers he feared most, the adult undergarments matted to his bony shanks like he was an infant, the green shit running down his leg. He'd put a slug in his head before he let that happen. He knew enough to know it had to be on your own terms. You had to own it. Owning it was everything.

When he opened his eyes he found his dead wife beside him, a shawl across her dead legs. Of course—today his youngest was returning. He had almost forgotten, but now it broke in him like a star, all crooked silver light.

"He's on his way by now," she said.

"Probably."

"Getting him a bus ticket. Be here in two days' time," she said. "And I tell you this, I'm glad it come out like it did."

He raised his coffee. "Half killing yourself don't make you no more a Christian than the next."

"Hush."

"It don't make you no more in the eyes of God."

"You hush that talk," she said. "You think the Lord ain't got you both on His mind?"

He stared into a dark that seemed to both begin and end a few inches from his face. "The Lord ain't never said boo to me."

"Elijah."

"The Lord ain't never said jack shit."

She seemed to study him from the depths of whatever place she occupied. "You got a black heart, Elijah Walker," she said finally. "You got the devil in you like a worm."

He opened his mouth, shut it. There was no use in arguing. He could sense the landing zone beginning to coalesce out of the lifting fog. He would be on the ground soon. He would be needed.

"Maybe," he said. "It don't matter no how."

"No," she agreed, "not now it don't."

It was freezing and what mattered was coming. His boy was coming.

In the men's room of the Greyhound station Malcolm Walker thought briefly of cutting himself. The mirror was shattered, and a sufficiently mean-looking shard had triangled itself into the corner, hooked and slim as the vein it would open.

Be done with it. Get it right this time, father.

When it passed he thought of Mary Ann and for the third time that morning considered calling her, then for the third time, remembered his refusal to see her when she had last visited. That had been the end of things; even within the fog of the hydrocodone he had known as much. Not that it mattered. Whatever small thing they shared had withered the moment she entered the church, their slow ruin made sudden in the shadow of his self-annihilation. That was, after all, his intent.

He left the men's room for the ticket office. He wanted a drink but there was nothing in the station. Somewhere down the road then. Roanoke, maybe, if he could last that long. He had started last spring with wine, a fruity merlot or a good claret one of the women would bring by the parsonage. By fall he was drinking a gallon a day. But that was finished too.

All that was left was home.

He stared at a map marked with fares and disclaimers, routes of blue lines that wiggled and stretched with vascular density, took his ticket and bag and walked into a waiting room that smelled like carpet-cleaning fluid, some vaguely carcinogenic detergent. He thought the child might be waiting for him but found instead a woman and her two daughters. She was a girl, really, nineteen, maybe twenty, with bitten nails and plastic shoes, her mouth loaded with golden bridgework, dull and intricate. A baby slept in a carrier beneath a blanket and a three-year-old pooled around the girl's feet like the train of a dress.

When the PA came on the girl gathered her children.

"Did they say Richmond?" she asked.

Malcolm nodded and she bit her lip and began to cry. When she stood she appeared stunted, somehow diminished in the harsh fluorescent light. She looked at her children with more exhaustion than judgment.

"All right." She pulled the girl up by her narrow wrist and lifted the baby carrier. The child's earrings sparkled. "This is us. Come on, precious," the girl said. "This is not a drill. This is not a goddamn test."

The bus crossed the beltway and took I-66 past concrete cloverleafs and rings of tract housing gone shabby with neglect. Thirty miles southeast of Washington there were new developments, prefab mansions crowded in fields of turned earth, I-81 an endless string of billboards. ALL-NUDE CAFÉ RISQUE. BATTLEFIELD RELICS. Country Skillets with 18 oz. ribeyes. His forehead tipped against the cool glass, past him the Shenandoah an ache of rolling pasture and Civil War battlefields. It was raining and he realized there had been something in the sky every mile of his trip south. Snow in Amherst and Hartford, sleet turning to rain as he left Grand Central and slipped down the eastern seaboard. Now it was snowing again, forty miles north of Blacksburg and the highway lined with decomposing memorials gone gray in the sleet—WE LUV VA TECH. PRAY FOR THE HOKIES. He took the print of Grunewald's *Crucifixion* from his bag and studied the tortured shape. The doctors had taken his New Testament and his copy of Leon Bloy's *Pilgrim of the Absolute,* but they had not found the print.

In Roanoke, he bought a carton of Camels and took a taxi from the station to an unpaved lane that wound up the ridge through a stand of tulip poplar. Jefferson Roddick's place sat on the crown of the hill past the tubes of a cattle guard, the house neglected and small with a wide front porch and a collapsing block stoop. Goats moved through a yard cluttered with junk, farm implements and an antique RC COLA drink cooler, bee boxes and trash, fishing line tangled in the low branches of a pine. There was no sunlight in the trees and snow melted in slim patches.

Malcolm found Jefferson at the shed out back, a slain doe tied to the rack of a Yamaha Kodiak, a larger buck limp on the concrete beside the four-wheeler. Malcolm stood at a distance and watched him cut behind the Achilles tendon, slide a spreader through the incisions, and pulley the deer so that it dangled from the rafters. A gout of blood fell from its mouth, thick and gelatinous, and splattered across the floor.

"Lung blood," Jefferson said, looking up. "See how dark?"

"You blew out the backstrap."

"Couldn't get a better shot."

Malcolm walked over. "Can I help?"

"Maybe get that bucket."

The bullet had entered just above the liver, passed through the lower cavity and entered the lungs, the entry wound a neat hole, the exit an explosion of fur and purple tissue. Jefferson glided the blade of his Old Timer around the penis and up the chest while Malcolm peeled the still-warm skin. Jefferson rolled his sleeves and tore out the rooted entrails.

When the deer were dressed they sat on the porch, Jefferson's rough hands pink and folded in his lap, his beard as short and uneven as his hair. Malcolm had known him years ago in seminary as the smartest person in a class of very smart people, every semester taking a full load while sitting in on four or five classes in philosophy and Russian studies. Jefferson had been ordained in the Southern Baptist Church and joined the navy as a chaplain where he'd deployed with a Marine battalion before being chaptered out on a psych discharge.

Malcolm blew into his hands. "It's freezing out here."

"You get numb after a while. You get used to it. Look here."

Jefferson took a fifth of Evan Williams from between his thighs, swallowed, and passed it to Malcolm. Tattooed on his left forearm, bright as jewel, beat the Sacred Heart of Jesus. "You know you look fucked up enough for both of us." He took the bottle back and drank. "Don't take that the wrong way."

"I had a bad run," Malcolm said.

"I heard you tried to kill yourself."

"That's what they tell me."

"That means it's probably true," Jefferson said. "You bring me anything?"

Malcolm took the Camels from his bag and Jefferson removed a pack.

"There's such evil shit in the air. I'm glad to see you, but you need to leave in the morning." He bit off the filter and put the cigarette between his lips. "You headed home?"

"For the summer. Dennis Turner got me a job at a school in Haiti starting in the fall."

"Dennis-fucking-Turner." Jefferson shook his head. A goat settled into a scratch of grass, legs curled beneath it like a dog. "You know it wasn't your fault," he said. "It wasn't mine either. All that shit they fed us about truth and beauty." He held out one hand and rubbed his thumb against his fingertips. "Pass that back."

They drank into the bright chill of afternoon on into the evening, then moved inside where Jefferson banked the wood stove with kindling and several pages from a Derrida paperback. The room was cluttered with books and papers. Two marijuana plants wilted beneath a heat lamp on the kitchen table. There was no sign of the child.

"This is your parents' place?" Malcolm asked.

"Was."

"They moved?"

"Died." Jefferson opened a tin of sardines and lifted a single fish, fingers bright with oil.

"What happened in Haditha?"

"I entered a heightened state of awareness is what happened." He pointed with one shimmering finger. "BioThrax IM straight into my shoulder. Anthrax vaccine but it was more like magic. The moment they stuck me I could think the future, see everything. I stopped holding services and had them bring me everyone they rounded up, men, boys, anyone. I smelled their hair and could see into their heads, know the crimes they were going to commit. I saw the entire insurgency bloom from first to last and started naming who would live, who would die. We lost a platoon leader and I had them take two hajjis down to the river." Malcolm said nothing and Jefferson took his eyes from Malcolm's face. "I'm not asking you to believe me."

They slipped toward night and then slipped past it, overtaken by darkness and the soft accompaniment of bells. When the fire died the room began to freeze and Malcolm lay on the couch and stared into the disintegrating light. Nights in the hospital everything would turn on him, his mind at war with itself, his thoughts a manic swirl of hymns and verses. No logic but an ocean of sound. He would wake and write something down, only to discover the following morning incomprehensible words scratched in a hand he did not recognize. A journey both in and out, but in the end it was a journey nowhere. There was no attending angel, no voice, only the wire-grid windows and bathroom stalls that would not lock, and in his second week it had occurred to him that perhaps Christ wasn't coming back. It seemed no great revelation.

He woke just before dawn, the room elastic with half-light, every object dematerialized. He felt certain it should have been morning by now, but in the stillborn cold he found no sun, only the figure of Jefferson crumpled in his rocking chair, his head wrenched forward as if his neck were broken, mouth snoring raggedly. Twisted around one fist was a length of parachute cord. It took Malcolm a moment to notice the Kabar knife balanced on Jefferson's thighs. He stood as quietly as possible, gathered his things, and slipped out the front door. The goats lifted their heads but did not rise.

Halfway to town he caught a ride to the bus station where he showered and changed. He came out tired but clean and carried his bag across the street to the Denny's, took a seat in a booth, and felt them look at him, the infinitesimal silver scars that checked his throat like bird tracks impressed in a creek bank, his scalded lips. Beyond that, he appeared normal enough: jeans and an Adidas windbreaker, good Tony Lama boots his brother Dallas had sent.

But they would know him. He had achieved brief fame: a grainy cell phone photo circulating through the right-wing blogosphere and onto cable news where he became the masochistic liberal priest, the hooded poster child for the blame-America-first crowd. The gesture had been pointless, of course, and he thought of the Iraqi child, of the sudden deconstruction of his face. If God took aesthetic pleasure in this, He was a God Malcolm could believe in, but He was not a God Malcolm could worship.

He used a pay phone outside the package store to leave Dallas another message, Malcolm's voice a whispery slish as he watched eighteen-wheelers rattle east along a span of overpass, the aluminum guardrails clattering like the hands of the old drunks, their noses wired with burst capillaries, little shelves of swollen livers notched on their sides.

He hung up, but didn't let go of the phone, and before he could stop himself he had dialed Mary Ann's cell.

"Please tell me you aren't coming here." He could hear her hand over the phone. She sounded underwater. "I don't want you coming here."

"I'm not."

"I'm sorry. That didn't come out right. It's just that I don't want you around Will is the thing."

"I'm not coming. I've left."

When he had begun to organize protests against the war she had been among the first to attend, eschewing the Episcopalian Christ for something more carnal, the greasy-haired socialist, the peasant from Nazareth. When the congregation's liberal conscience had been assuaged she had stayed; she had stayed when he was coming apart, first privately, and then publicly; and she had stayed when he fixed his eyes on the Grunewald. She had stayed right up to the moment he had attempted to become it.

"You've left?" she said. "So that's it, then? You just go?"

"I thought that would be better."

"Better for who?"

"Better for everyone," he said. "You, Will."

"You sound drunk."

"Give it time." He laughed and felt his eyes begin to tear. "That was a joke."

He knew her hand was off the phone now, out of the latex gloves and pushing the hair from her eyes. He thought of her outside whatever building she was cleaning that day, the parking lot scabbed with snow. Her fingers would smell like disinfectant; he could see them flying about her face. She would be dressed in scrubs and then undressed by the gathering morning light.

"I think I should go, Malcolm."

"I can call you later."

"I should just—"

"It's all right," he said. "We can talk later."

"Or maybe we shouldn't, I mean, if you think—"

"Think what?"

"Just don't call," she said. "Just please don't, okay?"

Inside, he bought a pint of Canadian Mist, put the bottle in his back pocket, and crossed to the Circle K where a black Tahoe with Georgia plates and an outdated CHELLIS FOR PRESIDENT bumper sticker idled in the parking lot. An old man in a Feed & Seed hat stood behind the counter, his skin pleated and ashen. Beside the register was a glass buffet case full of fried chicken and collard greens, the ham marbled with fat, the glass steamed and streaked with condensation.

"What kind of machine you driving?" the man asked.

Malcolm filled a fountain cup with ice and Coke. "What's that?"

The man nodded toward the Tahoe. "Your big rig there."

"That isn't mine."

"I'll bet she's hell on gas."

Malcolm put the Coke on the counter along with a pack of BC headache powders, three MET-RX protein bars, and a bag of Fritos.

The man lifted the chips. "Them Mexicans don't buy nothing but Miller ponies and corn chips. Every last one of em lives in the same damn trailer over by the lumberyard." He bagged the food. "Where you headed?"

"Home."

"Home's always a son of a bitch."

In the parking lot Malcolm topped off the cup with Canadian Mist, dumped in two headache powders, and fitted the top. He was not returning to his parish; he had no parish. He was headed back to the old man, to the church suppers in the low thrum of mosquito heat, to the pickups and potato salad. The freezers packed full of venison. Home, he thought. Home was always a son of a bitch.

The weekend was the last thing she owed him. Jordan decided that standing in her bedroom, bag packed and resting on the comforter. Leighton Clatter was coming for her that morning but it would be the last time. She'd survive. She had a little money and she had Roosevelt's knife. She'd pawn it if she had to. She'd survived before and she would survive after; it was just a matter of living within certain constraints, the discipline she'd managed at the spiritualist camp with Rose, the fasting and meditation. Two streets of palm readers and reiki healers crowded into mail-order Sears craftsmen bungalows—that had been the limits of her world. Wind chimes outside the Grand Temple. Tabby cats tipping over pie tins in the hush of afternoon. Everything since—it was all lower vibration.

She carried the bag into the living room and dropped it by the door. Her cousin Archimedes snored away on the couch, sweat floating on his chest, one arm pinked with claw marks. She'd heard them stumble in last night, how many she didn't know, a train wreck of laughing drunks high and playing whale songs on an iBook she saw balanced on the window sill. The room cluttered with bottles of Hennessy and an orange hookah. Newports and rolling papers dusted around a baggie greasy with resin and a few seeds.

"You're up." Archimedes's eyes were open and bulging, but otherwise he hadn't moved, thick arms crossed on the pile of his chest. "We wake you up last night?"

She gathered the papers in one hand and crumpled them. "I can't remember."

"Pretty early. Even for you."

"Leighton's picking me up."

"Shit." He raised himself onto one elbow and fell back. "I thought you were steering clear, baby girl."

"Yeah?" She was picking up bottles now, cigarette butts mashed and swimming within the glass. "Well, it didn't work out that way, did it?"

"It would be presumptuous for me to assume I understand your suffering."

"Jesus, go back to sleep, Arch."

"No soul intuits another's pain." He put his hands to the topknot centered on his skull, reached and took a Ziploc of pills from the floor. "I'd offer you something from the goodie bag but I know you got your particulars."

"Just go back to sleep. I've got everything I need."

"The American plenty. I hear you."

The kitchen was full of shit. No other way to think about it. Fast food trash, a silver beer can floating in the clogged sink like a buoy. She dumped the empties in the garbage, sat at the table, and drank warm chardonnay from a coffee cup. She owed Leighton the weekend, all right, fine, but that was all. Sunday morning she'd walk away; she'd survive. She'd done it before.

When he pulled to the curb she got in without a word. Leighton turned around and headed down Main Street where another knot of protesters marched outside his office, trust fund kids playing poor in their flannel shirts and work boots. But good for them. If they had nothing else to offer let them offer up their selves, bodies thrown into the gears of the Blue Mountain machine. She didn't care about the State Park land outside of caring that Leighton didn't have it, that Leighton failed, because, ultimately, that would be the only justice she would ever know. Just watching him fail, watching him fail and then crawling back into bed with him, dropped the next morning on the corner like laundry, a Ziploc of Colombian Gold and a few large bills paper-clipped to the sleeve like a parting gift.

"What?" Leighton asked.

They were passing Ken's Pharmacy with its neon R/X, the Rite-Aid, the white spire of the Lutheran church. Sleet turning to rain. The morning the gray of damaged tissue. She looked out the window and shook her head.

"Don't look at me like that," he said.

"I'm not looking at you at all."

"Don't get smart, princess," he told her. "Don't get above your raising."

When they started up the mountain she knew they were headed for The Settlement. She knew what it was about. She'd been once before and hoped never to return but that was all right, too, it was all right because it was finished, it was the last time, and after the weekend she never had to go back: not to Leighton, not to the high cathedral of his home, certainly not to this awful place where children walked naked across the filthy yard while their parents smoked crank and shot paper targets.

They took Highway 28 on to 76 into Georgia, a Forest Service gate, brambles scratching at the windows. She shut her eyes on the dirt road and felt the bed unfold in a series of ruts, the gravel washed into broad alluvial fans. Opened her eyes just once to stare into the green shimmer of pine boughs encased in glass—perfect crystals drooping toward the ground—shut them again when the pine gave way to naked hardwoods, the forest floor a carpet of leaves gone buttery with rot. The air was full of decaying Christmas, a childhood smell of Fraser firs dry and discarded on the sidewalk, up and down the street the day-after detritus of white pines and desiccated wreathes. Broken ornaments and scalloped glass. A confetti of stray tinsel. She missed everything and nothing about it.

When the Navigator came to a stop they sat in a clearing surrounded by evergreens, mobile homes circled in front of a collapsing farmhouse. A clothesline bowed with the weight of a frozen rug. A woman walked onto a stoop and stared at them.

Leighton cut the engine. "Just sit here until you get your shit right."

"I'm not getting out."

He drummed both hands on the wheel. His big rings, his big rings on her small face. "Get your shit right—" He spoke as if to a child. "—and then come inside. You're not going to sit out here like a spoiled brat. Is that clear?"

"Yes."

"I didn't come up here to fuck around, Jordan. You pull it together and come inside. There's someone you need to meet."

She nodded and he opened the door, stepped down into the mud and on across the yard where a man now stood by the woman. He was dressed in a western shirt and jeans, elaborately tooled boots, and Jordan watched Leighton climb the steps and shake his hand. They followed the woman into the farmhouse. When they were gone Jordan leaned back and shut her eyes.

She was almost asleep when the dog leapt against the window, paws planted on the glass. She fell back, then bent forward again. She could see its long canines bent like tusks, the ridged ceiling of its wet mouth. The barking was strangely muted, and she studied a slug of clear saliva that clung to the glass like a plastic worm. The dog dropped and reared again, paws sliding against the door panel. The drool shuddered. A woman grabbed the dog's collar—Jordan hadn't seen the woman come out; how had she missed this?—and the dog whimpered and dropped back onto all fours. It was a pit bull, all nerve and high-bunched muscle, and after a moment heeled by the woman's feet.

Jordan cracked the window.

"It didn't scratch nothing," the woman said. "It scare you?"

She had seen the woman before, on her previous trip, Jordan thought. The big brown eyes and an ear that appeared to have been gnawed in childhood. *Dark meat,* the woman had called her. They had been sitting on a patio behind one of the trailers. *I see you got a taste for the dark meat, Doc.* She motioned for Jordan to lower the window.

"He said for you to come inside," the woman said.

"Who?"

"Your man's in the house there. I got Elvis here collared. He ain't getting loose."

Jordan opened the door. The pit strained against the woman's grip, then heeled again.

"Go on," the woman said. "I got him collared."

Leighton was inside with two other men, the cowboy she had seen on the porch and a man nearer her own age, skinny and heavily tattooed in a TapOut T-shirt, his mouth collapsed around the absence of teeth. On the table a shotgun lay on a towel, the breech open, around it several red-and-gold shells upright as soldiers. The cowboy stood and Leighton introduced him as Brother Rick Miles. The tattooed man appeared to be asleep, slouched in a recliner with a glass pipe resting in his lap like a ship in a bottle. When Leighton began to lead her out of the room she pointed at it.

"Give me some of that first."

"Not that, honey. That's for the trailer trash. What do you have for her, Brother Rick?"

"Oh, I got something special for café au lait here."

"Something special," Leighton said. "How thoughtful is that?"

He led her to a wood-paneled room, a large waterbed in the center, sheets peeled back so that the bladder showed blue around the frame. Against the wall leaned a pair of antique leg braces.

"I don't want to do this," she said.

"You're trying me, darling."

"Please."

Leighton turned. "Brother Rick, one moment, *por favor.*" He shut the door and turned to where she set on the edge of the bed. "Do you know who he is, Jordan?"

"I don't care."

"Rick Miles controls all of I-85 from Atlanta to Charlotte. Nothing moves unless he gives the good word. Narcotics. Guns. He can keep people off our back. Do you want the Aryan Brotherhood up here, darling? How about Mara Salvatrucha?"

"I don't care."

"Jordan." He took a vial from his pocket and filled the cap. "Here."

"Please."

"Just because I'm feeling generous. Kindly do not dismiss my generosity."

She snorted the cap and he refilled it, passed it back.

"You're beautiful sometimes," he said, and touched her hair.

She felt it burn through her, raw enough to ignore Leighton's hand.

"Truly beautiful," he said.

She was already taking off her clothes. "Just send him in and get out."

He came in and undressed with his back to her, prim, she thought, until he pushed his way inside her and finally expired down her thigh, a bright streak like the dog's trail of saliva. She pushed him off and he dressed in the corner while she lay there sticking to the rubber bladder, the bedsheet a rope binding her feet.

"Your friends," he said, "have strange ideas."

"They aren't my friends. They hate me."

"There's going to be a war," he said, "no doubt. But I'm not so sure it's the war they're gearing up to fight. Of course, if you believe long enough the government is coming for you, eventually they'll prove you right."

"They probably hate you, too."

"Probably," he agreed, "but I'm concerned only with metrics. This bullshit ideology, that's all beside the point."

"What do you call this then?" She pointed at the silvery track he had left on her thigh but he was staring out the window.

"This." He shrugged. In his left eye was a blood spot, brown as old mud, as if he'd long ago gone dry from the inside out. "This is beyond the ideological. This is boredom, maybe. But I'm in the game now. I'll stick around and see what develops." He looked at her. "As a gesture."

"I need to get dressed."

"Of course."

She didn't speak again until she was back in the truck with Leighton and on the way to his house.

"So he's going to let you sell your drugs then," she said. "Or is he bringing you a truckload of guns? Which is it?"

He raised one hand as if he might touch her wrist. "Don't think this was something I desired, Jordan. Don't think that for a moment."

"You traded me so you can sell your drugs. You sold me to him."

"The deal was already done. And I don't sell drugs, darling."

"So what was I then, the handshake? The cherry on top?"

Leighton turned off the highway and onto the driveway that wound up to his house.

"He said it was boredom," she said. "That's what he told me."

"The Settlement has need of security, Jordan. We have to stay focused on the government. You know as much."

"You're crazy."

"When it's all we have left you'll understand why this mattered."

"I'm leaving you Sunday."

"Jordan—"

"I'm done with this. I don't care what happens to me."

He pulled to a stop in front of the house but left the engine running.

"There's going to be a point, Jordan." He grabbed her wrist but there was nothing violent in the motion; he was gentle now, the put-upon father, patient to the last. "There's going to be a point when The Settlement and the land are all we have left. I'm not trying to scare you but I want you to understand the gravity of the situation. When that time comes, Jordan—please listen—I want you beside me. I want to protect you."

She shook her head. "I think maybe you're the worst thing that's ever happened to me. I'm not coming back."

He cut the engine, took a bag of pills from his jacket and dropped them in her lap. "Darling," he said, "you are always and forever coming back."

Malcolm hadn't seen his brother in almost two years, but standing in the Greyhound parking lot in Greenville, South Carolina, Dallas Walker looked mostly the same, a little older but still vigorous, still the long-legged flanker with soft hands and good speed, the aging jock with his rangy arms and a square jaw. He was thicker, maybe, a heft that gathered at his center. At Georgia, he'd run like a man being electrocuted, and appeared to have traded that speed for bulk, a terrestrial heaviness that lumbered toward him. But if he was heavier, he was also a businessman now, partner in the largest real estate company in the upstate; the weight fit him. Money had come to him early in life, and he wore his wealth with a gentle insistence: the good old boy made good.

They shook hands and Malcolm put his bag in the backseat of the double-cab Dodge Ram.

The eleven years between them had always made him more an uncle to Malcolm than a brother, the guy with money to throw around, visiting home and buying beer for Malcolm and his underage high school friends. Dallas had just missed UGA's National Championship in 1980, a high school junior when Hershel Walker streaked past Notre Dame, but he still shimmered with the tag end of glory. Malcolm remembered sitting on the front porch with the old man, the TV dragged from the living room, watching Dallas take a punt around the corner and on toward the Ole Miss end zone, his mother inside, unable to watch, afraid Dallas would break his neck, afraid he'd crack his skull, afraid he'd blow out his knee. And then he had, of course.

"How's Randi?" Malcolm asked when they were on the highway.

"Randi." Dallas emptied a few sunflower seeds from a plastic tube into his mouth. "You know Randi, all red wine and pearls. I bought her a tanning bed last year. Spends half her time there and the other half driving to the Whole Foods in Greenville."

"She still working out?"

"Like she's anchoring the Falcons' D-line. She's amazing."

"What about Tillman?"

"Tillman." Dallas spat a sunflower hull. "Let me tell you about our glorious fat-ass uncle Tillman. I went up to see him a few weeks ago and I'm not kidding: he's at least five, six hundred pounds. Hurt his back and is just sitting in his recliner waiting for God to heal him. That nasty-ass little wife of his maybe half his age and running in and out, 'Oh, Tillman, Oh, Tillman.' He met that bitch on MySpace."

"He doesn't get to church?"

"Can't. Just sits there all day petting his damn rats and talking about God on the Internet. He kept texting me passages from Job till I told him to cut it out. The fat bastard thinks God's testing his faith." Dallas ran a finger inside his lip and fished out another hull. "You get a chance to see your lady friend before you left?"

"She didn't want to see me."

"The thing with her kid?"

"Yeah."

"That's hard shit, bro. I sympathize." He cracked the window and flicked shells into the breeze. "I know Randi wrote to you a little when you were in the hospital. She mention we won in court?"

"This was to buy the State Park land?"

"It's being appealed, but I think we're set. Got some hotshot outfit in Columbia doing our lawyering. There could still be another impact survey, but it looks doubtful."

"That's good, right?"

"It's damn good. We really need it right now. Last year we were selling lots at Chattooga Estates—two hundred K for sixth-tenths of an acre. A little air had gone out but until the market crashed it looked like we'd be fine."

"So this is the life raft?"

"We're hoping it keeps us afloat."

They rode for a while longer before Malcolm asked about Marilynn, Dallas's daughter by his first wife.

Dallas kept his eyes on the road. "I'm trying to quit dipping," he said. "I started dipping to quit smoking and now I'm chewing these things to quit dipping. If it wasn't for the salt I couldn't bear em."

"You still not seeing her?"

"Her mamma's making damn sure of that."

They took White Horse Road past an elementary school and a Baptist Church. Malcolm could feel the warm spread of the Canadian while Greenville slid past, hemmed behind a chain-link fence and frontage road. Houses and convenience stores. Telephone polls tacked with fliers for yard sales.

"I've been kind of worked up lately," Dallas said. "It's all stupid shit, really. But there's been so much going on. Some folks are pretty hot right now."

"This is about the land?"

"The land's on everybody's mind. Then with the inauguration and all. Did you watch it?"

"No."

"Stupid shit is all it is. Still, you reach a point and it ain't so amusing anymore."

"What about the old man?"

Dallas shook his head. "You know he's still too damn backward to live in the house, right? Well, I went and got him this enormous plasma TV, high-def. Sent the DirectTV guy back there. The damn History Channel so he can sit and relive his war twenty-four seven. Well, the guy goes back and Daddy almost shoots him."

Malcolm smiled.

"I'm serious," Dallas said. "He almost killed the man. And of course I'm the one who gets the call later wanting to know why some old man's on the porch waving a pistol." His arrowhead necklace slipped from his collar and he thumbed it back. "Anyway, me and Randi take the TV up there, this beautiful flat screen, and he stands there and tells us he doesn't want it. Treats us like a couple of aliens come down to abduct him. Randi was practically in tears."

"Well."

"'Well' is just about right." Dallas laughed. "'Well' is about all you can say for the man."

Dallas flipped the radio back on—WHORE, WHORE, WHORE, the voice intoned, TRAITOR, TRAITOR, TRAITOR—flipped it back off.

"There's a lot of people worked up about the election," Dallas said. "He won big down here in the primary. Say you didn't follow it?"

Malcolm watched the pines slide by with a boozy grace. "Not really."

"The Serpent, they're calling him. I don't know. There's just a lot of shit in the air."

Ten miles from home, Malcolm asked if Dallas would mind dropping him at Ed Bear's car lot.

"You in the market for something let me fix you up with a company truck. Got two more just like this."

"I appreciate it, but I just need something to putt around in."

"Well, you're still staying with us, aren't you?" Dallas asked. "Randi's set on it."

"I thought I'd check in with the old man, then go over to the house. Maybe air it out a little. He knows I'm coming?"

"He knows."

"He say anything?"

"The usual shit," Dallas said. "Check on him, but you don't need to be staying with him. The way he fucking looked at us."

"That's just him. He can't help it."

In the graveled lot of Ted E. Bear's Pre-Owned Cars and Trucks they found a '99 Nissan pickup with a camper shell and good tires, 2200! inked on the windshield. Bear took them up the steps of his double-wide past a cork board marked HOMETOWN HEROES and covered with photographs of soldiers and sailors and Marines, a single pimply-faced airman in desert fatigues posed by a stone inscribed KANDAHAR AFB. Malcolm paid from a roll of bills and pulled the Nissan around, left it idling by Dallas's truck while he hefted his bag into the front seat.

"You don't have to stay with that son of a bitch if you don't want to," Dallas said.

"I know," Malcolm said. "I appreciate it."

"Well, at least come over and see Randi."

"I'll get settled and come by Friday maybe."

"Friday's good. Leighton's having a party. We'll have a big time."

Out on the highway, road construction had stacked a line of cars by the turn to the Ingles and they stared at the shimmer of taillights on the wet asphalt.

"All right then," Dallas said.

They shook hands and Dallas turned for his truck.

"Hold on. I got something for you." He opened the passenger door and took something from the glove box. "I almost forgot."

He handed Malcolm a walnut box with a brass lock. Inside was a .357 Magnum wrapped in a chamois. Malcolm tried to pass it back.

"Keep it," Dallas said.

"I don't need it."

"Humor me then. Just put it in your bag there and forget about it."

"I don't even believe in guns."

"Well, I'm here to tell you they exist," Dallas said. "That happens to be one your holding."

Malcolm said nothing.

"Look," Dallas said. "I don't want to stand here and act like I know it all, but you heard about all the home invasions? Tweakers cutting their meth with Drano. Whipping their babies with clothes hangers. Meanest shit you ever heard. We got rednecks that just as soon shoot you as scratch their ass."

"Over what?"

"How about that roll you got? What was that, your severance?"

"A love offering."

"A love offering. Goddamn." Dallas walked to his truck laughing, shut the door, and rolled down the window. "Go see Daddy," he called, "but this weekend you come see us. Stick with your big brother and you'll be fine."

Dallas watched Malcolm's truck roll up the street and on toward the stoplight before he pulled onto the highway behind him. In the mid-nineties, Dallas and his partner, Leighton Clatter, had moved their offices from a Buckhead strip mall across the state line into what had once been a cotton brokerage. They had gut-renovated the building so that it had a raw, modern feel, exposed beams and original floorboards, recessed lighting and glass interior walls—an embodiment of the New South sophistication that animated Blue Mountain Realty and Land Development. Now there were protesters outside the entrance, kids with their Northface jackets and shaggy beards, girls whose underarms had never known the touch of a razor. It was all coming apart pretty damn quickly.

He parked on Main and walked the wet sidewalk past the Blue Ridge Bank to Common Grounds where he was to have coffee with a man from the Progressive Alliance. That was the deal: a cup of coffee and twenty minutes of pleading. But you have to sit there and actually listen to him, Dallas. Nod your head. Act like you give a shit. The man was the chief legal counsel for the state's largest environmental group, and Leighton thought a little honey might go a long way to preventing the group from filing for another environmental impact survey, a survey which would, of course, be approved, but would only further slow the development of the seven thousand acres Blue Mountain Realty had bought almost a year ago.

The State Park land backed onto Chattooga Estates and would already have been open for development as CHATOOGA: PHASE II had they not spent the bulk of the last ten months in court. Not that there would be much development: at most a few houses would dot the fringe. Dallas suspected that Leighton wanted the land for himself and was only using Blue Mountain to draw on corporate funds. Leighton was rich but counting legal fees they were already in for over eight million, debt leaking out of their collective ass and not a penny to show for it. But it was a massive tract, there was no denying that. Dallas had been considering inviting Malcolm up to walk part of the property—it would give him a good excuse to blow off the meeting—but his brother had looked rougher than Dallas had expected. Giving him the pistol seemed like the best and worst thing Dallas could do for him.

He stepped inside and gave his order to a white guy with dreadlocks and a green, yellow, and red Rasta cap, took his coffee to where Gresham Haley waited on a patchy velour love seat.

Walhalla had up and changed in the last decade and Haley seemed to embody the transformation. There were still stores selling Confederate bikinis and Dale Earnhardt flags, but with the rich second-homers came merchants offering lawn sculptures and blown glass ornaments. The Otasco the old man had owned for forty years had closed right after Home Depot opened on the bypass. The diners were gone. There was a Mexican restaurant and three pizza-delivery joints, but nowhere besides Hardee's to get a decent breakfast. A single feed-and-seed remained down near the old Southern Rail line, the big fifty-pound bags stacked and plastic-wrapped on pallets. Sweet feed and pellets of Marine protein rotting on concrete loading docks.

We've gone off and forgotten every decent thing we ever knew, Dallas thought. We got rid of the good and imported the shit. But he knew that it was his change, his responsibility. His and men like Haley. Dallas remembered him from high school as a giant head stalked on two weedy legs, a brainy track star who'd run all the way to Yale Law and then returned, Dallas figured, so that he might feel superior to one half of the population while feeling self-righteous about the other.

Haley was a self-proclaimed eco-warrior, but more than that he was a businessman, and Dallas thought they might deal reasonably with each other. Haley represented the conscience-stricken rich, those given to compromise. The true believers lived on the mountain, kayaked the whitewater all summer and managed sustainable Christmas tree farms come fall.

"What we want is consideration," Haley said.

"What you want is for this to stop."

"This isn't necessarily repugnant to us. We're not categorically opposed." Haley blew ripples across his drink. "And that sort of open-mindedness is rare. You should consider the rarity."

"The rarity?" Dallas smiled. He was on the couch facing Haley, between them a table covered with board games and a book of Vermeer prints.

Haley reclined into a mound of pillows and smiled. "You know we could hold things up almost indefinitely. I've got a judge in Easley who will hand me an order for a new impact survey in forty-eight hours—"

Dallas raised a hand to stop him. "Look, I don't want to be an asshole, but I promised Leighton I'd give you twenty minutes so how about you just tell me what you want."

"I just said what we want."

"You want your consideration—right. But consider me slow and spell out exactly what that means."

Haley shrugged. "Maybe a conservation easement on a few acres. You put, say, five hundred acres in our trust."

"Not happening."

"I've seen the plans, Dallas. You're barely developing the land. You could spare some trees."

"If we're barely developing it, then what's the problem?"

Haley held his mug with two hands. "Okay. So maybe you make a donation to the Alliance instead. Quietly, of course, and nothing outrageous. Let's just say three hundred thousand came our way. We might still complain a little in our newsletter but I assure you it would stop there. That little crowd chanting outside your office? They'd vanish overnight."

"Three hundred grand?"

"Ballpark."

"Three hundred grand for this to go away?"

"It'd be the best deal you've ever made."

"You want a bribe?"

"I think I've already covered that: we want consideration."

"Three hundred K worth." Dallas leaned forward. "The river rats know anything about this? The folks chaining themselves to the bulldozers?"

"I'm here representing a legitimate nonprofit," Haley said. "Not a bunch of greasy lunatics. Let's be clear on that."

The door jangled open and spat a mouth of winter air against them. Outside the light was changing, the first blush of pink rimming the sky. The clouds looked bitter.

"I could make you a hero," Haley said. "I know you're giving lip service to the green elements of Chattooga Estates."

"Can't do it."

"Can't or won't?"

"Doesn't matter," Dallas said. "Leighton wouldn't be onboard."

"Leighton's onboard."

"Bullshit."

"Leighton happens to be sitting right here in my jacket pocket if you want to talk to him."

"Fuck off."

Haley laughed. "He's bought off everyone else. What makes you think we're any different? But let me ask you something here, Dallas, and this is a serious question. How much is enough? How much money do you want?"

"All of it."

"That's not you."

"Every last dime of it. When I'm sitting on the Federal Reserve, that's when I'll have enough."

Haley shook his head. "That's not you. That's Leighton Clatter talking. I've known you all your life, Dallas, so don't give me that crap about the money," he said. "And don't give me the line about jobs or progress or anything else. This isn't some grand act of largesse on your part. You aren't doing anyone any favors here."

"Except maybe the five hundred folks who'll get construction jobs."

"You mean the five hundred Mexicans making three dollars an hour."

"Except the thirty-million-dollar increase in the tax base."

"Please. All you'll do is push up rates. You push the values up and people lose their land."

Dallas threw up one hand. "People don't want their land. Don't you see what I'm saying? They're sick of it. Driving twenty miles just to buy socks at Wal-Mart. I'm giving people a way out. This is a public service."

"I can make you into a hero, Dallas."

"No thanks."

"I know you and I know what you want. I can just see your daddy sitting up there opening his paper."

"You don't know me."

"Elijah Walker, just beaming thinking about—"

Dallas stood. "You don't know shit about me, Gresham. And your twenty minutes are up."

Haley clasped his hands in his lap, serene. "So what? You just walk out on me? We might talk it out a little first."

"There's nothing else to say."

"Except maybe that we need each other," Haley said. "Has it occurred to you yet that you're in enemy territory?"

Dallas looked around. The place was packed with high school students hunched over tablet PCs and iPods. Kids in Buddy Holly glasses and flannel shirts. Hipsters, the place had gone hip on him, and he wondered for a moment if a one of them had ever hit a blocking sled in full pads, or shouldered a sixty-pound rucksack in the Lejeune heat. They hadn't and they didn't care and now they had gone and made a dinosaur out of him. But that was all right.

"It's all right," Dallas said. "We probably need a place like this."

"Not here." Haley smiled. "I meant the State Park land. There are folks gearing up for Armageddon, holed up with their guns and bottled water. We get complaints all the time from hikers. You hear about the birdwatcher that wandered off and hasn't been heard from since?"

"You trying to scare me now?"

"We need each other. That's all I'm saying. Sensible people united against the heathen."

"Go fuck yourself, Gresham."

He laughed. "You'll be the one fucked, my friend. You got a forest full of survivalists up there. The last thing in the world I'd worry about are folks like me."

The eastern escarpment of the Blue Ridge is footed in the northwestern corner of Oconee County, the mountains rising slowly from the end of Main Street where the public pool and a Jehovah's Witness Kingdom Hall mark the city's limit. The vast low-ceilinged textile mills that once hummed night and day were shuttered in the eighties, the buildings marked with graffiti and straddling abandoned railroad lines. What remains are the water towers and a mill hill of identical shotgun houses, shabby with age and occupied by immigrant families a generation removed from the sweatshops of Mexico and Honduras. The Tire & Body Shop a tienda now, the windows plastered with posters advertising international calling cards and Western Union wire transfers. MEXICO, CENTRO Y SUDAMERICA.

Malcolm caught the red light by the Marine Corps recruiting office and realized he had passed the enlistment offices for all four branches of the service. There hadn't been any when he'd left, and he figured that had become the county's chief export: kids whose career choices were deploying to Anbar Province or putting out stock at Wal-Mart.

He left Main Street, passed Powell's Real Estate and Frasier's General Store, passed the Last Chance, an old biker roadhouse now owned by Florida investors—the sign out front read FRIDAY KARAOKE—and started up the mountain. The switchbacks wound through walls of hardwoods and scrub pine, the slopes cut with the occasional logging or fire road that inched through the forests. He drove slowly, the sun barely over the treetops and the blacktop slick.

Past the ranger station the road leveled and straightened, and people sat on porches with portable phones and police scanners, quilts across their laps, yards littered with garden gnomes and plastic waterfowl. In a couple of months the quilts would be gone and they'd be shelling peas into washtubs, box fans whirring, phones still crooked in the bend of their necks.

He took a left at the intersection of 28 and Whetstone Road, gained speed as he approached the higher elevations where the gated communities and vacation homes perched. When the last of the Piedmont mills had fled, the chief employment had become the construction of second homes for trial lawyers and surgeons out of Atlanta and Charlotte, hulking behemoths of stone and glass stilted on limestone crags and brokered, almost exclusively, by Dallas.

Malcolm hit his father's gravel drive hard enough to fishtail into the yard, the beagles on the porch waking, ears pricked. When he stepped out they barreled into the yard and twisted around his feet.

"All right, all right." He rubbed a furry pouch of gut. "Wait a second here."

He walked onto the porch and reached into a carton and removed several strips of beef jerky he tossed to them.

The cabin consisted of three rooms, a broad porch, and a narrow bathroom walled with Tyvek wrap. Originally it had been his father's hunting camp, built on the back forty after the old man had returned from Vietnam and needed a quiet place to sit in a deer blind and drink his Early Times. The house in which Malcolm and Dallas had been raised was on the far end of the property, situated off Whetstone Road and overlooking the orchards and pond. The Winter House, his mother had called it, since the old man had spent so much of his summers at the cabin. After she had passed he had abandoned it altogether.

She couldn't have lived with such awareness, she could hardly live at all.

Malcolm remembered her as incorporeal as weather, a cloud formation, some heat, less light. He had looked at her the way one might study a planet, some faraway celestial body, brilliant and glittering if only you could step closer, if only you were less removed. She had glided into a bridge embankment his sophomore year in high school, and from this he had retreated to the church, to books and prayers and suffering of the dispossessed, for he felt he understood the trauma of abandonment. The pilgrim child *in* the world, but not *of* it. His uncle Tillman had already been a lay preacher by then, on fire for the God Malcolm suspected his father had rejected, and like Tillman, Malcolm carried that same all-consuming flame. People thought his father incapable of compromise, but in truth none of them were. They were a family of zealots. And while it could be reduced to something chemical, some imbalance of serotonin, it might also be seen as the Hand of God. Either way it changed nothing, and Malcolm knew it. It was, after all, the reason he'd fled, leaving for the Northeast the day after his high school graduation.

The place looked the same as it had that day fifteen years ago, the limp clothesline and TV antenna splayed like a weather vane, a '65 Impala dull with primer deteriorating in the shed. Past it, wire helixes spiraled from the weedy garden plot. The bed of the old man's pickup was full of wet leaves and cans of WD-40. In the cab was an empty bottle of grape ripple and a few plastic-tipped Swisher Sweets.

The walls of the back porch were lined with canning, kraut and green beans, corn and chow-chow, bags of Purina. A box of Tide had spilled crystals onto the boards and he studied the unhurried resignation of its path, the blue ice floe that bent for the dial. It felt like what he was supposed to do, take notice of things, to prepare an accounting. He stepped past the washing machine and went inside.

The bathroom smelled like Ivory soap and shaving cream, the kitchen like Folgers Crystals. The old pot belly was gone but you could see where it had once sat, the flue entry a brown circle against the browner wall. The TV Dallas had brought sat boxed in the corner. Malcolm took a bottle of muscadine wine off the counter, left his bag in the bedroom, and walked behind the house. The door to the shop was unlocked and he took a Budweiser tallboy from the mini-fridge and sat on an upturned five-gallon bucket.

There was a workbench and a Troy-Bilt garden tiller, gas cans and bags of fertilizer, rakes, shovels, and hoes. Dallas's old weight bench was still in the back, a sheet thrown over it, giving it the look of a tiny, misshapen circus tent. The plates and dumbbells had long since gone to yard sales, but the bench was still there.

Behind the shed a footpath led through the pasture and down to the pond. Dusk was near, but he didn't know where else the old man might be. Growing up, Malcolm had walked with his father to the pond every summer Saturday. When he was older he started going in winter, barren days when the sky was gray and the rain shivered from the trees. He had gone then out of the need to be alone. The adult world had opened to him and what it had revealed was a world of secrets, formulaic whispers and hushes, all around him the noise of everything unsaid.

The trail came out of a pine grove into the damp bottomland where a few naked oaks and tulip poplars dangled over the water, aluminum lawn chairs spaced along the bank. At the mouth of the creek Malcolm stepped onto a narrow sandbar and half expected to see himself as he had appeared to the world, standing hooded atop the altar, hands outstretched and tentacled to the cables. Mary Ann's son, Will, had unlocked the parish doors, and when the congregation surged inside, clipped the wires to the car battery. *You do not enter paradise tomorrow, or the day after, or in ten years,* he had underlined in the copy of Bloy they had taken from him, *you enter it today when you are poor and crucified.* But that was over now. He was home, though it had taken his arrival to realize as much.

The breeze swished through the trees and ruffled the water and then all was quiet but for the faraway sound of the beagles running. He felt the wind against his face, his numb lips. If his father wasn't here Malcolm would have to walk to the house and he wasn't sure if he was ready for that yet. At some point in the hospital it had occurred to him that he had to forgive his parents in a way that he didn't have to forgive the world. Hate the world, fight the world, cry at the world. Fine. But forgive your parents.

"Daddy," he said, tentatively, and then louder. "Daddy?"

For years he had witnessed the old man's solitary offices. He was halfway to the main house before it occurred to him that he now understood them.

Several low-hanging pecan trees drooped in front of the house and limbs scraped the dead grass that lined the walk. The hedges were shabby and unkempt. Standing on the front porch with the bottle of wine, Malcolm thought he probably shouldn't have come. He sipped the wine and looked out at the boundary lines surrounding him—fence, road, driveway—and felt the narrow circumference of his life, the one hundred sixty acres his father owned winnowed to the few feet of porch beneath him. It felt smaller still.

He capped the bottle and walked into the yard. Behind the house were the remains of what had once been his mother's flower and herb gardens. Weeds grew like wires between the flagstones and a stone basin held a skim of ice, leaves glazed in the translucent freeze. He found the key beneath a flowerpot and entered to find someone had tarped what furniture remained. Dallas, he supposed, or someone Dallas had hired, the front room cluttered with the misshapen outlines of a couch and two chairs. The smells he remembered, the snarled lines of sight, but everything appeared smaller, bent under the weight of dust.

His parents' bedroom was on the first floor. The walls were pale yellow, the color of headache, the trim white, the floorboards polished heart-of-pine. There was a nightstand, two rush-bottomed chairs paired around the front windows, a heavy dresser filled with photographs. He took out one of his parents, the old man and his mother dressed for the Easter sunrise service. His father looked dour, late middle age stripping his hair and gums in unhealthy recession, his stringy body stuffed into a blue leisure suit so that he looked like a boiled chicken dressed for a parade. His mother looked more comfortable, if not happier, plump and pearled in her Sunday best.

In the closet were eighty-three pairs of her shoes. He pulled them out of boxes and from beneath the bed, a pair of pumps and two unmatched straw huaraches from the wardrobe, a single blue satin slipper from the bathroom. He assembled them, and in a way it felt like the sum of his mother's existence, footwear, expensive and cheap. In the hall closet hung a few of her dresses, and he lifted one to find his hand shimmered with sequins, diaphanous ovoids that fell from the material like confetti, bright as fish scales.

He had never really known her.

Upstairs, he let down the trapdoor stairs and climbed to what had once been his attic study. In the center, beneath the ventilation fans and pink-sheeted insulation, his 1/128th-scale model of the battle of Fort Wagner neared its bloody climax. He had spent his high school years constructing it, then abandoned its moral clarity for college. It looked the same: like a colossal train wreck, except there was no train, only war, the flags fraying and men leaning impossibly. The three-quarter-inch die-cast soldiers of the 54th Massachusetts climbing the papier-mâché ramparts where Confederates stared down the bores of narrow rifles and killed them like hogs. Colonel Shaw already in his ditch.

The summer before his mother died Malcolm had sat here with his father, around them dead horses split by grape and solid shot, red fingernail polish spilling from torn bodies.

"There was a man there." His father pointed with his glass. "Behind that dune right there. Remember we climbed it?"

"Yes, sir."

"Well, this man, no one knew which side he was on, but he was screaming such blasphemy, caught there between the lines, such profanity, that when he was finally shot dead—and who knows which side shot him—but when he was shot dead, both sides cheered." His father held up a wounded soldier. "Look in his eyes. If your eyes are sound, your whole body will be full of light."

Near a column of rebels, a tumbler held an inch of waxy bourbon, sawdust curled across the surface, a roach floating on its segmented back. Malcolm touched the plywood and it turned slowly, as elegant and veined as a leaf on an autumn pond.

Dallas had been here.

He imagined his brother sitting here, weeks or months ago, drinking and touching these artifacts, alone in this house Malcolm had fled in mid-stride, limping across state lines as if distance alone might salvage him. He picked up the jeweler's glasses, lifted a tiny man, and pretended he was God. The soldier was a dead man, or would be soon enough, a little splash of red nail polish fifteen years drying on his gray blouse.

"Everything will be all right," he promised. "Be patient with me."

The sound of a car broke his concentration, and he started down the stairs.

Through the window he saw someone in the driveway, but it was only when he was on the porch that he recognized her as Randi.

"Well," she said, "hello, stranger."

He stared at her and blinked.

"Malcolm?" She climbed the first step. "I'm freezing out here, you know that, right? I'm freezing and you're standing there staring at me like you don't know who I am." She walked onto the porch and hugged him, held his wrists and swung her hands onto his shoulders. "You don't look so bad. Skinny. Your lips are actually pretty."

"How are you, Randi?"

"Tired and cold." She let her hands fall. "Dallas said you were hiding out over here. I thought about calling your dad's, but thought I'd just ride over and find you." She looked at him. "You look as worn out as I feel. Can we at least go in out of this cold?"

She sat on the white-draped couch with her legs tucked beneath her, Malcolm in one of the armchairs, hands lifeless as deadfall. They talked about the house and the old man and Dallas's success in court. She asked about the woman he had left behind, the time in the hospital. It was nothing, he told her. A phase. A bad idea.

"Come on."

"I mean it," he said. "I was crazy for a while."

"Then what?"

"Then it passed."

"Don't say that. Things like that don't just pass." He said nothing and she stood and began to move around the room, then stopped abruptly. "Wait a second," she said. "I just remembered something. I can't believe I forgot. Dallas comes over here sometimes. Did he tell you that?"

She walked to the liquor cabinet beneath the built-in shelves and came back with a bottle of bourbon. "I'm gonna take this, all right? Just sort of out of sight out of mind."

"Elijah Craig."

"Is this a terrible thing to do in front of you?"

"Glad to know Dallas isn't drinking on the cheap."

"Be serious. Is this terrible?"

"Take it, Randi. It's fine, really."

She put the bourbon on the floor. Her sleeves were down to her finger-tips. "I don't mean to act like some helicopter mom or something. I shouldn't be treating you like you're six years old, I know. I just don't want to be like an enabler or something."

"It's all right."

"You know you never used to drink. I think that's why I was so caught off guard by everything. You were so holy. Is it rude to say that? God, I need to shut up." She took a bottle of Evian from her bag. "Actually, it wasn't even the drinking. It's that you were never the crazy one. I mean, not that you're the crazy one now." She stopped. "I'm trying to get past this whole suburban bitch in heels and pearls thing, and then I go and say things like this."

"Please just relax."

She put the water on the floor, stood, and sat again. "You get to this point," she said, "and it's like all the things you could never imagine when you were in your twenties or early thirties or whatever, suddenly you can imagine them. And it's not even that they're real that's scary. It's that they seem inevitable. I'm thirty-nine. You're what, like half that?"

"I'm thirty-three."

"You have no idea what I'm talking about. Or maybe you do. Maybe I'm being a bitch again."

He gave no response.

"How long were you at that church?" she asked.

"Almost four years."

"Almost four years. Wow." She stood, brushed the thighs of her jeans. "I'm not sure why I came over here." She walked over to the bottle of bourbon, looked at it, and walked to the window. "Do you know what's going on with your brother right now? The stuff with these protests, this State Park land. He's kind of shut me out of it and he never shuts me out." She sat back down. "Someone keeps calling him. He tries to cover it up, but I checked his cell."

"You should just ask him."

She smiled. "The thing about your brother, Malcolm, the two things, actually. He wants people to like him—that's one. Two, he doesn't want to disappoint anyone. Hiding things is oh-so-Dallas. He's Mister Non-Confrontational."

"It's probably nothing."

"Actually, there're three—and this really scares me, but this land stuff has made him so paranoid. He's like Mister Right-Wing Anger now. I can see him off somewhere just—"

"Just what?"

"Oh, Malcolm." She acted as if she might pat his leg, but instead put out her hands, fingers splayed, nail polish chipped. "Look at my hands," she said. "Look at the fingertips. I have scales."

"It's winter."

"It's scales. Look at them."

He took her hands, turned and released them, the skin cool and dry as fine-grain sandpaper. "It's windburn. Everybody's hands get chapped."

"Not like this."

"You're outside—"

"No." She pulled them back and balled her fists as if testing their dexterity. "It isn't just the weather. Or if it is, then something else is up because the weather never did this before. You can't make me feel good about this. This is age." She stood and smoothed the front of her jeans. "Have you been to see Tillman?"

"I thought I'd ride out there later. Dallas said he was in bad shape."

"He's going to die if he doesn't get out of that chair. That's the kind of shape he's in."

"I'll ride out and see him."

"Well, just remember this weekend."

"Dallas said Leighton was having some sort of party."

"Forget Leighton. Come to our house. We can just hang out and talk." She stared out the window. "I'm glad you're back, Malcolm. I'm glad you're safe." She squeezed his hand. "Try to go easy on yourself. It's not a sin to have thought you were something that you're not."

Elijah Walker was at Frasier's General Store picking through a basket of ninety-nine-cent trout flies when he saw Dallas's truck go by. He knew his youngest would be home that day but he couldn't sit still for it, just eating up the day, thinking of ways not to go back. That morning he'd left his dead wife in her rocking chair, unlocked the back door, and headed down the mountain. Now he watched the big Ram pickup roll past and dropped the fly he was holding. By the time he walked out the truck was gone, taillights bent around the next curve.

To hell with it, he wanted to say. But it didn't work like that.

Dallas had been almost a year old when Elijah had flown from Tan Son Nhut to Hawaii to Oakland, and it wasn't that so much that that kept him from going home as he didn't know what. The need to discard the self he'd become over there. Crawling through rice paddies and waiting for the close-air to hit the tree line. Crying in helicopters while another poor son of a bitch bled out on the cleated no-skid deck. He shouldn't have stayed away. To watch some-one die was to be baptized as human, nothing more. The bodies processed through Clark or Subic Bay. Now they all went through Germany on the way to Dover but it didn't change anything. He should have known, he should have gone home. Instead, he'd gotten into some shit with the law in Detroit and hadn't made it back until Dallas turned two. Pulled his life together. Got a job at the Otasco, then bought it outright. Close the store at six and come home to plow the garden. A good stable home from that moment forward. But if Dallas held those two years against him Elijah supposed he couldn't fault the boy's reasoning. Even with money life had been hard, though not in any way he could explain. There were years he drank too much, shoved money at them and walked down to the pond to spend half a Sunday just staring at the pollen grained across the surface. And there was Evelyn, wife and mother, there, but never really.

She had wrecked on a Friday morning, headed for the beauty shop when she hit a pool of standing water and locked down the brakes. Dallas had never forgiven him that either, though Elijah wasn't sure what the *that* was, for not somehow saving her, he supposed. Not that there was a thing he could have done. The paramedics hadn't even touched her, just waited on the firefighters and the boys with their acetylene torches. They cut her out and put her in a box. Closed coffin. Buried before the weekend was over. Preacher Dell standing over the grave: the last enemy to be destroyed is death. Barely cold and Elijah was ordering a headstone. He had rushed it, he knew as much, but hadn't seen he could bear it any other way.

Malcolm—

Malcolm was supposed to change things—a gift, an unexpected blessing—and Elijah supposed he had. Then Evelyn had slid into that bridge embankment and Malcolm, just like Dallas, had lit out first chance he got. When Elijah heard what his boy had done he hadn't been surprised. He was Tillman made over. Incapable of compromise. Still, the business with the antifreeze had almost broken Elijah's heart. He had almost drowned in sadness but when he resurfaced it was all anger. Just to hand it over like that, to give it away. He'd gone looking for someone to talk to after that, but all the VA had done was dope him up. Zoloft. Paxil. Then he'd found out Paxil was for folks who were suicidal and all that did was piss him off. He went off it cold. Not that it mattered. You can't medicate for regret.

He started his truck and pulled past Frasier's. On the front window were signs for Cash 5 and Mega Millions and Clean Sweep. They'd done away with video poker years ago, but a few of the faded posters lived on, tacked over by fliers for benefit suppers and missing yard dogs and bass boats marked down to $2,500, then marked down again to $2,200.

There ain't no bottom, he thought.

But he knew there was, and he knew he'd seen it. He just didn't like to think he'd ever see it again. Just that morning he'd pulled behind a car at the first traffic light coming into town and had by God sworn laying across the back glass in front of him was a human arm. A little Japanese hatchback with a severed forearm angled across the rear windshield. A moment later he'd seen it was just the wiper, of course, but it stuck with him, not so much the image—it hadn't really looked anything like an arm—but the fact that he'd imagined such. Dismemberment. Bodies in pieces. Was that where he was at?

He started up the mountain and made a left onto Whetstone and then another left onto Cassidy Bridge road, turned into the muddy yard of the El Shaddai Temple of the Holy Ghost and parked between a battered green Bonneville and a Ford pickup, the bed weighted with firewood. This was

Evelyn's church but he'd been coming on and off for the last fifteen years, more or less since she had passed. There was nothing official about the church, no regular choir, no bulletin or social committees. It was the sort of place Dallas and his fancy wife wouldn't set foot in. Or maybe they would, maybe he wasn't giving them any credit. Dallas was rich now but you couldn't fault a man his wealth.

Elijah liked the preacher, Clyde Dell, a man about his age who worked as a custodian at the high school, liked that he never had two nickels to rub together. Dell preached when the spirit moved him, healed when he was so instructed. Forty-odd years ago Elijah had watched Christ take that round, headshot and drifting face down in the rotorwash of a flooded rice field, elephant grass laid over like mown hay, and since then that had been all. An absence. That yawning God-shaped hole stuffed full with fairy tales. But listening to Dell he wondered if just maybe he'd missed something.

Dell had committed the Gospels to memory. He couldn't even read but could scroll back through every word of Christ's. Not that Elijah put a lot of stock in that sort of thing. His brother, Tillman, sat up in his trailer with his computer and Bible, and he was dying from it. Wouldn't get up for love or money. He said it like it was a joke but it wasn't. Enough thinking and you were finished. He'd seen a man's brain in Vietnam. The actual by God thing, gray and broken. There wasn't much heft to it, coming out the side of his head like an egg, and Elijah realized right then the brain wasn't what kept you alive. There were things beyond it. You've just lost the vision, old man. He who has eyes. Wasn't that the line?

The church was dim and warm, the screen of a space heater flexed orange near the altar rail. He sat on the back pew and nodded to the woman who sat at the opposite end—Mildred Carter—the only other person in the church. She had a thin cushion wedged behind her and appeared to be sleeping, doughy hands folded in her lap. When she moved Elijah could smell her, camphor and old age—he'd started smelling it on himself.

He thought about Malcolm. The truth was, no matter what he told Evelyn, he would be glad to have him home. After she had passed, Malcolm had been the still center of their mutual universe. Elijah and Malcolm, father and son. Dallas off in the Marines and already running around, but Malcolm home cooking supper or washing bedsheets, steady and upright. Elijah remembered him in front of the TV, nose poked up to the screen as if he might crawl inside with the little swoop-bellied Ethiopian children it took Elijah a moment to realize his boy was crying over. No, Malcolm wasn't crazy. He just felt too much. The antenna a bit too sharp. The eyes a bit too sensitive.

"Mr. Walker?"

He looked up into the tired face of Mildred Carter.

"Mrs. Carter," he said. "How are you?"

"Good as can be expected, I suppose. I'd complain if a body would listen."

"Yes, ma'am."

"It's funny what one will say to another. What one will put up with and another won't."

"I guess it is," Elijah said.

"Like when your boy called me the other day," she said. "Wanting to come see me and all."

Elijah turned to her.

"Your oldest boy, Dallas," she said. "Here I was in the kitchen and the phone starts to ringing and I pick it up and who is it on the phone but Mr. Dallas Walker himself. Right there calling little old me. He wants my land. I don't need to have no sit-down to figure as much."

He shook his head. "I ain't involved in any of that."

"Forty-four acres of good bottomland. I reckon he's about pissed his pants thinking about it." She clucked her tongue. "Papaw and his brother cleared that land in eighteen and ninety-nine. Hauled off the stones and plowed the soil. Them churning up old bones from the Cherokee like they was rotten potatoes. Old dad told me not a year before he passed that Papaw piled them bones and burned them, danced around them like he was half-Indian himself, which he might could've been. You think your boy took account of that?" He felt her look at him. "I's born in the big house in nineteen and twenty-nine but I doubt your boy takes account that, either. Course I heard all sorts of things about your boy. Bound to, I reckon." She looked back at the altar. "Heard all about the law getting after him."

"There ain't no law after him."

"Maybe not yet but what I heard is they will be soon enough. Him and that partner of his went and paid off the county commissioner's office is the way they tell it. Now he's went and got himself in bed with that group up the mountain. Them Tree of Liberty folk."

Elijah faced forward. The space heater reflected in the buckle of the paneled walls. The painting of Christ, knocking.

"I ain't got a thing in the world to do with it," he said.

He found Dell down in the basement kitchen, the room long and narrow with a low drop ceiling. The shelves were lined with gallon cans of Heinz Pork & Beans, ketchup, a jar of pickles suspended in a murky solution. Four metal columns flaking white paint stood at intervals.

Dell was mopping the linoleum.

"My boy's coming home," Elijah said. "Malcolm."

Dell looked up, surprised, then nodded.

"Today," Elijah said. "Probably already back looking for me for all I know."

"I think I might have heard something about that."

"He had some sort of fit, then tried to kill himself in the hospital." Elijah shook his head. He was sweating, had just realized it. "I don't know why I'm telling you. It ain't no secret."

"You want to sit down a minute, Elijah?"

"I don't know where I'm glad he's coming or not. Just a minute ago I was sure I was, but you get where you mistrust your own thoughts."

"You want to sit with me?"

"I got to get going here in about two seconds."

"Let's sit for a minute."

"I better just get on."

They stood for a moment, uneasy until Dell fixed his eyes on him. "I know you miss Evelyn the most at times like these."

"I do," Elijah said. "Dearly, I do. But maybe not like you're meaning, preacher."

Malcolm was on the cabin porch with a quilt draped over his shoulders when the old man came home. It was after seven and full dark. Sleet fell through the safety light.

"I figured on you flying down," his father said. "Been quicker."

"How are you, Daddy?"

The old man looked at him. "Let's get out of this cold."

They ate the leftover soup beans and cornbread and Hungry Man dinners heated in the microwave.

"Dallas didn't take you to see any of his good-time buddies?" the old man asked.

"Just brought me back."

"He didn't say anything to you?"

"Like what?"

"I wouldn't know." He raised his fork. "Boy don't tell me nothing."

"There's some environmental survey he's worried about."

"He ain't worried about no environmental survey. He just wants his back to the wall. Wants to feel like he's back on the ball field is what he wants. You know he's been on drugs since the day he got to Georgia? Steroids." He pointed with his knife. "Sat right where you're sitting and told me. Said he was hooked on em, hooked on being bigger than everybody else." He turned his attention to his plate. "I can't remember the last time he brought my granddaughter up here to see me."

"He brought you that TV."

"A TV ain't nothing but another thing." The old man exhaled, motioned at Malcolm's throat. "You're healed up, more or less."

"More or less, yes, sir."

"Your mamma would've been glad it come out like it did," he said. "But I ain't gonna sit here and lie to you, son. Making a fool out of yourself don't make you no more Christian than the next." The old man cut his country fried steak with his pocket knife. "I reckon you could get Dallas to take you on. He could probably use the help."

"I might be moving on," Malcolm said. "I have a job in the fall."

"This that job in Cuba?"

"Haiti. At a school down there."

"A school in Hay-tee. You get yourself half-killed, then half-better, and that's it: off to Hay-tee. I'd try to knock some sense into you but I'd probably die of exhaustion first."

"I didn't wish it this way."

"Didn't nobody," the old man said. "Rest assured."

Sometime later they heard the dogs rise and shift on the porch.

"Don't let me forget to let them in," the old man said. "It'll freeze tonight."

Malcolm nodded and for a while they ate in silence, listened to the wind gather and move the wind chimes, the trees.

"I wish you might explain sometime what happened to you," the old man said finally. "The hospital and all."

Malcolm shrugged. "I just lost it."

"No, you didn't. You ain't one to just lose anything." He put his hands on the table and stood. "It'd be a lot easier if you were."

Malcolm woke early the next morning, swallowed three BC headache powders, and struck out into the woods toward the creek. His father was still asleep in his chair, but Malcolm had heard gunshots and thought someone might have been firing at one of the bears that rooted through trash cans. The beagles were off running, so he walked alone through shafts of sunlight that fell through the trees and shaped a cathedral of sorts, the coming dawn backlighting the purple ginger and blue bellflowers that bloomed from the decomposing remains of a nurse log. Just below the house, he met the creek and followed it upstream until he found a small cairn of stones balanced atop a rock in the center of a still pool.

It was there he picked up the first swatches of blood.

The air was mineral-dense, and he followed the trail into a laurel thicket where bedded in the cool earth a coonhound lay on its side, its back hip blasted open. Dried blood had crusted the surrounding fur and turned the dirt wine-dark. The dog breathed slowly, struggling to turn one glassy eye on Malcolm before lowering it again to exhale into the dust. Malcolm stepped closer and saw a large wolf spider leg its way toward the animal's eye.

When he turned to go he saw the child sitting in the wet leaves with his back against the scaled trunk of a river birch. Malcolm had not seen him since the hospital.

"You're here," Malcolm said.

The child sucked air through his nose hole.

"I didn't know if you'd come," Malcolm told him.

The child said nothing and Malcolm started home.

The old man sat at the kitchen table drinking coffee from the metal cup of a Stanley thermos when Malcolm got back. Malcolm stood at the window, the yard gray and brown, the winter grass stunted and dead. Water dripped from the eaves.

"You're out early," the old man said.

"Thought I'd go over to the house. Maybe check on things."

"Storm's blowing up. Be six inches on the ground by the weekend."

"I'll get the heat on."

"Thermostat's busted." The old man pushed himself up from the chair. "All that space-age shit and freezing for lack of firewood."

When the old man staggered his way to the cabinet Malcolm saw he had been staring down at a wallet-sized sepia portrait of Malcolm's mother. He came back to the table with two glasses and a bottle of twelve-year-old Macallan's scotch.

"Every time I drink this I start to cry," he said. "The beauties of this earth."

"The wonders," Malcolm said.

The old man took a long swallow. "The goddamn wonders, indeed."

II.

At some point you had to get out. You had to get out, she thought, or it killed you. But that wasn't true. That was what Roosevelt would have referred to as one of her theatrical responses, her failure to exist beyond the performative, the reenactment of old wrongs, the slings and arrows and all-around bad shit laid on her by her nana. In truth, it wasn't so much that you were killed as warped, you bent in a series of compromises, each uglier than the one before. Though it wasn't so much your malleability that was at issue as the slow wasting of—and here she caught herself on the edge of theatrics—the slow wasting of your very soul. But this man—this white man—Luther Love was no more interested in such than Rose had been.

"You think I don't hear that drug shit twenty-four seven?" Love asked. He stood behind the display case and leaned toward her, hands planted on the glass. "You think I don't get tired of watching y'all come in here wanting and wanting what you can't get?"

But Jordan just wanted her knife, Roosevelt's knife, and she didn't see it beside the pocket watches and repackaged copies of *Call of Duty* and *Grand Theft Auto*. She had the fifty dollars to get it out of hock now, but if it was gone, she didn't know what would happen. She was coming off a bad jag—she had been dreaming of the bear again—and had a single Xanax left, but if Rose's knife was gone it wouldn't help. She'd spiral and she didn't want to spiral, Jesus, not again.

She smoothed two twenties and a crumpled ten.

"I just want my knife back."

"That knife's a piece of work," Love said. "It's crossed my mind a time or two to just hang onto it."

"You said you'd keep it for me."

"I did. But the thing with all you dopeheads." He scratched one gray temple and turned to unlock a cabinet behind him. "Y'all ain't the most reliable demographic." When he turned back around he had the knife in his hand but didn't yet pass it over. "This is a W. E. Pease," he said. "Look here. That's a Mortise handle. Every bit of it ivory. These are mosaic studs all along here."

"Just give it to me."

"This is a six-, seven-hundred-dollar knife. I did you a serious favor hanging onto this thing."

He slapped it into her hand and she pushed the money at him.

"Keep it," he said. "He came in and paid it off already."

She stared at him a moment. He was talking about Leighton.

"He said you'd run off," Love said. "But I guess you didn't run far enough."

She put the knife in her pocket and left, walked the length of the block to the Olympian Billiards & Cocktail Lounge. She felt the pang of losing Rose though it seemed almost sinful to evoke him, imagining him into shapes he had never occupied. More contortionist than lover. Less memory than ghost. They had fought, of course, fought because the Florida nights were stifling; fought because breathing was like pulling rags from your lungs, fought because everybody fought, given enough time. Fought because somewhere in this world— God only knew where—was a child whose name Jordan refused to speak. She had decided to forgive Rose, but standing outside the bar she undecided. He had cost Jordan her child, cost Jordan her life. But no use thinking about it now, she thought, and pushed open the door, not now or ever again.

It was almost six and the place was beginning to fill with folks shooting pool or drinking at tables, twenty-somethings in expensive hiking gear over from Greenville. They'd spent the day on the river or trails and would head home to their loft apartments and townhouses soon. Take their hybrid SUVs and four-thousand-dollar bicycles back to civilization. Playing tourist in the meantime. Anthropologists collecting banjo anecdotes for the next office party.

The older, grimmer local crowd sat at the bar and stared silently at a pay-per-view MMA fight. She doubted they knew what the letters stood for but surely in it they recognized their own lives. Faces bunched from working construction. Fingernails black or missing. They huddled in denim Carhartt coats and drank the cheapest beer on tap. Fifteen years making good money in one of the mills, then woke up one day to talk of layoffs and job retraining, except there were no jobs to retrain for. Life just pushed on. Their boys were men now and Jordan saw how this weighed on them. Tattooed and smoking meth or on foot patrol in Helmand Province—either way they weren't coming clean of it. Their daughters had babies and bought formula with WIC coupons. The old men might still go to church if their wives bothered with it but they were twenty years past belief, twenty years past caring. The shine comes off. That hard bright thing gone soft around the edges. You watch your babies grow up and fail you and honestly, what was left after that?

But Christ, she thought, snap out of it. The shit you carry around inside. The shit you project. Every old man wasn't her papa. Every life wasn't sunk into—she waved one hand as if someone might register the motion—into this. You sound like you're sixty years old and dying.

The animated swoosh of the Golden Tee video game brought her back and she took a barstool and ordered a glass of chardonnay. She wanted to do things right. That was all she had ever wanted. Right glass. Right wine. Everything in its ordered place. Calm and present. When she looked up she recognized the girl across from her, Karen, Kathy maybe. Five or six years out of high school and heavier than Jordan remembered her, lifting a Bud Light and freezing just before the bottle touched her lips.

"Oh my God, Jordan Taylor," the girl said. "Kim Strauss. Remember me? I was a year behind you in school."

"I remember," she said, and she did remember the face, if nothing else. "How are you?"

"Oh my God, how are *you*? I heard you were gone, like long gone to California or something."

"Florida. But I came back."

"I see that. You look great." But Jordan could tell by the way she said it she meant you look skinny, like sick skinny, girl, like HIV-I-can-see-your-skull-under-there skinny.

"Thanks," Jordan said. "How is everything?"

"The same," Kim said. "Always the same. Still see the girls in here like three or four nights a week. The one's that don't have babies, I mean. It's like one of those dances after the football games, you remember? Everybody so packed you don't even know who you went home with until the next morning and then you're like, oh shit, oh no I didn't." She took a drink of her beer. "Except I guess nobody has to sneak a flask in like Tommy Rich used to do if you remember that."

She didn't, and took an easy drink from her glass, slow but substantial, put the wine down when she felt the heat in her throat.

"So you had a man, I remember" Kim said.

"Rose," Jordan said. "Roosevelt."

"And that didn't?"

"No."

"Completely?"

"Completely."

"So you're like totally unattached?"

Jordan took another drink, nodded as she swallowed.

"Well, honey, that might work out just fine tonight. Look there."

A man smiled in her direction before he turned to the bartender. Good looking in a blue sport coat, his face a construction of right angles, his hair neat and flecked with gray. They were forever following her, older men, and she was forever indulging them, first Rose and then Leighton, dying on the rack of adulation.

"He don't even look like he's from Walhalla," Kim said. "Let me get out of your way before he wakes up and realizes he's in the redneck capital of the world."

"Oh, no," Jordan said, "please stay." But Kim was gone. The man watched her go, smiled, and moved to the now-empty stool, bourbon in one hand, wine in the other.

"I hope I didn't run her off," he said, and handed her the glass. "I took the liberty."

"What a gentlemen."

He smiled and she started to drink, remembered the knife, and dropped one hand into her lap to touch it through the denim of her jeans.

The man pointed at the drink. "Clos du Bois. I didn't misjudge?"

"Oh, no," she said. "A gentleman with a good eye."

"Or ear. I'm Tom."

"Jordan."

"That's a lovely name."

She batted her eyes wildly. "You can't imagine how often I hear that."

He gave back a sheepish grin. He really was good looking.

"I'm joking," she said, and left a little smear of lipstick on the rim like a gift. "So you're local, Tom?"

"Semi," he said. "I've got a practice in Atlanta that I'm gradually stepping away from. Got a place in the mountains now."

"You're a lawyer?"

"Reconstructive surgeon."

"Is that like a plastic surgeon?"

"Plastic surgeon. Sure, why not." He laughed. "You're something, aren't you? I'd like to fire you out of a cannon."

They moved to a table and Jordan drank a third glass while Tom rattled on about his time-share in Barbados. He was like all the rest who had bought second homes, rich and aloof, decked out in L.L. Bean and expensive loafers, probably spending more on Orvis fishing tackle than she paid all year in rent. She had lost the thread of the conversation and was no longer listening, no longer even looking at him but over his shoulder and around the room. The stereo wailed drunken country love and around them couples started to pair off, hesitantly, almost tenderly, she thought, not yet drunk enough to have forgotten what it means to be lonely. But when she looked out the front window she thought she saw Leighton's Navigator idling along the street, but that was the paranoia is all that was. Put it out of your mind, Jordan. Don't let it creep in.

She raised the glass so that it caught the overhead light.

Don't let it. Don't you dare.

But it had and she ran from the table and cut the line to the ladies room where she palmed water to swallow her last Xanax. A woman in a Mossy Oak ball cap and a black tank top looked at her in the mirror and asked if she was all right.

"Yeah," Jordan said. She was sweating but she was going to be all right. She was sweating but everybody sweated. It meant you were still alive. "Just saw somebody."

"Well, kill his ass, sister." The woman lit a cigarette. "They ain't a one of em worth the dick swinging between their legs."

"I have to go home," Jordan told her reflection.

"Don't let him run you."

"I just need to go home."

"Well, go home but don't let him run you."

When she walked back to the bar she didn't bother looking toward the street. It was dark now, and the window was a glossy mirror, a frame for sensible people laughing and drinking. She didn't need to hide. Tom was gone and she didn't need to hide. She had ways of disappearing in plain sight. You threw yourself against a wall and whatever stuck they accepted; meanwhile, the self slunk away, undetected. You didn't bother with any disguise. That was the secret: you didn't bother with anything.

She ordered a gin and tonic and when the bartender brought it she handed him one of the twenties. He was middle-aged and homely, a second-generation barkeep who appeared to have resigned himself to much less.

"I'd take that money and put it down on a bus ticket," he said. He looked out at the street and bent closer. "He was in here earlier looking for you."

When she asked who, he simply shook his head and walked away. She knew who, but this was theatrics, her performative state. She couldn't help it. She finished her drink and left.

She was two blocks up the street when she noticed the lights behind her and instead of playing coy she simply turned and walked toward them, watched the window slide down on Leighton Clatter. He had pulled into one of the angled spaces and she could feel the warm air radiate from the floor vents.

"I thought you might need a ride," he said.

"I'm walking."

"It's late to be walking."

"It's not that late."

He let his hand drift out toward her so that she saw the rings bunched on his fat fingers. "You're too pretty to be out alone."

"It's an affliction."

"Hilarious. You know you really should worry more."

"I'm fine."

She felt him stiffen and could sense the change in his voice even before he spoke: "Get in the car, Jordan."

He backed out and they eased up the street past Blue Ridge Medical Supply with its shower stools and electric scooters, Walgreens, the Gun Shoppe, the offices of the Department of Social Services housed down in the old fire station. They were building a new courthouse, four floors of courtrooms and, she guessed, holding rooms. The money was coming from property taxes levied on the new developments dotting the mountains that ringed town. The money was coming from people like Leighton.

"Did that little asshole in the pawn shop call you?" she asked.

"Who, Brother Luther?" He shook his head. "That would hardly be necessary. I have a long reach, darling."

She knew it was true. After Rose, she had come home and got her old job at the fish camp back, rented a dump on Short Street, spent her tips on rhinestones and cocaine. The night she met Leighton she was all lower vibration, strung out and in desperate need, and then someone told her Leighton was holding, and that was how she wound up with him. He was a disgusting man but she felt reckless, one remove from the worst desperation she'd ever felt. So in an attic room of wall studs and sheets of silver and pink insulation Jordan slid into his lap and kissed him while he slipped down the strap of her bra and licked around her dark nipples, heels grinding the floorboards as he swam into her.

She had spiraled after that, a down-racing arc that ended only when she was Baker-Acted in the fall. Her nana's work: three days in two-point restraints at Saint Francis in Greenville. After that were the attempts at normalcy, the friends who would take her home and try to teach her to how to live. Bridal showers and barbecues. Trips to the mall. There were girls' nights out that ended with Jordan unconscious or weeping; then there were no more nights out and then there were no more girls. She didn't miss it. *Sentimentality,* she remembered from the Jung she had read at the spiritualist camp, *is the super-structure erected upon brutality.* She didn't miss it one bit. She had simply called Leighton. She hadn't seen him for almost a year, but soon enough she was a kept woman, waking beneath the spidery blades of his ceiling fan, lying on his four-poster bed like a gutted fish. Later, he paid for her to get clean, but she never really got clean, now did she? She just went back to her grandparents.

"I've missed you," he said. "Got worried for a bit."

"Well you shouldn't have."

"Heard a nasty rumor that someone saw you all the way up in Asheville hanging around with the local filth." He kept his eyes forward. "I got so worried I almost went over and saw Littlejon, thought to ask him what had become of his granddaughter."

She said nothing, and he clicked the blinker to turn onto Short Street by the abandoned car wash. Someone had left a couch on the sidewalk and it was covered with garbage bags.

"I missed you, Jordan."

"You said that already."

He looked at her. "You're in one of your moods tonight. All right. I can accept that." He pulled to a stop outside the house she was renting. "But don't go slumming on me, and don't make me worry again, you understand me?"

She reached for the door and he grabbed her arm, switched his hand to her cheeks so fast she gasped, the meat of his fingers wringing her mouth so that it puckered like a child's.

"I'm refusing to take the long view. You understand me?" He dug his rings into her skin. "You don't run out on me. My patience is vast, but it's not infinite. Not at my age."

"All right," she managed to say.

"Good. But before you go I'd like an apology. Say you're sorry, Jordan."

"I'm sorry."

"Say you're sorry for making Leighton worry. Say you're sorry for breaking old Leighton's heart."

Her mouth was beginning to hurt. "Please," she said. "I'm sorry."

He nodded her head up and down slowly.

"I'll see you this weekend."

When he pushed her toward the door she almost fell out and then did, scrambling up as he peeled past the stop sign and out of sight. She straightened her coat and touched her front pocket; the knife was still there; she still had the knife, and thought of Rose and his Pilgrim angel, Rose dying on a rented hospital bed in Florida. For whatever else he was, he was hers. Or had been. But she had been so young, so young and so stupid. And what could she have possibly known, naïve as she was? She knew now you could love someone on the strength of being young. You could love someone because you are poor together, misunderstood together, lonely and cast to your own inadequate devices together.

Those days driving south when they would stay in bed until noon and then rise, bodies humid and feral with sex. You could love someone on the strength of all that, before the reckoning, before the petals wilt and then fall, first singly, then a mad shower that tastes like nothing so much as what is lost.

You could love someone on that, but not forever.

She unlocked the front door and walked through the kitchen and then room to room. No one was home. Archimedes had moved in right after he'd lost his job at Duke Power and with him had come a steady parade of his friends about whom the best thing she could say was that they tended to be temporary, coming and going so quickly she never bothered with names. The door to his bedroom was cracked, and she edged it open until it caught on the extension cord that ran to the empty fish tank, its dry seafloor cluttered with rocks and a busted pump.

The room was a mess—patches of drywall flaked onto the carpet beneath a sagging Bob Marley flag—and looking at it made her almost physically sick. She flicked off the bedroom light and watched the glow-in-the-dark stars flex on the ceiling. The room was a mess, the entire house was a mess, and what she was doing was living in filth. Her nana's expression. She was living in filth. Living in sin. But that was all right. She was here.

She was still alive.

Dallas was a peculiarly American sort of millionaire, impatient and uncertain, always parlaying this into that, getting bigger, stronger and richer, most certainly richer. He'd left UGA to spend three years in the Marines, lifting weights at an airless depot in Twentynine Palms and then, after his discharge, had moved to Atlanta to join a fledgling bodybuilding circuit that took him all over the Southeast.

When the circuit folded he felt things ending much as he remembered watching a traveling carnival end as a boy: with such sudden efficiency you are embarrassed for the nostalgia you felt five minutes ago; then it starts to rain. He wound up with a schmooze job at Jaguar's regional headquarters where he played golf and signed old UGA programs to dealers' kids before hitting the town. The Gold Club. Fan-Tasia. Peppered vodka and bowls of mixed nuts. Lap Dances in the champagne room. Then the IRS audit struck and it was that same carnival folding: goodbye, goodnight. The office was restructured, several execs were fired, and Dallas was out of a job.

Then he met Mr. Nu South, Leighton Clatter.

Leighton was not yet old enough to be considered a lecherous old man, but no doubt aspired to it. What he was, was a retired ophthalmologist turned restaurateur who owned a chain of over sixty restaurants throughout the Deep South called The Apple Cellar. The restaurants were situated just off interstates near malls and office parks, each made to look like a decrepit barn with antique yokes and scythes nailed on the walls. The waitresses wore aprons and bonnets, the men strung bailing twine through their belt loops. In the lobby gift shop were calendars and sepia prints and jars of apple butter. A broken-down wagon was hauled from lawn to lawn for openings and photo-ops.

"The New South's a parking lot," he had told Dallas. "I got the only place left where you can still find a mule."

Leighton was just beginning to buy up large tracts of rural land, and he needed a face for the business, someone to rub shoulders with investors and make appearances at county council meetings. Dallas would do the leg work and lend his name (if not his fast-fading fame) to the venture, while Leighton supplied the start-up money. It wouldn't be that difficult, they reasoned, and they had been right. All over the South, children were inheriting homeplaces they had neither the time nor inclination to maintain. That was where Dallas came in, swooping down like an answered prayer to buy old farms, erect a stone gate, dig sewer and water lines, and name the whole thing after exactly that which they had destroyed. GREEN VALLEY. DEER MEADOW. The hunger for six-tenths of an acre with a view of the Blue Ridge Mountains seemed insatiable. They'd moved the corporate office to South Carolina and Dallas had filled his new home with a liquor cabinet and a trophy wife to display beside it. For fifteen years he woke to an abiding sense of his blissful past. But when he woke this morning it was to the lit screen and soft vibrations of the Blackberry that rested on his nightstand.

This was not a good thing, and it took him a moment to orient himself: at home and in bed, Randi asleep beside him, hugging a pillow and curled like a burnt leaf. The room was drawn in soft darkness, hazy with a predawn light that seemed to fail past the edges of the drawn blinds, everything gray and then grayer. Compared to the room the blue screen lit brilliantly.

Dallas rolled onto his side and shielded the phone beneath the mass of his body. When it stopped he looked at Randi, relieved she hadn't woken. He didn't bother to look at the screen. He'd been getting the same text for weeks and knew it by heart.

Stay off the land. We are concerned only with your self-preservation.

The messages had started in January and he figured some asshole environmentalist had gotten his number and was fucking with him. Dallas would hear his cell go off in the other room, a single ring and then nothing except the message and UNIDENTIFIED NUMBER in the call log. He hadn't told Randi about it, but suspected she might be checking his phone. He couldn't be certain though, and had taken to carrying it with him everywhere, lugging it into the shower and down to the basement gym.

That Randi might find out scared him more than the messages.

He looked at the lovely taper of her body—one leg had slipped from the sheet, the white fabric darker where it rose and fell with her shape—looked at her and tried to remember the last time they'd made love. Christmas, maybe—Jesus, yes, Christmas it must have been. The fireplace banked, the day burning down and burning out, the memory turning to ash the moment he reached for it.

He almost touched her now but didn't. Instead he slipped into the bathroom and sent a plume of brown urine into the toilet, washed his face, and stared for a moment at his reflection. He'd been out late the night before—partying while she drove over to check on Malcolm, another disconnect, another moment slipped past—and the whites of his eyes looked runny and beaten. He drank too much, that much was clear. That he was a lazy, soft man he'd known for years, but that he looked like his father was the morning's revelation. It carried more sadness than surprise.

When he came out of the bathroom Randi was beginning to stir and Dallas dressed quickly, pulled on a T-shirt and gym pants, and padded barefoot downstairs and into the kitchen, where he stood on the cold floorboards and scooped protein powder into a shaker cup he filled with Ripped Fuel. Out the windows morning gathered tentatively along the treetops, all faded light, the sky overcast and raw.

When he heard the shower come on he climbed the stairs to his office. He had a routine—he wasn't avoiding Randi. He just had a routine, and if it meant he walked out of a room just before she walked in, well, shit, was that his fault? He tapped the mouse and the computer began to hum. *I'm just trying to get through the day, babydoll.* He said it to her at least twice a day. In the car, in the morning and at night, during that lull at lunch when they sat staring across the table, fingering flatware and waiting for plates of grilled tuna to fill the gulf. *I'm just trying to put one foot in front of the other.* And of course she didn't know the shit he was in.

Leighton had set up an RSS news feed so that any article mentioning Dallas, Leighton, or Blue Mountain Realty would be sent directly to his computer. This morning there was only one, a single blog post off a site called "X-Treme Mountain Savior":

> *If these assholes at so-called 'Blue Mountain,' are successful in raping this land—and if the Feds can't or won't throw them in jail—the precedent will pretty much destroy any effort to protect the last vestiges of Southern Appalachian forests. At least it's good to know that there are folks up there who will shoot these fuckers . . .*

He deleted the link. Why read that kind of shit? It was going to happen; it was already happening. The nutjobs trying to hold back the tide, Leighton was always saying. The fools telling the sun to stand still. It bothered Dallas, though. A hundred times a day he told himself he didn't care, and a hundred times a day it hurt, just a little, sure, a sliver of pain, but no less real. Because hadn't the whole world loved him once? Hadn't the world lined up to shake his hand? His entire life had been graced and he still had trouble imagining it any other way.

Then he remembered he'd left his phone in the kitchen.

He hustled downstairs and made it just before Randi glided in, enormous Gloria Vanderbilt sunglasses pushed into her wet hair, the former Miss Tennessee in an aquamarine track suit and a string of pearls.

She kissed his shoulder. "You didn't wake me up."

He dropped the Blackberry in his pocket, went to the sink, and started rinsing his shaker cup, clumps of powder dissolving against the drain. "I just got up."

"Somebody call?"

"Not that I know of."

She took a cardboard tube of orange juice concentrate from the freezer and began to spoon out bites. "I thought I heard your phone."

"You know that's pure acid."

She waved the spoon along her throat. "I have this gunk."

"You're going to ruin your teeth."

"I have, like, this gunk in my throat."

"What you have," Dallas said, "is six thousand dollars of cosmetic-fucking-dentistry. You ever think of that?"

She stopped in mid-bite and dropped the canister in the trash, turned, and plucked a banana. "I thought I might go back over and see Malcolm," she said after a moment.

"I thought you went over there yesterday?"

"He said you invited him to Leighton's," she said. "You didn't get those bottles out like I asked you, either."

He watched the reflection of his shoulder rise and fall in the window.

"I haven't made it over yet," he said. "But I will."

"Forget it. I got them myself."

He kept his eyes on the glass.

"I feel sorry for him," she said.

"Well, go back and see him. Nobody's stopping you."

She took a step toward him. "That cup's clean, baby. I think you got it."

He looked down. It was clean, had been clean for he didn't know how long. He cut the water and turned to face her.

"Go see Malcolm. I think it's a great idea," he said. "I'm sure it would mean a lot to him."

"Go with me then."

"I'm sorry about the bottles."

"Please?"

He put the shaker cup on the counter. "It'd probably mean more if it was just you."

The banana peel had folded over her hand, a flower, a perfect yellow star. She turned her hand and the flower was gone; it was just a peel now. She threw it in the trash, harder, he thought, than necessary.

"All right," she said. "I'll see you later then."

When she was gone he went downstairs and cranked the stereo to the classic rock station out of Anderson. The Ripped Fuel was beginning to take hold and he felt a lightness in his fingertips, his arms loose and almost foreign as the caffeine and ephedrine spiked in his bloodstream. He cranked the stereo and started skipping rope. When he had a light sweat going he loaded the bench press and pushed out a warm-up set and then another. He turned the music up. He felt it now, chest swollen and scalp tingling.

You know what I want.

Some days it was the only thing in the world he wanted. He loaded on Olympic plates and worked through five pyramid sets, cutting reps and adding weight. The music wouldn't go any louder, but shit, he felt so good it didn't matter. What he loved—what he'd always loved—was the clarity of training, the stop watches and scales. He could imagine no other form of objectivity, and objectivity was exactly what he needed. In the last few years he had come to realize that it might be possible to completely lose himself, to forget entirely who he was, to encounter his face in the mirror and have it bring forth a faint tremble that may or may not register as recognition.

The only answer that had ever truly satisfied was the gym.

There were times when he couldn't stop lifting. This was his attempt at
... ticism, at purification by pain: lifting past the warning signs, the shakes and
vomiting, lifting until you redlined somewhere between exhaustion and ecstasy.
He would work chest and shoulders. Bench, incline, and military press. Dips.
Shrugs. Side lateral raises. Chest flies. Upright rows. Abs. Forearms. Skip rope
until there was nothing left, then start over, pumping Cytomax and creatine
into his gut, cycling until there was neither motion nor form, just a little crust of
vomit on his shirtfront.

You know what I want: more weight.

Once in the Georgia weight room, Dallas was spotting a linebacker on the
incline press, screaming into his ear while he forced out his reps. They had
swallowed caffeine pills and spent the morning slapping each other in the face,
and on the third set Dallas bit the top of the linebacker's head, came away with
hair and bits of scalp in his teeth. Blood bubbled between hair follicles and ran
down the linebacker's face, but he had kept lifting, something rattling inside
him, too, and Dallas had thought: This is as close as I'm getting, right here.
This is heaven.

And he had been right.

He was feeling it today, too, sucking from a water bottle and moving from
the bench to the dip bar to the incline, where he slid on four plates—two hundred and twenty-five pounds—and lifted the bar. *I'm talking to you, bitch.* On
the third rep his nose started to bleed. He pressed out two more reps because
fuck you—you can't treat people like that. *Fuck you,* he yelled at his vibrat-
ing reflection. Randi was all pissed when all he wanted was to shield her. He
cracked out three reps and watched his eyeballs quiver in the mirror.

More weight. More weight.

But you can't treat people like that, the anonymous messages and online
posts. He started a burn-out set with one thirty-five, fell to the floor for a set
of push-ups. But why couldn't he just tell her? Why couldn't he just ride over
there with her? He felt his arms give and found his nose bleeding and buried
in the rubber mat, crawled across the room and pulled himself up on the squat
rack and started loading the bar.

But goddamn it: more weight—now, while he still could.

And if he couldn't just jump in his truck and follow her, what would that mean? He dropped into a set of squats. It wouldn't always be like it had been at Georgia, he knew that, first Dallas Walker, then Herschel Walker, one white and one black—*colored* the word they had used—and someone always making a joke or some dumbass comment. But he had been a star. Because he was good looking. Because lots of people thought he might be the fastest white man in the South. That he'd blown out his knee was perfect: it lent him a sort of mythic quality. *Who knows how far he could've gone? That son of a bitch could scoot.*

He dropped into another set and thought about Randi—he felt a sock pooling with warm blood—Randi brushing her teeth, sitting there in a powder-blue kimono watching the Home Shopping Network. "I'm always thinking about the day after tomorrow," she would tell him. "Tell me things I should already know."

More weight, more weight—it was beating in his head like a mantra now. *More weight.*

He was getting older, but she still looked like a nineteen-year-old fitness model with breast augmentation and a trust fund, a believer in eight hours of sleep and the power of acai berries, her very being the product of luxury and good grooming. Daddy the Memphis law professor. Mamma the social butter-fly. The private schools and two years at Sewanee before dropping out and moving to Atlanta.

They had drifted into this life.

He dropped into another set—*more weight*—but shit, his nose was really bleeding.

And if you drift into a life, how difficult is it to drift out? He had lived for a long time with the notion that he could somehow exist in a sort of stasis. Fuck-ing on hard beds and office furniture. These little fantasies of violence that run around the edges of things. But then the messages had started, and now Malcolm was back, and then there was his daddy staring at them the day they hauled up the TV like they just stepped off a spaceship—shit, he knew she'd looked at his phone. She had to have. She was too smart for him. She made too much sense. And what was happening to his eyes? He pushed out the last rep and decided to push out another and then another, decided he'd rather die than rack the bar.

*More weight, more weight—*but was it fading now?

Even his vision had tunneled. And was he alone? He was alone. And fuck—why was he on his back? And who the hell had vomited all over him?

He kept a folding chair in the basement shower for days like this, and crawled out of his clothes to sit beneath the warm spray until the mirror had fogged and his peripheral vision returned. When he stood, he thought his legs might lock, but he managed to get upright enough to hobble to the sink. From the medicine cabinet he removed a syringe and glass ampoule. He drew 40 ccs of Dianabol, slapped one butt cheek, inserted the needle, and drove the plunger. He held his breath; he always held his breath. When he was finished he collapsed onto the folding chair, naked and dripping on the linoleum, sweating again.

He was almost positive Randi had looked at his phone.

In the kitchen, he filled the blender with milk, strawberries, ice, creatine, and protein powder, and walked naked up the stairs, drinking from the pitcher. In the bedroom, he dressed, swallowed a 50mg Paxil tablet, and walked back downstairs where he filled a Nalgene bottle with bourbon. Cold late morning light stamped the far wall and laddered through the blinds, pale and paling.

It was after ten and someone was probably looking for him at the office by now—he was supposed to be looking at a piece of land in Westminster—but he thought maybe the thing was to get out and walk the land he'd been warned to stay off of, which, if any of this even fucking mattered, he happened to now own.

He left the pitcher in the dishwasher and took the bourbon back upstairs to the computer. He searched first for the missing birdwatcher Gresham Haley had mentioned and sure enough, there he was: Samuel Everett, fifty-three, resident of Spartanburg and lifetime member of the Audubon Society. Missing for five weeks now. When he searched for any regional environmental groups—the Sierra Club, the Chattooga Conservancy, Upstate Forever—he found just what he expected. The sites were largely useless and he narrowed his search to radical groups. Keywords: BLUE MOUNTAIN + STATE PARK + GUN + VIOLENCE. Change BLUE MOUNTAIN to DALLAS WALKER. Change VIOLENCE to FOREST. STATE PARK to ECOLOGICAL DEFENSE. He kept playing with the keywords and combinations and suddenly, inexplicably, the terms coalesced.

He was looking at a blog post linked off the main site of the Brotherhood of the Tree of Liberty, "a pro–Second Amendment, pro-Freedom, pro-America" organization based out of—Jesus, where was it? He couldn't find any info, no phone numbers, no addresses, just link after link to sites on antigun legislation, Waco and Ruby Ridge, Beau Chellis's failed presidential campaign. Dallas searched the page for his name and found nothing, searched for Oconee County and was linked to the Brotherhood of the Tree of Liberty's Manse Jolley chapter, headquartered at The Settlement, just across the state line in Georgia. The commanding officer was Shepherd Parsons. Dallas knew the name.

He knew almost all of the names. Love. Manning. Roach. There was even a Mr. Nu South. A bunch of neo-Confederate Sons of the South running around in the woods firing muzzle loaders and holding charity balls. They'd always seemed like a bunch of harmless rednecks, guys getting together at the VFW to listen to Bocephus and coon hunt, but there was he, Mr. Nu South with all his land and all his money. Dallas searched the web for the Manse Jolley chapter. Turns out they'd made an FBI watch list.

He walked back to the basement, past the weight equipment and into a small storage room. In the corner stood a Sentry twenty-four-gun safe the height of a grandfather clock and three times as wide. He wheeled the dial to 44—his old number at Georgia. To 3—the number of punts he had returned for touchdowns junior year against Ole Miss. Then 17—May 17th, in fact: the day his mother had hydroplaned to her death.

I am one morbid son of a bitch, he thought, and opened the heavy door.

Inside were his guns, collector's items mostly, antique Winchester rifles with silver inlaid on the stock, a Remington 12-gauge smithed for the nation's bicentennial, a Mannlicher Schoenauer 30.06 bought at auction. Twelve, maybe fifteen in all, and excepting one, none of them had ever been fired.

Dallas took a 1908 Enfield from its padded inlay and held it before him. The rifle had been carried from a hog farm in Long Creek to the killing fields of the First World War by Atticus Walker, his great-grandfather, and alone among the weapons it had been put to use. He looked down the sights at the hot water heater, returned the rifle, took out a small .38-caliber pistol, and put it in his pocket.

Uncle Tillman's trailer sat at the end of a rutted dirt road on a point overlooking the Cheohee Valley, the Airstream canted sideways to what had once been a front porch but now tailed off at an odd angle, as if the trailer had been lifted by flood and recentered along no known line. It was late afternoon by the time Malcolm arrived. Two pickup trucks and a battered Allis-Chalmers tractor with LOVE YOUR MOTHER and EASTERN BAND OF THE CHEROKEE NATION bumper stickers sat in the yard around a fire pit full of the burned slats from a packing crate, ashy beer cans, and a single empty bottle of Southern Comfort. Past this, the cliff fell several hundred feet down to the valley floor, the lower slopes forested but for a few houses scattered along the thread of creek that twisted through the bottomland. Down in the tree line, he made out an abandoned school bus, farther down the cathedral arch of a yurt.

Above it, mammoth houses crowded the ridgeline like teeth. Tillman had bought the point thirty years ago for a few thousand dollars when there was nothing on the mountain but a couple of hermits with Honda generators and four-wheel drives. Now half-acre lots sold for six figures, and a new blacktop highway ran up the mountain's spine, the homes accessible no matter the weather.

Malcolm walked back to the shrine he had seen driving in. Tillman had erected it just after moving here and had once, Malcolm knew, kneeled before it for hours a day, praying from the moment in the morning he walked up from the spot he left the school bus until the moment in the early afternoon he walked back down to it, a simple man-child, who, for whatever his failings, had managed to order his day around ceaseless prayer, constrained only by the comings and goings of children.

An antique bathtub stood on end, the lower third buried, so that it appeared an iron shroud. Within it stood a plaster Jesus, perhaps three feet high, robed, with arms extended. At his feet were several stones and arrowheads, a single turkey feather pressed beneath a plate of smooth shale. A few logs made for benches and in front of them the brushed floor remained packed and flat. But the shrine appeared in bad decline, Christ peeling, the crown of a bird's nest fixed between his back and the tub.

Malcolm turned back toward the house. When he passed the truck he saw the Iraqi child was waiting for him in the passenger seat, the wreckage of his face turned toward its pale reflection.

The child was silent.

Malcolm walked to Tillman's door, knocked once, and walked into a front of heat and body odor, the stench enough to twist his head. His uncle sat naked in a recliner, a nylon sleeping bag across his lap and a space heater by his big bare feet. He had always been a large man, but Malcolm guessed he had gained two hundred pounds in the three or so years since Malcolm had last seem him so that now he appeared a mountain of sliding flesh. The white chinchilla in his lap began to bark, and Tillman soothed it with one hand, his other on an open Bible. A smile pushed his pork-chop sideburns to the edges of his broad face.

"Malcolm," he said. "Praise the Lord. I'm so glad to see you, brother. Come in, come in. I didn't know you was even back in these parts."

"Just got back. How are you?"

"Oh, I'm fit as a fiddle. Tucked in here with my babies. Look here at Mr. Waffles. I want you to say hidy to my nephew, Mr. Waffles." Tillman looked up. "Ain't he something? I wish you would get you a seat." He shifted forward in his recliner and beneath the fold of one breast Malcolm saw the gray shape of an open sore, the infection creeping out from his back to reach like fingers around his sagging chest. He smelled like a dying animal. "Praise be. What a surprise. I thought for sure you were Maia. She's been gone two days and I'm just about to start worrying here in a minute." He shook his head in what appeared to be wonder. "My word, I am so happy to see you. I don't really get out much anymore and here I didn't even know you were visiting. Please get you a seat. And forgive me for not getting up."

Malcolm perched on the edge of an aluminum lawn chair. On the floor beside Tillman sat an open laptop, three near-empty gallon jugs of water, and a box of Ingles fried chicken. The box stirred and a gray rodent—another chinchilla—crawled out and scampered along the orange carpet.

"How are you?" Malcolm asked. "Dallas said you were down in your back."

"Herniated disk. Two of them devils, I'm afraid. But I want to tell you something, brother: my faith has not wavered." He was still smiling, one finger planted on the Bible, the other stroking Mr. Waffles. "It's got so bad I can't even get out of this recliner anymore. If it wasn't for Maia I don't know what I'd do. I wish she was here and you could meet her."

"Everything okay?"

"Oh, yeah. She went out Tuesday or Wednesday with her friends. She's got so many good friends. I hear em out there carrying on late. Sometimes she'll bring some friends in here to the back but they never bother me. She left me with some chicken and I been drinking down these water jugs. I'd offer you a Coke if I could get up."

"But what about your back? If you need surgery—"

"Oh, I couldn't leave my babies." Tillman stroked the white rodent. "Mr. Waffles and all these little boogers. Got four of em."

"And you're here alone?"

"Most often. Least it sure seems that way. But I ain't idle," he said. "I post sermons on the Internet, send texts out to folks. Bible verses mostly. But most of the time I just read God's word and pray. I'm waiting on deliverance."

"Dallas said he came up here a while back."

Tillman's smile disappeared. "Your brother's upset with me, I'm afraid. Said I was gonna sit here in my gathering excrement and die of a heart attack. I wish he wouldn't think that of me."

"He's worried about you."

"I know it," he said. "I do. 'But if you are pure and righteous and pray to God for mercy, surely he will answer your prayer.' I don't doubt the Lord will heal me. Now, let me ask you, Malcolm, you got you a cellular telephone?"

"Afraid not."

"Well, if you get one I want you to give me your number. I send out little messages. I know how life can discourage you."

"But—" Malcolm stopped. Outside he could hear cars pulling up, voices. "Tillman, I . . . Can I get you anything?"

"Maybe if you could fill one of these jugs here I'd sure appreciate it."

It was only when Tillman shifted his weight that Malcolm smelled the feces, a flowering vegetable rot that bloomed beneath him. He looked again at the jugs and realized at least one must be filled with urine. He took the one he was certain was drinking water and started refilling it at the kitchen tap.

"I'm gonna write down my number for you, Malcolm," Tillman said. "I'll write down my website, too, if you like. I'm just gonna put it all down for you here just in case you need it."

Malcolm left the jug filling in the sink and pushed aside the curtain that half concealed the bedroom. A mattress took up the entire space and across its surface a chinchilla dragged what appeared to be the milky skin of a condom gone crinkly with dried secretions. Several more empty beer cans were pushed against the window where a record player sat, the tune arm torn loose and the wheel now an ashtray for several cigarette butts and one shriveled joint. He picked up the cardboard sleeve of an album cover and dropped it back on the mattress. Van Morrison's *Astral Weeks*.

"You all right?" Tillman called. "Malcolm?"

Malcolm turned to find the jug overflowing. He cut the tap and returned the water to his uncle. "You're not drinking these days, are you, Tillman?"

"Alcohol? Lord, I ain't touched a drop in nineteen year."

"I didn't think you were."

Outside darkness had fallen, the trailer lit only by the pulsing orange grill of the space heater. Malcolm stood at the window. A bonfire was burning and he thought he could smell the honeyed funk of marijuana.

"Mr. Waffles is one tuckered-out little fella," Tillman said. "Let me cut on a lamp here."

"It's all right," Malcolm said. "I should get going anyway."

"I can let you hold this little booger if you like."

Malcolm stood at the window and stared out at the party. A woman wearing the kind of Native American headdress meant for children ran topless around the fire. The yurt was visible down among the bare trees.

They sat for a long time before Tillman motioned at the corner. "They's a boy-child sitting over there looking at you," he said.

"I know."

"He looks bad sick."

"He's dead."

"I ain't half surprised."

Dallas limped into the forest, the pistol and a bottle of Gatorade in the game pouch of his L.L. Bean coat, everything else back in the truck he had parked in a cul-de-sac at the end of the last paved road in Chattooga Estates. CHATTOOGA: PHASE II was a vast wooded reach of undeveloped mountain, no houses here, only a single serpentine road and the occasional survey flag. Past the limits of the Chattooga land stood the State Park tract, the seven thousand acres Blue Mountain had bought but did not yet possess, the land he had been warned to stay off. He had no idea what came beyond that, National Forest, perhaps. Miles of woods crossed with fire roads and the occasional plot of marijuana.

He followed the sunken trace of an old logging bed with no real destination in mind, just to get out in the chill air, maybe spot a few knolls that might serve as future home sites. The real work—the plotting of roads and sewer and power lines—would be subcontracted, but Dallas liked to think of himself as having a special talent for identifying the potential beauty in land, the artistry of imagining what a hilltop would look like with a slanting cobbled driveway, how the bend of an asphalt lane might fold into the shadow of dense hardwoods. Not that Leighton would allow anything to be built this deep in the forest. A few houses would ring the fringe—nothing more. Which, of course, made no goddamn sense money-wise. But Dallas suspected it wasn't so much about the money as Mr. Nu South's desire for a seven-thousand-acre backyard.

Past the logging road the muddy ground declined in a carpet of rotting leaves and glassy streams of snowmelt, one rivulet folding into another until a narrow creek ran in the fold of the land.

It could've been gasoline for all he cared.

It could have been poison, the entire valley a goddamn biohazard.

He stopped for a drink of Gatorade. Such a raw day, socks already damp and rain shivering from the trees. Everything naked and exposed. An ugly day. And they said he wanted to ruin this. He looked around at the brambles and scrub pine. They said this was beautiful. The folks howling over squirrel habitat for Christ's sake. The folks trying to stop progress.

They didn't understand. Cut the land. Ruin the land. Bleed the land. *Govern* the land was what he was talking about. Impose order, wrestle it out of the chaos of briars, the forgotten tangles of barbed wire grown into locust trees and oxidized to rust. He wouldn't turn back. Men had lived here. Now and then you ran up on the stone foundation of an old house, the trace that ran from home to shed. What he was talking about was nothing less than Man's Dominion. He was talking about the pioneer spirit. And here his wife was pissed at him and by God if his legs weren't beginning to cramp.

But he wouldn't turn back.

A triangle of tin hammered above a white blaze marked the State Park land. He picked up another trail and climbed the switchback—close enough to the highway to hear the traffic passing up on 107—descended again. Down in the draw near a footbridge an old man in soggy loafers and a toboggan glided the disc of a metal detector over the creek bank.

"You on private land," the man said.

"Yours?"

"Not mine. But not government, neither."

Dallas hopped the stream and kept walking uphill toward the ridge, sweating now. The sun was higher and what foliage remained laced a delicate filigree of shadows across the water. He guessed Randi was with Malcolm. His father would be out in his shop or walking the fenceline. He was a tyrant, but Dallas had always felt sorry for him, maybe because he knew his mother had never understood him. Dallas had always imagined her as some sort of houseplant, all stalk and vine. Kudzu maybe, the formless form that spreads and swallows.

His father was, at least for a while, something of a success. War hero. Businessman. Success enough, Dallas supposed, to allow his mother to assume the mantle of small-town queen, the society woman lovely enough what with her new dresses and hairstyles, her cable TV and supper-time subjects they could not touch.

Malcolm had been born late in their parents' marriage, years after a certain settling had occurred, the sediment drifting until there was only the legend of poverty and dust, the hard times. They were middle class by then, and because of that the past assumed mythic shape. He knew his father had been in prison just after coming home from the war. Stealing a car in Detroit. Joyriding. He did four months of hard time, and would have done more had a sympathetic judge not lost a son in the 101st.

After that, he had come home to South Carolina, to Oconee, the state's dark corner, and made a life selling mufflers and brake pads and gas caps to fit whatever you were driving. He seldom spoke of the war, and never about his time in prison, at least not in front of his wife. Rather, it was those moments in the woods, sitting in a deer stand that was nothing more than a piece of reinforced plywood hammered over two limbs, or those evenings Dallas slipped into the basement while his father played gin rummy with the other old-timers, the door-gunners and grunts that got hit first in the Ashau then, son of a bitch, in just about the same spot in some little hamlet full of doe-eyed girls and a company of NVA regulars.

Dallas crouching silently while proper nouns formed the crude outline of a life: the Early Times and amphetamines. Goddamn Hue. The talk of Jack Daniels and the bloody medevacs. Tallboys sloshed over an old wire spool tipped on its side for a table. Them gook motherfuckers the meanest you ever seen. Every last one of em.

He crossed the ridge and began to stride down the slope, taking willowy uneven steps, the wet leaves shifting beneath his feet. When he hit the bed of another logging road he angled away from the highway, then back toward it. If he got lost he could always hike up to the road and walk back. But he wouldn't get lost. He didn't have time to get lost. He had too much shit on his plate to get lost. This legal mess that hovered, this appeal, injunction, whatever the fuck it was called, this *legal attack* to stop construction of Phase II. It was bound to fail—*without merit,* the lawyers were always talking about how it was without merit—but it was a hassle he didn't need.

Some nights he would wake and find his heart a fist, eyes brittle as glass, and suddenly he couldn't breathe, stumbling to the bathroom, slapping for the wall switch, drinking water from the faucet until he calmed down. Randi would be sitting up in bed.

Baby, you all right?

I'm fine, go back to sleep.

But it was no joke. Men died over less.

He'd get worried and stay up half the night reading blogs about FEMA concentration camps or RSS feeds on ecoterrorism, fall asleep just before first light. He had his frailties. He was built like a brick shithouse, but his cholesterol was over 300—all the Dianabol and steak sandwiches. You factor in the stress—less had killed many a man.

He stopped down near the thread of a creek, the ground caked with toadstools and particulates of light scattered like wet coins. It was colder here, and when the valley narrowed to mossy limestone walls, slabs of rock folded as if in prayer, it became darker, too. He could no longer hear the traffic two ridges back but could hear the echo of water plinking into puddles. He thought of eyeless fish, the dead hand of evolution.

His socks were wet again and his quadriceps twitched, but he kept going.

Farther down the walls tunneled over him until he saw only a cord of gray sky. At the far end the walls receded, and he pushed through a laurel thicket into a small clearing overhung with fir trees and scrub pine where he stopped cold.

Something surrounded him.

When he moved his head, light caught and released the objects suspended in the empty air, the human flesh. He put one hand into his pocket, gripped the .38, and stepped forward. It took him two more steps to figure out he was looking at several naked Barbie dolls, perhaps thirty of them, hung on fishing line from the lower boughs, monofilament noosed beneath their rubber heads. Someone had attempted to paint one of the bodies purple, but had given up so that the figure appeared to wear wine-colored stockings. Dallas touched a foot and the toy twirled, a slow pirouette that wound the line in a motion unbearably lewd.

He crouched past them, gun in hand and arms out like a spider, ducking the figures that now and then brushed his hair, tan feet invisible in the ground fog. Past the Barbie dolls he found a picnic table cluttered with camping mess kits: rusted cutlery, empty butane cylinders for a Coleman stove, a large plastic pitcher full of rain water, and rotting leaves arrested in decomposition.

Stay off the land, he remembered.

Around the table the ground was cleared and brushed, a few silver tent stakes still in the mud, an olive tarp folded neatly over a dwarf pine. He looked overhead at the dense canopy and realized the camp would be invisible from the air. Sorry-ass junkies.

He figured the footpath led to marijuana plots but instead of plants found a rifle range, paper-bag targets in front of a berm dug out of the slope, a few brass shell casings he recognized as 5.56 mm, the round fired by AR-15s. He put one in his pocket and—

Jesus, had he heard something? He looked around into the still vegetation, heavy leaves glossed with moisture and barely ticking when the breeze barreled through.

Don't spook yourself here.

Stay off the land. We are concerned only with your self-preservation.

He squatted and listened. Don't do anything for a minute but just sit and listen, he told himself. Don't be stupid and don't be impatient.

The wind rose and fell and he strained to hear anything past it. Dogs—did he hear dogs baying? No, that would be the traffic. But he was a long way from the highway. Not even the sound of gunfire would carry that far. So what the hell did he hear?

His knee hurt like a son of a bitch, and with his free hand he drew out the Gatorade and slowly uncapped it, patted his pants pocket, and found a single Aleve. He licked off the fuzz and spat, swallowed the pill and swished with Gatorade, put the bottle back in the pouch, and raised the pistol. Just be sharp here. You've gone and walked up on somebody's hidey-hole and they won't be pleased if they find you messing around.

When he heard nothing he walked back to the picnic table. The accoutrements were rainbowed with rust, but it was clear they had been used in the near past, days maybe, a week at most. He looked for propane tanks or anything that might signal someone cooking meth but found nothing.

It didn't matter. It was time to go.

When he saw the ATV on the opposite ridge he knew it was past time. Dallas looked back once, then moved slowly through the limestone narrows and hustled up the slope over open ground. The man was in camouflage coveralls, his face hidden behind a mask, the four-wheeler idling beneath him. He revved the engine and Dallas began to jog.

He was sweating and out of breath when he reached the top, but didn't slow down, avoiding the switchbacks and plowing straight up, having already decided to make the road and get home that way. A cold deeper than his wet clothes had enfolded him and he needed out. He was almost back to his truck when he thought of smug Gresham Haley and his *sensible people united against the heathen.*

Malcolm spent that night at the old man's and the next day gathered his things and started down the mountain, stopping at a liquor store and the Ingles. In the produce section he ran into Ed Clark.

"Where's that sorry-ass brother of yours hiding?" Ed wanted to know. Malcolm hadn't seen Ed since high school, but he appeared unchanged, wearing gym shorts and a West Coast Choppers tank-top, his buggy full of Coors Light. "I see his pictures all over the county but never him. I been trying to get him to talk at this football reunion we're having. If you're in town you ought to come get shit-faced with us."

"I don't know."

"Now don't be a pussy on me, Malcolm. I know you ain't too busy."

"No, it's just I've been sick for a while."

"Oh, for real? Damn," Ed said, and something moved over him like weather. He looked at Malcolm's face as if all his hurt was written there. "You know I think I heard something about that."

"Just off my feet for a little."

Ed nodded slowly. "Somebody said something like that now that I think of it."

At the house, Malcolm filled the refrigerator and carried his things up-stairs to his old room, stripped the linens from the bed, and carried them to the laundry room in the basement, where he primed the well pump. By the shed he found firewood dry enough to light. He opened the chimney flue and all the windows, the sills covered with a confetti of dead bugs, the casements striped with peels of white paint.

The rest of the afternoon on into the early evening he dusted the fur-niture, cleaned the floors, and dragged a rocking chair into the front room. The refrigerator hummed to reluctant life, the compressor gagging and then pumping steadily, the interior bulb firefly dim. The ice trays had soured and he threw them into a Hefty bag along with the tarps. In his old room, he made up the bed and hung the Grunewald print above the headboard. The .357 Dallas had given him stayed in its walnut box beneath the nightstand.

It was not yet time for the gun, though that time might come soon enough. As a teenager Malcolm had known the truth of the old hymn, that the Redeemer did live within him, caged in his ribs and bulging heart. But if He was there now Malcolm intended to drown Him, to drink Him out, flooding Him through the veins and the pores. If he lived to Sunday he would put away the gun and the bottle, get a job. Resurrect his life and restore the house much as his father had restored it fifty years ago.

By four snow fell in bright helixes, and Malcolm shut the windows and drank bourbon. The room smelled like wood smoke, and he sat very still, the drink before his lips. He knew now that he had missed something—that in some essential sense his calculations had failed. But he wasn't sure how. It was pain without referent. Some mean trick of motion or spirit he had tried to whisper into Mary Ann's hair.

When the bourbon was gone he pulled himself off the couch and into the yard where snow was just beginning to accumulate. Along the ridges a last band of salmon rimmed the treetops while above it clouds massed. Snowflakes studded the pecan boughs like blossoms, and how beautiful it was, the crispness and sunless light, the cold clarity he had not felt since that last day in his church, and without intending it, he began to cry, softly and without any great sense of relief.

He was alone now. But in the end it would be better this way.

The truck caught on the second try, and he backed out and started down Whetstone Road past the grazing cattle and the trash-strewn weeds, a fireworks stand constructed from ply-board and marooned in a muddy pull-off, past the third- and fourth-growth pines, and on past a sprawling farmhouse where a sign offered shitake mushrooms and horseback-riding lessons. In an unkempt orchard of shaggy apple trees, he saw the feathering pennants of Day-Glo orange flags.

He turned off Whetstone onto Cassidy Bridge Road and crossed the Chauga River. The river was gravy brown, and past the bridge were fields and then a trailer park, a clutter of silver mailboxes beneath a sign that declaimed the Ten Commandments.

He slowed as he approached a black picket fence. Leighton Clatter had three hundred acres, most of which was pasture that swept to the hilltop where his monstrous house crouched amid the hardwoods. A sign read:

CLATTER FARMS
WHITEFACE BLACK ANGUS

But Malcolm saw only bison, burly filthy creatures that grazed the eroded slope.

He parked by Randi's Jaguar and started up the cobbled walk. The house was arched, its glass façade supported by massive beams, and on the porch he turned and looked out at the tea-set valley. What might have been crows or blackbirds lifted and finned against a wash of gray sky, a black shape, shadowing over the buckled field.

Inside, the party was in full swing, everyone in the sunken living room drinking and talking while Cannonball Adderley blew from speakers and a forest of glass bottles vibrated on a rolling cart. A field of lush heat radiated from the fireplace.

Randi saw him, put down her wineglass, and started over. Dallas intercepted her and Malcolm could see them arguing though he heard nothing beyond the music. Besides his brother and sister-in-law there was Leighton Clatter, a man and woman wearing matching body glitter and turquoise jewelry, and a young light-skinned black woman who appeared to be in her early twenties. On the wall behind her hung a massive bear skin, head and claws intact.

Leighton put his arms around the black girl, who stood, reached down and flicked off her red slippers, and started barefoot up the spiral stairs, a fingertip in each shoe, walking as if into the clouds. Leighton ignored her, a walrus of a man, centered on his leather couch, sweating.

"I swear to God," Leighton said, "I'm gonna wind up just like that Mexican lady on *Cops*. You know the one I'm talking about?"

The body-glittered couple laughed. Two more women, large-breasted in skimpy animal prints, came out of the kitchen and a few more men and women circled the periphery of the living room, a black-and-white feist at their heels.

"Malcolm, you big outlaw stud," Leighton said, "you made it. Dallas, your brother made it." He hooked a thumb at Dallas. "This guy," he said. "You believe this guy? Have a seat, Malcolm."

The two women from the kitchen circled the doctor and perched beneath his arms.

"Malcolm, Malcolm, Malcolm," Leighton said. "Come here, player."

Malcolm stood to shake his hand and Leighton pushed a woman in a leopard-print unitard out of his lap. The woman pawed the air and purred.

"Why don't you be Malcolm's girl tonight?" Leighton told her. "Malcolm's a real 'why-is-there-something-and-not-nothing?' kind of guy." He handed Malcolm a glass. "My first wife, I'd always believed in the sexual plenty, if you know what I'm saying. But then it got to a point: no sex. We weren't even touching. It was like I'd washed up on some beach. Kelp. A dead jellyfish. I lived three years with all this marine imagery before I had the sense to file. What's the moral of this story?"

Malcolm said nothing and Leighton gestured with his drink.

"*That's* the fucking moral right there," Leighton said, and put two blue pills in Malcolm's hand. "Let me ask you something though, serious for a minute."

"Leave him alone," Dallas said.

"Hey, Dallas? Go fuck yourself, all right?" He turned from Malcolm to Dallas. "What we're doing is having a conversation here. What we're doing is communicating."

"Leave him alone."

"Hey, Dallas? How about you sit quietly on your ass and enjoy my hospitality? Is that too much to ask?" He turned back to Malcolm. "I don't mean to be rude but I've got to know. And I should say it's because I'm a student of these things, so to speak. The spiritual world, the ethereal. There are nights I sit up and read the Desert Fathers."

A woman put on an Edith Piaf song and Leighton turned to her.

"Listen, sister, that negativity puts my chi in disharmony," he said. "My shaman has been very clear on that point." He turned back to Malcolm. "I can ask?"

"Ask."

"Because I have to know: when you drank it, did you think you'd ascend to the right hand of the Father?"

Jordan stood in the bedroom and waited for someone to hurt her. She'd been alone for what seemed hours but now Leighton, Rick Miles, and another man stood near, figures along the hazy fringe of sight. They weaved, grazed her skin, pushed her on the bed. She wasn't surprised. She knew what it was to be pushed. After Rose had died, Jordan had followed a man to a little coastal town in Brazil. His friends spent the winter surfing and crawling into her sleeping bag, high on cheap homegrown. You accepted it. Passed out along the dunes, woke to the chewing of sand fleas and the gloom of early morning tidal fog. You moved on.

She could hear the party downstairs. The music was distinct. Whatever man was on top of her was not. You separated. You compartmentalized. She shut her eyes and thought of Brazil, the memory catching like a hangnail, the days of nothing but drum fires and sand bedded in her scalp. Smoking blunts outside an abandoned roller rink, the air full of cannabis and the exhaust of portable generators.

They let her sit up on the bed long enough for her to run a line, pushed her back again. She watched the ceiling fan and realized she had never put her shoes back on. This gnawed at her. The pale soles of her feet. The hint of intimacy. As if they were experiencing her as *her*, something more than the corporeal, the inner self she had buried very near Rose's little plot overlooking the Grand Temple. Someone tried to kiss her and she twisted away. A hand on her chin. The pain then, though she knew the pain had been there all along, awaiting its release, that moment it might find form.

When they were finished she sat alone on the bed and fished her underwear from the tangle of sheets, the room spongy but beginning to cohere, lamps, desk, a framed painting aligning at right angles. It was her body that remained strange, ill defined and vaguely foreign, so that finally she examined herself in the wardrobe mirror. They hadn't intended to injure her and they had not. There were men who intended injury and men who intended subjugation. Only her clothes were damaged, the waistband of her underwear bare and stretched, a band of elastic exposed so that it left a ribbon of puckered skin below her stomach. She slipped them back off, pulled on her jeans and shirt, and sat on the bed. She needed to be still, to compact things back into the sphere that was Jordan, for at that moment the fraying she felt gathering at the edges of self might conspire to leave nothing behind.

Last Things.

The notion of apocalypse had come to her the night before she and Roosevelt had joined the spiritualist camp. In a shabby hotel outside Orlando, they had made love, and she had come while beneath him, something that didn't happen so often anymore, and in that moment of flying together and flying apart, she had felt death very near. The feeling had vanished after her return, but lately there had been a growing sense of finality, the last evolution of what had taken shape that night in Florida.

Now, she thought her way back, their stumbling onto the bed, kissing until her jaw ached, the steady gathering of clothes on the floor, the steady disappearance of every scar mapping what she'd come to consider their mutually stalled lives. She thought hard. If there was indeed to be nothing left she wanted to memorize every detail, then walk away and never turn back, to vanish into the lure of what Buddhists called Unbeing. It was like a seduction, the notion holding such sway over her, the idea of easy nothingness, that she had to resist it constantly.

She was still sitting on the bed when a man staggered into the room and leaned against the doorjamb.

"I'm closed," she said. He looked at her with bright eyes. Everything about him appeared slurred—the pink lips and disheveled clothes, the small scars that laced the base of his throat—everything but the eyes, the eyes burned. She screamed at him again and a moment later a woman hooked his arm and Jordan listened to them stumble down the stairs. Right then she decided to drive home that night. The weekend was the last thing she owed Leighton but at that moment she decided she didn't owe him that, not anymore.

She stepped into the bathroom and was washing her face when she noticed blood on the collar of her shirt, the lightest of sprays, a mere drop, two perhaps, more brown than red. No matter. She would wash it out with ammonia and whatever detergent her nana had, brush her teeth, and clean her clothes.

This is horrible, she told the eyes staring into her own. But it is not me.

Sometime later Malcolm was in the hot tub kissing a woman while snow vanished on the burbling surface. Someone had put a bottle of champagne in his right hand and he drank from it while Dallas slept in a lounge chair, a beach towel over his boxer shorts. At his feet, a pistol lay on a folded Bulldogs sweatshirt.

The woman straddled him, poured champagne down her chest, and pushed her slick breasts toward his mouth. Plastic cocktail swords lay scattered around the tub.

"Crazy," she said. "So crazy."

Behind them spread the houselights, the spindly shadow of deck rails elongated and vanishing in a crush of dark. A row of Palmetto trees, snow in the folds of yellowed fronds. Malcolm wasn't sure how he had gotten here, though when he looked around he saw his pants hung over the edge of a picnic table, folded neatly. Vaguely, he remembered swallowing the two blue ovals, their chalky taste in the back of his throat. There was something about Randi's face, yelling maybe, lipstick on her teeth. *Go home. Take him home, Dallas.* Randi angry, though he couldn't remember why. Something about the black woman he had seen climb the stairs, another argument, he thought. Another something.

In the truck on the way back to the house, the woman hung her head out the window and into the biting night air, swallowed, choked, and then began to puke, smearing the upholstery and streaking digested salad greens down the rear quarter-panel.

He put his eyes back on what he thought was the road and leaned into a fan of defrosted glass. Snow blew in through the open window and he wasn't sure about how he'd gotten to the truck. He wasn't sure about the headlights, either, whether they were on or not, but managed to pull onto the shoulder. He put one hand on her lower back while her stomach spilled in sudden plumes. When it was over, she swished with a beer and spat onto the orange snow.

"We're good now?" Malcolm asked.

She nodded and threw up again, hair tinseled with puke.

She was drunk again by the time they made it upstairs to his room, the fire out and the windows silvered with frost. Malcolm lay on the bed beneath Grunewald's Christ while she unfastened his belt, the act heartbreakingly complex. She leaned forward and cupped his head like a baby, one soft nipple on his forehead. It was almost hard by the time he had it in his mouth. He kissed her breasts while she worked down his pants, glossy hair spilled down one bare shoulder.

"You look like you might need this bad," she said.

He tried to smile, lying on the bed with his erection softening against the fierce cold while she slipped out of her pants and settled back on top of him. From somewhere she took a condom and rolled it onto him, smoothly, expertly, the chap of her cracked lips glistening when she licked them.

"Do I know you from somewhere?" Her panties were studded with plastic rhinestones and below her belly button a tiny butterfly unfolded its yellow wings. She put her hands on his shoulders. "Seriously. I know you."

"No, you don't."

"I look at you and I'm like: Wow. I know this guy." She started kissing him, stopped abruptly. "Oh, my God. I know exactly who you are."

"No, you don't."

"I looked at that picture a thousand times. I saw you on the news."

"Please shut up."

"My sister was in Iraq."

"Please," he said, and shut his eyes.

Elijah watched the headlights flare and dim, a window squared in pale white and then nothing, the truck and house lost in the shapeless dark, hours from dawn and snowing. Malcolm was finally home and Elijah watched for a moment longer but there was nothing else.

"Dallas's had him out I'll bet you anything."

"You need to quit worrying about it and get on to bed," his dead wife said.

"I got a good mind to ride over there tomorrow and check on him."

He reached into the bright chill of the refrigerator and took out a can of Coke and a slice of American cheese, walked to the back door and unwrapped the cheese slice.

"Go on and rest," he said. "I'll come in a little."

"Elijah—"

"I won't be long."

When she was gone, he walked out into the yard and looked into a ceiling of endless winter sky, velvet and deep with falling snow. Walked past his equipment shed and past his dormant garden, the furrows grained with ice, down to Malcolm's old rope swing where he wiped away the rain and sat. It creaked, gave but held, and he drank his Coke, thought of his boys gone so wrong.

When he went to crush the empty can he found he couldn't, his arthritis too bad, his hand too old, too old and too damn useless. There were times he felt himself growing old like a tree, long and gnarled and brittle. Everyone else turning dumpy and pale, but not Elijah. In the bright glare of Hardees, he would watch the housewives in line for biscuits and gravy, herding their fat impatient children. They would turn to puddles while old Elijah just knotted up and one day burned.

He stood, the seat of his pants damp, and found his hands almost locked, nerved with shallow pain, so that he opened the kitchen door with his thumbs, closed it, and fought with the chain until he gave up. In the bedroom, he opened the closet on Evelyn's bright dresses and heavy winter coats bagged in plastic. He'd brought it all over just after he moved in. Lonely one night and just wanted to be near it. A shoebox full of discarded lipstick tubes. One of her brassieres folded over the closet rod, a big chunky thing with wires and clasps. He remembered the day she came home with it from the JC Penney, but now lacked the courage to touch it.

She'd always wanted things he couldn't give her.

He could see her across the room in her rocking chair and slowly removed his shoes and socks, lay down atop the covers with his pants on. On the nightstand a glass of water bled onto a lace doily, and he watched the sliding condensation that leached outward, a ring of material darker than the rest.

"He needs to get the heat on." He waited but she did not speak. "I might ride over tomorrow and make sure he's warm."

"I see what you're thinking," she said.

"He ain't got sense enough to get a fire going."

"That ain't what you're thinking about."

No, he was thinking about the war. While she was alive, he never spoke with her about it, but he could see in the purse of her mouth what she could not voice: why do you dwell on them times? Why are you still thinking about it? You're a morbid man, Elijah Walker. It's been ten, twenty, thirty years. But he knew he would never leave that flooded paddy. He was the paddy every bit as much as the paddy was him, having not so much traded places as melded whatever energies they possessed.

"You're morbid," she said. "Get up and be useful."

And he knew he should, but even imagining the act was exhausting. You get tired all over, he thought, tired somewhere behind the eyes. He remembered the advice they'd given them at survival school: don't think too far ahead, just do the next right thing. But the next thing wasn't always easy. And he sure as hell wasn't willing to touch the question of right.

Malcolm woke alone and slatted in clean light, his hair crowned with sweat. Above the headboard Grunewald's Christ appeared a twisted insect, broken and pinned, a spider caught descending the wall.

He found the woman in the bathroom, snorting cocaine out of the convex of one black fingernail. "What?" she said. "Last I checked this was still a free country."

He spat into the sink and she lifted her hand.

"I know all about you, Malcolm Walker."

Downstairs, he made a fire and went into the kitchen where he drank coffee, ate loaf bread, and tried to reconstruct the night. There was still the outline of an argument with Randi, something by the hot tub that would not come into focus. Some matter surrounding his willful self-destruction. Some question of his desire to drink himself into oblivion. He ate another slice of bread and when he felt full took a bottle of bourbon upstairs where the woman lay in her panties, the sheets peeled back to reveal the mattress, the room full of Pine Sol and sweat. They lay in bed and drank the bourbon, sweating despite the cold.

He woke again in the afternoon and they drank and listened to the snow plow out on the highway. In his mind sat long monoliths of darkness, hours wiped from memory.

"Why did you do it?" she asked him.

"I don't know. There was never a voice."

"There never is."

Along with the cocaine she had two Oxy 80s and a Viagra.

When he swallowed both she started laughing and laughed until her voice faltered and he realized she was crying. Then it all began again. They had sex for what seemed hours, in the bed and against the wall, on the stairs and on the floor, in the bed a second time. By the time the woman passed out he was raw and exhausted. His heart fluttered and his erection hurt. The bourbon was gone but he was perfectly sober.

He showered and drank several glasses of water, slow sips so that he could breathe through his constricted chest, ate the rest of the loaf of bread, and felt the furnace of his skull expand and contract. Upstairs, he took the .357 Dallas had given him from the walnut box. The handle appeared to be mother-of-pearl inlaid with the figure of a coiled snake. He put the pistol in the waistband of his jeans and watched the faint rise and fall of the woman's chest. She was naked with the sheet pulled so that it bisected her body and when he touched her skin he found it beaded with icy sweat. He covered her and left.

It was night when he walked out of the house and he was sick of himself, sick of being, his erection plastered to his thigh and his heart swollen. The moon had risen and banks of dirty snow were pushed along the shoulders so that he kept to the narrow centerline, pastures on both sides of the highways, skeletal trees assembled in little gatherings of darkness. Beneath a security light he saw cows bedded around a feeding ring and when they saw him they began to bawl and a few rose, pleading, he thought, moving toward him as if on life they laid the better claim. Beyond them the mountains waited, patient as stone.

He breathed the cold air and felt somewhat better, his heart still ballooned but downshifting, his groin raw but no longer aching. He supposed it would be quicker to simply take the pistol Dallas had given him and shoot himself in the temple, but he wasn't yet ready for that; a sense of curiosity hung around the endeavor. If he saw morning Christ would live and he would accept that, quietly, and without any great show. What he would make of it he did not know, only that he would neither seek God nor beseech an absent Father. He would simply exist, quietly, in the hollowed shape. But he had the pistol and did not think he would see morning.

The horizon lit, a faint rising glow, and it took him a moment to realize a truck was approaching, topping the rise and slowing as its headlights swallowed him. Snowflakes wheeled in the glare, and he stepped back into the slush and watched the truck slow, the window gliding down.

"You broke down?" the man asked.

Malcolm blinked. The man was familiar though it was impossible for him to say how he knew him, an elderly black man, one gnarled hand on the wheel, the other fingering the side mirror. He wore a Carhartt watch cap and a bulky corduroy jacket.

"Just out walking," Malcolm said. "I needed some air."

"Well, it's all black ice down around the river. I wouldn't get my air down around the river. You don't need a ride nowhere?"

"I'm all right."

"I liked to not see you topping the hill there. Good way to get yourself hit."

"Sorry about that."

The man looked at Malcolm's feet. The cuffs of his jeans were wet and the burnished eyelets of his boots caught the glare of the headlights.

"All right then," the man said.

It took a moment for Malcolm to realize the man could see the handle of the pistol, the mother-of-pearl iridescent and slick. When the truck pulled away the slush creaked beneath its tires and the old man was two red taillights, failing in the distance. When he was nothing, Malcolm turned for the house.

In the morning the snow was gone and the bed empty. He searched for his wallet and found it on the stairs beside an upright boot that still held ice forked in the tread. The Nissan pickup sat in the front yard, one bumper buried in a tangle of hedges. He had no idea what had become of the woman.

He drank tap water and built up the fire. From the kitchen window he could see the porch light of his father's cabin, a half-mile away. He ate two baloney sandwiches, swallowed three headache powders, and drank glass after glass of water.

In the bathroom upstairs he stared at himself in the mirror. His eyes were brilliant spiders of blood, his face ashen. A cold sore had blossomed on his lip, opening like a night flower, bright and apologetic. When he twisted his head the scars along his throat shimmered, glossy sandbars climbing pale skin, and he fingered one, doubting, like Thomas, but believing, too, amazed at the scarecrowing of his emaciated form.

But the revelation was not his body. There was something larger, something he had forgotten or failed to understand. His head ached and his mouth was dry but he went on standing there until it hit him: today was Sunday.

He was alive.

III.

What was left of the snow melted in the shallow pools that surrounded the El Shaddai Temple of the Holy Ghost. Malcolm was late—the sound of singing came through the cinder block walls—but that was a good thing; he didn't want to speak to anyone. To be here was enough. They would see him. They would know. Here was their wayward child come home at last, the light they had sent out into wider world to collect degrees and wisdom and a wealthy congregation in a state most had never visited. That wider world had broken him, of course, burned away his fat and arrogance as perhaps they had known it would, so that he was reduced, stripped bare—they might believe—for his trip through the Eye of the Needle.

He knocked the ice from his boots and slipped into the back pew. Most of the church was gathered at the front singing from hymnals or playing instruments, piano, three guitars, an autoharp, everything just as Malcolm had left it: the wood paneling, the glowing space heater, the painting of Christ knocking on a closed door.

When the choir sang *I've got a mansion, just over that hillside* he knew they were irreconcilable with the world, square pegs in the round hole of existence. They were dreamers, fools for Christ. The elderly in Velcro tennis shoes; the young families who sat closer to the rear behind a row of severe-looking Hispanics, father and mother, daughter and son, faces fixed as if awaiting sentence; the single elderly black couple; the small girl who crawled along the floor showing the tarnished buckles of her plastic shoes. Near the front, the old man sat stiff and silent, hands resting—Malcolm knew—across the Bible his wife had carried for better than forty years.

It was only after his mother had passed that the old man had put away his Early Times and combed his hair. Before she died, Sundays had been for cutting brush or plowing, running his antique Cub Cadet through the morning fields, then sitting in his shed drinking tallboys and sharpening mower blades. There was always something to file or paint, a worn fitting, a bushing gone soft. Malcolm saw the old man in his blue coveralls diving into the wreck of his Impala, the Braves on the radio. *Look at me here, son.* Rising from the engine block to scratch his nose on a greasy forearm. *I don't need a preacher to tell me there ain't a thing new under the sun.*

When the singing was over a man began to pray and hands went up as if for balance, palms open to the Lord. A woman raised both arms and the loose skin swayed like a sheet drying on a line. *Oh, Jesus.* There were the sick and unchurched. The shut-ins. The lost jobs and heart attacks. Meth-addled children glassy-eyed and adrift. Pray for them. Pray for the tired parents who had stroked out walking from the Coke machine back to the weave room at Piedmont Quilting. Pray for the cousin whose trailer had burned to its cinders. Pray for brother Tillman still down in his back and bad hurting.

Malcolm saw the black woman stagger into the aisle, hands aloft, and realized the man beside her was the man who had stopped for him last night, Malcolm's discarded angel. *Good way to get yourself hit,* he had said.

When the prayer was complete the hands came down and the preacher stood and moved not to the pulpit but to the orange carpet in front of the altar. He carried a Bible but did not open it, a muscular, white-haired man with long sideburns and thick-rimmed glasses named Clyde Dell. He had been the preacher as far back as Malcolm could remember. He had also been one of the janitors at Malcolm's high school.

"I don't know where the Lord has something for me today or not," he began. "I woke up this morning with a tiredness down in me, something that lay deeper than sleep, and I just lay there staring up at the ceiling with Annabelle there beside me, all tired and worn out. Like the Lord didn't have no use left for me." He raised the Bible slightly and for a moment it trembled in the air, no theology but the blood. "But we all know that ain't true, brothers and sisters. We all know the Lord's got something for all us"—his hands and voice rose in unison—"We all, every one of us—amen!—know that the Lord abides in our presence. We know Christ is among us right now, brothers and sisters." His voice wavered and righted itself. "We know we doth dwell in the house of the Lord." He was screaming now. "We know—amen!—brother and sisters that Jesus Christ has died for our sins, crucified and risen, so that we might dwell in the house of the Lord."

Tell it, called a voice.

Bless him, Lord.

He threw back his head to show a throat rivered with veins, his glasses bright discs of light. "We know," he screamed, "that the Lord Jesus Christ who was crucified for the sins of us all, then resurrected on the third day, is here among us. We all know—"

A woman near the front stood, raised her hands, and began to stomp her feet.

Jesus, Jesus, Jesus.

"—that our Lord God and Shepherd is here among us right now—amen!—among the lost, among the sinners, the forgotten and the forlorn—"

Jesus.

"We know that the Father did not lift up the Son to earthly glory but lowered him—amen!—to the mire of human suffering. We know, Lord Jesus."

He was breathless, doubled with his hands on knees, the Bible against one thigh, before he rose up again, screaming as if stricken, running down the aisle and back to the pulpit, eyes full of animal light. The church was on their feet now, calling and waving.

Bless him, Jesus.

Malcolm began to sweat, the air dense and heavy.

"We all know, brothers and sisters," the preacher said.

The piano began, quietly and then stronger—*Softly and tenderly, Jesus is calling*—how had he not seen the woman step up the aisle to the keys?—while around the altar men and women collapsed onto their knees, stricken.

—calling, O sinner, come home—

Then Malcolm was walking.

He kneeled at the altar and rested his forehead on the polished rail that smelled of linseed oil, turned to see a dandelion head pressed on the bottom of a man's boot. The preacher began to intone and Malcolm shut his eyes. "Oh dear Jesus, we kneel before you today. Oh dear Jesus, we come on our hands and knees, sinners all." There were murmurs, affirmations. A woman said, *Help me, Jesus.* Malcolm looked up from the rail at the painting of Christ knocking at a door, his pale blue eyes and long flowing hair, alone in a city of sandstone and blown glass. "We pray for your forgiveness and mercy, dear Lord. We ask your sweet pardon." Malcolm waited for Christ to move, the eyes to shift, the body to descend from the frame, but nothing happened. The heater knocked to life. A woman began to weep. *Oh, Jesus, oh, Jesus.* But he was nothing, a reproduction, inks on canvas. He was a reproach.

Malcolm lowered his eyes to the silver chain that looped from a man's wallet to his belt. The dandelion head lay crumpled on the floor. So I go it alone, he thought, and realized he had thought all along Christ would be waiting for him at the last moment.

"Except a corn of wheat fall into the ground and die," the preacher said, "it abideth alone: but if it die, it bringeth forth much fruit."

His face was strained and ecstatic; his neck bulged above his collar, glasses off, waving them in the air, crying Jesus—amen!—yes, Jesus and Malcolm felt sweat prickle his scalp. The night before he had attempted his self-crucifixion, after he had said his prayers, after he had prepared the black hood and battery cables, he had kneeled before Mary Ann and washed her feet, one and then the other, dipping them in a small tub and toweling them dry. He saw now how arrogant that had been, and how useless.

"Amen!—wherever two or more gather in my name," said the preacher.

Then Malcolm felt the brightness, looked up but could not see. The altar and pulpit were hidden in a brilliant glow and he felt a warm bath of light on his face though he no longer heard the wailing and praying. The warmth crawled his skin and began to move inward past muscle and bone and deeper still, tunneling into his organs. Through his eyelids he saw the fine tracery of veins, narrow and delicate, and he felt lifted bodily though his fingers remained clawed around the rail. His heartbeat rose and subsided, and he blinked at the altar and pulpit which had returned now, the men and women around him. The light was gone and the circle was beginning to break up as people turned for their pews, exhausted and weary, trudging like heavy-footed animals.

Malcolm stood, felt the room tilt, threw out his hands to catch himself against the wall. He was drenched with sweat while behind him stood the remnants of the huddle, hands uplifted. In the center a voice screamed for forgiveness. Past them Malcolm saw the old man sitting in his pew, dry-eyed and impassive. He wore a starched button-down, his sparse hair plowed with comb lines.

He looked at Malcolm and Malcolm turned away, fumbled along the paneling, crying now, until he felt the door that led to the basement. He staggered down four steps and crashed into the silver insulation that lined the unfinished landing, planted his face against a wall stud, breathed raw lumber, and began to cry.

It was gone now; He was gone, having floated cleanly from the body. Malcolm felt abandoned, but strangely relieved, too. He made to tuck his shirt in, to become, again, somehow respectable, presentable, while through the door came the muffled sound of wailing, loud enough to break his empty heart.

He walked down the stairs to the bathroom, washed his hands and face, and opened the door just in time to see a woman cross the room and disappear up the stairs. It was only a fleeting glance, but he knew without a doubt it was the light-skinned black woman he had seen ascending the stairs at Leighton Clatter's two nights before. Through the floor Malcolm heard the piano, footsteps; the service was ending. She had ducked out of the altar call just as he had, and he needed to talk to her about that. He hadn't felt so certain about anything in months.

The basement door opened behind the church and he hustled past a picnic shelter and propane tank, rounded the corner, and followed her into the gravel parking lot crowded with pickups and cars.

"Excuse me," he called. "Excuse me."

She paused, and for a moment held his gaze before she started walking again, thrusting her hands into gloves.

"Excuse me," he said.

She was reaching into her pocketbook.

"I thought maybe we could talk for a minute," he said when he caught up to her. "I saw you at Leighton Clatter's."

She was still reaching into her pocketbook, still walking, breath pluming like smoke.

"Then I saw you just now in the basement and just thought maybe if we could talk for a second."

"Why?"

"Because maybe"—She had her keys out now and he saw tattooed on the web of one thumb the shape of a small star. "I don't know. I had a pretty rough night and think I might owe you an apology."

"No, you don't."

"I think from Friday—"

"I said you don't."

"Maybe if I could just introduce myself."

She stopped by a Camry, powder blue and scuffed with two mismatched hubcaps. "I already know who you are." She fit her key into the door lock. "I heard all about you."

"Really, what did you hear?"

"I need to get home."

"You're not going to hurt my feelings," Malcolm said. "I'm curious what you've heard."

"You're not curious. You're just trying to be funny."

He tried not to smile. "I'm trying to be funny, true. But I'm still curious."

"All right." She faced him, her eyes chocolate and streaked with silver as if shattered from within. "You're the guy who strung himself up like the photograph from the prison. The hood and everything. I saw the photo."

"Maybe not my finest moment."

"Funny. I thought you'd say the exact opposite."

"I tried to kill myself," he said.

"I didn't ask anything about that."

"This was in the hospital." He smiled and felt the cold sore crack. "I drank antifreeze. Basically an entire gallon. They had to pump it out of me. My kidneys should've failed."

"I've got to go."

"These scars." He motioned at his throat. "I had to have surgery on my larynx."

"This is making me uncomfortable."

She twisted her key and nothing happened.

"Sometimes you have to blow on it," Malcolm said.

"What?"

"The lock. It freezes sometimes."

She twisted harder and the lock popped open. "Not today," she said.

A minivan backed onto the highway. All around them cars and trucks were starting up. Across the highway blackbirds sagged a length of power line.

"I don't even know your name," Malcolm said.

"Goodbye."

She sat down and tucked her dress beneath her. He leaned on the door frame and smelled coconut air freshener. The ignition began to ping.

"Seriously," he said. "Just a first name."

"Jordan."

"Jordan, Jordan, Jordan." He tapped one finger on the roof. "You're Littlejon Taylor's daughter."

"Granddaughter." She pulled the door and he had to step out of the way. Exhaust billowed from the tailpipe.

"I think I saw him last night."

"I think you're crazy. And now you're scaring me."

"I was out walking."

"Goodbye. Seriously this time."

"Do you always come here?" he asked the glass. "Every Sunday? Because maybe I'll see you again."

Her window came down two inches and he felt a stream of warm air rising from the heater vents. "Let me be clear on something," she said. "Friends of Leighton Clatter are not friends of mine. All right?"

"Perfect, because he's not my friend." She kept her eyes forward and he felt the car shift into reverse. It crunched backward, compacting the gravel, and straightened on the highway. He watched it roll past the trailers and the dead honeysuckle vines.

"Bye," he told the air.

When he turned the old man stood beside him, a small bear in a denim jacket zipped to the neck, the knees of his jeans glossed. He had shaved the gray stubble from his hard cheeks but looked older for it, brittle and gravity-stricken.

"You all right?"

"Yeah, I just." Malcolm pointed up the road and let his hand fall. "Do you know her?"

"Not to speak of. Run off years ago with old what's his face that drove a eighteen-wheeler, then come home without him."

Malcolm said nothing and the old man reached out for his sleeve but let his hand fall, empty. "I saw you at the altar," he said. "You looked scared."

"I was," Malcolm said. "But I'm not anymore."

Jordan spent Sunday night at her grandparents' house, she didn't know why. Stretched in her childhood bed and not waking until after ten. She was sleeping more and more these days, sleeping without dreaming of the bear, and maybe that was her system realigning itself or maybe that was the depression. She brushed her teeth and washed her face but didn't bother changing out of her nightgown. No one was home, but it was more than that, it was a clinging childhood, the reversion she underwent every time she entered the house. Here it was all nightgowns and bedtime prayers and glasses of milk. It was easy enough to understand. It was because of her nana and papa. It was because they didn't believe in her. They had loved her. They had fed her. They had raised her. But they didn't believe in her.

In the kitchen she fixed a bowl of raisin bran and stared out the window.

There were hinges in her life, she saw that now. The day she met Rose, the day they took her child, the day Rose passed. But the underlying bedrock, the lowest strata, was always her grandparents.

She rinsed her bowl in the sink and tipped her head against the cool window. It was going to rain but she didn't care. Let it pour. Let it flood. There once was a girl. No, she thought, there once was a man. There once was a man and I loved him and lay down with him and when I climbed from his arms I carried within me his child. Seventeen. A year older than Jordan's mother had been when the same thing happened to her, as if Jordan had failed to evolve, or evolved in a stutter of regretful half-steps, and only enough to delay the inevitable. Jordan's mother's name was Ainsley. She was white, and Jordan had met her exactly once. Her father's name was Joseph. He was black, and she had met him exactly never.

Rose was Roosevelt Hawkes. She had met him the spring she turned sixteen, and though he was dead now, she thought she still loved him, though perhaps only in the way one loves a lodestone, a burden that gives meaning. At sixteen she had needed a witness to her life, maybe that was all.

The day they met she was outside Head's Grocery & Superette. The store's bell chimed and she looked up into his radiant face, silvered sunglasses pushed up into a nap of hair, the sun behind him hazing a corona of bronze light so that one ear was translucent—so unfair, seeing him like that, already counting down the options left to her.

"I ain't seen you since you were a child." He drove an eighteen-wheeler and owned a brick bungalow behind the library. "Littlejon did right to hide you, girl."

"He hasn't exactly been hiding me."

They wound up back at his house, side by side on the bare mattress, a blue comforter thrown over a curtain rod, waking with an embroidered flower pressed into her cheek and a hurtful dampness between her legs. The pain alone enough to wed them.

I want to love you, fuck you, hurt you. I adore you.

She had believed in it then. But what she wanted to believe in now was rapture. That she had felt it—sudden and in full bloom—blush up her neck and into her face. The next day she showed up unannounced, and from there it went on for the next year, fucking him the first day and last day and every day in between. Fucking him until the morning she realized what fucking meant.

She walked down to hall to what would have been her daughter's room, stood on the threshold and imagined the pink comforter bunched at the headboard, the toys and dolls pushed into neat piles. Her daughter would be seven now, was seven, somewhere she was seven. Only not here. Rain began to pelt the roof. She didn't care. She had to work that night but had nowhere else to be. Sleeping more, she thought. What was that a sign of? Or was it a sign at all? She had never been good at signs.

She had been three weeks late before she had even realized she might be pregnant, her first notion coming the day she raised her hand in Mrs. Smith's first period French class, *yes Jordan?, the restroom ma'am?,* feeling it swell inside her with only the slightest awareness . . . *all right go, but be quick about it,* and then it was all vomiting and swelling while girls in sweaters a size too small conjugated verbs *Je suis Tu es* and Jordan heaving out her future, watching it splatter, before the little jets of water came to wash everything clean and the bowl was crystal again and that was a sort of salvation.

Wipe your mouth on the back of your wrist, wash your face in the sink, thumb back your straightened bangs just as you hear the hall monitor's high heels ticking along the tiles, *What are you doing?* hear the knock *What are you doing in there, young lady* and it comes shifting out of you again right into the basin to splatter the mirror. *Are you sick? Oh, my God, child,* ghost pale with flecks of vomit on your sleeve, wipe your mouth on the back of your wrist a second, a third time, while the girls in sweaters a size too small keep conjugating *Nous nous nous sommes . . . I think, yes, let's get you to the office, you poor child, Come on now, no reason to be embarrassed, What you've done is caught some stomach bug—*

But what she had done was miss her period.

There was nothing to drink in her grandparents' house. She thought she might have something in the car, though, and crossed the yard between the gingko trees, male and female separated by a wide gulf of lawn. Across the road, cows were bedded in the grass like orphans. The rain was soft and in the car she found a bottle of wine and the baggie Leighton had given here.

She poured a glass and washed down a Xanax, took her wine and stretched out on the couch while rain blew against the windows. There once was a man, she thought, and this is how a life falls apart: sitting at a concrete picnic table outside the Dairy Queen, her sundae melting into a bleary puddle. Rose had offered to pay to get it fixed but she hadn't wanted it fixed. Instead, he'd reached into his pocket, removed a jeweled clasp knife, and set it on the table. "That right there, it's yours now. That knife's worth every penny of six hundred dollars."

She refused to touch it and he took the knife back. The weather had suddenly turned hot and she felt it on her neck.

"What do you want from me?" he had asked and she still remembered her answer: "Just for you to get in your big rig and drive off. That's all I'm asking."

And that's all he'd done.

She shut her eyes. The room was dark, only the dim light that fell through the curtains to honeycomb the carpet. The room was dark. The wine was warm. Rain fell. A series of declarative statements that ended in this: they took her child on a Saturday.

She pulled herself onto her feet and looked out at the garden where all was gray. Rain beat the dead stalks, swayed the weeds, ticked up puffs of dust.

Rose came back for her the following summer. A year had passed and the child with the name Jordan refused to speak was months gone. Rose touched her face. She let him.

"I ran away," he said, "I know that. I did wrong. But I ain't come back for no reason but to talk to you, Jordan, so why don't you tell me what I can do? Please, baby."

That night she met him at Head's Superette and it was there that he told her of his Pilgrim angel. He'd been in a wreck somewhere out west and an angel of the Lord had pulled him from the sinking cab and sent him home to resurrect the life he had dispatched. *Lord done put me on a path,* he said. *I'm going to Florida and He wants you with me.*

She went. But why? Because she could. Her lacquered Pine-Sol dreams always calling. A house with curtains. A brick bungalow behind the library. *Away, away.* South through Georgia toward Savannah and on past the cranes that towered along the harbor, past the broad expanses of wetland and the gates to the entrances to golf courses and beach resorts, the vast colonies of the secluded rich. US-1 to I-95 with the windows down and James Brown in the tape deck. She could feel the backs of her thighs sweat against the slick upholstery.

You know I feel all right. You know I feel all right, children.

It was just outside Savannah that she told him to keep driving, it didn't matter where, just drive, baby, please, let's not stop.

"My heart feels drugged," she told him, "scary and heavy."

All night, they saw billboards for alligator farms and orange groves, the land braided with dry creek beds, tangles and thickets that doubled back on themselves. Bridge pilings and the legs of docks sank in the mud beside signs for family campgrounds and all-night truck stops. She shut her eyes tight and then tighter.

Just drive. Please, baby. Don't stop.

North of Jacksonville, they got a room at a motor court two blocks off the ocean. There was cigarette ash in the sink and a TV remote bolted to the nightstand. Outside, the air blazed. White-hot light jumped off the chain-link fence where Jordan sat by the pool, rail thin and wearing gold hoop earrings big as bracelets, in the cooler beside her a liter of Bacardi rum and a six-pack of Coke. She rubbed her body with baby oil and spent the day drinking and throwing ice cubes into the pool.

That night, a storm blew off the ocean and the next day the parking lot was littered with palm fronds. Beards of Spanish moss hung from the gutters or died in shallow pools. They walked along the beach and the ocean was flat, no breeze and not a wave all the way to the horizon where kids rode Jet Skis in the gray surf.

She got drunk in St. Augustine and leaned into his arm as they made their way up Cordova Street.

I want to love you, fuck you, hurt you. I adore you.

South then: Daytona, Cocoa, Vero, West Palm, Boca Raton and its long sweep of dunes. She kept the window down and in every gas station bathroom wrote on the mirror in lipstick. HELP! KIDNAPPED!!! GOING NORTH ON 95. RED CHARGER. TN PLATES. Every word of it a lie, every mile another regret, all the way to Key West where she crawled across the mattress like a starving cat. She loved it there and what she remembered later was the sun's heat, early and diffuse, the hardness of her body in the shower afterward. The subtropics and a sky full of stars: all fingertips and ice melting in a watery drink.

After two weeks they started north to settle into a life—a house with curtains, a brick bungalow behind the library, *away,* she whispered at night, *away, away.* They wound up in a spiritualist camp of psychics and mediums in central Florida. The heat was wet and lustrous and she came to realize that she did not so much love Rose as revere his ability to carry her. But he had carried her here. Everywhere cats and women with press-on nails, men who had sex in Wal-Mart parking lots and went home to wash their white jeans in the sink.

He told her it was in God's hands.

Soon enough he quit eating—that was in God's hands, too—and grew thin and wizened, his eyes pocketed, the bonework of his face articulating a papery geometry. Standing on the porch barefoot in Levis he appeared a stalk of dying corn. When she touched his arms parts of him fell away, ghosts of dried skin, a confetti of discarded self.

She followed him to healings and transfigurations. Heaven and hell were states of consciousness. But she believed hell to be the communal dorm of shared toilets and box fans, the white rice and four-gallon tubs of cole slaw, the giant samovars of instant coffee. In the dorm at night they would hear others making a sweaty love and Rose would touch her face with a single finger. *There is no fall,* he told her, *no fall, no sin.* She thought of leaving, but could not, not yet. He told her she was beautiful, a reflection of the very Image. *Be patient, girl.* After a year they could petition for a private room.

She tried. She took classes on meditation and healing and learned that her desires were lower vibrations. Only harmonious living within the community could attune her life with the higher vibrations of the spirit. She read sacred texts and was instructed to subsume her desires to those of the camp. Around that time her hair started falling out and she would find it on waking, plucking wiry strands from the mattress ticking (the desire for a pillow was a lower vibration), and she was glad for it meant she was suffering. Rose lived on thin tea and tins of butter cookies. When he meditated he collapsed into another state, rigid and distant and then absent, his eyes shut as his soul scratched against the Wheel of Being.

She tried and tried, but could not, and one night convinced him to ride into town. She told him she wanted to go. *We can't. Where would we even go?* Anywhere. Just anywhere, please. *Can't do it,* he told her. *The Lord got us on a path.*

But it was not any Lord she understood, and one night she wandered down to the retaining pond and there, amid the brackish water and migrating arctic terns, was raped by two white men, jowly citrus farmers who had pulled off the highway to take a piss. When they were gone, she curled onto her side and felt them ooze out of her like wet sand.

When she exhausted her tears she stared into a night sky blurred with her crying. Who was this God? If God existed, she wanted to hold Him with the lightness of a dancer, close enough to absorb the radiance; she wanted God descending, slow as a feather. She pulled herself off the wet grass and began crawling back. She decided to stay. She decided to forgive everyone.

She endured, meditated, and prayed. Had her future scrubbed from the frying entrails of a cat, lifted from her palm, foretold from weather and air. They revealed everything except that Rose was dying of pancreatic cancer. The devil was in his bloodstream, he told her, testing his faith, and one evening she watched the tremor of his pulse cross the top of his hand.

"What does the silence feel like?" she asked him.

"Like God." He tried to pull his skeletal hand away. "I can't explain."

She sat by his side for the fourteen weeks and three days it took him to transmute flesh into spirit, to become a scarecrow, and then to become nothing. When he passed the world was suddenly cold and spare, the palm fronds drying to husks on the sidewalk. Goddamn February and her Rose dead on a rented hospital bed. She put his knife in her pocket and kissed his closed eyes.

Like God, she thought. *I can't explain.*

Monday morning Malcolm passed the entry gate to Chattooga Estates and turned by the waterfall that coursed through the manicured landscape. A quarter-mile from the river began the federal corridor where you could not so much as camp, but Dallas had managed to build his gated community as close as legally possible. A few homes reared from the hills, high-ceilinged monsters of stone and glass that edged above the tree line, but most were hidden beneath fir and spruce. He found Dallas in an empty cul-de-sac, a plat spread on the hood of his pickup. Another truck sat behind him in the far curve while out in the woods two men moved among the trees, spray-painting dwarf pines and dotting the leafy ground with Day-Glo flags.

Dallas looked up and back at the plat. "Hey now."

Malcolm stood at his shoulder. A can of Cheerwine balanced on the contour of the hood, holding down a corner of the plat that showed a field of intersecting lines, blue whispers and neatly scrawled numbers.

"You looking for me or just out loafing?" Dallas asked.

"Wanted to talk to you, actually."

One of the men walked out of the woods wearing jeans and a black sweatshirt, a yellow-eyed wolf airbrushed across the front.

"You mind letting me finish what I'm doing here?"

"Of course not," Malcolm said.

He stepped a few feet away into a spill of sunlight. Spring was coming—the last late snow melting, April a few days distant—and he could feel the air brightening. He looked back at Dallas who kept his head down. He wore the same khakis and windbreaker as the day he had picked up Malcolm, the cuffs of his pants folded awkwardly above work boots. Past him, along the edge of the curbs and storm drains were posts marked with lot numbers, the ground beyond scratched with orange instructions for septic tanks and driveways.

"You know you got Randi real upset the other night, the way you were running your mouth." Dallas kept his eyes on the plat. "If you weren't family I might have knocked the shit out of you." He looked up. "Probably should have anyway."

"I can't remember a thing." Malcolm touched his tongue to the cold sore, the Braille-like strawberry that parted his lips. "I'm sorry."

"She go home with you?"

"I'm not even sure when she left. I'm sorry about the whole thing."

Dallas stared at him and waved away the apology. "Forget it," he said. "You were lit. We were all lit. I shouldn't even say anything. Randi was pissed at me for inviting you over in the first place, then you show up and I try to stick a drink in your hand." He rolled up the plat and threw the Cheerwine can in the truck bed. "You want to walk down here a ways? It's two stakes marking the back of this lot I need to find."

The understory was beginning to flower, tentative green leaf and new shoots, broad rattlesnake plantain, elderberry and stands of shiny mountain laurel, poison oak braided through the thickets.

"Here's basically what I did." Dallas whipped the ground with a branch he had stripped bare, the plat tucked like a scroll beneath one arm. "Basically you came back and I just decided the thing to do was act like nothing happened. I didn't give you a chance to say anything. See if you can read this. We're somewhere near the back line." He handed Malcolm the plat and started walking again. "What I should have done is just got things on the table. But shit, you tried to kill yourself, brother. That one's not in the playbook. Can you figure that thing?"

Malcolm found the cul-de-sac and a stand of hardwoods.

Dallas nodded and went back to whipping the ground. Behind them came the sound of a truck starting.

"I guess Randi was already feeling bad about going over and taking that bourbon out of the house. Which, I'm sorry—I know I should've taken care of that before. But then I go and invite you to Leighton's, fix you a drink." He touched a rotten stump with the toe of one boot. "Somehow it hadn't occurred to me that drinking was the start of all this."

"It wasn't, actually."

"What was it then?"

"I don't know, but drinking wasn't the start," Malcolm said. "Drinking was an effect. Not the cause."

Dallas stared at him, turned and walked on. "Tell me when you think we're near it."

They found both stakes and Dallas knelt and tied a length of plastic orange ribbon to each. "I got shit on my mind," he said. "I don't mean to get all pissy. I'm not myself."

They started back toward the truck.

"What was it you wanted to talk about?" Dallas asked.

"I wanted to ask about a job."

"For real? Wouldn't take a truck, but you'll take a job?"

They were almost back to the road, close enough to see that the survey crew had departed.

"What could you do?" Dallas said.

"Whatever you needed."

"Assistant to the chief?"

"Assistant to the whatever."

"I'd be shitting you if I didn't say you're probably overqualified for digging ditches."

They came out of the forest into the early warmth.

"I just need something to keep me stable," Malcolm said. "It doesn't matter how small."

"Well, I can always use you for something. I don't pay shit."

"Neither does sitting at home."

"You still got that job in the fall? Cause I don't think this is anything you want to make a career out of."

"This would just be for the summer."

They stood with Dallas's truck between them, traces of heat rising off the hood, the air spiked with pine. The sky breathed, the clouds open and spreading. Winter seemed to have disappeared in the time it took them to find the stakes and walk out.

"Just come down tomorrow and we'll get you started." Dallas opened the cab door. "And maybe say something sometime to Randi, too. It doesn't have to be anything big."

"I'll talk to her."

"Just whatever," Dallas said. "It's not my business." He threw the plat across the seat and Malcolm watched it loosen, one end dilating like an eye.

"I really do appreciate it."

"We gotta stick together, bro. That's all there is to it."

That night Malcolm drove back down Main Street, turned by an abandoned car wash onto the side street, and stopped outside a small clapboard house where he was almost certain Jordan Taylor lived. A party was going on inside the house and James Brown's "Night Train" filtered through the window screens.

Malcolm knocked three times before the door opened on a massive black man in baggy shorts, flip-flops, and an Oakland Raiders T-shirt. His hair was pulled onto the crown of his head into a perfectly symmetrical topknot.

"You the pizza man?" he asked.

"No, sorry. I'm looking—"

"Cause you the pizza guy you done forgot your pie."

"Actually, I'm looking for Jordan Taylor."

"And I'm mean hungry about now."

"I'm sorry," Malcolm said. "I'm just trying to find—"

"I'm giving you a hard time, cousin." The man hiked one jowl and let it fall. "You looking for Jordan. I hear you. But check it out: she ain't here. She working tonight."

"She's coming back, though?"

"At least theoretically. You a theory man?"

"I'm not sure what you mean."

Behind the man James Brown screamed.

"I just mean do you have any interest in hypotheticals: will she come back? Won't she? You familiar with Schrödinger's Cat?"

"I'm just gonna wait out here if that's all right."

"You just gonna roll up and sit on my porch?"

"Or stand. If that's all right."

"I'm fucking with you again," the man said. "Go on and sit. We a democracy. We all about equal opportunity."

When the door shut Malcolm leaned against the banister and brushed aside the moths that dusted the floorboards, their bodies broken and flightless. He was happy to wait. It was the first warm night of the year and people were out on the sidewalks and in yards. He sat down in one of the wicker chairs and sometime later Jordan appeared in front of the house.

"Father," she called from the walk. "You again."

He stood abruptly. "Please don't call me that."

"So my stalker has a name preference." She smiled, walked up the steps and flattened her lips, serious. "Are you persistent or just bored?"

"What if I said both?"

"I'm not sure I'd be flattered."

"Both, but not equal parts?"

"Then I'd want to know how long you've been sitting out here."

"Before you filed the restraining order?"

"I wouldn't want to be rash."

She looked at him and he couldn't tell if she was amused or angry.

"If I caught you off guard yesterday I'm sorry," he said.

"So you did come to apologize?"

"No. Yes." He smiled. "I just saw you and—"

"Come on." She took her keys from her pocketbook. "We might as well talk inside."

Malcolm followed her into the house, the wood-paneled living room crowded and warm, Otis Redding on the stereo. At the coffee table a man crushed a Ritalin tablet, ran the line on a pizza box, and daubed what was left on his gums. The guy with the topknot collapsed in a beanbag chair, hookah by his bare feet, wide eyes wandering the ocean of his face.

"I didn't mean to interrupt the party," Malcolm said. "I heard the music but—"

"This isn't a party," Jordan said. "This is like nightly." She nodded at the man with the topknot. "These are Arch's friends. My cousin, Archimedes, pride of the family. Has a master's in electrical engineering from Clemson, but does everything in his power to embody every racial stereotype at once. Isn't that right, Arch?"

Archimedes looked at her. "We about to spark a bowl. Ask your boyfriend is he hungry?"

"Come on," she said to Malcolm.

He followed her through the laundry room, the subfloor bare, the walls threaded with copper piping that led to the hot water heater. One window was sheeted in polyurethane and the air was sticky with fabric softener.

On the back porch a man slept on an army field cot. Malcolm could see the slouch of his gut and the little hurricane of baldness that swirled on the crown of his head.

"God," Jordan said. "They're everywhere. You think they might at least stay inside. Just ignore him." She sat on an Igloo cooler and motioned for him to take the rocking chair. The man shifted in his sleep.

"So," she said. "This is a social call? Or you just stopped by to say hello. Or you just what exactly?"

"I don't know."

She smiled. "Someone out there I could check with?"

"I just saw you at church and—"

"Wait. I've already heard this part."

"Right. Sorry. But, I just got back to town and then I sort of—" He felt something pulse behind his eyes, then, much lower, something stirred, nausea, the smell of mothballs and warm decay. In the pockets of his mouth he tasted wine and for the first time in months actually desired a drink. Somewhere, he knew, Mary Ann was drinking alone, Will asleep on the couch. Malcolm looked at the man grunting out his dreams.

"Ignore him," Jordan said.

"I just saw you at church and recognized you from Leighton Clatter's. You're a friend of his, I guess, and I thought—"

"I'm not a friend of Leighton Clatter."

"Right. Sorry," he said. "But honestly, I'm not really here for any reason. I just sort of stopped by. Then I thought maybe if you wanted to do something sometime. Maybe get something to eat. Some sort of non–Leighton Clatter thing."

She bit her bottom lip and he put one hand on his stomach.

"You all right?" she asked.

"Could I use your restroom? I'm sorry."

He went back inside, through the party and down the hall, and into the bathroom where he swallowed a handful of water. There were entire days at his church when he would feel the absence of panic, a still center clear as morning air. But more often there was this: moments of nausea and fear, a trembling want that sent him from his study to the phone booth–sized bathroom where he kept a bottle of wine. Later, when he became self-conscious and then embarrassed to be hunched over a sink, he put the wine in his desk and drank it from a coffee cup. The old women would bring boxes of crullers and bagels from the bakery downtown and he would sit smiling and beneficent, old at thirty, his porcelain mug amid the thimble tubs of cream cheese and plastic tableware. Behind him—always behind him—hung Christ, broken-bodied and lean as a garden snake, observant, perhaps, but no less silent.

When he felt calmer he walked into the hall.

"You get lost?"

He turned to find Jordan. "No. I'm sorry. I just—"

"I'm giving you a hard time. Come on."

Malcolm followed her into the kitchen where a bottle of vodka stood on the counter amid cereal bowls and plates filmed in syrup.

"I have a weakness for kitchens. You can talk in kitchens," Jordan said. "Everybody except you, apparently."

"I'm sorry."

"You apologize too much," she said.

"Right. Sorry."

"Hilarious." She lifted a scrub brush and pointed with it. "Look, I know you've had a hard time. I shouldn't stand here and pretend like I don't know what happened to you. I pretty much said as much yesterday."

"I'll tell you anything you want to know."

"But the thing is: I don't want to know anything. I feel like I already know too much. Don't you think everyone does?" She dropped the brush back in the sink. "I don't mean that to sound so harsh. I know you just got back and all." She looked at the yellowed curtain that hung above the sink, above the hand soap and dish detergent, then down at the octagons patterned on the linoleum. "I'm sorry," she said.

Out the window, Malcolm watched the underside of a new leaf hanging below a hummingbird feeder and lit with streetlight, pale and veined and no larger than the ear of a child; the leaf was translucent with light. It shivered and was still.

"I should probably get going," he said.

"I didn't mean for that to sound so harsh."

"It didn't," he said. "Thanks for the talk. Maybe I'll see you at church."

He walked down the front steps onto the sidewalk and was near the car wash when she called his name. He stopped and saw her coming up the walk, barefoot, arms hugging her chest.

"All of that came out wrong," she said. "You just sort of caught me off guard."

"Again."

"And please don't say you're sorry. There's just this sense that you could sort of hijack me right now. Like emotionally. I was with a man for a long time and a lot of things went wrong. Like all lower vibration. Now I'm in this place," she said. "Like not exactly a dark place, but it's still a place. If that makes any sense."

"It does. We might even be in the same place."

They stood in the gloom of the car wash vacuums, the night gathered around them. A car passed, a rug of blue light beneath.

"You really want to do something?" she asked finally.

"More than anything in the world, I think."

"Why?"

He ran the toe of one shoe along a sidewalk crack. "You're making this hard."

"You had a very blue aura standing on the porch. I couldn't see it at church but I saw it tonight."

"What's blue? Calm, maybe?"

"You know the Shaver Center in Seneca, the rec center? I meet with a group there. Wednesday nights at eight."

"Like a church group?"

"Like a meditation group, I guess. You ever meditate?"

"At one point, yeah."

"Maybe bring a pillow." She looked at his face as if recording it. "You know you seem remarkably all right for a man that's been through what you have."

"I'm not."

"So this is an act?"

"Pure façade."

"You're not bad at it."

"I think it's probably my last best chance," he said.

Dallas sat on the edge of his desk and blinked slowly, socked toes pressed into the ash carpet. His office was on the third floor and looked out onto the lobby below where track lighting spread wands of light over the brick walls and brass-potted ferns. Malcolm had almost disappeared into a cushy black leather armchair, a cloth deposit bag marked BLUE RIDGE BANK in his lap. He fingered the zippered teeth and watched Dallas walk to the glass and back again, tracks disappearing in the thin shag.

"It's not going to bite you," Dallas said. "Seriously. You've got to look at some point."

Malcolm opened it far enough to see several sleeves of cash, tight bundles of one-hundred-dollar bills in wrappers that read US $10,000.

"You see what's going on?" Dallas asked.

"This is a bribe."

"That what you think?"

"You just handed me a bag full of money, Dallas. Gave me an address to deliver it to. What do you expect me to think?"

"I expect you to have a little faith. You think I would get you involved in something illegal? You think I'm involved in something illegal?" Dallas bent forward and spat Skoal into a Mountain Dew bottle, made a show of wiping his mouth. "Excuse the language, but that's an insult is what that is. I don't claim to understand you, Malcolm, but that right there is a fucking insult. You're the one asked for a job if I recall correctly."

Dallas hung his head and shook it. "I'm buying some land," he said. "A lot of land, actually, in a lot of places. And it's just me. Not me and Leighton. Not Blue Mountain." He put the pale starfish of one hand on the glass. "We may be in a little trouble here and I'm not just talking about this environmental stuff. This whole State Park thing—we had to jump through some hoops to make it happen, and now some heat might be coming down. I've got a few letters from the Savings and Loan, stuff I never even knew about but it's got my name on it. You follow me?"

"I'm not sure."

"I'm saying it's possible there were some bribes paid, more than possible," Dallas said. "But that isn't one of them."

He sat at his desk and planted both forearms on the blotter. By his left elbow was a ceramic bulldog in a red jersey, a pumpkin-colored football between its paws.

"We'll be in court once more—which should be fine. But after that there's probably going to be an investigation and it's possible that it'll be federal. I don't think I have anything to fear personally—I haven't done anything that even whiffs of wrong. But Leighton may have, and at this point the less I know the better. I don't ask about his shit," Dallas said, "but we're legally incorporated and if he does get caught it comes down on both of us. Leighton wants this State Park land bad. Has for a while. He's rich, but he's not rich enough to buy it on his own. You know his damn Apple Cellars have been losing money for the last five years. You know that?"

Malcolm shook his head.

"Well, it's got me worried," Dallas said. "So I'm shifting my money out of Blue Mountain and buying things up individually. That money you got there, that's three hundred large for a fifty-two-acre spread outside Chattanooga." He rested his head in the glove of his hand. "Needless to say this is strictly between us." He stopped, motioned at the deposit bag. "Technically, it's all in

Randi's name. But there's nothing illegal about it. I'm a free citizen buying up land. I wouldn't bribe anybody."

"I understand."

"This'll keep you busy for a while; then I'll find something else for you." Dallas fished the dip from his mouth, wiped his gum, and flicked the wet mass into the trash. "I'm a little worked up," he said, "I know. Still, I wouldn't bribe anybody. I'm not that stupid. Despite appearances." He reached into a drawer for keys. "Let me get you a truck."

He was west of Chattanooga when he spotted a lone mobile home in a field of waist-high grass, pulled onto the gravel drive and parked behind a Mack truck cab, its chrome bulldog tensed with light. A woman in the porch swing stood and walked inside, and by the time Malcolm got out a man was coming down the block steps, leaning into a cane, the woman behind him. The man stopped on the walk, barefoot in blue jeans and Titans sweatshirt.

Malcolm introduced himself and the man looked him over. The right side of his face had slid toward his jaw, eyelid and cheek wilted to the steady sag of his chin. The woman stood a step behind him in housecoat and flip-flops, half hidden by his collapsing bulk.

"I won't not invite you in." The man's eyelid twitched when he spoke. "I'd just as soon you take that money and be on your way, but I won't behave like no animal."

The next day he drove into north Georgia, the countryside flattened into brown pastures. There had been little rain, and the creek beds were sandy and dry, bleached driftwood washed onto bars amid paper bags and flattened McDonald's cups, a few cows ankle deep and bawling. The weather had grown strange, and around nine Malcolm shut off the heater and rolled down the windows. By eleven it was ninety and the sun not so much fell in shafts through the birch trees that overhung the road as glowed behind them, burning the leaves with green light, an oppressive persistence that wobbled the blacktop. Heat rang off the door panel and he rolled the window up against the red clay that dusted the fields.

He stopped at a farm near Hiawassee where he paid the balance on seventy-seven acres of frail third-growth timber.

"You don't want to get out and walk the property line?" the old woman asked.

She sat in a porch glider with a fat calico in her lap and oxygen tubes looped up her nose. Inside, a home health nurse scrubbed a casserole dish.

"No, ma'am," Malcolm said. "I just need a signature."

On the way back he listened to gospel talk radio out of Toccoa as he passed the ranch houses with four-wheelers and porches crowded with washing machines. He lost the station in one of the resort towns lined with boutiques and coffeehouses and that was just as well. He felt at last that he was learning to be both *in* the world and *of* it, and it was the process of making every life a commodity, every exchange a transaction. The idea was to narrow the geometry down to a tight sphere, a few people you cared for, and, beyond that, a world you did not.

He left the signed papers on Dallas's desk and was on his way out when someone called his name: Leighton in his office, the door open and a bottle of J&B on his desk.

"Come in here a minute," he called.

It was almost six and Malcolm could hear people leaving the building, footsteps down the stairwell, the soft ping of the elevator. A tide of departing engineers and agents, cell phones clipped to belts, power suits and expensive hair, all heading out for the evening.

"Come in here, Hollywood. I'm not going to bite," Leighton said again. He looked up from a blotter scribbled with names and phone numbers and swirls of blue ink, advertisements for insurance companies and pharmacies. "You know we never got that chance to talk the other night." He wore a rumpled seer sucker, his eyes fat as boiled eggs in the sloppy construction of his face. He filled a paper cup and offered it to Malcolm. "You got famous there for a bit, didn't you?"

"Infamous, maybe."

"Infamous." He laughed and liquor spilled over his wrist. "That's the gospel according to FOX News. But what say you, brother? You off the sauce?"

"Despite it all."

"Despite it all, indeed. Was it dear sweet Jesus that got you straight?"

Malcolm said nothing and Leighton rocked back in his chair, behind him a glass wall, behind that the empty reception desk below. "Well, He has yet to address your brother. Good ole Dallas still loves a nip. What's he have you up to?"

"Running errands."

"Errand boy." Leighton took a drink. A string of spittle glistened on one cheek. "So does that mean he's scared yet?"

"Of you?"

"Don't be a smartass. Of the whole damn contraption. Dallas's spent his entire life this close to being the big dog. But there's just always somebody a little bigger. He doesn't understand that's life. He takes it personally. He's never gotten what it means to be a man. The biggest muscles. The woman with the biggest boobs." He raised a palm as if in supplication. "Don't misunderstand me. I love your brother, but I don't see him making it. This thing is coming down. Systemic collapse. There are people doing the math on this. People way smarter than me. Ninety percent of the world won't go to bed hungry while the other ten percent gets fat watching YouTube. They'll be at the gates. They'll be clawing to get inside. Me, I'll have my own army. My monsters against theirs. If I burn they'll sure as shit know why." He filled another paper cup. "Is that what it was about with you? The hood and the battery cables? The whole Abu Ghraib wonderfuck?"

"It wasn't that."

"Well, it should have been. You understand you fucked up, right?" He drank. "You good-hearted liberals were sitting around writing white papers on political correctness while the jobs went to Guangdong Province. Talking about Jesus but playing that consumer game like everyone else. Which is fine. It's a fun game. But you shouldn't have spent your days acting like you gave a shit about the common man. You shouldn't act baffled when they want someone like me."

"Want you for what?"

Leighton wagged the bottle. "You sure?"

Malcolm shook his head and Leighton refilled his own cup.

"I know folks," Leighton said, "I have friends—they would gladly die over an idea. Not even a thing. Not even a person. At least I'm in it for the thing." He crushed his paper cup and drank from the bottle. "Ultimately," he said, "this is about systems of control. That's what they tell me. The illusion of freedom within the larger context of tyranny. Letting the prisoners rearrange their furniture and all that." He motioned with the bottle. "Were these like the people in your congregation?"

"Some of them, I guess."

"So what happened then? And I should say I have my own theory."

"Fire away."

"See, I think you took all that progressive talk seriously. You forgot that deep down the only project anyone is committed to is his own comfort." He smiled. "I saw through all the other bullshit years ago. It's like the houses in Chattooga Estates. They're green, yes, but only up to a point. There's a façade of environmental responsibility. But the moment it runs up against luxury— fuck it. We go with luxury. That's what you didn't see."

"And that's your theory."

He smiled and took another drink, wiped his mouth on his sleeve. "The more aggressive the state becomes, the more repressed the individual. When the state becomes violent the only response is for the individual to answer in kind. It's a zero-sum game, but we didn't invent it." He laced his fingers and fired them out. "Collapse the system. That's my theory. Those assholes at Lehman Brothers did more for the poor than you and your Jesus ever dreamed of."

He leaned forward and Malcolm saw that he was wet, the neck of his shirt soaked, his arms ringed with moons of sweat. "You know we're really not that different, Malcolm. Except maybe I'm the one with true faith. I believe in the apocalypse whereas you believe in good mental health and a positive attitude. You still believe you can reform things. On Earth as it is in heaven."

"I don't believe in anything."

Leighton rocked back in his chair and laughed. "You're too gentle, my friend. Even your lies. You should find another line of work before you get swallowed."

On the third day he drove to the home of Mildred Carter, the unacknowledged grandmother—the white grandmother—of Jordan Taylor; but Malcolm was here because she was the owner of forty-four acres of hardwood fronting

Chattooga Ridge Road. They sat in the formal dining room, a musty closed-off space of brown and orange carpet and dusty blinds, afternoon light slatted over the heavy table and on to the breakfront filled with china patterned with tiny blue flowers. It was hot in the room and motes of dust hung in the still air.

"I seen you at church. You're the one that went off to be a preacher."

"Yes, ma'am."

"There ain't nothing goes on I don't know about sooner or later." She took a sip and returned the glass, her face vined with age. "Your brother called and called wanting my land, but I never figured he'd come hisself. I know all about your brother, too. Calling me up sniffing around. Government took old dad's river land in nineteen and seventy. Ain't nothing down there now but a bunch of hippie boys don't look no different than girls, all of em floating around in their fancy little boats. I always knowed somebody would come calling for the rest." She held out her hand. "You got something for me to sign or not?"

She sold the land for three thousand an acre, and Malcolm came home to a letter confirming his position teaching Bible and ethics at the Servants of All Ministries School, Grande Goave, Haiti, the job offered, praise be the Lord, on the recommendation of Professor Dennis Turner, a great friend to the Haitian people and all brothers and sisters in the blood of Christ. The accompanying brochure showed glossy photographs of block churches and brush arbors roofed with heavy-gauge vinyl, skinny children and women in bright headscarves. And mud, everywhere mud, churned in the roadbeds or baking on the deforested slopes. *We await your arrival with great promise and good faith. Praise be the Lord.*

He sat for a while studying the photographs and the grainy depiction of the northern coast of Haiti, then slid it back into the envelope and put it beneath the bed in the walnut lockbox that held the pistol.

Praise be the Lord. Even if He is not.

Wednesday evening, while Randi climbed her StairMaster, Dallas drove downtown to Luther's Main Street Pawn & Redeem where he parked beside a van dull with gray Bondo and several bumper stickers, one of which read: SURE YOU CAN TRUST THE GOVERNMENT. JUST ASK AN INDIAN.

The store windows were covered with iron, a mismatch of delicate filigree and heavy prison bars. Inside was a poster of Geronimo sitting his horse—

FIGHTING DOMESTIC TERRORISM SINCE 1492—and beneath the counter were several small pistols, .25 and .22 caliber, a nickel-plated .38. In the adjoining case, gold Kruggerands were spread on a beach towel beside video games. The walls were covered with stereo equipment, bicycles, guitars, and hunting rifles. Luther Love sat by the cash register with a Cabela's catalog and a stack of old BEAU CHELLIS '08 campaign stickers.

"Help you?" he asked.

Dallas hooked a thumb toward the street. "I like your van out there."

"That's a '82 Dodge conversion." Luther folded a page corner and looked up, a pair of reading glasses hooked on his nose. "I didn't know it had a fan club."

"Well, your stickers mostly."

"I've had those for years. My ex stuck on most of em."

"I'm Dallas Walker." Dallas extended his hand and the man took it in a limp shake, his palm smooth as butter. "Were you a Chellis man?"

"Still am. If God don't strike this Sodom down first that'll be the man to get us on track. There's a rumor he's coming back to these parts."

"Can I have a sticker?"

"They ain't much use now." Love passed an open hand over the pile. "Take three or four if you like."

Dallas slipped one off the top. "Let me ask you something else if you don't mind. Somebody told me once you refuse to pay taxes."

"Who told you that?"

"I can't even remember."

"Well, I don't guess it's any of your business, but I ain't ashamed of it either."

"Like a moral thing."

Love shook his head. "I just refused to be robbed is all. Take the money I earn and give it to the folks on welfare."

"I hear you."

"The women with crack babies and all. I work for a living."

"I'm right there with you, bro."

Love stood and removed his glasses. "You see that over the door there?" He pointed past a fully assembled swing set to a sign that read: US CURRENCY ONLY. "Everything passes through here is cash money. I don't need Uncle Sam's hand in my pocketbook. Did you want to look at buying something?"

"Maybe those watches."

Luther removed a velvet-lined tray of women's watches.

Dallas held one up to the light. "This is a Patek Phillipe. Is this for real?"

"I wouldn't stock it otherwise."

"That's for the high rollers." Dallas put the watch back on the tray and lifted another. "I also heard you might know Shepherd Parsons, runs the Tree of Liberty outfit up on the mountain."

"I know Parsons. I've only lived here my entire life."

"I was wondering how I might get in touch with him."

"Why? Because you a Fed?"

"Because I'm sympathetic. I'd just like to talk with him."

"Well, you don't need my permission."

"I hear you," Dallas said. "But I thought maybe you could tell me some things."

"You ain't interested in these watches, are you?"

"Maybe let me see that one. I might take that one for my wife." He picked up a worthless Timex, the second hand frozen in place. "I've asked around, but can't seem to track Parsons down."

"He lives just past Long Creek toward Clayton. I don't reckon he's hiding out."

"Does the Brotherhood ever meet?"

A bell sounded and Dallas turned to see a man and woman step inside. The man held a red-headed garden gnome on his shoulder as if it were napping.

"Don't want it and don't need it, folks. Seriously," Luther said. He turned to Dallas. "They a benevolent society. Not much different from the Shriners. You want to track down the Shriners too?"

"I know they get out in the woods a little, shoot guns."

"I don't know anything about that."

"Really?" Dallas said. "Cause I hear they might have some sort of camp?"

"Like a hunting camp?"

"More like a training camp."

"Training for what?"

Dallas put his palms on his chest and smiled. A blue Schwinn hung from its front tire, suspended like a trapeze. "Like I said, I'm sympathetic. I'm on your side."

Luther looked past Dallas. "I'm serious," he called. "Don't even bring that pointy-headed thing up here."

The bell sounded and the man and woman were back on the street.

"So maybe if you could put me in touch with him," Dallas said.

"People bring the most ridiculous shit."

"Can I call him?"

"Parsons you still talking about? He ain't got a phone."

"You for real?"

"FBI sits on that shit. Got a CB radio but you won't get him on that either. Best thing to do is just ride over the VFW Hall."

"They won't mind?"

"They have potlucks about every week."

"Potlucks but no phone," Dallas said.

"I reckon if the Feds want to sit down and eat cornbread they can sit down and eat cornbread," he said. "It ain't no secret gathering. We might have an A-rab for president, but we still got the Constitution."

"I'm right there with you on that."

"This is still the United States of America.," Luther said. "We ain't quit being no city on a hill. You want to see him so much just ride over and talk to the man."

The following evening Dallas did just that, driving to the VFW Hall on Highway 28. The block building sat beside the Last Chance, and when blue laws closed it at midnight on Saturdays the crowd took coolers from their pickups and step vans and simply moved the party across the graveled parking lot. Just before seven the place was mostly empty, a few pickups and a Pontiac Grand Am hitched to a trailer of scrap metal, coils of wire, and sheets of aluminum. Beneath the awning, a Harley leaned on its kickstand, the seat alligator, the gas tank tangerine metal-flake.

The inside of the club appeared a bare warehouse, a dim room of tables and folding chairs scattered across the concrete floor. Two men shot pool beneath a black flag that read: MEKONG DELTA BROWN WATER NAVY 1969. One of the leather pockets on the pool table had been replaced with a tube sock.

Shepherd Parsons sat at a table with a younger man Dallas suspected might be his son, cans of Natural Light and V-8 spread in front of them. The younger man—a boy, really—had a scratch of red beard, though his upper lip was clean shaven and pale.

Dallas walked over and introduced himself.

"Luther Love said I might should be on the lookout for you," Parsons said.

"Word travels fast, I guess."

"He got me on the two-way last night." Parsons motioned at an empty chair. "Sit down with us. I don't stand on ceremony with nobody but the preacher and the undertaker."

Dallas sat. Parsons topped his beer with tomato juice. He was a rangy man with a silver wire-brush mustache perfectly groomed, his hair in place and his denim shirt tucked into his jeans. His hands appeared gigantic. The boy looked shiftier, his coat-hanger forearms tattooed with the markings of a Maori warrior and what might have been the face of James Earl Ray. When he smiled he was all dead teeth and yellow gum.

"This is my youngest," Parsons said. "Joe Don."

"Call me Shit-Toe," the boy said, and spat into a can of Diet Coke.

Parsons took a drink from his beer and swallowed visibly, his throat twitching. He was almost skeletal, his gauzy skin marbled with blue veins and stretched over an elegant elastic frame. "Luther said you wanted to ask me some stuff about the Brotherhood."

"I just came to talk. I'd like to find out what you're about."

"Well, let me tell you then. I just passed my fifty-eighth season honoring the birth of our Lord and Savior Jesus Christ and I don't much beat around the bush, not anymore. What we're about is nothing less than freedom itself."

"I hear you."

"I spent twenty-one months in Southeast Asia. Lost a chunk off my left foot in the tunnels around Cu Chi and was grateful that was all. All so some hippie on a college deferment could smoke homegrown and screw my girl-friend." He put one oversized hand on the table. "I hope you won't take offense, Mr. Walker, when I say I doubt you have the foggiest fucking clue what I'm talking about when I say freedom. You familiar with the expression 'participatory fascism'?"

Dallas shook his head.

"Know anything about the Patriot Acts?"

"No."

"You vote?" Shit-Toe asked.

"Every election."

"Fucking stupid," Shit-Toe said. "The only vote you have that matters is the one you cast on *American Idol,* asshole. If voting mattered it would be illegal."

"That's enough," Parsons said. He looked at Dallas. "There's a line in Alexis de Tocqueville about government keeping the people in perpetual childhood. You read de Tocqueville, Mr. Walker?"

"Afraid not."

"You're living in state-imposed ignorance, man," Shit-Toe said.

Parsons stilled him. "'It covers the surface of society with a network of small complicated rules,'" he said. "'Men are seldom forced by it to act, but are constantly restrained from acting.' That was almost two hundred years ago. You have any idea how worse things are now?"

"I don't know."

"We endure more state repression and control than at any time in our history."

"I think I'm starting to get a sense of that."

"All due respect, I find that hard to believe. Otherwise I think you might find yourself striving for something besides what you've been brainwashed to call progress. All progress has done is cut us off from who we are. Run us off the land. Run us down to the rest of the world. Buy your shit at Wal-Mart and put your neighbor out of business. Watch television made by folks who think you're nothing more than a dumb redneck. Pay em to make fun of you, then plug your little speakers in your ears and pretend it all doesn't matter. Worship Apple. Bow to Google and Microsoft."

"I hear you."

"You hear me yet you persist, Mr. Walker. Corporate America's dropping iron fragmentation bombs in Iraq because you're too busy on Facebook. They're shipping jobs to China and blowing the tops off mountains because you won't bother to look up from your goddamn iPhone. Manufacturing's collapsed, but Goldman's got the keys to the Fed. Half the population's locked up. Put the blacks in prison, the kids in schools no different from prisons, put the old folks in retirement homes."

"My Daddy's sitting at home right where he wants to be."

Parsons smiled. "I don't mean to come after you personally. I mean this in a general sense." He paused for a moment. "What the hell. You're Leighton Clatter's business partner, ain't you? Leighton's an old buddy of mine. You want to learn, why don't you come up to The Settlement and go hunting with us? We have a big to-do every April 19th," Parsons said. "We're going to drop a couple of bucks. There's a ten-pointer I've seen twice."

"They're out of season," Dallas said.

"Fuck seasons." Shit-Toe's head still rested on the Formica. "The only seasons we acknowledge is those accorded by the wisdom of God Almighty."

Parsons quieted him, resting one hand lightly on the boy's cheek. "Out of season is the point," he said. "You think your great-grandfather listened to the government?"

"Hunted when and what they said." Shit-Toe raised his head and took a can of Kodiak from his pocket. "Let his family starve cause some faggot bureaucrat cared more about deer population than about people?"

"But your family isn't starving," Dallas said.

Parsons laid one hand on the table. "Don't miss our point, son. This is a statement about freedom, about government overreach. You want to know more, come hunting with us. We're hard to find but I'll draw you map."

"We're the Manse Jolly chapter," Shit-Toe said, "and if you don't know about Manse—"

"That's enough." Parsons stayed him a third time, hand to cheek, and the boy was suddenly and perfectly still. "This is same fight that started in 1861 and now it's run up through Waco and Ruby Ridge. Thomas Jefferson was the prophet of government tyranny."

"What's April 19th?" Dallas asked.

"Patriot's Day," Parsons said. "Concord and Lexington. The ATF's slaughter of the innocents. The Oklahoma City bombing." He bowed his head as if in benediction. "This has been a long fight."

Every day it grew warmer and after three days of walking fenceline and sitting on the cabin porch Elijah got in his truck and started down the mountain. He'd seen not a soul since Sunday and had stayed home thinking Malcolm would show up but then he never did. Elijah had driven over to the house Saturday to make sure he was warm and Malcolm had walked onto the porch and acted like he hadn't recognized him. Some girl behind him squinting and scratching herself, little butterfly tattoo right there where her T-shirt didn't quite meet her underpants. Both of them barefoot and stoned to the moon on whatever dope she must have peddled. The next day at church Malcolm hadn't seemed to remember it and Elijah hadn't said a word. Just went home and talked to his dogs until he quit talking to them. When he'd started again, he'd found his voice rusty with disuse and realized if he sat there much longer he'd get sorry as Tillman. Which scared the ever-living shit out of him. So he'd shaved and ironed a pair of Wranglers and got moving, finding, as he drove the back roads, eruptions of flower. Yellow jessamine and lady's slippers. Bee balm and red-tipped Indian paintbrush. The world waking up. Without him.

He passed the iron frame of the old Highway 76 bridge, rusted and narrow and twirled with climbing vines. There was a new concrete overpass now, a uniform span wide and ugly and white as bird shit, silent as he glided across into Georgia. Germans had come up from Charleston to settle the Piedmont but it was Scots-Irish who had settled the mountains. Hard-drinking sons of bitches. Mouthy. Quick to fight. They'd shot Cherokee and then, when the Cherokee were all run off, took to shooting each other. Periodically they went off to kill Germans or Vietnamese or Iraqis but they always came back to shooting each other. A sort of sacred calling. Jesus and a good .30-.30. Less now, more civilized, he supposed, but it persisted. He'd seen enough not to be bullshitted on that count.

He drove to Clayton for the hell of it, turned around and drove back, still early by the time he was in Walhalla. He caught the red light by the Kawasaki dealership. ATVs, motorcycles, Jet Skis, three-wheelers. The place was usually populated by men in Dickies and bib overalls, long goatees flowering down their throats, heads shaved and bolts driven through their noses. Elijah had seen one with a series of three or four silver hoops embedded in his lip, looked like an old catfish with a beard of five-pound test lines. The place was quiet this morning, and he watched a giant American flag unfold itself in the breeze.

Farther along, he passed an empty lot full of brown men huddled and drinking coffee. Day laborers waiting to spend the day hanging drywall or cutting grass at one of the golf courses. Dallas didn't even cruise the lot anymore.

Had his own Mexicans. Found him a Mexican boss living in a four-bedroom ranch with his wife and kids. All his hired Mexican hands living ten to a single-wide, piled onto air mattresses and fold-out couches. Which just went to show you that nationality and home ultimately didn't mean shit. Elijah had learned that over there, the girls in their *ao dais* waiting just outside the wire in Da Nang, got their brother working as their pimp—it was about money, then and now.

He parked at the Country Cupboard, a square block building rung with pickups and a few county work trucks, shovels and orange water coolers strapped to the beds. The place was full and loud and he sat in a booth and ordered coffee and eggs and bacon and toast. Waited for his head to clear. The cobwebs of several days in near silence thinning in the noise of old men and cutlery, daddies in Red Wing boots kissing their wives and kids goodbye and then off to dig another sewer line or shingle another roof. He finished his breakfast and drank a second cup of coffee, savoring it, feeling it pool in his stomach. He hadn't eaten much all week and the food sat heavy. He tipped his head against the plastic seatback and felt his eyes nodding, looked up to find the waitress refilling his cup.

"Thank you, ma'am."

She smiled at him, lipstick on her teeth, support hose. She looked tired but kind and he watched her cross the room, eased back his head. It was an indulgence. Old age, he thought. A dying man. There was a time when he wouldn't have blinked in public, let alone shut his eyes. Big bad Elijah Walker. Back from the war and tearing his knuckles up on whoever's face got in his business. You'd see him around town with his hands scabbed open, working the Otasco register with his thumbs. Now it was the arthritis. Which was some form of justice, he supposed. All of it coming back to you. The little bald-headed monks they'd see in Saigon. Putting your Marlboro out in their begging bowls. The animals they'd shot. But he hadn't meant it. Young, dumb, and full of cum. You don't put a rifle in a boy's hands and not expect him to go wrong.

He was on his way out when someone called his name. Several big-bellied men in button-downs, wiping their jowls on napkins. A couple so skinny they appeared to be scarecrows.

"Elijah," one said. "Sit down with us a minute. We got you a chair right here."

Five of them. Men he recognized but could no longer place. He'd probably known them since grade school but had forgotten their names decades ago.

"I need to get on," he said.

"Just sit with us two minutes," the first said. "Charlie here was just talking about your boy."

"I got two boys."

"Well, sit down and fill us in on things. We were talking about Dallas."

"That punt he took back against the Gamecocks," another man said. "That boy that got in front of him's head still ain't quit ringing."

"He ring his bell, did he?" said another.

"He knowed he was hit. I'll say that for it." He looked up at Elijah. "Sit down with us."

The man pushed out a chair and Elijah lowered his bulk. He could feel the torn upholstery even through his jacket.

"Charlie said he's due in court one more time. You know about this?"

"It's that sorry-ass environmental group out of Greenville," the one who must have been Charlie said. "They've give him shit for a solid year and all the man wants to do is give people jobs." Charlie looked around and the other men nodded. "If you left it up to them we'd all be sitting around starving and bird watching like that asshole that wandered off. People need work. People are tired of it."

"What's he say about it, Elijah?" another man asked.

Elijah looked at him. He could almost place this one. Coke-bottle glasses and a face like a fish. Someone who came in the store, maybe. Or his wife had been friends with Evelyn. The Ladies Auxiliary. The Walhalla Garden Club.

"He mostly keeps his business to hisself," Elijah said.

"That's exactly how it should be," Charlie said. "Let a man work and leave him alone. There's plenty enough out there that are looking for ways not to."

"Sitting around on the welfare," the third man said.

"The welfare. SSI and TANF. All of it. It ain't no wonder this country has gone to shit."

Elijah was outside and walking to his truck when someone came out of the restaurant behind him calling *Mr. Walker! Mr. Walker!* He wore a sweater and khakis, a good deal younger than the others, mid-forties probably, Dallas's age.

"I wanted to speak to you, but didn't want to say anything in front of them," he said. "I'm Chris Banks. I work at the Savings and Loan?"

Elijah opened the door of the truck and faced him. He looked like one of the Mormons he had seen out west after getting back, clean cut with shave bumps and a receding hairline. He remembered them from Utah and Colorado, men with their flattops and American flags, persistent and unbending patriots.

"Anyway," he said, "I went to school with Dallas and always thought a lot of him. We were never really friends, I mean, but I always sort of kept up with him."

"I'll tell him you asked after him."

"Oh, that's all right," Banks said. "I mean that would be great and all, but really what I wanted to say. I wanted to ask you." He smiled with a sort of missionary zeal, little sprouts of acne around his small mouth. "I had just heard some things, about Dallas, I mean, and I had gotten—I don't know. I guess I was just a little worried about him."

Elijah climbed into his truck. "Well, he's a big boy."

"Oh, definitely. I definitely know that. But—" He looked at the glass doors of the building and back at Elijah. "I'm breaking all sorts of laws just saying this, but that partner of his, Leighton Clatter?"

"I don't want to hear it."

"I understand that, sir, but I've got a friend that works at NationsBank. He pulled a spreadsheet for me."

"Not interested."

"I'm not even sure Dallas knows what all his name is on. They'll be an account." He shrugged. "Then the money just up and disappears. If I didn't know any better I'd say someone is laundering money."

"I don't want to hear it and I mean it," Elijah said. He put one hand on the open door as if to shut it. "I appreciate it, but it ain't my business."

"Well, maybe you could just get him to call me."

"I'll pass it along."

"Just let me get you a card."

The man took out his wallet and Elijah shut the door and started the engine, dropped the column into reverse.

"My card," the man said and held it to the glass, but Elijah was already backing onto the highway, thinking about what a mistake it was to leave home.

At ten minutes before eight, Malcolm got out of his truck at the Shaver Recreation Center and carried a flat camping pillow across the asphalt. The evening was cooling but still held the day's warmth, spring air swelling out over the baseball diamonds where banks of sodium lights sent broad wands onto the grasses and the pebbled walking track where women swished by in nylon track suits.

Inside, the foyer bustled with parents and kids in basketball jerseys sucking on sports bottles, the air full of popcorn and sweat. A men's adult-league game was going on in the gym and a few wives and children sat in the metal bleachers. Malcolm waited for the game to shift ends and crossed the baseline, passed through a dining hall where senior citizens crouched over paper plates, walkers and canes oddly marooned along the lengths of the folding tables, then walked down the hall to a small room where several people stood around a table eating cookies and talking.

Pillows formed a circle on the floor and along the far walls were prints of Jesus, Buddha, a menorah, and a photograph of the cube-like Kabah in Mecca. The people appeared to be mostly early-middle-aged professionals, though a woman who was perhaps seventy, silver hair swinging to her waist, sat on a cushion not far from a teenage boy with one side of his head dyed a marshy green. There was no sign of Jordan.

After a moment a man caught Malcolm's eye, folded a chocolate chip cookie into his mouth and walked over, chewing and extending his hand. He wore a saffron robe over mountaineering pants and river sandals. A blonde goatee triangulated the point of his chin.

He offered Malcolm a place to drop his pillow, and assembled the group. When they were seated he folded himself into the full lotus, an elongated man who seemed to embody expensive enlightenment, spindly and slim wristed with a plume of ponytail at the base of his neck. Just as he began to welcome everyone the door opened and Jordan slipped in with an apologetic duck of her head. She sat on her pillow, smiled at Malcolm, and stared down at the tiled floor beneath her.

"Don't be in a hurry," the man told them.

Afterward, he walked with Jordan along the rubberized trails that wound through the park between the backstops and bleachers. It was dark and the night had softened. Only a single softball diamond was illuminated. Bats swarmed the coppery klieg lights while a lawnmower sped across the outfield.

"You know you don't sound that much like a preacher." In her hands was a copy of *The Cloud of Unknowing*. "Like someone with all those degrees."

"Just two."

"Just," she said. "Like that's nothing."

Along the edge of the woods honeysuckle laced a wall of kudzu so that the air was heady with flowers and gas.

"I'm still wondering why you followed me that Sunday," she said.

"I'm still wondering why I was there in the first place."

"And?"

"I like to think that I'm inching back toward life. A year or so ago I reached the point where I had to cut certain things off if I was going to make it."

"What kind of stuff?"

"A lot of stuff I was raised with. Certain ways of thinking."

They stopped and watched the lawn mower slide away from them, skate across the grass, then return chasing yellow headlights.

"I thought maybe sometime we could do something," he said. "Maybe dinner or something. Coffee."

She looked at him and bit her bottom lip.

The headlights moved over her shoulder, lit the down along her neck, and were gone, back toward the far end, the signs that lined the outfield wall. BLACK'S ELECTRICAL SUPPLY. THE BANTAM CHEF. The distance marker too distant to read.

"I wasn't thinking it had to be any big deal," he said.

"No."

"Just get together."

"Yeah," she said. "I'd like that."

"But?"

"But I guess—okay if we keep walking?"

Past the diamond the trail steepened until they looped the outer perimeter of the parking lot, past them the elementary school playground with its swings and slides, three Dumpsters docked unevenly against a concrete loading bay.

"I don't know how much of this you know," she said. "This is kind of awkward, but the whole thing with Leighton Clatter. This is all the past—completely the past. But I've had—I don't know. An up-and-down life, I guess you'd say. I had a daughter with a man. She was put up for adoption. And then I went to Florida with her father and he—" She stopped by a split rail fence, flecked at something with her thumbnail. "Last year I did thirty days in the Rosewood House," she said. "I had a pretty intense habit."

They could see the extent of the fields here, the needled patchwork of dugouts and concession stands. No one else was walking.

"This bothers you?" he asked.

"A little, yeah. It doesn't bother you?"

"You're talking to a guy who tried to kill himself. Not a lot goes past that."

"So we're just a couple of fuckups?" She put one hand to her mouth. "Sorry. I shouldn't say that."

"No. I think you're probably right. But just the same let me ask you this: Jordan Taylor, are you free Saturday night?"

He saw the unwinding of her face, the spreading lips and lifting cheekbones. He saw her smile.

"Not this Saturday," she said. "I have some things. But how about the next?"

Friday Malcolm drove downstate with Dallas to look at a tract of land in McCormick County and by noon they stood on a knoll above the creek, its surface broken with shatters of light, a necklace of splintered sun. Along the timberline stood the skeleton of an abandoned deer tower.

"It's pretty land," Dallas said. "Rolling hills. Got this nice creek."

They walked down to the water and watched it break over stones smooth as blown glass. The wings of a dragonfly blurred but the insect did not lift.

"They've got kids in Asheville but they don't want it. The kids never do." Dallas thumbed the beaded sweat from his lips. "Mark my words, they'll be in an old folks' home in six months' time. You see the old man's hands shake? You don't come back from that."

They stopped back by the old couple's house, then drove out to the highway, rattled over the pipes of a cattle guard, and stopped. The road was clear as far as Malcolm could see, but Dallas made no move to pull out, letting the big hemi engine idle while grains of dust settled on the black hood in intricate geometries.

"There's something I need to tell you about," he said finally. He scratched a fingernail on one of the Styrofoam coffee cups in the holder. "We got something in the mail yesterday. It was there when Randi got home or I would've grabbed it. Look in the glove box there."

Malcolm found the letter, read it twice, and slid it back into its envelope.

"This is a death threat," he said.

"It's this damn State Park land that's got everybody shitting their britches."

"You need to give this to the police."

"That's exactly what Randi said."

"She's exactly right."

"The police never do shit." Dallas's left arm rested on the window sill and for a moment he grabbed his head, thumb on one temple, forefinger on the other. "There's been some stuff for a while. Stuff on the Internet. I think somebody got the number to my Blackberry. Randi doesn't know about any of that, but she opened this before I got home."

"You have to call the police."

He shifted the truck into DRIVE and pulled out onto the highway. "The police ain't gonna do shit."

"Jesus," Dallas said when they were back in Walhalla. They were passing his office and he pointed to the parking lot. "Looks like we're gonna have to stop for a minute."

Randi's car was parked around back and Malcolm followed Dallas up the stairs to Leighton's office where Randi sat on the leather couch. Leighton slouched in a rolling chair, a bottle of Wild Turkey by his socked feet.

"Speak of the devil," he said.

Randi stood. "I brought him a copy," she said. "Don't be mad, all right? Leighton has as much a right to know about this as anybody." She sat, looked at Malcolm. "I guess he showed it to you?"

"Yeah."

"Jesus Christ," Dallas said, and sank into the leather couch beside his wife.

Malcolm stood by the door while Leighton mumbled on about the direct mail that had circulated for weeks, the phone and email threats. The freaks. The gawkers and stalkers.

"When Baptists start using the Internet," Leighton said. It was meant to be a joke. Instead of a punch line he pulled the stopper from the Wild Turkey. "Seriously though, this scares me. People might hate Dallas in an abstract way, but ultimately they need him. He's progress. He's the American dream." He pointed the mouth of the bottle at Dallas. "People are hot over this State Park thing, partner. So maybe we take this as a warning sign. People do not threaten the Dallas I know, and here you've been threatened. Therefore we shift our thinking, our precautions."

"I can take care of myself."

"Just listen to him," Randi said.

Leighton pinched the bridge of his nose. "Dallas. Jesus. Somewhere—I don't know where, but somewhere a man is sitting in a tiny room, some rat-hole place—no windows, no air—and all over the walls: You. Dallas Walker. Your picture."

"Listen to him, baby," Randi said.

"This is how these things start. This is how the little man proves to the world he's still alive. The little tree hugger with his hemp sandals and a mail-order thirty-aught-six. Look. I know some people who do personal security. Let me make a call."

"A bodyguard?" Dallas said. "Are you serious?"

"He's interested," Randi said. "He's just tired right now. He barely slept last night."

"I'm right here beside you," Dallas said. "Don't act like I'm not in the room."

"Listen to me, Dallas," Leighton said. "I'm talking about a man's thought process here, about the mechanics of his thinking."

"He's interested. He's just stressed."

"Thank you," Leighton said. "You make my point. Dallas is stressed, and possibly in danger, and next week he's getting a sidekick. Think of yourself as a superhero. Your husband is a superhero, Randi."

"I've always thought so."

Dallas spread his arms, palms out, and looked at them. "People: I'm right here in the goddamn room."

"A bodyguard would—"

Dallas put up a hand to stop him. "I can take care of myself. Trust me. I'll take some precautions."

"I hope so," Leighton said. "Because they're going to be taking shots at you. That's going to be the one constant."

IV.

Dallas took a drink of Johnnie Walker from his Nalgene bottle and watched the land slide by, the massive billboards staked in pastures, cloud shadows that lumbered across yellowed grass. The meeting was in the Sunshine Diner in the parking lot of the old K-Mart building in Anderson and the goddamn cows had him nervous, the entire county nothing but tract housing and dairy farms. He had spent the morning trying to draw lines between what he saw as the cardinal points: the State Park land and the texts, the camp and Mr. Nu South, the letter—the death threat, but he could barely stand to think of it as such.

He stopped at a Sonic in Clemson, and south of the city it began to rain and he drove eighty through the downpour, shivers of rain peeling off the windshield. The weather broke just outside Anderson and the sun burned behind the clouds though the day remained overcast, the air gray and gummy with heat as he passed a string of empty storefronts. Going-out-of-business sales and boarded window frames. A child chasing a dog outside a brake shop. He pulled into a strip mall parking lot just as the sun slipped the clouds and silvered the puddles.

Inside, he took a seat at the counter among the Sugar Daddies and beef jerky. A woman came over and flipped open a small pad.

"We done serving breakfast, hon," she said.

"I just want some tea."

"Sit still a minute."

The door rattled and a woman walked in wearing a black T-shirt with the picture of a bearded Middle Eastern man, cross-hairs centered on his forehead like the mark of the beast. A few minutes later a man took the seat beside him and leaned forward.

"So," the man said. "You the fella rang me up."

"I'm the one."

"Well, you looking to buy something or just window-shopping?"

Dallas looked at him.

"Got folks window-shopping these days," the man said, "asking to put shit on layaway like I'm the JC Penney."

"I didn't drive all this way to pull your chain."

"Come on then. It's all out in the truck."

He followed the man out to a Toyota pickup with a camper top. The parking lot was nearly empty, all the stores but the diner closed, only the occasional car that passed on the highway. The man dropped the tailgate and zippered open a heavy duffel bag. He took three rifles from the bag and unrolled the beach towels wrapped around each.

Dallas pointed to the second, its laminate stock splintered and held together with duct tape. "What happened here?"

"Laid some poor son of a bitch out cold, I reckon," the man said. "That's a Chinese knock-off. AK-46. You ever in the service?"

"No."

"Here I was in the FFA one day and suiting up for Nam the next. Raising a hog at the time. You ever see a hog die?"

"How hot are these?"

The man pointed with a stub of finger. "The AK and that SIG there might have some residual warmth. But the numbers are filed off if that's what you're asking."

"They can't be traced?"

The man picked the gun up by its shattered stock. "The AK's a choice weapon. Knew a fellar headshot with one," he said. "He looked like a sideshow but he lived. Now a hog dying." He put the AK down. "It's a sight. You stick one it's like as not to squeal like a woman." He picked up the third gun, a machine pistol. "That's a TEC-9. Modified, but bought free and clear."

"How much for the TEC?"

"Four hundred. You'll find it in pawn shops for less, but it won't be modified. Feel it here." He handed the gun to Dallas. "Nine by Nineteen Parabellum in a thirty-six-round clip. That's your Columbine gun, right there. A brutal little motherfucker. You want, I'll throw in some ammo. Got a box somewhere."

Dallas passed the gun back. "Cash only, I'm guessing."

"Cash or gold if you got scales on you."

"Let's stick to cash."

While he counted out the money the man rolled the gun back up in its beach towel. "You want I know a fella that might could get you something heavier," he said. "He's running a special right now. Got an SAR 48 Heavy Barrel. Fires a seven-six-two round. Same shit NATO carries. World falls apart it'll be a comfort knowing all that ammo is out there."

"I'm fine with this."

The man put the TEC-9 in a paper grocery sack and the rifles back in his duffel bag. "You change your mind you be in touch. You got the email? I know an old hayseed in Jackson County, barely got running water but got the email. Uses it to keep up with his grandyounguns."

"This is all I need."

"Well, call me back if anything changes." The man closed the tailgate to reveal his weathered CHELLIS sticker. "It's some crazy bad shit out there," he said.

The following week Malcolm picked up Jordan Taylor and headed up the mountain. The land was mostly National Forest broken by the occasional apple orchard or pasture, green and breathing, the air thin and fragrant as they declined toward the Chattooga. Spring was inching up the mountain and a few stands of rhododendron were studded with white blossoms while wild flowers grew along the graveled shoulders.

They parked at the Winter House, took the rods and tackle and a backpack from the bed, and walked down the path to the pond, the woods so thick with glossy mountain laurel and rattlesnake plantain the undergrowth nearly swallowed the trail. They set their gear on a chaise longue by the aluminum lawn chairs and rubbed on bug spray and threw out their lines. In the back-pack he had a bottle of wine he opened and poured into a plastic cup for her. He drank ginger ale and watched the bubble of his sinker sway in water the color of thin tea.

"My grandparents raised me," she said. "My dad was gone and my mom—well, you know about my mom, I guess."

Her childhood had been the community's open secret: the one thing everyone knew but never spoke of, as if nodding were enough. If anyone did speak, it was the old women who whispered in church, the rustle of a skirt, a hand lifted to a face heavy with rouge and eyeliner, pinched behind a Sun-day bulletin—*now you know it was Littlejon's wife wouldn't have no truck with raising that child*—or standing over mixing bowls in kitchens overflowing with knick-knacks and grandchildren too young to understand. The one secret that was no secret—*they up and took that baby from her*—spilling before her so that she tripped into life, uncertain and vaguely apologetic, but for what she could never say.

"When I first figured out she was my mother, this white woman." Above her head a dragonfly levitated on translucent wings. "I mean I had known something was different about me. Of course, I had known that. But then when I finally had what was like this definitive answer."

She shook her head and the dragonfly floated away. "I don't know. It was strange, like she was part of my life but not really. Still, I was subject to it all, if that makes any sense. Like she was the texture of this whole other world I might have lived in. And then when I got pregnant."

Malcolm looked at Jordan and back at the water. In another week the surface would be dusted with pollen; stray cattails would scratch the surface, the ground littered with buckeyes.

"I used to come down here," he said. "I would just sit for hours."

He told her about Mary Ann and Will and what he had done, about talk-ing to Will about God.

"The God Talk," she said. "And you haven't heard from her?"

"Last time we spoke I told her I'd call."

"Will you?"

"I can't see any good that would come of it."

Around dusk they heard the sound of faraway machinery. He knew what it was immediately, and it carried in its low thrum a tiny star of hope, as much promise as to be born again. A few minutes later the old man's Cub Cadet emerged from the trees and bucked down the rutted path opposite them. The tractor stopped by the earthen dam and the engine went silent, the grill tinseled with torn leaves and a single yellow wildflower. The old man sat there as if sitting a horse, looking at them and then out at the water and the darkening sky. A sliver of moon had risen and hung pale and thin above the pines.

"I got the dogs penned and thought I might ride down and see what y'all was catching," he said. "Y'all catfishing?"

Malcolm stood. "Hey, Daddy."

"Malcolm, I wish you might come over and give me a hand down, son. I just about can't climb off this machine no more."

Malcolm helped him down and the old man limped over, two rods in one hand and a paper sack in the other.

"Evening, ma'am," he said to Jordan. "This boy treating you all right?"

"Good evening, Mr. Walker."

"He don't treat you right you let me know about it."

"He's been pretty good so far."

"What y'all fishing with?" he asked Malcolm. "Plastic worms? You ain't gonna catch nothing on no plastic worms. You're wasting this lady's time. Reel that in if you would, ma'am."

She handed him her rod and he took a sliver of raw chicken liver from a container in the sack, cast the line, and handed it back to her.

"Yours too, Malcolm."

By the time Malcolm's line was baited and cast something had struck Jordan's. The rod doubled and she staggered along the bank, laughing and almost falling in.

"That's a fish right there," the old man said. "Pull up and reel down, honey. Pull up and reel down."

They netted the fish, a solid twelve- or thirteen-pound cat with a head wide as a fist. Malcolm held it beneath the gills, gray and slick and barely curling.

"I want you to look at that," said the old man. "That right there is what we call a fish."

When she saw the blood in its gills she stopped laughing.

"But you have to let it go," Jordan said. "You have to throw it back."

"Catch and release." The old man nodded. "We honor that."

Malcolm eased it into the reeds where it splashed into the dark water. The old man sat in a chair and blew cigar smoke around his head, a spot of shaving cream visible on his collar. The sky darkened and tree frogs and cicadas began to sound.

They fished in near silence for the next half hour, and when they had caught and released three more the old man pushed himself up and tipped his hat.

"I appreciate y'all letting an old-timer sit." The tractor coughed to life. "You might want to check them lines, Malcolm."

"You want me to ride up with you?"

"Sit still. I'm all right."

When the tractor lights began to dim Malcolm stood and wiped his hands on the back of his pants. "I should help him get in. Do you mind?"

"I'll just wait here," she said. "Hurry back."

He jogged up the trail and crossed the yard. The cabin lights were off and he was almost to the porch steps when he saw his father in the rocking chair.

"I seem to have gotten stuck," he said. "Set down and can't get up."

Malcolm took off his boots and helped him inside. He expected his father to protest, but when Malcolm began to unhook the galluses of his overalls he made no complaint, only sat on the bed with his bare foot touching the floorboards, frail and slightly fetid with the heat. One clavicle narrow and brittle as a child's.

"She seems like a good one," he said.

"She is."

"Don't let her sit too long."

"Let me just help you here."

He was slightly out of breath and Malcolm walked him into the living room to the recliner, then brought him a glass of water. In his chair he appeared a small bird, flightless and terribly vulnerable.

"Go on," he said. "I'm fine here. Old is all. Old and just about laid up sorry."

When Malcolm got back the moon had fully risen and he could see that Jordan had finished the bottle of wine. She was sitting on the chaise longue, leaned back on her elbows.

"He's all right?"

"Asleep, I think."

"It was sweet of him to come down here. Sweet of you to help him like that." She touched the fabric beside her. "Come here."

He sat by her and felt the heat through her jeans. She moved so that she straddled his waist and they leaned together back into the giving fabric, kissing. He slid her shirt up and then off and when she reached for him he kissed the star on the web of her hand. He felt her hands on his fly and realized his own hands had unbuttoned her jeans. She kissed him again.

"We can get on the blanket," he said.

"This is all right."

He was inside her then, and they made a shy sort of love, as if coaxing out some fragile thing debating its own birth. When they were finished she put her warm mouth in the crook of his neck, and when he kissed her again he tasted the familiar long-ago taste of grape, one thing lost, one thing found.

After that there were no more trips to make or land to buy and Malcolm spent the next few weeks clearing brush and weeds around Chattooga Estates. When the rains began he sat in the cab of his pickup and watched it dance on the hood and streak the windshield, while down in the draw of the land the ground sketched an open wound, damaged but alive, green and teeming, the creeks rushing. The rain fell and the logging road turned to brown paste, soft enough to trap the Bobcat that was uprooting scrub pine. They pulled the tractor out with a tow chain and a big CAT D6, watched the rutted tracks fill with water, and went home.

He started spending his mornings walking the banks of the Chattooga, coming along the day's early edge, that moment past dawn when motion has not yet overtaken the stillness of night, moving along the rocks and out into the braided shallows where milky river stones warped by the current's motion formed a pebbled bed, the surface ringed with the rise-forms of feeding trout.

Besides the child, he was mostly alone, with only the occasional boaters or random party searching for the missing birdwatcher to break his concentration.

One morning he clamored over a rock jumble just below First Ledge. The sun was behind the trees but bright enough to see the ferns that grew through sandy cracks in the rocks, tendrils stripped by the current so that they spooled like floss. Just below the falls, a massive eastern hemlock had fallen into the river to form a half-moon of beach. Approaching, he could see the plumb line of something reared from the sandbar at a slight angle, a log, it appeared, buried by the wash only to have the last few feet resurrected.

When he climbed down he saw the curve, the defined prow and gunwales, and knew he was looking not at a log but at a dugout canoe. The wood was slick and soft, bloated with generations of burial, and he ran one thumb along the perfect simplicity of its length. Its width was no greater than the distance from fingertip to elbow, nothing wasted, its lone adornment a carving on the bow of some sort, but gone soft with the years until it was impossible to tell what it might have been. Bear or bird of prey, eagle, fish, rock, tree.

"Look at this," he told the child.

The child crouched on a rock, hugging his knees and breathing audibly, while Malcolm watched the sun rise over the trees and plait the river with gold light.

"He's speaking again, isn't He?"

"So what are you doing all day?" Jordan asked him one evening.

He had driven down to Moore & Moore Fish Camp to meet her at the end of her shift and they sat at a folding table in the prep room, the walls lined with bags of House Autry seasoning and Styrofoam cups.

"A lot of nothing," Malcolm said. He had a plate of catfish fingerlings and a few hushpuppies. "I read, go see the old man."

"I still can't believe you call him that."

"I call him Daddy to his face."

She smiled. The door was propped opened and they could smell the evening, flower-bright and cooling.

"But seriously, a lot of nothing doesn't sound so bad right now." She took a hushpuppy off his plate. "Maybe one day I'll get in on that."

"I wish you would."

"Maybe I will."

"I'm being completely serious," he said. "We could take a trip somewhere."

"Where would we go?"

"Where would you like to go?"

"Anywhere but here."

He saw her weekday evenings but never on Saturdays. They meditated
every Wednesday night, but he had yet to return to church. He had yet to pray,
either. But through the meditation he was beginning to sense something he
had not felt in years, something he had lost in his rage for outrage, and what
it was, was the possibility of God waiting somewhere past silence. The God of
stillness. Malcolm held out for that faraway emergence that might yet gather
along the atmospheric edges, then move steadily across the land, over the
crumpled rimrock of the mountains and on across the pine ranges, widening
out over the pulp forests and cow pastures and acres of asphalt parking lot, the
gentleness of the enduring suitor.

Mornings, the old man ate cornflakes and drank coffee, made toast on
the stove, tended to whatever it was he tended to, and was back in his chair
with an afghan thrown over his legs by the time Malcolm would walk onto
the porch around ten, stomping his feet and slinging water from his arms so
that it beaded the porch boards. Rain hammered the roof and knocked down
the wide heads of sunflowers so that they lay soggy and decomposing in the
mud. The dogs on the porch like piles of wet laundry. The air gauzy with gray-
green light.

One morning Malcolm set up the TV Dallas had brought.

"How's the world sitting with your hotshot brother?"

"Good, I think," Malcolm said. "He's waiting on a court date about this
State Park land, but seems all right with things. How are you today, Daddy?"

"Wet," he said. "Damp, leastways."

"I went up to see Tillman the other week. He's not doing so well."

The old man sat with the paper in his lap while the dust settled on the
floor like a rug. "If he's too stubborn to help hisself I don't know how nor why
he expects God to fix him."

In the afternoons Malcolm walked the Chattooga in rain so fine it seemed to hang in place, curtains of mist as insubstantial as breath. The river had risen above the stone outcroppings and into thickets of laurel, the current brown and swollen, a single throated rush that hurried debris beneath the skeletal bridge. It looked nothing like the Chattooga and more like some sluggish western river unloosed, flat and headstrong and growling. He combed the bank but saw no signs of the canoe. It was buried beneath the river, lost for another two hundred years as perhaps it should be.

One evening Preacher Dell came out to see him and they stood in the evening grass and drank glasses of tea while fireflies lit the back field.

"How is Miss Annabelle?" Malcolm asked.

"She's hanging in. Eat up with the cancer, but hanging in." Dell shook his head. "The poor girl, everything she eats I have to run through the blender."

They walked down to the orchard, the apple trees swallowed by kudzu and climbing vine. At the edge of the tree line they looked back toward the house that stood in dark relief against the sky, light bent around the roofline.

"But it is beautiful this time of day, isn't it," Dell said. "Evening land, my Daddy always called it. Like night was its own country. This beautiful evening land."

They started back toward the house.

"You know it doesn't have to all be suffering, Malcolm." The house's long shadow stretched down the declivity of the land. "I fear maybe you'll miss the beauty in this life. There's terribleness, I know. But remember that there's beauty, too."

Dallas took the Highway 28 bridge and crossed the Chattooga just as the water began to crimson with dawn. Fir and spruce trees lined the bank, stout and overgrown and casting jagged shadows across the surface as he crossed the state line into Georgia. In a padded case beside him was a 30.06 rifle, a box of cartridges, and the map to The Settlement that Shepherd Parsons had drawn. He had told Randi he was walking a piece of land—he was lying to her on more or less a daily basis, but he liked to think it was only temporary, and only for the greater good—but today was Patriots' Day, the nineteenth of April, and Dallas was going hunting with the Manse Jolly chapter of the Brotherhood of the Tree of Liberty.

He passed the empty hulk of a building that had once housed a garment mill, deserted now, the jobs all gone to Guatemala or Malaysia or Honduras, passed horse farms with big vegetable gardens in side yards, tomatoes staked and corn already knee high, trailers with satellite dishes mounted on fence posts. A sheriff's deputy waited in his car on the grassy shoulder of Rock Crusher Road and stared into his radar gun. Dallas eased off the gas and raised one finger.

He turned onto a narrow one-lane road and drove beneath a canopy of oaks before turning again, this time onto a dirt road by a sign that read: NO TRESPASSING NO HUNTING NO FISHING. He passed an open Forest Service gate and came out of the woods into open pasture at the edge of which sat a sprawling farmhouse. The rear of the house was sheeted in roofing tin, and below, on his caving porch, sat an old man, a Martin .22 flat across his knees.

Dallas slowed and hung one hand out the window. The old man sat in his rocking chair, two beagles asleep at his feet.

"Headed down to Shepherd Parsons's place," Dallas called.

"You work for the guv-ment?"

"No, sir, I certainly do not."

Past the house the road narrowed to a washboard of twin dirt tracks that reentered the woods. He let off the gas and coasted. A pack of dogs barreled out of the woods to mirror the truck. They disappeared back into the trees just as he entered the clearing.

In the yard were several mobile homes, behind them a large two-story house. Dallas parked behind a pickup and got out. A moment later Shepherd Parsons walked around the house carrying a rifle, his coveralls unzipped to his waist.

"Mr. Walker." He extended one hand. "Good of you to join us. The boys are all out back, but step in here a minute."

They crossed the house's broad porch and entered the front room. A Confederate battle flag hung on the far wall and on a side table sat what appeared to be the skulls of several loggerhead turtles. There was something ghostlike about the triangular eye sockets and Dallas felt some vague identification. He knew he carried within him the seed of his own annihilation. But he didn't believe in it. He had already decided that if he came through this he would declare himself a survivor, had decided it, in fact, the moment he had passed the Forest Service gate. If he walked out he would become one of those hard-edged men, those men whose eyes hold the immensity of all they have experienced. It would give him ballast; it would anchor him. But staring at the skulls it began to feel less like a pose and more like one of those things granted only after you renounced its existence.

Parsons took two beers from the refrigerator, passed one to Dallas, and sat down at the table. There was muscle on Parsons's stringy frame, but mostly he looked like a survivor, loose-skinned and nicotine brown, wiry as a man who had survived weeks adrift in a lifeboat living off bottled water and high-calorie energy bars.

"Not too early for you?" he asked.

"Not on a holiday."

Parsons lifted his beer. "I was ten years in the service and fifteen more doing contract work before I got sent to Washington. I feel like every time I sit down to have a cold one I'm toasting being home. Cheers." He finished the beer and threw the empty into a wire basket, took a Coke from the refrigerator and a bottle of Jack Daniels from the cabinet, took a sip of Jack and chased it with Coke.

"I learned all I needed to know about the federal government direct from the horse's mouth. All those silver-tongued bastards. You talking about some marvelous bullshit when they flap their lips." He lifted the Jack. "I did a lot of jobs in Central America through the late seventies into the eighties. Went to Iraq for some contract work, then some shit went down and I got called home. Spent an entire winter staring out at the parking lot, waiting on some bureaucrat to hand down my fate. Probably the worst time in my life. I cut a deal to avoid prosecution and came home."

Dallas looked around the room at the books on political philosophy and U.S. history, primers on the Cherokee removal, a copy of the Federalist Papers.

"I just say all this so you'll know that when I talk about freedom I'm not bullshitting around," Parsons said. "Some of these boys are. They want to get out in the woods and play soldier, shoot cans, and drink beer. They might be angry as hell. They might have lost their job to Mumbai and their house to the bank all so some hedge fund manager can keep his compound in the Cayman Islands, but they're still just bullshitting around. Most of em. But a few know what's at stake. They've seen it. You think you know what it's all about, then you go over and see your buddy blown to shit by an IED. You see a little girl burned up on her way to school by a JDAM."

He took a drink.

"You do some terrible things for your country, then come home and find out your country doesn't give a shit. You got no job, no home. The federal government's too busy bailing out Wall Street to worry about the fact your wife left you when you tried to choke her in your sleep." He shook his head. "A few of em know what's at stake. You look like you might too."

Around the house the yard was beaten clay, flat and hard and embedded with what little gravel remained. Five trailers sat in a half-circle and in front of them several men and a few women sat on their tailgates or in lawn chairs, drinking beer and holding rifles. Parsons introduced him and led him around to the back of a Bronco where a man sat in a camp chair, reading.

"Brother Rick," Parsons said. "I want you to meet somebody. This is Dallas Walker. He's new up here."

Rick Miles stood and offered his hand, his right forearm tattooed with the words *JUIF ERRANT*.

"Dallas this is Rick Miles. Rick's on loan from—who are you loan from, Rick?"

"The universe," Miles said.

"The universe. Be more specific."

Miles shrugged. "I'm just floating through, chief. Trying to be a good boy."

"Rick not only supplies us with a lot of hardware," Parsons said, "he's good about sticking around and making sure everybody knows how to use it."

"What you in the market for, pilgrim?" Miles asked Dallas.

Dallas's reflection warped along the edges of Miles's mirrored sunglasses. "Nothing, I don't think."

"Nothing, he don't think." Miles turned to Parsons. "He's charming."

"Don't give him any shit."

"Ah, my humblest apologies, sir. But you still got to replace those sorry-ass AR-15s, Shep. It's like you're living in the Pleistocene."

"I know it."

"And hustler here don't need a thing?"

"We're just bagging some deer this morning, civilian-style. You coming along?"

"Don't need to sit in a tree to feel like a man," Miles said. "You know that. I'm going to sit right here and think about my own death, get that yellow taste of finitude beneath my tongue."

"How lovely," Shep said. "How poetic you must feel."

"It's why Americans are children. They can't sit two minutes without their little whirling gadgets. If you can't sit still you can't sit with your own death. And then you can't own it." Miles grinned. "I got a tape of that Nick Berg kid getting decapitated. Al-Zarqawi and his crew. It's like staring at the sun."

Shep turned to Dallas. "Let's get moving."

"I'm telling you," Miles called after them. "You can be repulsed by the blood and the squealing, but not by the act. The act's pure poetry."

They sang a round of "Onward, Christian Soldiers," and walked out in groups of two and three, filed through the power company right-of-way and fanned out beneath the massive steel towers. Dallas walked with Parsons and his grandson, a boy maybe eight years old and carrying a Winchester .07-8mm, a slim black rifle with a barrel the color of smoke.

A half-mile down Dallas climbed into a tree stand that overlooked grass and scrub pine, his rifle across his lap. Parsons stood on the step below him.

"You see a game warden, don't act a fool," he said. "We can always bail you out for poaching but not for murder."

"No worries."

"We'll be down to your left. You get a shot you take it. Don't wait on us."

Alone, he watched a thunderhead pull its shadow over the folds of land, the cloud moving toward him and then over him. Randi was up by now. She had probably called his cell but he'd left it in his truck. Wondering what he was doing—and what the hell was he doing? Playing at breaking the law, playing at defiance. All his life he'd lived with an abject fear that he would be left out, that somewhere something would go down and he'd be standing on the sidelines. It didn't matter what, so long as he was in it. He'd had football but never had a war, and what he wanted more than anything was blood on his face, the future in his gut like a seed, hard and turning, always threatening to flower and kill him before he could eat the world. The future was bloodshed, and he was heir to this violence. He thought himself a simple man: he just wanted to be in the shit.

He raised his rifle and ran the scope over the field, past the purple wild-flowers laid over by the wind, past the traces of tire tracks that ran to a fenced transformer, on to the edge of the trees where he saw Parsons and his grandson, their backs to him, side by side in the tree stand, Parsons's arm around the boy so that they appeared as one, joined at the shoulders. All of it seemed so normal.

Dallas sat in the stand until the mosquitoes found him, checked the safety on his rifle, climbed down, and started walking back. The day was hot and be-neath the power lines he could hear the low hum of the voltage overhead. He stopped for a moment to rest on one of the concrete pads and thought of the bumper stickers he'd seen on the trucks in the yard. I LOVE MY COUNTRY, BUT FEAR MY GOVERNMENT. AMERICAN BY BIRTH, SOUTHERNER BY THE GRACE OF GOD. BEAU CHELLIS: LET'S TAKE BACK OUR LAND. A slogan painted on the walls of the VFW hall: THIS COUNTRY WAS FOUNDED ON GOD, GUNS, AND GUTS—LET'S KEEP ALL THREE. A couple of hymns before marching out to blast away the morning.

He stood and dusted the bottom of his pants. It was probably ten by now. He felt like a fool.

The Settlement appeared nearly empty when he got back. Dallas unloaded his rifle, slung it over his shoulder, and was heading toward the cabin to see if Parsons had returned when someone called his name. He turned to find Brother Rick Miles walking over in flip-flops and a red T-shirt that read UN-CLE SAM'S MISGUIDED CHILDREN, a shotgun slung across his back.

"Hey, boss," Miles said. "Back so soon."

Dallas looked past him. "You seen Parsons?"

"Haven't seen a soul." Miles reached for the strap of Dallas's rifle. "Let me see that scattergun you're shouldering there, soldier."

Dallas passed him the rifle and Miles opened the bolt and peered in.

"This new?" Miles asked.

"Never been fired."

"Now me," Miles said, "I prefer the employment of an antique firearm to all others. If I could carry a muzzle loader I think I might transcend this current incarnation." He clacked the bolt shut. "But this ain't bad."

Dallas took the rifle and Miles unslung the shotgun.

"This is a Mossberg 930." He patted the stock and handed it to Dallas. "Combat grips. A composite stock. This ain't your granddaddy's shotgun."

"It's nice."

"It's nice, Jesus. You know, you seem a little out of place up here among the heathen." Miles took the shotgun back. "Not quite pork rind enough for this outfit."

"How do you figure that?"

"Fingernails are too clean. I tell Shep all the time: dirty fingernails breed infestation. Infestation breeds disease."

"I need to get on."

"Disease breeds death. It's like the great chain of being."

"Tell him I was looking for him."

Miles spat between his feet. "Well, don't let me keep you."

Dallas turned to go.

"Are you looking for shit to get into?" Miles called. "Cause I'm saying, don't get above your raising, you know? Don't get out of your league." Miles stroked the Mossberg like a pet. "They're going on the hajj, partner. Shep and the good doctor. These aren't rational actors we're talking about here. I don't know if that was clear to you or not, but they're about to step in some serious game."

He was back around front when Parsons found him.

"I was afraid you might have left," he said. "Didn't see anything?"

"Quiet morning."

Parsons stroked his white mustache. In his right hand was an Igloo cooler strapped shut with a bungee cord. "You got a minute to sit down? I don't want to keep you, but there're some things we should talk about."

"All right," Dallas said.

"You can leave your gun in your truck."

Behind the house several pit bulls were out of their pens, running or playing tug-of-war with heavy lengths of rope. A dog hung by its teeth from a tire swing, its gray body roped with muscle.

"You have dog fights up here?" Dallas asked.

Parsons dismissed it with a wave of his hand. "Just another blood sport."

"You know it's against the law."

"A lot of shit's against the law. You of all people should know that."

They passed the pens and turned toward an aluminum building. Dallas could hear a woman laughing, and through a line of hedges saw the aqueous surface of an above-ground swimming pool.

"What's over there?"

"Partying is all," Parsons said. "You don't care about that."

Past the hedges the pool was a blue jewel. A topless woman splashed in the water while a man Dallas recognized as Shit-Toe slipped down the sliding board, a bottle of champagne clutched in one hand. A girl in leg braces slumped in a beach chair.

Inside an old barn were two four-wheelers and several push mowers, square hay bales stacked to the tin roof.

"Can you ride one of these?" Parsons asked.

"Been a while, but I'll manage."

"Just don't tailgate me. I don't want anything up my ass."

They reentered the power company right-of-way, turned onto a narrow trail, and started downhill through the hardwoods. The trail disappeared and they bumped over the uneven ground. Finally, Parsons stopped on a ridge that overlooked the valley. He cut his ignition just as Dallas pulled beside him.

"You know where we are?" Parsons asked.

A stream wound through the land below them, a slow-moving platinum slur brilliant with the midday sun. Dallas looked at the valley and back at the direction they'd come in. He guessed they had covered maybe three miles.

"No idea," he said.

"Look closer," Parsons said, and fired the engine and started down the slope.

When Dallas made it down Parsons was already off his four-wheeler and untying the cooler he'd lashed to the rack. Parsons walked down along the creek and entered a laurel thicket. Past it stood a picnic table.

"How about now?" he said.

Dallas looked around him. The creek was drier than when he'd been here before, and they'd entered from the opposite end, but it was clear where they stood.

Parsons took two forties of Michelob from the cooler, dumped water from a citronella candle, and lit the wick. He cracked the beer tab and sat at the table.

"How far back is it, you think, to the State Park land?"

Dallas held his beer. Water trickled over his hand but he couldn't feel it. "Maybe three miles?"

Parsons shook his head. "Not even two. Sit down. We might as well thresh this all out. Rick Miles saw you down here," he said when Dallas was seated.

"I don't know what you're talking about."

Parsons took a drink. "Let's cut the bullshit. You walked up on us. It happened."

Dallas shrugged. "You're closer to the highway than to the Park land."

"That's true," Parsons said. "Encroached on from all sides."

"You know I wouldn't have even been in here if it hadn't been for the messages y'all kept sending."

"What messages?"

"I thought it was time to cut the bullshit," Dallas said. "The messages on my phone."

"Somebody was calling you?"

"Texting me. Telling me to stay off the land."

"I don't know anything about it, but it sounds like the sort of bullshit Joe Don would be into." He waved away a horsefly. "Just to fuck with you would be my guess."

"Just to fuck with me?"

"He's misguided like that. He scare you?"

"He scared the shit out of me."

Parsons laughed. "Well, good for him. Good for Joe Don."

They sat drinking and watching the sunlight collect in bright scraps.

"I'm sure you've seen the plans in the paper," Dallas said. "Leighton's against any building off the entry road. We don't come anywhere near the property line."

"I've talked with Leighton about it. That's not my worry, some kid with a .22, squirrel hunting, walking up on us. Some folks are concerned but not me. Like you say, somebody's more likely to wander down from the highway."

"What's your worry then?"

"My worry is the surveying."

"You got no worries then. The survey work's done. The appeal was dismissed."

"Don't you have some sort of hearing coming up in a few weeks?"

"It's not a hearing. It's an appeal for a hearing. It'll be dismissed."

"Yet I keep hearing things," Parsons said, "rumors, persistent whispers. What if somebody gets an injunction and they run another impact survey? These goddamn environmental groups."

"It won't happen."

Parsons pointed with his beer can. "We'd have Feds two ridges over. You'd get folks down along this creek examining the watershed. They'd be all up and down this valley." He finished his beer and crushed the can. "We'll fight if it comes to that."

"It won't come to that."

"That's not what I'm hearing," Parsons said. "Leighton's been after me for a while to get you up here."

"Mr. Nu South."

Parsons looked at him. "I told him there wasn't any use, that you'd come around eventually, but now I hear you're playing peekaboo with some lawyer when all you need to do is return a phone call."

"Gresham Haley. He's harmless," Dallas said. "I guess Leighton's in this pretty deep."

"He's not into anything he doesn't want to be. Leighton's been very generous."

"I somehow missed that."

"Sounds like you missed quite a bit, Mr. Walker." Parsons pointed in the direction of the highway. "I can see em using this just to get at us, the whole thing cover to violate our rights."

"I'm telling you. It won't come to that."

Parsons took another beer from the cooler and popped the tab. His coveralls were unzipped again and his bare chest matted with the wreckage of mosquitoes, wine-colored blotches scratched with translucent wings. "They're all for some Colombian fighting Monsanto but you put a gun in a mechanic's hands and suddenly what you got is some ignorant wife beater, some drunk backwoods asshole who won't wake up and join the twenty-first century. Since the election we've gotten all sorts up here. I'll not lie to you. Drug pushers. End-of-the-world Rapture folk. All sorts. But if it brings me closer to securing this land I'll tolerate em for the time being and let me tell you why."

He pointed with his can.

"Look up that ridge, Mr. Walker. Look at this land. Picture five hundred families moving here. Picture five hundred families who believe in what's sacred, folks who don't want their phones tapped by Homeland Security or their children raised by Oprah. We'll have the watershed. We clear a little land and manage the game and we'll have a secure food source. I'm talking about our own little kingdom here, independent of the outside world. We'll pick up everybody America's discarded. The poor, the homeless—they'll have a home. The hungry—we'll feed em, work the fields shoulder to shoulder. We'll go out and get them. Go to the prisons, go to the asylums. We'll build an army out of all the folks corporate America doesn't give a fuck about. And we'll train em right here."

"What does Leighton want out of it?"

"Leighton's a classic narcissist. He wants to be king." Parsons took a drink. "Don't look at me like that. I've made my compromises and I'll continue to make them until this land is secure. After that it's a different world. You understand me?"

"It may not be as bad as you think," Dallas said.

"Or maybe it's worse."

"I don't think it is."

Parsons laughed. "I went out and saw him when he came through town last year for the primary," he said. "The Serpent, I'm talking about, that A-rab Hussein motherfucker. Gave a stump speech right off Main Street, and let me tell you what I did. You know the old Five & Dime? Tallest building in town. I climbed up on the roof. Goddamn Secret Service and state police everywhere and I climbed up there with an M-14 and put the crosshairs on his black ass. Just sat there and watched him." Parsons drained his beer in a long slow swallow. "If they come down in here," he said, "you go get you a gun."

"I got a gun."

"Get you a bigger one."

In late April, Malcolm convinced Jordan to go with him to Charleston. He woke early, walked the streets until nine, then headed back to the hotel to find Jordan cross-legged in the floor, *A Course in Miracles* open in front of her, her iPod playing some sort of rhythmic drumming. Seven beats per second, she had told him. It was primal, the rhythm of the earth's core. She looked up and smiled, lithe and trim in a tank top and pajama pants. The note he had left still sat on the nightstand by the phone.

"Good walk?" she asked.

"Hot already." He propped one foot on the bed and untied a shoe.

"There's so much energy here," she said without looking at him. "So much psychic trauma."

"This was a major battle. A siege. It went on for days."

"It's like the whole area is the scene of one giant dislocation." She kept her eyes on the screen. "It's like only when something is taken from its context can you truly see it. And everything here has been knocked off its foundation. I dreamed about the bear last night. Like it was waiting to tell me something."

They made love atop the duvet and walked to the Aquarium. It was lunch time and they had the place mostly to themselves. They climbed the stairs to the large freshwater tank that occupied the entirety of the third floor. The tank was in constant motion, fish circling at all strata, ignoring the long dip net gliding along the bottom. They watched the trout and catfish, long sleeks of muscle patterned like snakes. Alligator gar drifted near the surface like deadfall limbs, and Malcolm studied their archaic form. They were older than he had ever imagined, and more beautiful too, and he found his eyes tearing as they looked at him without recognition, his shape held in the gloss of their eyes; and then he understood: they did not need him. They did not understand him. And they would go on another million years after him. His life as insignificant as starfall.

That evening they walked to a Thai restaurant on Upper King. When they got back to their room Jordan took a baggie of marijuana from an Altoids tin and lit an incense stick. They sat on the floor at the foot of the bed with their backs against the comforter. The air conditioner spewed glacial air that seemed to vanish in the heat floating through the open balcony doors.

"The bear keeps coming to me," she said.

He took the joint from her, held it, let his head loll back onto the bed. On the floor an ice bucket sweated.

"We should shut the sliding doors."

"The room is nonsmoking." She took back the joint. "It came last night and wanted me to follow it. If you follow your dream totem to whatever place they take you, the totem will give your message. It means something in your life has to change. Or is going to change, I guess."

His eyes felt brittle. "I feel like I should shut that door."

"Sit still. And 'perceive in sickness but another call for love, and offer your brother what he believes he cannot offer himself.'"

He stood but made no move to the balcony.

"'Miracles are merely the translation of denial into truth,'" she said, and it took him a moment to realize she was reciting something from her book. "'If to love oneself is to heal oneself, those who are sick do not love themselves. Therefore, they are asking for the love that would heal them, but which they are denying themselves.'"

"Is this a message for me?"

"Sit," she said again, and he looked down at her, legs folded beneath her, a ribbon of bra strap visible where it had slid from beneath her tank top. Sweat beaded along her upper lip and just behind her ears. "Please."

She offered up the joint. Instead of taking it he walked to the hall door and stared for a moment at the map posted there. IN CASE OF FIRE a stick figure directed the way to the nearest exit. Beneath that was the checkout policy. The room was indeed marked NON SMOKING.

In the closet he found a portable baby crib stowed beneath the garment rack and ironing board.

"There's a baby bed in here," he called. "A crib."

"I want to know what you told that boy at your church to get him to help you," she said. "The God Talk. What did you tell him about God?"

At the mention of Will, Malcolm felt something clench, the sense of having overlooked something, a crucial detail left unattended. He thought of those summer nights with Mary Ann before everything had gone past him, the porch swings and old records spinning into static, of kissing her and tasting grape Kool-Aid. Where he stood, the chap of her lips, the way she canted her head. How he never learned to listen.

He walked barefoot into the bathroom and turned on the overhead light, stared into the glare of the mirror. "A crib."

"You tried to kill yourself. You actually drank a gallon of antifreeze," she said from the other room. "I want to know what you told him. I want the God Talk."

He cut off the light and stood in the door. The room was full of darkness, shadows tipped from the ambient light of the parking lot.

"If you'd drunk like half that much you'd be dead," she said. "Do you remember telling me that? Sit down. Don't shut the balcony."

"Let me see that."

He took what was left of the joint between his finger and thumb and sucked, felt a balloon of heat center itself deep in his chest and expand outward. The incense stick had almost burned down, a thin line of white smoke willowing up.

"What do you dream about?" she asked when he was beside her again.

"I can never remember. I dreamed about storms for a while, but not for months. Tell me about the bear."

"I think there's a bottle of wine in my bag if you want it." She put a hand to her face. "God, I'm so phased."

He opened the bottle and poured two small measures into plastic cups.

"You don't have to drink it if you don't want to," she said.

"A little is okay. Tell me about the bear."

"I'm just waiting. If there's a message there or not. I don't know."

He sipped the wine and was strangely relieved to find he couldn't taste it. He took another drink. "Like a message from God," he asked, "or a message from yourself?"

"I don't know. How much difference is there?"

He shook his head though there was no way for her to see this, her left hand on his thigh now, the slight scratch of her fingernails. He thought her pupils must be enormous, black wells lustrous with tears. She would look younger than her few years, giant-eyed and childlike. Or would they be tiny? He was no longer certain.

"'The simplest definition of God,'" he said, "'lies in the idea that truth and meaning are one and the same thing.'"

"That's you saying that?"

"That's Alain Badiou."

"But you believe it?"

"At one point. I'm less certain now."

Her hand slid up his thigh to rest absently against his pelvic bone, nothing sexual in the motion; it felt almost sisterly. He fought the urge to get up. For some reason he wanted to look again at the crib. He thought if he could look again he might find the Iraqi child sleeping there, an infant again, his life restored.

"'Each of us is guilty before everyone for everything,'" he said, "'and I more than the others.'"

"Badiou?"

"Dostoevsky."

"Don't talk Dostoevsky," she said. "Don't talk anyone but you. You really don't remember your dreams?"

"Not for a long time."

Darkness closed over them. The heat abated and the shadows were gone but it was the darkness he noticed.

"Where is it you go?" he asked. "All those weekends."

"Why are you asking me?"

"I just wonder."

"I said if you trusted me not to ask."

"I do trust you," he said. "But I wonder, too. I'm sorry."

"Don't apologize. Don't go through life apologizing," she said. "Tell me something: what will we do when we get back?"

"What do you want to do?"

"I'm asking you."

"Live a good life. Raise vegetables. I'm cautiously optimistic."

Easter came and went in a shower of crenelated blossoms, dogwood petals that dusted the yard, gathering without reference to the crucified Lord. In May, a letter arrived postmarked Roanoke, VA. It was from Jefferson Roddick.

So you are going to Haiti and I am not. And you are going to save some child's life while I do not. So be it. You should know, however, that while you may rescue some child from the slaughter bench of history that ultimately your kindness will not matter: the child will suffer, the child will die. That is to live by works. But you should also know that if there is salvation we are saved by our belief that though the act does not matter, it simultaneously matters immensely. That is to be saved by faith. Do not judge yourself by what matters here, Malcolm. History is a hard teacher, but in the end she is false. The temporal is an insufficient realm. So save someone. Do your useless good. Know that it does not matter. But know, too, that it matters more than anything else. Grace comes from the ground up, Malcolm. If it comes at all.

Malcolm read the letter a second time, put it back it in the envelope, and walked inside, the possibility of Haiti a distant fever. The house felt cavernous and empty, a mausoleum filled with useless antiques. He paced the rooms and finally sat on the porch to wait for Jordan. When she arrived he took her upstairs to the threshold of his bedroom.

"What?" she asked.

He spread his arms as if to indicate all that stood about them. "Move in," he said. "Abide with me."

PART TWO

V.

After the rains the summer grew shaggy with heat and in the evenings Malcolm sat alone on the porch while Jordan meditated upstairs. Three weeks had passed since she moved her scant belongings into the Winter House, and they settled into a life, an easy routine of working in the yard and eating dinner on the back porch. She had cleared and tilled the gardens once tended by Malcolm's mother, and though it was late in the season when she planted, green shoots climbed from the churned earth. Jordan quit her job at the fish camp. Malcolm worked a few days a week for Dallas, but there was little to do until Dallas's appearance back in court.

There was no need to be elsewhere. There was some money, a little but enough, and there was the large empty house that cost nothing to embody. And there was work here. Soon they would can beans and corn and peppers, and as the days progressed and the shoots spiraled and lengthened to tendrils, Malcolm began to perceive the contours of a new life. They would buy a milk cow and chickens, chop wood for the winter. They would live quietly and simply, tending their house and land. He imagined the future's shape as existing behind some transparent screen, a possibility, a shy magic yet to be conjured. If he squinted just enough, if he ignored just enough of those moments when she locked herself in the bathroom, or the way she looked at him, lips formed around a question she would not ask, if only he accepted their shared life as a series of slippery glances, then he could believe in it.

Mornings, he still rose early to walk the river and fields, returning to find Jordan pruning the fruit trees. While she worked, he began the restoration of his sprawling diorama of Fort Wagner. In part, it was an act of completion, but perhaps more than that it was the need to impose order on all aspects of his life, to make the crooked straight. In the evenings, he waited on the porch and watched the thunderheads cross the sky, the eaves strung with Tibetan flags meant to lift their prayers. Slivers of stained glass in the gingko trees wheeled triangles of light across the yard.

Tonight, it was not yet raining, but it was warm and humid, and in the distance heat lightning broke, vast sheets that illuminated the surrounding fields. The wind blew and the flowers in the beds feathered and ticked. He leaned back in his chair.

You could go crazy this time of year.

The thought splintered in his mind, and for a moment he felt ridiculous even though he knew it was true. It was that desperate time, violent and unpredictable. The season of wet heat and hair that matted against damp necks. It was the time of year when people snapped.

He looked out at the asphalt, heard the weathercock on the roof spin, pushed down the thought. Despite everything, he was happy, waiting to walk upstairs to make love to a woman he was beginning to believe he loved, willfully ignoring her manic fits and bleeding nose, the complications gathered around and against him.

Such ignorance had not been necessary the first week. The first week had been bliss. The second week certain issues had emerged, bright triangles that flamed in some ancillary space, the mind's trapdoor swung open on a dark corner. By the third week he'd learned when to walk out of the room.

But most days things were good.

Most days, he ate lunch in the kitchen with Jordan, then followed her upstairs where they made a fierce and silent love. Afterward, they would lie twined, the windows up and the room dull with heat, sticking to the wet sheets that peeled from the mattress.

He liked to watch her when she rose from the bed. He liked to watch her move across the room, the brief moment she paused in front of the mirrored closet door. The white sheets and the hourglass stain of their lovemaking.

If it was hot enough they showered together, and on these days Malcolm thought: this is heaven, the Kingdom of God within me and all around me. He stood behind her and lathered her back and shoulders, reached around to soap her stomach and breasts, let his hands slide over her mocha skin. Something telepathic in the gesture, fingertips to temples.

Listen to me. Understand me.

She was several weeks into *A Course in Miracles* and around their room she placed candles and mirrors. At night, she sat cross-legged in the floor and meditated. When the voices became too much she smoked pot for a reprieve.

"It gets so loud sometimes," she told him, "these lower vibrations."

The hours folded one into the next and he went days at a time without seeing the child. The days were good. It was the nights that undid him.

Some nights he woke to find her locked in the bathroom, crying. Other nights, he woke to find her impression in the mattress, the weight of her absence unbearably sad. She would be in the kitchen, staring listlessly at her reflection, or wandering the yard barefoot. Once he found her manically scrubbing the flagstones. *I can't sleep, get away from me, don't touch me, get away from me.* There were moments when she moved with the slow submarine grace of undersea life, and others when she was frenzied.

They went back to church on a Sunday evening—a healing service, Jordan's idea—arriving at dusk, the parking lot of El Shaddai crowded with cars and pickups and a battered school bus painted sky blue so that the official markings showed as faint ghosts. The sanctuary was a dim roar of lamps and box fans arrayed at the ends of pews, everyone standing, a cluster of Church of God men and women having arrived—Malcolm guessed—on the bus and now occupying one corner of the room. Hairnets and long dresses for the women. The men in boots and pressed jeans. Preacher Dell stood before the altar with his hands upraised and eyes shut, around him a chorus of amen and hallelujah and amen and thank you, Jesus. Malcolm and Jordan sat by an open window and Malcolm watched moths climb the rusted screen. Was it true what they said—and who said it? he had read it but couldn't recall where—true that it wasn't light they sought but the deeper darkness that lay behind it? An optical illusion, then. A trap that drew them on to self-incineration.

Preacher Dell summoned forth those seeking the Power in the Blood and men and women began to move forward. And then Jordan did. Malcolm followed her up the center aisle where she stood behind an overweight man in sweatpants and a *Return of the Jedi* T-shirt. An elderly woman, one of the Church of God women, whispered in Dell's ear and Dell nodded and whispered back, placed one hand on the woman's head. The other hand he extended toward God. The knot of people did the same, one hand on the woman's back, the other palm opened to the coming of the Spirit. *Oh, Jesus,* Dell began to intone, and Malcolm lost him, a hail of garbled talk, the shock of the woman collapsing back into the waiting arms. The man stepped forward and Dell prayed and the man began to sob so that his body trembled, arms and neck and the fat that hugged his waist. When he turned to wipe his eyes on a prayer cloth anointed with oil, Malcolm realized Jordan now stood before Dell, eye to wet eye before—Malcolm felt, but could not say—the throne of judgment.

Jordan whispered into Dell's ear.

"Tell them," Dell said and murmured something inaudible. "Tell them, child," Dell said again.

"I can feel the devil," she whispered. "I can feel the devil on me."

"Tell them," he counseled.

She spoke louder: "I can feel the devil climbing over me." And then shriller, higher, summoned from that place to which Malcolm had once descended: "I can feel the devil climbing all over me, up and down my back."

"In the name of Jesus Christ the crucified and risen Son of God on high who shall sit in judgment of the quick and the dead," Dell called, "I command you Satan and your legions of darkness away from this Child of God."

Jordan screamed. "I can feel him!"

"Away!" said Dell.

"I can feel him!"

"Out!"

She began to twist, hunched forward as if trying to flip the devil forward onto the orange carpet. "I can feel him, I can feel him!"

The preacher bent to study the space between her feet, then suddenly stood upright and pointed down the aisle. "Open up those doors," he said. "He's off! Open up those doors and whoop that devil down out of here!"

Jordan was stomping, something caught in her throat, half-terror, half-joy, while around her men and women bent, hands on knees and cheering, as if watching her grind the devil into the thin shag. When she began to kick the devil toward the door they began to scream louder. *Kill that devil! Whoop that sorry devil on out the door!* Dell marched before them and stood in the threshold, arms extended, head back and eyes shut. "And I call upon the Holy Spirit—amen!—now and forever here in the—"

She fought the devil down the aisle, a tangle of hair and sweat and tears and the manic whooping, and when he was gone, and the doors shut, fell onto the carpet and wept.

"I've never felt anything like that before," she told Malcolm in bed. "I don't know if I ever want to again." She was curled against his length, one warm thigh across his waist, a single sheet against the ceiling fan that rattled above them. Her left hand crawled up his chest and came to rest in the hollow of his throat. "I'm so tired now. It's like everything—I don't know. Like everything drained out of me, good and bad—and what I realized is that maybe what I'm after is too much. It's like I don't even realize what I'm asking for."

"You should rest," Malcolm said. But despite his words felt an erection bulge beneath her thigh, tightening until it felt like iron.

"I can't even be sure that was me."

"Who else would it have been?"

"I don't know," she said, "who was it for you?"

He said nothing and she shifted her thigh, glided down her hand and took his erection in her hand, held it without moving.

"Do you believe it?" she said.

"Believe what?"

"God. The devil." He felt the slightest of movements. "All of it."

"I can never really say," he said. "Not anymore."

"You shouldn't have to say." She was slowly sliding her hand up and down. "It's not rational. It isn't something you can defend or reason or argue." He felt as if he would burst, but grew only harder beneath her patient hand. "What were you preaching up there?" she asked. "Was it Socrates or was it Jesus? If you take the teaching away from Socrates he's just a man. But Jesus is still Jesus."

His erection was painful and he tried to think of something else, the bubbled hood of the Church of God bus, the greased windows that must have brought them singing up the mountains, old hymns, Blessed Redeemer, P'wr in the Blood, the night streaming in and pulling hair from beneath their careful riggings: *farther along we'll know all about it, farther along . . .*

"Isn't that enough?" he said.

Her hand waited and then began to move again. "Isn't what enough?"

"Just to be a man. Just to be a human."

She put her mouth on his stomach and he sensed her downward movement. "I don't know," she said from somewhere beneath the sheet, and he felt her hot breath on him. "I thought once that it was. Or no I didn't." She nipped at him and he shuddered, a tingle running up his spine. He would lose it in a moment. He would lose everything. "I've always known it wasn't enough," she said. "I thought that at least you understood that."

Three days later he found her along the creek bank, the water silvery and ghostlike, the silk of her nightgown pressed to her body. He crept behind her, stopped and called her name. Something in the way she stood put him on edge, something about the pillowing light.

"You don't need to worry, baby." She didn't turn as he approached. "Just look at the water."

"I want you to come back with me."

"I'm fine. Just look at the water."

River light moved across her eyes, the current unspooling and rolling away. Malcolm took her by the arm. The air drowsy with heat and honeysuckle.

"Living water," she said. "I baptize you with water, but a man comes after me—"

"Jordan."

"Do you remember that first night with your dad, that night when we walked down here? You remember you told me about that boy at your church. The God Talk."

"Jordan—"

Her laugh dissolved into something like a gasp. "It just looks so damn inviting. I was just lying there sweating and so hot and I thought about what you must have told him—and then all I could think about was the water."

He would lead her home only to find her gone the next night, or the night after that. But he was patient, and studied her eyes the way a farmer studied sun and sky, glossy and distant one day, restless and gathering the next. He would endure.

Tuesday morning was all procedural bullshit as far as Dallas was concerned, motions granted and dismissed, a lot of silly gavel beating while Gresham Haley stalked around the courtroom and begged for an injunction. They broke for lunch and Dallas met Randi at the steak house just down the street.

"Jesus. I'm thinking this was a bad idea."

"Dallas, honey," she said, "the judge'll throw this out."

He pointed with his fork. "They're talking about me over there. They keep looking at us."

"They're not looking at us."

"It's hot. I'm sweating." He put both hands on his hair. "I'm thinking we should go."

She forked greens into her mouth. "Eat your lunch, baby."

"Did you see the folks on the steps waving their posters?"

"He'll throw it out."

"This group," Dallas said. "The Progressive Alliance. They're just pissed because I got the land before they could. They aren't the quacks chaining themselves to fucking trees. I can respect those people. They're idiots, but at least they're putting something on the line. The folks I can't stand are these lazy assholes paying their fifty bucks a year to the Sierra Club, then squatting in their five-thousand-square-foot homes feeling righteous because they recycle."

Randi looked at the nearby tables and back to Dallas. "Please keep your voice down."

"You know they came down here and ate up these mountains, just absolutely built on every hilltop they could find. Swallowed the lakes. I know because I sold em the land. But now that they've got theirs they want to pull up the drawbridge. No more developments. Save the fucking planet. Stop global warming."

"Please, honey," she said. "I promise you he'll throw it out."

Dallas filled his mouth with beef, slid out the fork so that the tines shined with saliva. "Then why hasn't he yet?"

She touched his hand. "Go home with me. We'll fix a drink, celebrate. You know it'll be dismissed."

And it was. Just a few minutes after reconvening the judge found no grounds for further delaying the development of the State Park land and dismissed the appeal. Dallas shook his lawyer's hand, stopped by the restroom, and walked out to face the protesters crowded along the sidewalk. If he'd been a little older he could have gone to Nam—he thought that standing there. A decade younger and he'd be in Iraq. He wondered how it might have changed things, a war. Instead he'd gotten this: the flip-phones and American flags, the screaming.

He called Randi from his truck but instead of heading home made the hour drive to the far shore of Lake Keowee. He had a lake house there—a double-wide, really, but nice enough: underpinned with a screened porch and a yard full of pines—and liked to get away every so often. He drove slowly, passed through Clemson and Six Mile, backed down the public ramp, and eased the boat off the trailer. It was too damn hot to be out, the sky a blistering white, the lake as empty as the parking lot. A Bass Tracker in a far cove. An aluminum johnboat creaking through reeds. The South Vegas Bar and Grill was still shuttered for the season but the giant lake houses appeared occupied. The last time he'd been up they'd been mostly abandoned, stilted above yards full of autumn leaves and deadfall limbs, ski boats raised on hydraulic lifts and covered with tarps, and it did him good to see life returning, spring cranking into summer.

He motored toward the spillway where the gray surface folded away in a wash of falling water. One hundred yards out he cut the throttle and just let the son of a bitch drift, took a pull of Johnnie Walker and cast a spinner toward the bank. When the wind blew the water white-capped but other than that there was only the slow wheeling of the rod.

But that was all right. The quiet was soothing. He felt more alone than he had in ages and was happy for it. He guessed Randi was running on her treadmill: sweaty and panting and pissed that he wasn't home yet. If he left her alone she'd run it out. He envied that; that had once been him. The years at Georgia on through the Marines and the bodybuilding circuit—that had been him, buying Johnson & Johnson baby oil by the gallon, sleeping in Econo Lodges and inhaling the leftover sweat of old prizefighters gone to seed. He had lifted weights in every dim and sooty gym in the southeast, every anger or fear diminished by the steady accretion of steel and grit. He thought of those moments onstage, oiled and dehydrated and so cranked on ephedrine he felt his shoes scrape the ceiling. In many ways, football had always been a scam, a team sport, a place to hide. But alone onstage—that was something else entirely.

He reeled in when he saw the bass boat coming toward him, two good old boys running around with a pair of Evinrude 120s mounted on the back. They cut their motor and glided over.

"Any luck?" one asked.

"None to speak of."

Dallas could see a litter of plastic worms and vials of rainbowed Powerbait.

"Been tied up down by the bridge," said one. "Catching em as fast as we could reel em in. Eddie caught him a six-pound smallmouth. Big old monster son of a bitch."

"I'll give it a look," Dallas said.

"You do it, buddy."

But instead of making for the bridge he headed to the dock, drove up to the lake house, and fixed another drink. He walked through the house, bare feet in the deep pile of the chocolate carpet, knowing all along where he would wind up.

The bedroom walls were pressboard paneling whorled with knots and eyes so that it looked not so much like wood as cut from a tree but wood as imagined by a manufacturer, wood two removes from existence. On top of the liquor cabinet was a photo of his daughter, Marilynn. Thirteen years old now. He didn't like to get into it but there it was. There *she* was. He'd been circling the photo for the past hour and knew it. It was hard, though. She lived in Atlanta with her mother, Dallas's first wife, and though he'd sent several gifts at Christmas he hadn't seen his girl since the fall. That was his fault. It was all his fault, truth be told. He had always wanted to be a good father and thought at one point he might turn out to be. Now he knew otherwise. It had slipped past him. He'd messed around, neglected them both, but there had been a moment, he thought, a chance. One night when Marilynn couldn't have been more than two Dallas had gone back to check on her. It was a random thing, peeking into her bedroom after she was asleep, not something he did often. She'd been a little shit that day, no-no-noing him into submission. Usually she was a sweetheart but she'd been a shit that day, and he guessed he'd felt a little guilty.

So he'd gone to peek in only to find her head wrapped in both the blanket and sheet and even though Dallas heard her breathing he had imagined her near suffocation. He pulled down the covers to find her head soaked in sweat. And then he was soaked in sweat because it was just a random thing, complete chance really, that he'd walked back here, and suppose he hadn't? For a moment he'd had to lean against the wall and watch her breathe. He had just grazed it, and the realization was stunning.

It was all so goddamn fragile.

Now, he felt neither excitement nor pain, only an intense sorrow, and then he felt that sorrow drain from him, pulled as if by gravity, and he felt nothing at all. He and Randi had decided against children, which is to say he had refused her. She had wanted one, he knew that. But he'd fucked up once and didn't want to relive it. So Randi pays for the sins of my past. I fuck up and Randi suffers for it.

As always, he thought.

He fixed another drink and started looking for something to eat, found a frozen steak and a bag of chunky frozen vegetables he thawed in the microwave. He needed to go see Marilynn, would, in fact, now that things were fine with the land. Fucking Gresham Haley. He'd lost, of course, but his words were beginning to haunt Dallas.

The steak spat and hissed in the pan and when it was ready he sat down at the table, cut the steak and found some butter in the fridge to spread over the vegetables. His phone buzzed with an incoming call but he let it go to voicemail. Randi looking for him. He guessed she was done running by now, twelve or thirteen miles down some nonexistent road. And here she wanted to know why he couldn't sleep. Jesus Christ.

That was her question: why don't you sleep, Dallas? Why can't you rest, baby?

She'd laughed about it but it wasn't a joke. The Barbie dolls with their invisible nooses. Those 5.56 rounds in the mud. These people were serious. It wasn't some bullshit game. Haley had been right: the legal wrangling was the least of his worries.

He didn't head back until he knew Blue Mountain would be empty, parked around back and walked up to find Gresham Haley on the couch in his office, a bad dream sweating onto three thousand dollars of leather upholstery.

"You?" Dallas said.

"Pretty fancy show in there today." Haley was dressed in running shorts, a T-shirt matted to his chest and a sports bottle of Gatorade between his hairy thighs.

Dallas looked out the door to his secretary's empty desk. "How the hell—"

"She let me in," Haley said. "I caught her on the way out."

"Well, she's fired next time I see her."

"Actually, she did you a favor."

"Letting you sweat up my couch?"

Haley shot a jet of liquid into mouth. "Sorry about that. I was running and had this sudden need to speak."

"And you couldn't call?"

"I've done nothing but call. I left you messages."

Dallas leaned against the corner of his desk. "Yeah, I got them."

Haley nodded slowly. "I didn't know if you had or not. I didn't hear back."

"You filed a fucking lawsuit against me. What did you expect to hear?"

Haley said nothing and Dallas walked to the small bathroom tucked in the corner. "You want a towel or something?"

"You know I still hold two Yale records," Haley called. "The two-mile and the three-mile."

Dallas took a towel from a wicker cabinet. "I thought it was all meters now, the 3200, the 5K?"

"I'm just saying you're not the only athlete around."

"I never said I was." He threw Haley the towel, the man too slow to react and the cloth flapping against his shoulder. "You come up here to talk sports?"

"I came up here to help you since you can't seem to help yourself." He wiped clean one arm, spirals of dark arm hair. "I came up here to warn you."

"Why don't you go home and take a shower, Gresham? You call me and I promise I'll pick up."

He toweled dry his Gatorade. "This is gone pretty damn far for you to take it so light, Dallas."

"Are you drunk?"

"I was out running," Haley said.

Dallas walked over and took his bottle, smelled it. "What is this? Vodka?"

"Arctic Mist and Grey Goose."

"You're all class, Gresham."

Dallas passed it back and Haley reclined on the couch and propped his Nikes on the armrest. "Yes, indeed, that was a pretty fancy show. The way the judge danced around all morning like he gave a shit. Then he gets his lunch and out goes the appeal."

"Can you even walk?"

He held the bottle above him. "I like the blue. The blue has a calming effect." He sat up on one elbow. "I didn't see your partner today."

"Get up." Dallas pulled him onto his feet and leaned him against the window overlooking the reception area, his amorphous double on the couch, a black blot smeared against the brown leather. "Get up and go home."

"I know all about Leighton Clatter, Dallas. You may not but I certainly do."

"I'll help you as far as the door but that's it."

"You need to understand some things, my friend."

"Walk."

"Like your account with NationsBank."

"I don't have an account with NationsBank."

"Like the Savings and Loan behind the post office? Their records on you are about this far from getting subpoenaed."

"Just fucking walk."

He got Haley into the hall and then the elevator.

"What I don't understand," Haley said, "what I absolutely don't understand is why you are even with these people? You realize they're opposed to the very system that's made you rich?"

Haley was starting to slide down the wall.

"Don't sit down," Dallas said.

"Let me ask you something"

"Get up. Don't sit down."

"Have you heard of a guy named Rick Miles? Brother Rick, they sometimes call him."

The elevator door opened on the lobby.

"Get up, Gresham."

Haley unfolded like a marsh bird, a skeletal construction of knees and elbows. "Brother Rick happens to be a major player in both the narcotics and firearms industries. A sort of middleman who connects people with suppliers. 'Moving weight,' they call it. Rick is a man who moves weight. Why don't you ask your partner sometime if the name means anything to him?"

"All right."

"'All right.' That's all you've got? 'All right?'" He burped into a cupped hand. "There's no creeping socialism, Dallas. You think corporate America would tolerate socialism? You think they see that as a viable economic model? No one is coming to take your guns or your land. They're just a bunch of junkies and crazies. They're paranoid, my friend."

"Start walking."

"You really think it's going to revive the housing market? Is that the angle?"

They stopped by the door.

"What the hell do you want from me?" Dallas asked.

"Do you even realize you are protesting against the very system that's making you rich?"

"You said that already."

"I'll bet you get up in the morning and think the Invisible Hand brushes your hair."

Dallas opened the front door. "Is this about your bribe?"

"We are so far past that, my friend. This is about keeping you alive."

"I seem to be doing just fine in that department."

"Except you're not. Except you're ignoring all the warning signs. You remember that lost birdwatcher I mentioned?"

"Samuel Everett."

Haley crossed his arms and leaned against the front glass. "Well, well, you've done some research, I see."

"What about him? He got lost and now he's bear food."

"He's not bear food."

"He fell off some ravine and he's rotting in a ditch."

"He didn't fall off anything."

"What are you saying, Gresham? What does this have to do with anything?"

He peeled off the glass and smoothed down the shorts bunched around his thighs. "I think you know what I'm saying, but then maybe you deserve it.

I came up here to give you one last chance to get out because I'm telling you right now: I'm stopping this thing. I'd like to see you come clean of this, but then again maybe I don't. This is starting to repulse me."

"What happened to that sudden need?"

"Just remember when it all falls apart that I tried to help you."

"If you were trying to help me you wouldn't be extorting me, or trying to stop the development for that matter."

Haley stumbled onto the sidewalk. "Has it ever occurred to you, just once in that big dumb jock brain of yours, that maybe I'm trying to stop the development in order to keep you alive?"

"You don't owe me any favors, Gresham."

"You're right about that," he said. "We can at least agree on that."

A little after eleven Jordan stood in the bedroom door and waited for Malcolm to look up from his book. She couldn't speak to him; she knew that now. But if he would only look at her she thought things might still be made right. She couldn't say how or why. She knew only that the Last Things might be stayed.

He was reading Simone Weil because someone in seminary had referenced her once. He was backtracking. That was what he told her: *I'm backtracking, picking up the things I skipped past.* But he wasn't backtracking; he was becoming himself. She had thought he was like her but he wasn't, and knowing that, she knew such mysticism was lost on a man who—in becoming himself—demanded the concrete, his life the steady accumulation of data, receipts, and printouts to store in file folders and a fireproof box.

Look at me, she thought.

She had spent the last hour in the kitchen drinking chardonnay and scrolling systematically through the television, loop after mindless loop until she heard the cessation of footsteps and climbed the stairs to stand here and be ignored.

He licked the tip of one index finger and held it just above the page.

"I thought," she said.

He looked up "Didn't see you standing there."

"You didn't look."

He let the finger fall and smiled. "You coming to bed?"

"In a minute."

She stood in the bathroom for some time, studied herself in the mirror, looked away, looked back again. Finally, she cupped water to her mouth and swallowed the last Oxy 30 left in the baggie Leighton had given her. She would spiral, could see already the velocity she would gain, the inevitability of crashing, how the flameout would wash her back, how it was already tugging at her. Her skin itched, she had started noticing that. It didn't matter how much lotion or oil she used. Her skin itched and she knew what it was about. There was no choice now. She would call Leighton, go to him.

Except no.

Except what did it matter?

She stood in the threshold and saw that he had taken up his book again.

"You coming?" he asked.

"Actually, I thought I might ride downtown. To the grocery store?"

"This late?"

"We need some things. And it really isn't that late. I mean you're reading and all."

"Okay," he said. "Be careful."

And that was all. She stood in the door and watched the fall of his face, back to his page, back to his life. Okay. Be careful. Go out and do whatever the hell you want. Go waste your life while I sit home with my book and my God, happy and loved.

She took Rose's knife from the nightstand and slipped on a pair of sandals.

"I'm leaving," she said.

He seemed not to hear.

Then she was just driving. But it wasn't to the grocery store; it wasn't anywhere. All her life, night had a sort of narcotic pull, the lure of whatever lurked just past the last angle of light. She turned on the radio. Sam Cooke. Otis Redding. Marvin Gaye and Tammy Terrell. All the Motown she had listened to with Roosevelt. She thought of him often, though he was less memory than smell or taste, some little trigger she would encounter and suddenly she would be beside him in his truck, cutting school to drink grape ripple and French kiss at every stop sign. Since that day in Florida she had clicked her life away, an abacus of switched beads, as if in their movement she would find—what?

She had no answer, and instead of thinking drove back down the mountain and along Main and onto Short Street. Near the corner, she passed an open garage where a man sold roast beef shaved beneath a heat lamp, a rectangle of yellow light you could smell from the end of the block. She'd been there once with Archimedes and some of his friends. This was right after Arch had been fired and he'd blown his last paycheck so that everyone arrived loaded on little pink tablets of bring-me-joy embossed with pineapples and palm trees. They'd wound up making a scene and she guessed she wouldn't be welcome among the families eating off card tables and paper plates. Not that she particularly cared to be, but there was something in the tension that hurt her, being associated with Archimedes and his thug friends, all of them crowded into a shotgun house on the edge of Little Mexico.

The Chamber of Commerce, the police, the land developers, they all wanted them out, the blacks and the Mexicans—at least they had that in common. Impediments to Walhalla as a resort town, the Gateway to the Blue Ridge, the last stop before hitting the Chattooga. They wanted boutiques and gourmet delis, but had just another southern scar hollowed from the inside out. Thirty years ago the mills had employed over half the town and down Main Street were department stores and soda fountains, but that world had collapsed a generation ago. Or that's what they told her. It was before her time, and true or not, all she'd ever wanted was out.

She turned left by the car wash and passed several antebellum homes, beautiful white plastered things, layered and airy as wedding cakes. At the end of Main, down near the city pool, was Head's Superette & Grocery, and that was where she was headed because that was where it had all started, that was where she'd met Roosevelt.

Ever since returning from Florida she had felt its gravitational pull. Rose and his Pilgrim angel. Her seventeen-year-old incarnation—the self she couldn't have back. She would start walking and wind up here, stop without intending it, trying to conjure the before time, listless and glassy-eyed between the island of gas pumps and the cracked highway, the bank of scabby grass blue with streetlight.

Her headlights cut the blush of dark.

I won't go in, she thought. And then she did.

The floor was concrete, the smell faintly metallic and dry by the long bins of fruit, the out-of-season watermelons and cantaloupes and shucks of Silver Queen that lay as if in coffins, neatly displayed in the dusty light. She had forgotten the smell—moving past shelves of deviled ham and baked beans, now past boxes of cornflakes and Corn Puffs—she had forgotten the smell but it was coming back, and she moved without thinking to the glass cooler that lined the far wall, took out a Dr Pepper and found a bag of salted peanuts on the rack behind her.

"We're about to close," the girl at the counter called.

The girl at the counter—Jordan didn't recognize her, frizzy red hair pulled back in a ponytail, a few freckles scattered across a broad face. She had a book in front of her, a textbook of some sort, and Jordan strained to read what appeared to be a random alphabet of letters and numbers. Math equations of some sort—Rose would have known. Behind her sat a playpen, empty but for a wadded blanket and stuffed Big Bird. Jordan looked past her to the shelf, the cigarettes and blister packs of medicine, the envelopes of Levi Garrett and rolls of Copenhagen and Lotto 7 scratch tickets.

"This all?" asked the girl.

"Where's the old guy who used to run this place?"

The girl shook her head. "It's two seventy-nine. You want a bag?"

"He ran it for years. Did he sell it or something?"

"I've only been working here since Christmas. You want a bag or not?"

She went outside and sat on the bench. The night Rose returned she had met him here. He'd been in a wreck somewhere out west and an angel of the Lord had pulled him from the sinking cab and sent him home to resurrect the life he had dispatched. She had chosen the place because it was the same bench where they'd first met, the same squat trees, heavy and green-leafed and rustling. For the first time in months she had felt a circling to her life, an arc that found shape in the failing honeyed sunlight. Roosevelt's face shredded with the branch shadows, forearms on his knees, hands open, pleading with her there in the gloaming.

Listen to me, girl.

He had been working for Dreck's Trucking, making long hauls from Atlanta up to Oregon or sometimes Washington State, trying *to save up a little something, baby. A little something for us.*

Except there is no us, Roosevelt. Now listen to me, I don't think you're listening—

Oh, I'm listening, Rose saying this now, *I'm listening good.*

Roosevelt driving through blizzards of rain and half-snow that turn mouse gray on the asphalt and then brown with exhaust. A scattering of trucker pills boring out his ears and shuddering his heart. Coffee and White Crosses and Ray Charles in the tape deck. *Listen, baby. I mean it. No one else knows this.* Jordan hearing it all over again. *No one else in the world knows—* she mouths the words for him: *this story.*

He leaves Spokane just before dawn, early April and I-90 still wet with the last of the spring snow, and is somewhere in Idaho when he hits the patch of black ice, and it's just this feeling of slipping away, this sliding, and not just the truck, but his whole life, the last few years, meeting Jordan, his child being born—everything. Just slipping. Going now: goodbye. And he isn't even scared. *Not a bit I wasn't, baby. I kept remembering something my granny would always tell me growing up. Grace. Spent a whole life running from it and there it's the first thing comes to me: 'not mercy, child, oh, no.' Well, I felt that then. I knew then what she meant. Like I had found it—grace—and it was the only thing in the world that mattered, the only thing worth finding.*

The cab goes thirty or so feet off the bridge into the black water. The trailer catches on the mangled guard rail, but the cab tears free to plunge the rest of the way. Splash. Darkness. *Damn, baby. Just like that it goes. It sank so slow. It was strange. I reckon I probably could've climbed out if I'd wanted to. I don't know. I just sat there. The water looked so damn cold.*

So Roosevelt watches the water line rise above the cab windows and fill up through the floorboards and thinks of his new baby girl. The rescue squad arrives, pulling ropes and hypothermia blankets from the back of a pickup, and Roosevelt thinks about Jordan, alone with her grandparents and a screaming child. The Idaho State Police block off the highway while a red helicopter marked NEWSHAWK circles overhead. A team of divers make their way up from Moscow, but all Roosevelt feels is the denim of his jeans grow heavy, and then his underwear, his shirt—all of it like a glove closing over his heart.

He inhales the cold, the weighted blackness that swims into his lungs.

He needs it. Somehow he needs it.

Strangest thing, the sort of peace I felt. I gave it all up to the Lord, and then he gave it all back.

The accounts varied, but witnesses agreed that a man wearing what appeared to be the stark, black dress of a Pilgrim had stepped from the bank opposite the gathering onlookers and waded out into the water, emerging a few minutes later with a limp and unconscious black man slung over one shoulder like a forty-pound feed sack. Rose was left on the bank, rolled gently onto one side so that the water could drain from his lungs. The man, who witnesses guessed stood anywhere from seven to nine feet, disappeared into the cold dead scrub leaving behind not a trace, not so much as a footprint in the soft mud bank.

I was awake inside the whole time. It was so cold my skin was hot. I felt myself burning, my hands, my eyes. Then I felt sleepy. And then he had me. My angel.

Years later, she would trace to that moment the despair that now laced her heart, sitting just behind her breastbone, a feeling so precise she felt as if she might touch it and somehow right the entire world with nothing more than the laying on of hands.

I know I screwed up bad, girl. I know we lost her. But maybe we can get us straight, me and you.

She'd almost laughed at him. I want to love you, fuck you, hurt you. I adore you.

And now Malcolm and his goddamn Simone Weil. Like he could fake his way back to mystery, to the wondrous horror of his attempted crucifixion. But she couldn't leave him, not yet anyway. She wanted the God Talk; she wanted what he wouldn't give her. He would ruin her if she let him. But she couldn't leave just yet. She took her phone out and scrolled to Leighton's cell. She could push a button and fix everything. That easy magic that might float her for weeks—she could absent the bear, she could absent everything. And how simple it was—neural chemistry. Not God but dopamine. Instead of a savior, serotonin.

She shut her eyes until she heard his voice.

"It's bad," she told him, "it's like a thousand times worse than I ever thought."

"So your little Messiah couldn't save you?"

She held the phone away from her ear. "Please, Leighton."

"Where are you?"

"This is just for right now. This is just for tonight."

"Where are you?"

"Across from the city pool? The convenience store there?"

"I can have someone pick you up in ten minutes."

But he came for her himself, picked her up, and started up the mountain.

"I almost feel sorry for the boy," Leighton said. "He's busy playing house and has no idea, does he?"

She put her forehead to the cool glass. "He knows as much as he wants to know."

Leighton turned off the highway onto the Forest Service road, a slew of gravel behind them as they rolled toward The Settlement.

"What do you have for me?" she asked.

"Everything. Be patient."

"I need something bad, Leighton. I need it now."

When they pulled up to the farmhouse she saw Rick Miles and Shit-Toe sitting in rocking chairs, waiting on her.

"I don't want to remember a second of this," she said.

"You won't."

She grabbed his wrist. "I'm serious. If they're going to touch me give me enough to put me into next week. I can't take this home."

He smiled, opened the door so that the dome light glowed and she could see that the men on the porch had stood, gentlemen suitors, kindhearted slavers.

"And where else would home be?" Leighton asked.

When she laughed it came out like a yelp and she thought, Oh, God. She thought, Oh, God, I have to go somewhere.

I have to go away.

I have to go home.

I have to—and stopped because she had no answer.

He started the tractor and eased out of the shed past the disc plow and a line of discarded push mowers, an old camper shell like the molded hump of a snap turtle. It had rained two days prior but Elijah hadn't cut the bottomland all spring. It was probably thigh high and thick with snakes. But more than that he wanted out of the house. He was spending too many days in the recliner with the TV on mute, newspaper on his lap like the thinnest of blankets. Just didn't seem to have the strength to get up. Wasn't eating. Wasn't sleeping. At night he'd sit in the chair and worry about Malcolm and Dallas, what the boy at the diner had said, the one from the Savings and Loan. *Then the money just up and disappears.* Evelyn peering through the darkness like an owl. You got that meanness down in you, Elijah Walker. But she didn't know. When she had first appeared he had thought she could see into him, understand his thoughts. Now he knew she could not. The other side was just that: the other side.

He'd see it soon enough. That morning he'd stood naked in front of the mirror, first time he'd done it in God knew how long, and what he'd found was death. Its cold proximity. His abdomen swollen and rumpled above the blue map of his scrotum. He thought of how it felt to have survived the war, bringing his flesh home, triumphant, but less impressive now. Home to rot. The souring meat of his body collapsing in stages. Renal failure would be last. He'd go quick after that. Which meant his dignity might outpace his body, if only by a second.

He backed to the Bush Hog and dropped the PTO. He had rigged one of the old push-pull collars years ago but the son-of-a-bitching thing was hard to operate. Old hands. Claws, really. He couldn't get the pins in and then did, climbed back on and started down the trail to the bottom. He'd bought the land just after he'd come back, one hundred and twenty acres. Had blown his discharge pay months ago and had to borrow every dime. Could have bought two, three hundred acres if he hadn't been scared. Easy credit back then. But Evelyn had been against it, she wanted to live in town, one of the old Georgian Revivals on Main Street. Ivied columns. Walk to the pharmacy. Walk to church. He blamed her but in the end he'd done what he wanted. Which had always been true.

He'd spent two years restoring the farmhouse, several months building the cabin. Dallas just a boy then, three or four years old and dragging a hammer in the dust. Come home from work and get to work. This back before they convinced everybody that work was beneath their dignity. Back before they got us ashamed to have dirt under our nails. Work now the sole provenance of the Mexican. Working their asses off for three dollars an hour. Which is why the white man has gone to hell. But it had been different then, he'd done it, spent weeks refinishing the floors, took a month to pull off the rotting asphalt shingles and replace them with sheets of Galvantine, half a year to build new kitchen cabinets. The main bath had swallowed him, occupying the better part of a summer, but in the end it had been a masterpiece.

Evelyn had hated the place until town started going to shit. Lot of petty crime when the jobs dried up. Then bigger stuff: B & E. Armed robbery. Little old ladies losing their jewelry boxes or having their husband's gun cabinets emptied. Piedmont Quilting had brought a thousand Mexicans over the border, then shut their doors when the INS came knocking. Biggest immigration bust in state history, had to herd them into the city gym and damn if it wasn't hard not to feel sorry for them, hustled like that. The workers chasing the jobs and the job chasing cheaper workers. Everything in Honduras and Guatemala. Eight years of Reagan and folks got desperate, stole Social Security checks and sold pot and soon enough were cooking meth. She'd started liking it then, the isolation. Planted the flower beds and an herb garden, took to growing roses.

The trail emptied out into a broad field, hardwoods on three sides and the creek flowing along the fourth, a few scrub pines cropped along the edges, but he could live with that. He wasn't planting. He was cutting just to cut. The tires squished into the mired ground and he lowered the deck and switched on the blade. Grasshoppers springing in front of him. Something rustling in the grass, rat or snake. Wasn't big enough for a beaver. More often than not he saw turkeys, gobblers, and a big tom flared and prancing, but he figured the noise to have scared them off. He didn't get down here too often anymore. It had been different before, of course. He'd fished the creek and pond two or three times a week for thirty years. First alone, then with Dallas and then Malcolm. Pulling horny head and creek chub out of the dark holes eddied behind rocks. Dallas had started bringing girls down when he was about fifteen. A sleeping bag wrapped around a bottle of wine he thought he was hiding. The rods and tackle box just to complete the act. Elijah never said a word. Watched him go and just smiled. Ignored Evelyn when she started in. Malcolm had been different. He was maybe five when Elijah had first stocked catfish and there were some in there now big enough to take your arm off. Thirty- and thirty-five-pound mudcats with whiskers long as your forearm. But Malcolm hadn't cared about the fish any more than he'd cared about the girls. He'd just go down and do what? Sit, Elijah guessed. Stare at the water and the sky, lost to the world.

Elijah made several sweeping circles, pushed the throttle, the engine coughing and surging forward. He was getting dizzy, the heat maybe, or the fact that he'd had nothing in his stomach for forty-eight hours but black coffee and Loratab, and he knew he needed to finish. Get back to the house and eat something, try to rest. Maybe find something in the medicine cabinet to help him sleep. He started sweating and then stopped, suddenly cold, and he knew that was bad. Started shivering. Saw something move in the tree line.

He pushed on the throttle.

Don't get lost in your head now. Stay sharp.

He edged the throttle again and watched the exhaust pop the rain cap up and down. Something was definitely moving in the tree line, then in front of him, then around him. A yellow cloud hovering like dust before they came down in a fit of temper, and for a moment he thought he really had entered a yellow haze of pollen. But the cloud was alive, stinging him, and he crouched low against the steering wheel, looked up to see muzzle flashes in the tree line. Shit. The heat of contact fizzling to cold. The acidic tang of fear, caught in the open and around him men falling without sound, crumpling, the chaos of crawling. The dead like dancers in their awkward poses, pretzeled in the mud, and the old man conjured certain referents that existed beyond the yellow jackets he had stirred. A colonel on the dusty LZ of a firebase, behind him a giant map of the teardrop valley: *Victor Charles is a wily adversary,* he told them. *And now we're digging right into his shit, gentlemen.* He clung to the tractor, waved one arm above him. Then someone opened up with the 60 and the tree line shredded. Someone else on the radio for fire support. Still they were everywhere, dug in, little goddamn slant-eyed gooks with their Chinese rifles. He felt something on the back of his neck and then on his arm. The pedal was jammed and he realized he was falling not from the back of his tractor but from the lurching APC, wounded, and with all the strength left in his dying body the old man took the grenade from his rig and slung it toward the trees.

His arm traced a long arc and there was a moment of appreciation, watching the graceful parabola of flight; then he felt the ground rise to meet him, sunk in the dark mud of the bottomland, looked up to see the tractor motoring on, crumpling, now, into the disintegrating ambush and the waiting creek.

That evening Malcolm and Jordan hiked into the wilderness around Ellicott Rock and camped at the confluence of the North Fork of the Chattooga River. The land gentled into a lazy crescent of sandbar that reached toward the opposite bank without ever quite realizing it. The river was high with spring rain and along the edges long grass folded beneath the surface like unkempt hair. Farther out it eddied and deepened so that the bottom disappeared in darkness.

Just above the bank they lay out their groundsheet and pitched the tent. Rocks ringed an ash mound topped with the metal wiring of a charcoal grill, and around this flat river stones. Malcolm scrubbed the rusted grill with sand while the river steamed, the heat flat and thick. Jordan was in the tent and he knew better than to bother her.

At dusk they cooked skewers of tomato, pepper, and squash. Darkness fell and Malcolm banked the fire and they moved down the slope away from the heat. They were both sweating, the air heavy with mimosa blossoms that wheeled and curled on the surface.

"Let's swim," she whispered.

She was up and in the water before he could touch her, head disappearing and resurfacing. They floated into the center of the pool, above them the pulse of stars, the red streak of a meteor. When he plowed his fingers through her hair he felt the sand bedded in her scalp, put his hands around her stomach and realized she wore nothing, her body sleek and moon-bright.

"What is it you want to tell me?" she said. "It's all right to say it."

He said nothing and they crawled to the bank—at least it felt like crawling, a slow paddling forward, his chest pressed to her back, the entirety of his life, he felt, compressed to this simple motion—and began to kiss. She lay very still and was dry when he entered her, a tentativeness to their lovemaking that ran past comfort and on toward fear. He touched the star on her hand as if it might rise without him.

Afterward they lay on their sides, awake and breathing. They dressed and Malcolm lit a Coleman lantern, the orange flame pressing their shadows into the trees.

"I was walking downriver from here," Malcolm said. "Back in the spring when it rained so much. And I came over this ledge. The rain had washed out the bank and there was a canoe there, just the tip of it. A dugout canoe maybe—I don't know—two hundred years old. There were carvings on it. It felt like this incredible gift. Like seeing something holy." He smiled and put one finger on her hip. "We can have a life together, Jordan. We have a house. We could have a child."

"You forget I've had a child."

"It would be different this time. It would be ours. What I would do," Malcolm said, "what I would do every morning is stand over her crib and touch that little beautiful groove that runs from her lips to the bottom of her nose."

"So she's a girl?"

"I don't even know what it's called, but I'd touch it every morning."

"That's not the way it works," she said.

He reached for her but she shied away. "You know you walk through the world like you're weightless."

"Like I glide."

"No," he said, "not glide. I've seen women glide. It's something else."

"Something mysterious?"

She was mocking him. He didn't care. When you are sincere it is possible to not care, he thought. That is to be in love. "I don't know," he said. "It's just something I feel about you."

She stood abruptly. "We need to dress before we freeze." She dusted the sand from her thighs.

"Sit with me another minute."

"Malcolm—"

"Sit with me."

"This is ridiculous, Malcolm. This is you doing something terrible to me."

In the morning they hiked back to find the voicemail on Malcolm's cell phone was full of messages from Randi. "It's your father," she said on every one. "There's been an accident."

Elijah Walker listed left off his pillows, a patch of pearled sky visible through the window behind him. Dallas leaned into the old man's sleeping face, while a nurse stood by the bed and adjusted a drip bag.

"Think he knows I'm here?" he asked. "Think he even knows who I am?"

His father was a scarecrow of a man, a pale question mark bent beneath the thin sheets, a riddle Dallas could not solve. Light played along the slope of his skull down to the yellow bruise that cushioned one eye. He had not treated his father well. He knew this. But Jesus, it's not like he treated us well either.

"I kind of feel like something like this happens, and after that it's all—I don't know," he said. "You crash your tractor, lay in a field for God knows how long. How do you come back from that?"

The nurse said nothing, and when she left, Dallas took out his cell phone and stared at the screen. After two days of dialing he still hadn't tracked down Malcolm. He shut the phone, opened it again. His knee throbbed but he was going to have to live with that, at least until he could get a drink.

Old age, he thought, and looked at his father.

Along with several bruises and abrasions, the old man had separated his shoulder. Otherwise, the fall from his tractor had contributed only to the discovery of a strangely distended abdomen, a mass of ugly protrusions signifying cancer of every stripe. He must have known for months. At least a year, the doctor had said, probing his stomach, the old man unconscious. This kind of metastasization doesn't happen overnight, no way. The MRI would happen in the morning, but surgery appeared unlikely. There were issues like age, the strength of one's heart.

Dallas looked up from his phone. The thin hospital gown appeared to cover a welter of fruit, all rounded ends and odd protuberances. His father looked tired and old. His heart was probably suspect. When you allow your body to reach this point, the doctor had said, it says something about your willingness to—and then caught himself and said nothing more.

Dallas pushed out of his chair and dialed Randi. For the last twenty-four hours, while Dallas sat by his father, she had been attempting to reach Malcolm.

"Anything?" he asked.

"I left like a million messages. I think at this point we just wait for him to get back. How's your dad?"

"Asleep right now. The MRI's tomorrow."

"Are you staying?"

"Probably not," he said. "It occurred to me a little while ago that his tractor is still down in the field. Can you meet me over there? Help me get him some things?"

He hung up when he realized his father was awake, eyes cloudy but comprehending.

"Dallas?" he said, his voice a thin grating. "Sit down, son. Sit down."

"Hi, dad."

"Where's your mamma, son?"

"She's not here."

"Say she's gone already?"

His father seemed to stare at their reflection in the window, two lonely pilgrims, dusty and seated along the shoulder of some empty road, and for a moment Dallas wondered what it might be like to hold his father, to feel his shrunken form sprawled across Dallas's lap. The sharp angles of his father's hip bones, the faint reek of body odor and urine. The constriction of tubes and cords as he pulled the old man against him. He wanted to hold him but couldn't bear the thought of touching him.

"Dad?"

He was asleep again. Dallas watched his chest rise and descend, then let go the breath he hadn't realized he held. For a moment he had thought his father dead.

He drove home through rings of streetlight, the evening smoldering, concrete burning quietly while the last of the sunlight seared the cyclone fencing that wrapped a construction site.

Randi's Jag sat idling in the old man's yard when Dallas pulled in. She had the windows up and air blasting. What appeared to be a champagne flute was in one hand. He tapped the glass and listened to it whisper down.

"The front door's locked," she said.

"You try the back?"

"He already hates me. I can't stand the thought of snooping through his house."

"What are you drinking?"

"Prosecco."

"Jesus, Randi."

"I'd already opened the bottle when you called. I couldn't just leave it."

"Just go through the back and find him some things. T-shirts. Underwear. I'm going to try to get the tractor back up here."

"I don't know where he keeps anything."

He put his fingertips on the door frame and removed them, a touch, less than that. "Just dig around. Please. I'm not asking that much here."

"Dallas, honey—"

"If I can get this thing out I'll be back in like fifteen minutes."

He started down the path, paused behind the house until he heard her car door open and shut, and walked on. The trail was little more than a brown scratch in a riot of green, barely visible in the early twilight. He batted at a spider web and wiped the silvery filaments from his face.

The trail bottomed out by the pond, the near shore lined with lawn chairs and old rod mounts, and Dallas walked upstream picking through the kudzu and poison sumac until he spotted the hazy bulk of the tractor resting in the creek. The Cub Cadet sat in perhaps a foot of rushing water, the front left tire having sunk slightly deeper than the others, but otherwise it appeared fine. He traced the twin ruts that ran from the bottomland where his father had been plowing, on through the brush where they gouged into the mud and disappeared in the water.

Then he just stared at the tractor, stood on the bank and studied its dematerializing shape, the lines and right angles blurring in the failing light, slashes of green leaf hanging from the engine block. There was a rock about halfway between the shore and the back right tire, and he stepped for it, felt a spasm in his knee, swung his weight forward and climbed onto the machine.

The seat and console were covered with shredded leaves. Bits of mica and sand covered the manifold in a fine patina, dry and glinting. He felt the key in the ON position, and it occurred to Dallas that not only was the gas tank probably empty, the battery was no doubt dead as well. And now it was almost full dark, a last band of light, tree frogs going, cicadas.

The front tires settled deeper into the creek bed. He knew the tractor wasn't going anywhere. He started to stand and cracked his knee and fell back onto the vinyl seat. He would have to walk back up in the dark and get a gas can and a battery charger, find a flashlight in the house, and it probably still wouldn't back out. Once the ground dried out he could get the Bobcat in here and tow the damn antique—maybe that was the thing.

But instead of getting up he simply sat there, let the night take firm root. He listened to water bend around the tires and imagined the sound of it, the sudden veering, the reconfiguring, on toward the pond and over the spillway and on toward what? He realized he had no idea. He had grown up on this very land, fished and camped here, brought girls to lie on a Coleman sleeping bag in the shade of the big hardwoods; he had lived almost half his life here and had not the slightest idea where the creek went once it funneled through the dam.

It came over him that this was the reason someone was going to kill him. This was the reason someone somewhere waited with their mail-order rifle and gut full of hate, because, in the final count, Dallas Walker was not a thorough man. Dallas Walker was a lazy man, the kind of man who might continue to let things spill past him with neither care nor curiosity for what came after. Damming a creek—the old man had dammed the creek sometime in the early seventies, a young man himself then, married and home from the war. Damming the creek with no concern for what lay downstream.

Of course, Dallas knew that wasn't true: his father would know. His father would have known before even considering the idea. He would have walked the land, talked to neighbors, consulted maps. Dallas would've just paid someone to mound the dirt and then sat and watched the water collect; but his father had done everything himself, shaped the bank, regulated the spillway. Whatever consequences flowed beyond were intended.

In the distance he heard a car horn: Randi looking for him. But he made no move to stand. The pain in his knee was just starting to subside and he saw no reason to rush things.

Was there really someone out there who wanted him dead? Probably. And he didn't blame him. He hated the man, but he didn't blame him. If it wasn't him it would be someone or something larger. The government, perhaps. He believed about half of what he heard on the radio and was beginning to doubt Leighton believed any of it. *Leighton's a classic narcissist. He wants to be king.* Dallas hadn't received a warning through his Blackberry in weeks and guessed Parsons had taken care of that. Gresham Haley hadn't called since his visit and there was no reason to suspect he would: he had exhausted his legal recourses. The RSS feeds monitoring the Internet had fallen off as well. But that didn't mean they weren't out there.

He twisted the key to OFF and back to ON just for the hell of it. When he climbed down he missed a rock and soaked both his shoes and pants cuffs.

Randi sat on the back porch banked in shadow when he walked into the yard light.

"You all right?" she called.

"Damn thing wouldn't start."

"I honked the horn."

"I need to go see Tillman. He needs to know about Daddy."

"You couldn't drive it out?"

"That damn tractor is thirty years old if it's a day." He stepped onto the porch. "I've told him for ten years now I'd get him a New Holland if he would just use it."

"You're soaked."

"He's too damn stubborn is what he is."

"Baby, your pants."

He looked at his khakis, darker below the knee, and raised one loafer. Bubbles gathered and burst beneath the tongue. "I took a little tumble," he said. "Nothing major."

"Oh, baby."

"I'm fine. Let's go home."

"You fell?"

"Let's not talk about it," he said. "Let's just go home."

When the old man was finally discharged it was not to his home but to that of his youngest son. To the room Elijah Walker and his dead wife had occupied so many years before: the same wrought-iron bed frame, the same dresser and chairs. Malcolm mounted a window air-conditioning unit and replaced the decrepit ceiling fan while Jordan went over every hard surface with Murphy's Oil. They installed a phone, bought a radio and small television, raised the windows, flipped the mattress, and washed the sheets. When they were finished the room smelled like a forest, airy and bright with new yellow curtains bellied inward. The old man could die in comfort here.

For he was coming home to die. There had been, and would be no surgery. His body was consumed with cancer, but it was also tired. I'm sixty-seven years old, for God's sake, he told them. Don't probe me or stick me. Just let me alone. And excepting a feeding tube in his stomach, they did.

On the day of his discharge Dallas picked him up from the hospital and drove him up the mountain. While Jordan settled him in his new room, Malcolm and Dallas walked onto the porch, the window unit whirring behind them.

"He thought he was going to the cabin?" Malcolm asked.

"He said not word one, bro. Not a single complaint."

"He's bad then."

"He ain't bouncing off the walls. But he's a tough old bird yet."

"You all right?"

"I'm struggling with it," Dallas said. "I keep telling myself he's too damn proud to die."

Malcolm said nothing.

"I've got to see Tillman at some point," Dallas said. "He's going to take this hard."

That evening Malcolm carried first a rocking chair, then a lawn chair into the bedroom. When he came back with several pillows the old man was awake.

"You don't have to do that," he said.

"Raise up," Malcolm said. "It's suppertime."

"Go eat at the table."

"Raise up and let me fix this" He slid the pillows behind him and eased back his delicate frame.

"Go eat at the table like a civilized human being."

"You gotta eat, too."

"You put that aluminum chair in here you look like some redneck trash."

Malcolm smiled. "I'm glad you're here, Daddy," he said, and without realizing what was happening—without meaning it, though he did mean it—kissed a liver-spot on the old man's head. They were both silent for a moment before Malcolm went back to slapping at the pillows.

"Okay," the old man said. "Damn, son. I said okay."

That night, the three of them ringed the television and ate cream corn, tomatoes, and biscuits, lifting it to their mouths and chewing in silence. But it was a good silence, Malcolm thought, a comfortable silence. They left the rocker and lawn chair and every evening Jordan carried back two plates, Malcolm behind her with his own, thinking: we have found something here, a rhythm, a way forward.

On the mornings when the old man couldn't eat, Malcolm crushed Regalin pills and pushed cans of Glucerna through his father's feeding tube. When he was back asleep Malcolm climbed to the attic while Jordan dug in the flowerbeds. Eventually, she would come inside, bits of dark soil falling from her dress. Paisley gardening gloves and a sun hat. Cotton dress damp with sweat.

"How is he?"

"Sleeping."

"Good." She pulled off the gloves and ran cold water over her hands. "Come out here and look at this."

The garden grew abundant, almost profligate with its reckless haul of tomatoes and peppers.

"You realize it's crazy early for tomatoes like this," he said.

"Apparently I've got some sort of touch."

She led him through the rows naming the plants, the eruptions of flower. "Silver Queen." She touched the silk of the husk. "Everybody always talks about how hard it is to grow corn, but look. Row after row, tasselling."

It was weeks before he realized he had forgotten what dirt smelled like.

One morning Malcolm was repainting horses in the dull roar of the ventilation fan when Randi found him, at his shoulder before he realized she was there. He was wearing jeweler's glasses and looked up at her through eyes whaled to enormity.

"I didn't hear you come up."

"Dallas is downstairs." She looked back at the trapdoor. "They're just sitting there sort of not talking. I think that might be what they need, though. To just sit and not talk." She sat down on a crate of books. "I didn't see Jordan."

"She's out back somewhere. We have fruit trees now. Or had them. They were swallowed by kudzu."

"I hope I get to say hello."

"I don't think she's hiding. She probably just didn't hear you drive up."

Randi picked up a three-quarter-inch Confederate by his boots. "Is he still wet? You've got red all over him."

"He's been shot. One of the wounded."

"That seems terrible." She set him down and wiped her fingers as if to cleanse them. "I've been getting on Dallas about coming over," she said. "He's moping. Hardly been to the office lately and this is supposed to be the busy time of year. He's staying away from Leighton, which is probably a good thing. But he still hasn't been to see Tillman."

"I can ride out and talk to him."

"So can Dallas. He's Dallas's uncle, too."

"How is he otherwise?"

"Dallas? A little less crazy, I guess. A little less paranoid." She grabbed a truss and pulled herself off a sinking box. "But only a little. It's like he's become such a realist. He still dreams—I know he still dreams—but something gets in the way, you know? I don't think it's fear. I think it's just that sense of—" She shrugged and he knew at that moment she was talking not about Dallas but about him. Except it wasn't realism; it was vanity. The child had shown him that too, his vanity, as surely as he had shown him the antifreeze in the supply closet. She looked at him. "You seem happy, Malcolm. You seem like you've got a good thing here."

"I do."

"You're in love. That's wonderful. But be careful, all right?"

July came in shocks of green heat, and with it Jordan opened the house, washed the windows, and began to paint the upstairs rooms and then the kitchen, fans blowing the odor of matte enamel out into the sultry air while the old man lay in bed and listened to the drone of the faraway radio she had tuned to a pop station.

"Is she going to paint in here?" he asked Malcolm. "You should let her paint in here. Put up the windows. Get the fans going."

"The smell might make you sick."

"I am sick. I might as well talk to somebody."

So she did, spreading a bedsheet for a drop cloth and moving along the baseboards to do the trim. The old man sat up in bed and talked to her.

Malcolm stayed clear but occasionally would stand just outside the door and try to hear what was said. Stories, mostly. Jordan's long anecdotes about her grandparents she still saw every Sunday at church, about her own childhood, happy moments he suspected had occurred only in her mind. His father spoke of his own childhood and Malcolm realized he had never heard his father talk so much, and never without the anger that had floated so long just beneath his words.

"You have to let things go," Malcolm heard him say one day. "All that ever-loving shit that hangs around you. It has to dissolve."

"'The end of desire is the end of suffering,'" Jordan said. "The Buddha said that."

"The Buddha was right."

Saturday evenings she disappeared only to return in the late afternoon on Sunday, bright and brittle as the fingernails she broke clawing at her dry skin. One night Malcolm and the old man watched her go down the front walk and waited as her headlights crawled the wall.

"You shouldn't let her go out like that," his father said. "You should keep a woman like that at home."

"She can do what she wants. She's an adult."

"I'm just telling you. She's told me things."

She came back the next day with a dropper bottle of Ativan and two re-fills bags.

"He's going to need this," she told Malcolm.

"Where did you get that?"

She sat cross-legged on the bedroom floor, the ceiling fan spinning and the curtains bulged. "You drip it." She held it up to her mouth as if to demonstrate. "Like just a drop or two, and then the whole world glows."

Several days later they all three sat watching the local news when a map appeared, a line originating in Idaho swept down through the Southwest and then into Texas and on into the Deep South where it bent through the northwest corner of South Carolina and turned for Georgia and Florida. The screen flashed to a reporter standing on a street corner in some depressed sun-drenched town, hair plastered in a wet mop while behind her a parade of Winnebago and Airstream trailers pulled by F-250 pickups rolled across the screen. White faces hung from the windows.

"Once seen solely as a fringe candidate in the last year's presidential race," the woman said, "Beau Chellis and his 'My America' tour is suddenly on everyone's mind. In his bus crossing Middle America, Vietnam hero Colonel Beau Chellis is now being trailed by his own army of converts and followers. Some claim as many as five thousand."

"We want to become involved in the direction this country is taking," said a man onscreen. "The idea that we want to 'take over' anything is nothing but scare tactics generated by the socialist left-wing anti-American media. What we want to do is rescue Christian America and the Constitution. This is for our country as much as it's for Jesus."

Following the group was a band of far-right anarchists: a tribe of survivalists, radical libertarians, 9/11 truthers, and apocalyptic prophets who called themselves the Soldiers in the Army of God. The doomsdayers wore holstered Brownings and carried 30.06s on their backs. The camera panned over assault rifles spread on a tarp, AK-47s and discarded M-16s, Israeli-made Uzis. A banner read: THE RIFLE IS THE TOOL OF THE PATRIOT.

The image gave way to a list of towns and dates.

"They'll be here in five days," Jordan said. "We should go down and see them."

"No way," Malcolm said. "These people scare me."

"But think of it as a big joke. It could be fun," she said. "Like a parade. You'd like to go wouldn't you, Elijah? Drive down the mountain and see the campers roll by. Maybe get out of the house."

"I wouldn't mind loafing a bit," the old man said.

"We should do that," Jordan said. "All of us. Just get out a little. We should be doing it right now, in fact. What do you think, Elijah?"

"I ain't getting any younger."

So that afternoon they lifted him into the Nissan and drove to Main Street, the old man between them, Jordan feeding him ice chips. Malcolm had helped him from the bed—something he did daily, getting the old man to and from the bathroom—but there was something in the act of easing him down the front steps and into the July heat that made apparent his sudden frailty.

It took Malcolm halfway down the mountain to realize what had been evident to the others from the moment Jordan had first suggested the trip: that this might well be the old man's last, that hereafter he would sit in resignation, awaiting the halt of organs, stalling and then failing resolutely, the final collapse that would come slowly and then all at once, overtaking him like wildfire. Jordan, arm across the backseat, stroked Malcolm's neck once and let her fingers rest against his collar bone.

Malcolm looked at her. "Where to?"

"I thought we might ride up to Hardee's," she said. "That be all right, Elijah?"

"That would be fine, I reckon."

They parked outside and Malcolm put his hand on the ignition. "I could go through the drive-thru. You want a coffee, Daddy?"

"Let's just go in," Jordan said.

Malcolm followed her inside where he stared out the window at the old man.

"Look at him," Malcolm said. "He's not moving."

"Let him sit there for a minute without you staring," she said. "He used to come here mornings after your mother died. I want to take him to his cabin for a while. Let him see it."

"How did I never know he came here?"

"You were off in school, getting educated."

She looked briefly out at the old man and then ahead at the bright counter. The place smelled like French fries and detergent. A teenager dumped a bag of frozen Tater Tots into the fryer basket.

"He knows he won't see it again," she said.

The old man's cabin appeared no worse for his absence. The drive was washboarded by the rain but the grass was cut and twice Malcolm had been over to Bush Hog the bottomland. The Cub Cadet was back beneath the shed, and the beagles had been adopted by the man Dallas hired to mow the yard.

"You want to get out, Daddy?" Malcolm asked.

"Just go look around for me, son. Make sure everything's all right."

"I can help you around the yard."

"Go on," he said. "Both of you. Check on my tractor. I'll honk if I need you."

Jordan and Malcolm walked around the house to the porch. The land was impossibly green, the trees leafy and bright. Jasmine climbed the trellis where they sat in rocking chairs and looked over the land that sloped beyond them down to the pond and back up to the house where they lived.

"We're right there." Malcolm pointed. "That clump of pines. You're garden is right behind those silver maples. You can see all this in the fall. We'll come up here then."

She patted her legs. "Come here."

"This is good of you, Jordan. To treat him like this."

"Come here," she said.

He sat on the arm of the chair.

"Kiss me," she said, and she tasted of coffee, faintly acrid, but sweet, too. "Let him sit for a little while longer."

"I'm glad we did this."

"We'll do it again the day they come through."

But on the day they came through Jordan was gone. Malcolm came in from walking along the river to find his father propped up in bed, alone.

"She say where she was going?"

The old man blinked twice. "I heard her pull out. I reckon she thought I was sleeping."

They waited all morning, though Malcolm knew all along she wasn't coming. The last three days had been an ugly devolution of paranoia and vomit. Finally, in the afternoon, they drove to Main Street and parked by the Bantam Chef. A few minutes later the caravan rolled down the street like a liberating army, a highway patrol car out front, blue lights winking, behind it Chellis's campaign bus, the old Colonel wearing his green beret and waving from the skylight. After the first few motor homes an actual parade materialized with flatbed trucks and church floats spangled red, white, and blue. Men and women on the sidewalks cheered the classic cars and street rods with glasspack mufflers. Hands hung from windows and waved American flags while Lee Greenwood blared from some open storefront. Behind them came the smiling, well-armed Army of God, NRA and POW/MIA flags draped down the sides of Econoline conversion vans, pistols holstered on hips.

The parade rolled on to Greenville where Chellis was holding a rally.

Malcolm and his father sat until the last vehicle passed and the street was again empty but for the silver streamers and candy wrappers scattered in the gutters.

"Well," Malcolm said, finally. "That was something."

They sat in the hush of late-afternoon heat, backs adhered to the upholstery.

"I thought we might see Dallas, Daddy," Malcolm said. "Thought maybe they'd whisk him off to some full-auto-machine-gun paradise."

The old man said nothing, eyes fixed on the street.

"I'm just making a joke," Malcolm said.

"Take me home," he said.

"I didn't mean anything by it."

"I know you didn't. But I still don't want to hear it. Don't want to see it, either. Don't want to see town or nothing."

Malcolm started the engine. "Well, I promise you this," he said, and dropped the truck into reverse, "you won't see it again."

It felt like the cruelest promise he would ever keep.

VI.

She knew several churches were running buses from the Shaver Center to the Chellis rally in Greenville, and she climbed onto one and collapsed into a seat, the Ativan just beginning to reach through her like long fingers, delicate and cold. A man and woman—white man, white woman—leaned into the aisle to talk to her and she said something back, loud, maybe, and they didn't look at her again.

When the bus began to move someone started to sing "God Bless America." The crowd took it up and Jordan began to sing, too, shouting the words because she was underwater now and could hear nothing beyond the din of noise that sounded from within her, the firing of synapses, the unregulated—it felt unregulated—throb of her heart. She looked out through dim lamps, the world hazy and soft at the edges, but in the end it was like everything else: things happened or they didn't. At night, they would make love and lay twisted in the sheets because this had become her life. Weed the garden and wash her hair. Swallow Oxy 30s and talk to her plants.

It was only context, she thought. Circumstance.

She sang louder and by the time they made Greenville the couple had moved to the front. The other seats around her seemed to have emptied too, and she stumbled down the steps into the late-day heat, no longer concerned about Malcolm.

She had left while he was out, but she knew he would forgive her. He couldn't help to. He would give her the gift of his Christian forbearance and dignified superiority. He would give her everything but what she needed most: the God Talk. The explanation. The words he must have told the boy who clipped the battery cables in the church. Instead of an answer she would be sentenced to Malcolm's patience. She would come back in the whispered tick of night, mere hours from dawn, and he would be calmly waiting for her.

"Talk to me, Jordan," he would say. "Help me understand. The way sometimes you're so—"

The word, she knew, was *mysterious*. He wouldn't say it, but he had said it before, said it often enough for her to know what was next. In the past she had always responded by rolling her eyes, but thought now—someone was trying to sell her some sort of red, white, and blue pinwheel—thought now that perhaps she had missed something, that perhaps he was really trying to make clear some thought just past the edge of articulation, some truth that began just after grammar left off. But she had never learned to listen.

She pushed away the pinwheel and tried to get her bearings.

The plaza was already beginning to fill. Families, quartets of teenage girls, bus loads of senior citizens. Kiosks sold AMERICA FOR AMERICANS T-shirts and buttons and flags that read ONE NATION UNDER GOD. There were stands for corndogs and funnel cakes and Slushies. A team of men in blue jumpsuits put up an outdated CHELLIS FOR PRESIDENT banner.

Oh, she should have listened. She—

Someone walked out onto the stage and a cheer went up. It sounded muffled and dull and fantastically sad, and at that moment she thought perhaps that she might yet love Malcolm like she had loved Roosevelt, and then she was sure of it. She felt something spreading outward and what it was, Jordan realized, was love in its purest form. She shook with it, her love spilling across the luminescent plaza to consume the familiar geometry of street and brick. Her nana on the couch reading the Gospel of Mark—she did not hate her. Her papa in his little corrugated-metal bass boat—it wasn't his fault. She felt love envelop her, rounding over the shapes and curves to map the night, running to the edges of the crowd until it was swallowed by noise.

The man on stage raised a hand. "Folks," he said, "folks, good evening."

She tried to listen, to be still. She needed that stillness she had felt on the bus. If she could find that stillness, if she could hold it—so many times growing up, listening to Percy Sledge or riding around with Roosevelt, she would feel it then, and if she could only cage it so that it was within her, even as she walked out into the world, if only she could keep it, everything, she knew, everything could be different. But now—

"... I am so pleased to see each and every one of you tonight, and what I'd like to ask first, I'd like to ask each of you to stand ..."

That night—she was thinking of that night in the attic full of cardboard boxes and pink-sheeted insulation—that night she had fucked Leighton Clatter in a fit of cocaine grief. What else might she have done? When she had first made love to Malcolm she had thought: I am constructing a new life. I am building on the ruins of my past.

"... and to the Republic, for which it stands ..."

She looked around her: everywhere hands over hearts, hands over hearts.

"... under God, with liberty and justice ..."

The thing about Malcolm, it suddenly occurred to her, was that he didn't want a wife: he wanted a riddle, a few truncated lines to decrypt and salvage by the force of belief. The same had been true of Rose. After he died she got in his car—her car, now—and took his knife—her knife—and headed east toward the ocean, washed up in a seedy resort town south of Daytona, slept in her car until she got work at a beachside bar and grill.

She moved in with four other servers, two women and two men, unrolling her sleeping bag onto the filthy couch of the tangerine cottage. After a few weeks she started taking Vicodin and running lines of coke with one of her roommates, Jared, and that December followed him and his friends to a little coastal town in Brazil where they spent the winter surfing while she sat in a rattan chair and smoked cheap homegrown. They passed out along the dunes and woke to the chewing of sand fleas and the gloom of early morning tidal fog. Jared shirtless and sunburned and gnawing through another vampire weekend, a dream hoop inked over one slouching pectoral. When he blinked she heard his eyes click.

One night they got loaded and lay on their blanket to watch the moonrise and that evening she found herself standing in the ocean, the wet hem of her dress wrapped around her knees. She felt the weight of things, finally, and when Jared came to take her from the water she started screaming and put her nails in his eyes and he struck her and then the tide was running over her, diluting the coppery taste of blood until even that was gone, and she was alone in the outgoing surf.

The weight she had felt was Rose.

But it wasn't Rose who had ruined everything: it was her nana. Jordan had been a child, nothing more, barefoot with blades of wet grass clinging to her slim ankles, a smile creased in the bottom of one foot.

It was her nana's fault.

It was God's.

Another man was on stage now. Cuff links—she was near the lip of the stage and saw his cuff links flare in a band of canister light.

"My brothers and sisters," he said, "what an honor and privilege it is for me this evening to introduce to you one of our own, a fellow brother, a fellow believer, a God-fearing patriot who has shed his blood battling the godless atheistic socialism that is once again threatening our very hearts and hearths. A man convicted that we must turn back to the beliefs and principles handed down by our forefathers. A man who Lord willing will be our next President of the United States—"

Cheering and more cheering and then out came a little man in a green hat.

"Colonel Beau Chellis," said the man with the cuff links, and she watched Chellis stride across the stage like Jesus Christ—but He was just another man, wasn't he? Which meant there was no use praying about the child whose named she refused to speak, no use thinking of how she would have loved her, how she would have raised her. *Please, Nana, ruin my life. Take away the only family I might ever have.* Roosevelt had said once that the past and future were only illusions; there was only the present. But Jordan imagined not that there was neither present nor future, rather that there was only the past, what *was* lived out through eternity. A single mistake became a thousand mistakes. What *is* hardening to densest bone, settled, and then set, so that what *is* was nothing more than what *was,* lived a little later. It made her hate herself. Despite the love she felt, she knew there was always this other self she couldn't slip free of, the girl who always got it right. Just a little stronger, a little braver, just a little more Jordan than Jordan could ever be.

She watched the man on stage lean toward the microphone.

"I am a man," he said. "A man no different than you. A child of God standing humbly before you tonight, my brothers and sisters, not merely as a former candidate for the highest office in this our blessed land, but as a humble servant of our Lord who has sworn to return this nation to its rightful owners—" The cheering began again. "—not to the humanists professors shuttered in their ivory towers or the corrupt bankers sealed in their Wall Street brokerages, but to the good and decent, God-fearing citizens of the real America—" And she was underwater again, the dull roar reaching her through fathoms of waving light, the stage and crowd behind an opaque screen.

She needed out.

She started to move but felt herself stumbling, crashing; there were hands on her, grabbing, pushing her up. *Lady? Ma'am?* She pulled herself upright and felt the flash of something, there for just a second, less than a second: a moment. So love, then. I'm posing a question, she thought, to God. How long does it have to endure to confirm the statement, the act? Who was to say what was enough? If she'd given herself to Roosevelt in twenty-minute increments, the totality of their life together equaled nothing more than a few fused days. Choking on the honeysuckle and wisteria. Feeling a root hard in your lower back while he moved atop you.

Her lost daughter she loved only with her secret heart, the one she kept hidden behind the first. Her love scripted across her flesh. Malcolm she might love, but didn't know what that meant anymore.

But where was she going? Someone—two people, two white people, two white *men*—were leading her along the edge of the crowd. She could feel their fingers curled around her upper arms, marching her like a child. Then she was in front of someone, a nurse of some sort, a mesh tent with a couple of ambulances parked behind it.

"I thought maybe she was dehydrated or something," one of the men said, "then I looked at her."

"Look at her eyes," the other man said. "She can't understand a word we're saying."

The woman—a white woman, a nurse—raised a penlight and beyond it Jordan saw her warped face bent around the edges as if seen through a keyhole, peeking in at her nana, peeking into the communal bathroom in Florida (she would wedge a chair beneath the lockless knob and soak in the greasy claw-footed tub for hours).

"Can you bring her over here?" the woman asked. "She's probably just drunk but we should run fluids to be safe."

They reached for her and Jordan was gone.

She jerked free and ran along the plaza's edge onto the sidewalk past the food carts and vendors. A few heads turned to watch, but when she reached a grassy rise at the end of the park she turned back to see that no one had followed. Her heart spun as if tacked to a wall—a child's game, the pin-the-tail-on-the-donkey she'd played once—and when she looked back she felt something grave and thick moving through her, and what she wanted to avoid was the thought that some larger intelligence or force—she didn't have the word for it—but some larger *something* had conspired against her, arranging the stars so that their courses might somehow collide and wreck. She wanted to believe in randomness. She wanted to believe in the terrible luck that had befallen her. She wanted Malcolm's God Talk empty of God, but suspected something different. If there is a God, she thought, He is most certainly a man.

What does the silence feel like?

Like God. I can't explain.

She stood with her hands on her hips, panting and thinking of Rose. The day he died something within her had folded itself away saying *I will be with you, but I will not be of you.* She had thought something might develop within her then, some opening that would reveal the secret, sitting at his bedside and racing toward that ugly end, some place without the distrust and hurt. She had listened to his breath rasp, catch, and expire in a faint huff, and now that he was dead she knew it was like a candle blown out so that there is no flame, only a curl of dissipating white smoke.

She heard the man's voice over the loud speakers.

". . . my brothers and sisters, let me say then that I am not here to be meek. I am not here to turn the other cheek. Jesus will return with a tongue of flame to cut down His enemies, brothers and sisters, and He expects us to act in his stead . . ."

Sudden applause and she saw that it was over, the small man waving in bursts and camera flashes. Watching it exhausted her. She was thirsty and tired and somehow it was more than she could stand. She started walking toward the buses and was back near the stage when she stopped cold. This feeling, she thought. Again. And right then she was back in her nana's bathroom, that spring morning she had squatted barefoot on the cool bathroom tiles, peered down into the bowl, and waited. Counting the days and then weeks until her life seemed constructed around the mathematics of chance.

The bear had led her here.

She had felt as certain then as she did now, and with that certainty came a surge of happiness. Then, almost as quickly, her heart begin to corrode, just a little, but with that sense of inevitability, too, of knowing that once it began it would not stop, that everything was tainted now with this—was it fright? A little spasm of unrealized grief? She knew it wasn't hope, not anymore. Life is strange, she thought. It struck with the clarity of original thought: how cruelly strange, this life. I am not the first to know how absurd life is. But that doesn't make it hurt any less.

The bear had led her here.

She knew it without the slightest caution and wondered only if the Universe intended it as gift or torment. But she could suspend such judgment, at least for the moment. She wiped the tear she hadn't felt falling, sat down on the sidewalk, and put her hands against her stomach to better feel the child growing within her.

They left the rally in a limousine Leighton had rented for the occasion, around them hundreds of RVs and a mob of protesters and counter-protesters, signs on one side that read JESUS LOVES US ALL and THOU SHALL NOT JUDGE, and on the other, past the blue sawhorses, JESUS HATES FAGS. A man walked down the street in a T-shirt marked: FROM TIME TO TIME THE TREE OF LIBERTY MUST BE REFRESHED WITH THE BLOOD OF PATRIOTS.

Dallas looked at them and thought of the war he'd never had, screwed the top off his Nalgene bottle, and took a long pull of Johnnie Walker.

"Ridiculous," Leighton said. They turned onto Academy where the local NBC affiliate was setting up a long boom mike in the parking lot of the Bilo Center. "Just look at them. I got a tumor the size of a watermelon eating my cerebral cortex, and these fuckers are chanting. I wish Randi could've made it. Randi has a calming effect."

Dallas took another pull. "You know this isn't her thing."

"What, politics?" Leighton began to lick the time-release coating from an OxyContin. "The rally?"

"All of it. The whole circus."

"The circus is democracy, my friend. This is America you're looking at. These people." Leighton rapped one knuckle on the smoked glass. "Look out the window here. These people have been beaten down for as long as anyone has bothered to notice. White trash. Trailer trash. No one to look down on. And everyone needs someone to look down on."

"So you give em the immigrants, the gays—"

"The liberal east coast effete, absolutely. Anybody and anything different. Tell them their kids will grow up to be Spanish-speaking homosexual welfare recipients. Tell them the Feds are coming for their assault rifles. You know George Wallace's line about crowd control?" Leighton paused. "You give the poor white the nigger and the nigger Jesus. Well, Jesus is still in business, but if you want this power you've got to find a new nigger."

"It's goddamn depressing."

"It's the world, baby. It's happening. You don't have to believe it to use it." He held the OxyContin before him and closed one eye.

"You're spoiled, Leighton," Dallas said. "Life has spoiled you."

"Please. Like you're not living off the fat of the land. When's the last time you didn't get what you wanted?"

"How about the time you got me in an eight-million-dollar land deal, then decided not to make a fucking dime off it. You remember that one?"

Leighton studied his pill. "You know it's more complicated than that."

"Like how?"

"Like it's possible there's going to be another impact survey, and that's just the first thing."

"No way."

"Listen to me—"

"Don't fuck with me, Leighton," Dallas said. "Haley had his day in court. He lost."

"It's not for sure, not yet. But I want you to talk to Gresham."

"All Gresham wants is his money." Dallas put his hand to the glass and let it fall. "Let's just pay him and be done with it."

"I've already paid him. What he wants is to talk to you. What he wants is an apology."

"For what?"

"Who gives a fuck for what? He has the power to make this go away and we need to be kissing his ass."

"We never should have touched that land," Dallas said. "We got greedy."

"Greed is all we have, my friend. Our comforting spirit. Nothing matters until you can buy it, sell it, trade the motherfucker online."

Dallas put his head against the cool upholstery and wished for Randi beside him, her hand on his destroyed knee, the scratch of her fingernails. "But what does it matter?" he said. "They what? They come in, walk the land, check the plats."

Leighton smiled. "You're missing the larger import."

"They take water samples. Big deal. We've been through this before."

"You're missing the point, my friend. It isn't so much about the survey as it is about our friends nearby."

"Your friends."

"My friends? I was given to understand you paid a visit."

"I paid a visit but that's all," Dallas said. "We're businessmen. If they don't want a couple of state engineers in the woods—"

"Federal. A couple of federal engineers. And I doubt there'll only be two."

"State, federal—it's their problem, not ours."

Leighton studied the pill. "My shaman said something very thought provoking recently. He sees me dying violently, but he imagines it a sort of beatific death."

"What's the second thing?"

"About my death?"

"About the land," Dallas said. "You said that was just the first thing."

"My shaman, he said: it can't just be about the money."

"It can just be about the money. The money is the only thing." Dallas's head had fallen against the window.

"We're not putting any houses in. We're going to preserve that land."

"So your buddies can sit around and poach deer? You know you really fucked me over, Leighton. Running around buying land for these assholes."

"Like you weren't fucking me? You think I don't know about all the land you've been buying up. If you're looking for some sort of hedge against what's coming I can assure you that's not it."

"Is that what the whole bodyguard thing was about?" Dallas said. "You get a minder to watch me close, make sure I don't dig into the State Park land."

"The State Park land secures the back acreage." Leighton had turned conciliatory, his voice level. "I'm trying not to be too disappointed it took you this long to figure things out."

"You never said shit to me. I thought this was legit." Dallas looked at him for a long moment. "What's two?" he asked finally.

"Two is this: we're going to get indicted."

Dallas put a hand to his face and removed it. He had become suddenly self-conscious of his gestures, his pose just that: a pose.

"We're going to get indicted," Leighton said, "and we can go quietly into that good night and spend the next twenty to thirty getting sodomized with a broomstick at Broad River Correctional, or we can fight."

"This is insane. We have lawyers for this. We cut a deal."

"We're past the deal-making stage."

"If we're not developing the land, fuck it. We don't need it. We give it up."

"We're not giving it up. We're going to defend that land, Dallas. We're going to defend ourselves."

"Are you actually talking about shooting someone?"

Leighton shrugged. "People get shot all the time. It's random. It happens. What I'm talking about is a principled stand."

"This is insane."

"We give warning. We contact the media. If anybody crosses the property line we exercise our constitutional rights. The people are with us on this."

They were in Easley now. Baptist churches and strip malls. After-school Tae-kwon-do and Pizza Hut Express. Orange tiger paws fading off the asphalt.

"I've got to talk to Randi."

"I'm thinking of bringing in the Colonel. Having him on consult."

"I want nothing to do with this."

"We'll meet at The Settlement, have a powwow with Shep Parsons," Leighton said. "Plan our moves."

"I'm telling you right now. I'm not in this. I'm getting my own lawyer."

"Just hear Shep out," Leighton said. "Then make the call."

Randi was on the treadmill in the basement when he got home, the TV on QVC and a fan angled into her face. She pulled out her earbuds when he she saw him.

"You're home," she said. "How was it? It was good?"

"It was fine."

"I want to hear all about it."

"No, you don't."

"Seriously. I do." She wore gray UGA sweatpants and a plunging red sports bra swept with a half-moon of sweat. She bent her face to the edge of a towel and wiped away moisture. "I'm so glad it went well. We should go celebrate."

"Actually," Dallas said. "I think I'm gonna take off for a bit."

"Okay." She mopped her face a second time. "Just let me finish."

"That's all right. I think I might hit the gym. Lift a little."

"Lift here."

He shook his head.

"Lift here and we can celebrate after," she said. "It'll be fun."

"I need to get out."

"You've been out all day."

"I'll just break a sweat and be back."

"Well, if you can wait like—" She looked down at the display. "Nineteen minutes I'll be done here. You can lift while I shower."

"How long have you been on that thing?"

"Two hours and eleven minutes."

"Jesus, Randi. You lifted before that?"

"Delts and quads," she said. "Just let me finish and I'll come with."

She was soaked, skin slick and gleaming, and he thought of her in the walk-in shower, head back and shampoo streaming from her hair. He thought of all the times they'd made love down here, then thought of that first night he'd seen her at the 24 Hour Fitness in Atlanta. He had never known anyone who worked out as intensely as she did, not at Georgia and not in the Marines, not even on the bodybuilding circuit, and he loved her for that intensity, but feared her too. Just a little, he thought. She existed on an edge he had never quite touched, as if she were privy to an entire country that lay somewhere past the point his will surrendered. He looked at the glass sliding doors that opened beneath the back deck. He needed to leave before he embarrassed himself.

"I won't be long," he said.

"You can't wait half an hour on me?"

They were selling earrings on the television, turquoise spangles that looked like something you might bass fish with. A woman held them to her ears and squealed.

"I'll call if I'm late."

He drove to the Gold's Gym in Seneca. It was a thirty-minute ride and he had everything he needed at home, but kept a membership for days like to-day. Leighton had rattled him and he needed that communal uplift that always came with shared sweat, the music loud, everybody slapping each other and yelling shit. The caffeine and testosterone overload. He drank a Ripped Fuel and listened to the Drive-By Truckers, windows down and arms twitching by the time he hit the parking lot.

Inside, GunsN'Roses banged off the weight room walls and shook the floor-to-ceiling mirrors that twinned the dumbbell rack. There were fat guys in tank tops and forty-something moms sitting on leg machines and staring at cell phones, but there were also serious lifters, male and female alike, and he loved the serious ones, the ones pushing through sets of dead lifts or doing squats until they dry-heaved in a trashcan.

Tonight, he lifted back, biceps, and hamstrings, moved from pull-downs to dead lifts to curls. Bent-over rows. E-Z curls. Leg curls. Preachers and cable rows. He did a hundred incline crunches and was at the water fountain when a man walked over and extended one hand.

"Dallas Walker, right?"

"Right here, bro."

"Shit, I thought that was you. Ed Clark," the man said. "I graduated a few years ahead of Malcolm. I see your billboards all the time."

"That's me."

"Damn, but it's good to see you in the flesh. I remember watching that game against Liberty your senior year. You remember this? You ran for four touchdowns in the first half, then sat on the bench and laughed your ass off. I think you had something like one hundred and forty yards by halftime."

"Liberty was always soft."

"You're still lifting, too."

"Now and then. Nothing strenuous."

"Shit. Look at you."

Dallas shrugged. "I try to stay mean."

"I was talking with Tim Smith. Tim over there if you know him." He motioned to one of the men congregated around the incline press, goateed and wearing a shirt that read ANIMAL NUTRITION. "We were trying to remember how many times you repped two twenty-five your senior year. I swear to God twenty-three sticks in my head."

"That was it. Twenty-three."

"Goddamn. And how much did you weigh, like two twenty?"

"One eighty-five, brother. I put on weight in college."

"Goddamn. Twenty-three reps."

Clark shook his head and Dallas dipped to the fountain. His sweat was beginning to cool and he could feel his muscles stiffen. The Ripped Fuel had drained through his system and now the adrenaline was fading too. He needed a shower. He needed to get home. Rain spattered the front window, the sky beyond the color of damaged lung tissue, iron gray and fissured with light.

"How many you think you could put up now?" Clark asked. "Reps, I mean. Like you say, you still got that meanness. How many you think?"

"None," Dallas said. "Zero reps."

"Bullshit. You look game as hell to me. Come try it."

"I better get home."

"Come on. I bet you can still do twelve reps. I know you just lifted back, but seriously, you're Dallas-fucking-Walker."

Two minutes later Dallas was flat on his back beneath the bar. It was always like this, some asshole egging you on. But I should be past it, he thought. I should act like an adult. Stand up. Walk away. Instead he did a warm-up set with one hundred and thirty-five and shook out his arms while they slid on plates. Ed Clark spotted him while Tim Smith and another man he didn't recognize stood in front of him, arms crossed, the fucking disbelievers.

On the first rep he knew he was in trouble. The weight felt heavier than it should, the bar uneven. He forced it up, exhaled, and lowered it again. By the third and fourth rep he was feeling better about things, limber and strong, his fingers loose around the crosshatched grip. Control the weight. Everything fluid. Breathe and push. He pumped eight and then nine, paused, pushed out a tenth. Ed Clark stood over him yelling, a rain of white foam feathering down. Dallas forced out an eleventh rep and held the bar in the up position and panted. Sweat buttered his upper lip.

"One more," Clark chanted. "One more, baby."

One more. There was always one fucking more. He fixed his vision on a tube of fluorescent light and set his chin. He knew he didn't have one more in him but lowered the bar anyway. That was what being game meant, going past that point where reality left off, tricking the mind so that it might in turn trick the body, and he'd spent his entire life being game, trying to please people and then suffering for it. His coaches and bosses. The old man. Randi and Leighton. And look where it's gotten me, he thought. He was going to jail if someone didn't shoot him first. But fuck it. He was game.

The bar touched his chest and he felt it go up and stick, his arms at right angles. He gathered himself, arched his back, and pushed again. The weight began to rise, but at the same moment he felt a needle of pain finger up his spine, every muscle in his back clenching and releasing. He racked the weight and sat on the bench.

"Holy shit," Clark said. "That was badass."

In the last push a thimble of urine had leaked into his underwear, and now something felt wrong in his back, cords of forgotten muscle stretched slightly off center, the spine compacted. Clark and the two other men went on laughing and congratulating him while Dallas started for the shower.

Ed Clark waited for him when he came out. "We're gonna knock back a few cold ones at the Main Street Garage. We'd sure enough love for you to come drink with us."

Dallas dripped on the tiles, barefoot, naked but for the arrowhead necklace and a towel around his waist, his toenails yellow and ridged. "What time is it?"

"Like barely eight. What do you say?"

"I should probably get home. The wife."

"Come on, man. It's early. The wife'll still be there. That's the thing about wives."

Dallas lifted his gym bag from the locker and found a tube of Speed Stick.

"What's wrong with you, biggun?" Clark asked. "You look all down in the mouth."

"I'm all right."

"Check it out. Let me cheer you up a little." He took a plastic baggie from his pocket and placed a pill on the bench. "That right there's on the house."

Dallas picked it up. "What is that, Darvon?"

"Darvon's banned, I think. That's Percocet."

"Will it blow up my heart?"

"Only if it's a bomb." Clark smiled. "What that'll do is put hair on your chest. Make your pecker hard."

"That's what I need."

"We all do, brother."

"Well, I guess it's a Percocet sort of day." Dallas dry-swallowed it. "Thanks. I'll try to get over and meet y'all."

"Don't try, do." Clark stood. "I'm gonna have a beer waiting on you."

Walking out to his truck Dallas felt like a wounded animal, something tired and ragged dragging itself along the forest floor. The rain was light but he was damp by the time he climbed inside. He took out his cell phone and thought of calling Randi but didn't. Instead, he just sat there, hands heavy as slain doves. The interior smelled of new leather and the mint of his deodorant. He shut his eyes. The gun was beneath the seat and he felt himself nearing the zero of truth. What it was, he wasn't certain; he knew only that it would be something final and inescapable and it would fill every pore with light.

He opened his eyes and listened to the rain on the roof.

He liked the stillness, then suddenly didn't and turned the ignition so that a thousand devices woke to mechanical life: GPS, radio, wipers. Lights and motion and sound, all blessed distraction, all blessed noise.

He parked beside the Main Street Garage and hustled through the rain that fell harder now. The joint was a barely refitted service station and the two bay

doors were up so that water splashed onto the concrete and forced the pa-
trons back toward the bar where they sat beneath a stained-glass Rumpleminz
shade and several potted bonsai trees. Ed Clark had two Coronas sitting by a
pack of Marlboros and passed one to Dallas, who drank it in one slow swallow. After the second beer he started feeling good and bought a pitcher and
then another and soon enough was laughing and talking about Coach Dooley
and the Sugar Bowl and that man-child Hershel Walker running with a tire
hitched to his twenty-seven-inch waist. He loved that story about the two
Walkers, a couple of hungry country boys, one white and one black, and how
someone once had said something about that being the way of the world or
end of the world or some shit that had just been hilarious at the time.

Somewhere around his fifth or sixth beer his cell phone bleeped and Ed
Clark put his elbows on the table.

"That's you, chief."

"What's that?" Dallas asked.

"Your phone. Somebody's looking for you."

"Wife, probably," said another man, Tim maybe, or the other guy who
was starting to look a little mean, eyes narrowed, scarred fists on the table.

He had a text from Randi.

WHERE R U?

He waved over another round, rocked his chair back onto two legs, and
kept talking though no one seemed to be laughing anymore. But fuck it, he was
having a good time. By the time the second text came he was almost too drunk
to read it.

MISSING YOU

CALL ME

He looked back up to find two of the men gone and the third lurching
toward the bathroom past the pool table and a couple of girls drinking margaritas. He poured what was left of the pitcher into his glass and drank. The
man wobbled out of the bathroom and past the table, nodded at Dallas, and
was gone. Dallas pushed himself out of his chair and took the pitcher to the

bar. His knee was beginning to ache and he could feel the shallow twitch of nerve endings in his back. He put the pitcher on the counter.

"What you drinking there, cousin?" the bartender asked.

"Whatever's on tap. Bud's fine."

"On your card?"

Had he given the man his card? The slot in his wallet was empty; he supposed he had. The man put a new glass mug in front of him and Dallas filled it. He asked for the tab and took the pitcher back to his table. He was thinking now of Malcolm. He needed to tell Malcolm about Leighton and Jordan Taylor but damn if he wanted to do that. He'd get Randi to. Randi could handle that sort of thing, gentle, good-hearted Randi. He never should have left her, should have waited for her to finish, climbed into the shower and then maybe onto the bed. When was the last time they'd made love? Weeks. A month, maybe. No: longer, much longer. But he wasn't going to let things keep sliding. CALL ME CALL ME. Jesus, he loved that woman, and his baby brother, and his hateful Daddy. Even fat-ass Uncle Tillman. He loved them all if he was honest about it. Forget Leighton and the indictment and everything else—he could still turn this thing around.

He walked to the high-top where two women in jeans and halter tops were drinking margaritas, cigarettes and lighter by a laminated card showing drink specials. He started talking, beautiful bullshit just flowing from his lips, and they were laughing—he had them laughing—and everything was just as it had always been.

"I wish I'd met you a decade ago," he told one.

She cocked her head. "Except I was twelve."

He kept talking, his voice getting louder, then noticed that they had stopped laughing, too. But he had to tell them one more thing, and leaned forward so that the table shifted and something splashed onto his shoes. Slushy ice. Yelling. He was almost certain one of the women was yelling at him but he couldn't understand why. Then a hand clamped his shoulder and he looked into the broad face of the bouncer.

"Don't be the cause of no ruckus," the man said.

His head was shaved and a yellow earring fell from one lobe like a slant of watery sunlight, ridiculous, but beautiful.

"Me?" Dallas asked.

"Ain't nobody looking for trouble tonight, certainly not these young ladies."

"I don't ever look for trouble."

"That's a good attitude right there. Now just lower the volume about three clicks and leave these women be," the man said. "Just walk right on by."

"I hear you."

"Behave like a gentlemen."

"I hear you. I'm leaving."

Dallas walked out and was halfway to his truck when he gagged, bent forward, and vomited onto the wet asphalt. He rested for a moment, palms on knees, and ran his tongue along the grooves of his teeth. When he felt stable he went to straighten up and that was when everything caught. The pain was instantaneous, laddered up his spine from tail to chin, every muscle contracted just as it had on the bench except this time there was no release and his body was captured at a thirty-degree angle, his back out.

He staggered to the truck, reclined the seat, and collapsed so that he stared at the oblong bulb of the dome light. He was breathing needles, every inhalation washing him onto a beach of suffering before towing him out again, a dying man, drowning in the leathery air and the smell of secondhand smoke. He worked his cell out of his pocket. He thought of calling Randi, but knew he wouldn't. And where were those assholes from the gym? Gone, he knew. Fuck em. The best thing was to wait, maybe sleep a little, sober up and see if his back would unclench. He shut his eyes.

Now, he thought, would be a good time to sleep. Not to rise, not to piss, but to sleep. Blackness. That falling away when you're seven years old and day crumbles into night and night into day and then your mother is shaking you awake. But he couldn't sleep and the more he thought about things the angrier he got and the angrier he got the more he knew exactly whose fault this was. And he was tired of it. By God, he wouldn't stand for it, not for another second, and eased the phone up by his face so that he might dial Gresham Haley.

It was late that night when the phone rang. Malcolm carried it out onto the porch and sat in a rocking chair.

"How's dad?" Dallas asked.

"Asleep. Is something wrong?"

"No. Just wanted to check in. I'm sorry to be calling so late but I'm wound pretty tight right now and I need to ask a favor," he said. "But first I want you to know I'm not trying to drag you into anything. I just don't know who else to ask."

"What's wrong?"

"It's not exactly what's wrong, just that there's a little meeting tomorrow night. This is with Leighton and some folks he knows and basically I just want another set of ears to tag along, sort of just take the whole thing in."

"Should I ask what it's about?" Malcolm said.

"Probably not. I've just about scared the shit out of myself thinking about it. What do you say?"

"So long as dad's okay."

"Good. That's good. I appreciate it," Dallas said. "So how is he?"

"He never says anything but I know he'd like to see you."

"I was by three days ago."

"When he was asleep. You need to come by and sit with him. Stay a while," Malcolm said. "You and Randi both. He talks about both of you. He's changing."

"Bullshit. He don't change. Listen to me, Malcolm: me and that guy, I got boxes on top of boxes and in every one of them are issues with that man. I got a closet full."

"He's changing. He's changed."

"He's too old to change. Tell him I'm keeping his place up," Dallas said. "I told him the other night, but I doubt he remembers it."

"We took him over there the other week and let him see it, Jordan and me."

"There's probably some things you should know about her, Malcolm."

"Like what?"

"Let's talk tomorrow. I'll pick you up maybe nine, nine thirty? What time is it now?"

"Late."

"Shit. I shouldn't have called. I just couldn't sleep. Randi ran sixteen miles on the treadmill this evening. I feel like the whole world's got out ahead of me."

"I'll see you tomorrow, Dallas."

Jordan was awake in bed when he walked back upstairs.

"What did he want?" she asked.

"For me to go to some meeting with him tomorrow night."

"What kind of meeting?"

"Something with Leighton and some other people. He said he didn't really know what it was about."

"Then why does he want you to go?"

He sat on the side of the bed and shrugged, a self-conscious gesture, invisible in the dark. "I don't know. He said he wanted another set of ears. I think he's in some legal trouble."

He lay back and shut his eyes, arranged his hands on his chest.

"Don't go," she said. "Stay here tomorrow night."

"I need to go with him."

"No, you don't."

"He's worried, baby." He rolled onto his side to face her outline. "He needs me."

"To what? To just sit in the car?"

"Maybe. Come on. It's late." They lay for a moment though his eyes were no longer shut. "Why shouldn't I go?" he asked finally.

"Because I finally received my message, my dream totem" she said. "And if you go I'm afraid I'm going to do something terrible."

"What are you talking about?"

"It's so loud right now. I hear these things, these vibrations."

"What do you hear?"

"Just stay near me. I know where he's going to take you, Malcolm. I've been there. If you go, something terrible is going to happen."

He heard in her voice what he thought might be tears and put his ear against her ribs, moved over her stomach. "He's just worried," Malcolm said. "It'll be a few hours at the most."

"I'm telling you, there's this bad energy now, all this noise." She raised her head. "What are you doing?"

"Listening. Go to sleep."

His ear was against her heart.

"It's not good, Malcolm. Please understand me. When I was out tonight—"

"Shh."

"Listen to me."

"You don't have to explain anything."

She dropped her head back onto the pillow. "I'm going to ruin us."

"No," he whispered. "No, you're not. Sleep."

He could feel the warmth coming off her skin, the last traces of oatmeal soap.

"Malcolm—"

"I can hear everything," he said, "and everything's fine."

Dallas didn't wake until after eleven, sore and hungover and alone, the world filmed in a Percocet haze that was slow to lift. He lay on his back and followed the blades of the ceiling fan, exhausted. All night a single nightmare had haunted him, a vision of his future self, stripped and emaciated and sheared of muscle, a spindly dying man, and he wondered to what extent he was seeing the future because it felt, he realized now, more like it was imagining him than he was imagining it. He showered and found Randi in the yard standing over a dead grackle, the body stiff but unmarked, a single drop of black blood crusting the bill.

He touched her elbow and smiled. "Can we talk for a second?

She blew a strand of hair from her face and looked up at him.

"Can you take those gloves off?" he said. He kept smiling, brighter and brighter, he hoped. "I can't talk to you in those gloves."

"You know, you're scaring me, smiling like that."

"I'm not smiling like anything," he said.

She peeled off the gloves, wadded and dropped them, and then they stood like that, Dallas smiling, both of them listening to the gloves crumple open by her feet.

"I have to go see Leighton tonight," he said finally. "We're having a little meeting."

She studied his face before speaking. "I want to know what's going on."

He tilted his head.

"I want to know what the hell is happening here, Dallas. The phone calls, the letter—"

"I'm not sure what you're talking about."

"I know something's happening and I know it's bad."

"Everything's going to be fine."

"Then take me with you tonight."

"I can't do that."

"If everything's going to be fine, take me with you."

"You know I can't do that."

When she looked at him he could see her lip quivering. It was anger, he thought. It wasn't fear.

"You're lying to me." She said it so quiet he found himself leaning in. "You're lying to me and you've been lying to me I don't know how long."

"I'm gonna get this straightened out."

"Get what straightened out? That's what I'm asking you."

"I'm gonna get this straightened out tonight and then I'm gonna take care of all the things I've neglected. Daddy, Tillman, you—"

"I don't want to hear your bullshit, Dallas." She put both palms in the air, bent down and used one of the gloves to pick up the dead bird by the tip of a wing so black as to appear blue, an oil-like sheen to the torn feathers, almost iridescent. She held it between them. "I don't want to hear it."

He reached for her elbow. "Let's go inside."

"Let me throw this poor thing away," she said. "This is starting to disgust me."

"Let's go inside for a minute."

"Let me throw this away."

He followed her around the house to the garbage can. "Randi?" he called. "Come on. Don't be like that."

"I'm not being like anything," she said. "I'm throwing away a dead bird."

She dropped the lid and balled her fists on her hips. She was flushed and sweat dotted her upper lip, tiny opaque beads that trembled when she spoke.

"Come on," he said.

"I'm not an idiot," she said. "As much as you might like to think so I'm not. You think I don't see what's happening? Leighton and all of this land, Dallas, and what does he want to do with it? Have you even thought about that?"

He touched her elbows. "I'm gonna get everything straightened out tonight. The land, everything."

"No, you're not. Your father is about to die and you haven't even mentioned that to Marilynn. The simplest thing, Dallas, a phone call, you can't even make a phone call and tell your daughter that her grandfather is about to die."

"Randi—"

"You're not, baby. Don't you realize that? I know you and you won't. You'll just hang around the edges, not really in, not really out. Scared to death you'll miss something. Scared to death someone'll think less of you. Mister Non-Confrontational to the bitter end."

"It won't be like that," he said.

"Look at me, Dallas. What's happening here?"

"You know sometimes, baby, sometimes I think: if I'd had a war. I think about that a lot. Nam. Iraq. It might have been different with a war."

"This is gonna hit you, Dallas."

"It won't be like that."

"This is gonna hit you," she said. "This is gonna hit us both. All these years you've listened to Leighton."

He laughed. "Baby, I believe about one-third of the shit out of Leighton Clatter's mouth."

"But it's the wrong third, honey." She raised her hands as if she might touch his face. "It's always the wrong third."

Instead of touching him she spread her arms, palms forward, and right then he realized where he had seen the figure from his dream: it was the same figure that hung above Malcolm's bed.

Jordan waited in the kitchen, one of Malcolm's old sweatshirts pulled over her pajamas, a silver ankh around her neck. She held a coffee cup in two hands and when he leaned to kiss her forehead he saw tremors feather the glossy surface.

"I can see a red aura coming off your brother," she said. "It's like flames. Be careful, all right?"

He pushed open the screen door. "Don't worry if I'm late."

Dallas sat in the truck, drinking Johnnie Walker. "She didn't mind you tagging along?"

"You don't want to come in and see Daddy?"

"I hate to bother him so late."

"He's still awake. He knows you're out here."

"We had a good visit last time. I think I'll leave it at that." Dallas shifted the truck into gear. "We have a way of screwing things up if we talk too much."

They took Chattooga Ridge Road to Highway 76 and on through the dark fields. Barbed wire strung around ranch houses and trailers. An Amoco station at the crossroads. A big CAT excavator in a muddy field.

"We need to get the land settled before anything happens to him," Dallas said. "I don't want Tillman's bitch wife getting so much as a blade of grass."

"This is what you wanted to talk about?"

"I don't even want it, but I sure as hell don't want her to have it. I could buy out anything daddy might have willed him," he said. "You'd have the house and the thirty-five acres. I'd own two-thirds but we could just leave everything as is."

"I'm not worried about the land."

Dallas drank from his bottle. "I'm just trying to prepare for this. This is gonna land hard on me when he goes. I can already tell that."

They were in Georgia before Dallas spoke again. "What'd you tell her?" he asked.

"Jordan?" Malcolm flicked his eyes at his brother and back to the passing fields. A dark quilt of apple orchards and horse farms, a few beef cattle bedded beneath a barn light. "Just what you told me," he said. "That you wanted someone around, an extra pair of ears."

"I'm not trying to drag you into anything."

"I know that."

"There's this guy," Dallas said, "Gresham Haley. He's a lawyer with the Progressive Alliance. Well, last night I called him. And sort of lost my shit, just really went mad dog on him. I may have fucked up big time."

They turned onto a Forest Service road and then a road marked PRIVATE DRIVE, completely dark now except for the flash of their headlights roving like bright eyes in the pie tins nailed to trees. They ground through the shallow bed of a creek and stopped by a cattle gate.

"Can you get that?"

Malcolm swung it open and shut it when Dallas lurched past.

"They call this place The Settlement," Dallas said.

"Who does?"

Dallas said nothing and they drove in silence until lights appeared in the trees ahead, a soft glow diffused by the understory becoming squares of window, symmetrical and bright as they grew closer. He pulled to a stop by the trailers, cut the ignition, and took another drink from his bottle. "Shit," he said very quietly. The yard was full of cars. A brown minivan with its bumper fixed with duct tape. A pickup jacked up on mud tires and massive shocks. Christmas lights were strung along a brush arbor, two looping cords of red and green globes lit like distant moons. Behind it all loomed the two-story farmhouse.

They listened to the engine fan tick.

"I'm going to be indicted," Dallas said finally. "It's pretty clear at this point."

Malcolm looked at him.

"I've got this sense it's going to be bad," Dallas said. "Fraud. Bribery. Maybe some conspiracy stuff. Leighton's into a lot more shit than I ever dreamed. The Savings & Loan bullshit. Then there's this militia group. I always thought they were just a bunch of rednecks drinking Busch Light and shooting tin cans, but . . . " He cracked his door and the interior light flashed. He took a pistol from the dashboard, slid it into his back waistband, and looked at Malcolm. "I'm not trying to drag you into anything."

The yard was a confusion of cars and old lumber piles. Rotting shingles. Orange trees sweating inside plastic bags. The sizzle and stink of garbage and fried fish. A girl laughed through a window screen and called out at them. A yard light came on.

Another voice. "That you, Mr. Walker?"

A man tromped down the stairs. Dallas shook his hand and introduced him to Malcolm as Shepherd Parsons, the man who runs this whole outfit.

"Have I seen you around?" Parsons asked Malcolm.

"Probably you have," Dallas said. "I've got him working for me now. Leighton in there?"

"Down this way." He started toward the far trailer. "He wasn't sure if you'd be here or not."

"I said I'd be here."

"That's what I told him," Parsons said. "One other thing. The Colonel's with him. Colonel Chellis." Parsons looked at Malcolm and back to Dallas. "But that goes no further than right here."

They were near the last trailer when the first cry went up, a lamentation, plaintive as a wounded animal. There was silence, then another cry followed by the beating of feet.

"Jesus, they've really started up now," Parsons said. "They'll get the dogs to baying if they don't watch out. Let's go around back."

Outside the trailer a man sat on a camp stool, smoking.

"Brother Miles," Parsons said. "You remember Mr. Walker?"

"Do I remember him? We're practically cousins."

"You coming inside?"

Rick Miles stood. "That's not my bag, chief."

Malcolm followed Parsons and Dallas up the concrete steps and into a tiny kitchen where a Hispanic man stood wrist deep in thawed chicken, the room stiff with heat and the smell of fry grease. He quartered a bird and dropped it with a soft thump into a mixing bowl of flour.

"Brother Pablo," Parsons said.

The man wiped his hands on a towel, one forearm covered with white puckers of scar tissue it took Malcolm a moment to recognize as cigarette burns. "Brother Parsons," he said. "How are you tonight, sir?"

"How long they been at it in there?"

"Long enough, but I expect a lot longer before they done."

Parsons pushed open the door and looked at Dallas and Malcolm. "I told you we get all types up here."

In the next room a prayer service was underway, men and women crowded into the narrow living room, most sitting but a few leaning against the paneled walls. A child slept facedown in the green shag of the carpet. It was dim, but Malcolm recognized the mandolin player from El Shaddai, eyes shut and hands clasped as he swayed atop a piano stool. All appeared drunk, heads barely tethered while a girl floated across the carpet on leg braces, her shadow twisted on the wall. She was tiny, barefoot in jeans and a T-shirt, and spoke with what Malcolm thought a heavy Eastern European accent.

"Hear me, hear me," she chanted. "Pestilence shall be across the land."

When she turned he realized that she was not a child but a woman, young and attractive with a mane of wavy blonde hair. "'But before all these,'" she said, "'they shall lay their hands on you, and persecute you, delivering you up to the synagogues and into the prisons, being brought before kings and rulers for my name's sake.'"

She leaned forward, hands on the coffee table, balanced against the glass on bright fingertips as lovely and awkward as bird feet. The crowd seemed to lean in with her.

"And it shall turn to you for a testimony. Settle it therefore in your heart, not mediate before what ye shall answer: For I will give you a mouth and wisdom which all your adversaries shall not be able to gainsay or resist. Here me, hear me: Jesus said, Whoever is near me is near the fire."

Parsons opened the door on the warm night. "They ain't in here," he said. "Come on."

They followed him down to another trailer where he stopped by the concrete steps and turned to Dallas. "I know he's family," Parsons said, "but the Colonel's peculiar about company."

Dallas looked at Parsons and at Malcolm. "You mind waiting out here?"

"I don't mean to be an asshole about it," Parsons said. "In fact, step in the house and wait if you like. Get out of these damn mosquitoes."

"I'm fine out here. I'll wait in the truck."

"Well, the door's open if you change your mind."

Malcolm walked back to the truck and sat in the passenger seat. A few minutes later people began to file down the steps from the prayer meeting, get in their cars and trucks, and start up the road. When the last pickup was gone the woman came out, dwarf-like and hobbling, her leg braces clattering. She crossed the yard and headed for the house, her face lit red and green and taking shape as she stepped beneath the Christmas lights. When she was inside Malcolm got out and followed her, the night suddenly and magnificently quiet as he climbed the front steps, found the door unlocked, and stood for a moment on the threshold to softly hello the darkness. The glow of the safety light showed a plaid couch. An empty gerbil cage sat on a table and when he touched the exercise wheel it sounded not unlike the woman's braces. Above the table hung a Japanese ceremonial sword, the blade engraved with dark ideograms.

"Hello," he said, again, softer still.

An interior door was propped open and he walked in, let the door swing shut behind him so that he stood in utter blackness. I am defeated, he thought. But he walked forward, hands trailing down the ridged pressboard, walls buckled with the moisture he smelled in the carpet. There was a sense of nearness. The child. I am defeated, he told himself. But he did not stop.

A few steps in he became aware of her shape occupying the far end, gray in the graying light. When her hands came up he felt something rough graze his arms, dry fingerpads as she pulled him into the room where a bed sat covered in a burgundy sleeping bag and an electric lantern burned on the floor. He stood by an armchair and studied himself in the mirrored surface of a picture frame, a dim form, wisps of hair raised on end. Moths had eaten the chair's upholstery, fashioning a pattern of perfectly round holes up the seatback, ordered as animal prints, and he put his finger in one. This was his new awareness, his all-knowing. The peculiarities and daily humiliations that would consecrate his life.

She moved behind him. He waited.

A clock ticked off the seconds, while another, above the bed, unwound. A third hung on the far wall. The room full of clocks and their patina of fine dust, so still it took him a moment to realize the hands had been torn free so that no shadow crossed the faces; he was hearing their inner workings.

Then he felt the woman behind him, felt his body go rigid in a way that almost surprised him, his sudden response. She drew closer but he did not turn.

"You said something." His lips were near the glass. "In the other room. From the Gospel of Thomas."

Her reflection kneeled on the floor and filled a chalice from a pitcher.

"What are you doing?" he asked the mirror.

She pointed to the floor in front of her.

He turned and she said something in a language that sounded vaguely Russian, something shaken from the cold shores of some faraway Baltic state. She spoke again, pointed to the ground.

"I don't understand," he said.

She came to him and led him to the edge of the bed where he kneeled beside her. She smelled like a clean animal, something groomed and domestic, and when she lifted her cup he did the same. The wafers lay on a cloth napkin and he saw this now for what it was, the blood and the body, and shut his eyes and drank.

"I will smite the shepherd," she said in her misshapen English, "and the sheep of the flock shall be scattered abroad."

Parsons led Dallas to the pool he'd seen on his previous visits. On the deck Leighton, Chellis, and Rick Miles sat collapsed into the rattan furniture squared around a wicker table. Insects whirring around a bug light. Citronella candles glowing with a papery light. Leighton had a box of cigars in his lap. A bottle of Laphroaig scotch sat by his feet, past it a ring of empty glasses arranged like the fundaments of some nearly forgotten faith.

"Just in time, Dallas," he said.

Dallas took a seat while Parsons moved to the edge of the deck, leaned against the banister and lit a Marlboro, his face lit and then extinguished, plowed over with darkness.

Leighton raised the scotch and a glass. "Colonel?"

"Just like that, soldier," Chellis said. "Neat."

He turned to Miles. "And you, sir?"

"I can't imagine countermanding the Colonel."

He fixed Dallas a drink and they all four sat with their scotch and cigars.

"Ah, God," Chellis said. "I wait for these moments. Escaping the mob." He shook his silver head. "Escaping the people."

"They love you," Leighton said.

"They love me. They love me, Rick."

Miles saluted with his drink.

"Ah," Chellis said, "but we're in a bad place, our America, and my sense is that regeneration will come only through holocaust."

"We've reached that point," Leighton said.

"We've reached that point, indeed. It's why we're here, is it not?" Chellis turned to Dallas. "You're quiet over there, soldier."

"Dallas is a little stunned right now," Leighton said. "I dropped some harsh reality on him and I don't think he's recovered. Reassuring him is one of the reasons we're here tonight."

"You're stunned?" Chellis asked Dallas.

"You could say that."

"That's all right," Chellis said, and finished his drink. "Be stunned so long as you absorb. Absorption is the seminal act. Fill me up if you would, kind sir."

He held out his glass and Dallas poured the scotch. Chellis drank it down. Dallas poured again and this time the Colonel let the glass rest on the slope of his paunch, the liquid catching the candle flame and pulsing with a mellow burnished gold.

"You two are in some shit," Chellis said. "Parsons, too. I'm correct in this understanding?"

"At one point we were out of the shit," Leighton said. "I thought we were, at least. I thought the shit had come and gone."

"Like a lovely lady," Chellis said.

"But now the shit seems to have descended."

"So what's next?" Chellis said. "What's the next step, Mr. Walker?"

Dallas took a sip. "There is no next step."

"No next step?"

"I told this to Leighton already: we let the lawyers handle it. We put it in their hands."

The Colonel nodded. "But what if the Feds come sniffing around?"

"We take steps," Leighton said.

"You take steps," Dallas said. "I'm out."

Leighton leaned forward into the candlelight. "Except you're not."

"Gentlemen, gentlemen." The Colonel shut his eyes. "Let's think pleasant thoughts. Good memories and positive vibes. I have one for you: I'm imagining them in their *ao dais* out along this little place we'd hit just outside the wire. Danang I'm talking about, '67, '68. What do you say, Richard?"

"Before my time, Colonel."

"Indeed. It's my truth. But the truth isn't always what happened, gentlemen. There is intention, possibility, what *might* have happened. The truth is what is experienced, and experience is simply a product of memory. Maybe truth is only for God."

"Maybe the truth is God," Miles said.

"Ah, Richard. I met Rick—when did I meet you, Brother Rick?"

"Right after the Iraq War started, Colonel. I was at one of your events."

"Santa Fe."

"Albuquerque, I believe."

The Colonel swirled his glass and drank. He wore a rumpled suit and looked like he'd just come in off an all-night flight from some weary rustbelt city, Cleveland or Detroit, a place with a burnt-out ghetto and indicted mayor. "Albuquerque," he said. "In Albuquerque we raged against the madness of the crusading military-industrial-entertainment complex, knowing all along they had their eyes on us. Knowing it was always just a matter of time." He looked at Miles. "I recall you were a contrarian son of a bitch."

"Yes, sir."

"Shep?" Chellis called. "Shepherd? Can you join us, soldier?"

Parsons had drifted out into the yard, a pinprick of cigarette, nothing more. "I'm right here, Colonel," he said. "I'm listening."

"Good," Chellis said. "If it runs to its logical end you can count on Shep."

"It'll run to its logical end," Miles said. "This is the federal government we're talking about."

Chellis sighed. "I knew I didn't have a chance in hell in the election. Felt the same way in Bangkok in '84. We were going over the border to look for all our brothers left behind. POW. MIA. All of em. I knew I didn't have a chance there either. I suspected all along the Arab would prevail."

"But these Feds," Leighton said.

"The key is to maintain a high profile." Miles grinned.

"Don't agitate, Richard," the Colonel said.

"I'm serious," Miles said. "You gotta get the TV trucks set up in the yard. The boys at CNN calling the place a compound."

"Richard—"

"I mean big, Colonel."

"Big like Ruby Ridge," Dallas said. "Big like Waco." He could feel them looking at him. "That's what you're talking about here. You're talking about a massacre."

"You're a naysayer," Leighton said. "You've gone negative on me."

"I haven't gone anything," Dallas said. "I'm out."

"You step away now," Miles said, "and it only gets worse. This can be your Lexington and Concord. Otherwise they handcuff the invisible hand."

"Handcuff it," said Leighton. "Cut it off."

They sat in the suffocating darkness. Dallas downed his drink and stood. "You're all crazy, talking like this. No offense to you, Colonel."

"None taken."

"I admire you're service, but I can't be a part of this."

"We all do what we must, soldier." The Colonel's head lolled onto the back of the chair. "Ultimately, Shep will take care of things. I knew Shep all the way back in Nicaragua. It's normal to be afraid. Just do what Shep tells you." He swallowed his scotch. "May I address you gentlemen?"

"Without question," Leighton said.

"No. With question. Always with question." He held his glass out to Dallas. "Another refill, Mr. Walker. My drink appears to have absconded on me. Yes, thank you. And please sit down. Please sit down, sir. No one is going to hog-tie you, at least not tonight." He drank the glass down. "This is final stage of human history, gentlemen. Many thought it would go on forever, but the truth is, we are at the end of things. Five hundred years of enlightenment, gone. The age of democracy, gone. Western values like freedom and autonomy. Complete my sentence, Richard."

"Gone."

"Gone, indeed." His eyes shut and for a moment he began to snore. "The same principle," he said suddenly, "the same principle that put running water in a billion homes has led to the inflation of everything. The more there is of something the less it matters."

"Democracy has a finite timeline," Miles said.

Chellis lifted his drink. "You remain depressingly prescient, my friend. But I think it's clear to all we've entered a spiral of finality."

"Birth pains," Leighton said, "earthquakes throughout Asia Minor. A single world government. People are doing the math on this."

"There are people doing nothing but." Chellis lifted his glass. "Nevertheless, the future is systems of soft control. Give away your privacy to the Internet, give away your guns and your land to the government, give away your wealth to the corporations. Bit by bit give away your freedom and finally give away your individual self. But note the giving. You give it away."

"Except for us."

"Except for us," agreed Chellis. "From us, they take it."

"Except they won't," Leighton said.

"Ah, but they will," Chellis said. "But in the end you won't care. Inflation makes things matter less, and the logical end of inflation in a pseudocapitalist world is mass consumption. It is centralized control. So where are we then? The short answer is that this is the age of confusion. We can know our position in history but what the hell else? Contradictions should now define us. We have a God in love with the so-called popular culture to which we thought He claimed an aversion. A post-God religion. Liberal-conservative."

"Colonel?" Miles said.

"Republican-Democrat."

"Colonel?"

"What, goddamn it?"

"You're raving, sir."

"Well, I'm drunk, Richard. What do you expect of me?" Miles stood and walked into the darkness while Chellis held his glass out to Dallas. "I'm just saying these aren't labels. They're attempts at wishful thinking. There is only one distinction that will, without fail, determine whether, like after the age of antiquity, we descend into the dark ages or move forward. Would you like to know what that divide is, Mr. Walker?"

Dallas looked at him. Chellis's eyes were glossed and bright, slick cue balls in the sunburn of his face. He was crazy. Dallas saw that now. They all were—wealthy and angry, well armed and well educated, but no less crazy for it—and it came over him that it was not the men threatening him he should fear but the men surrounding him, pleasantly drunk and plotting a very private apocalypse.

"That divide is between those who still believe in the idea of freedom versus those who have given up on it. We mustn't confuse our enemies, gentlemen." Chellis leaned forward and burped. "We must not stake out our positions in ignorance. But just as surely we must kill every nonbeliever." The Colonel turned to Dallas. "I'm given to understand that you were something of an athlete, that you knew glory?"

"In a very small way," Dallas said.

"Glory is a silly bitch," Chellis said.

Malcolm thought he must have passed out because when he woke he was on the bed with no sense of things, the room and time both having collapsed around him so that the particle board ceiling seemed to hang a few inches from his face. He had sweated through his shirt and all over the stiff pillow and when he tried to raise his head saw the woman sitting in the corner, holding the Iraqi child and brushing what little remained of his hair, carefully combing his black curls away from the empty eye socket. She kissed his head, however lightly, lips brushing his torn scalp, and then kissed him again, and then again, as if the act alone might render him whole.

Malcolm let his head fall. For the first time in months he had dreamed the hospital dreams, the comets and meteor showers, the unstemmed rains of poisonous gas. The pipes had been busted in the back shower and he knew one of the old men kept his stash beneath the drain. A seventy-seven-year-old Hungarian, English as a fourth language, needle tracks behind his knees. The world lit by crank, its collective suffering strung like a chain of beads.

He pulled himself onto his elbow, found his shoes, and staggered up the hall into a kitchen cluttered with baskets and ceramic animals. A slant of light parted the curtains and lay across the dead eye of the stove before folding into a sink streaked with rust. At the table sat a woman he recognized as Mildred Carter, Jordan's grandmother, the old woman he had visited months ago, her head bent over a plate of gray biscuits while her jaw worked methodically, laboring like an animal. When her jaw stopped he saw that swallowing would be an ordeal and it was. She lifted a plastic glass of tea and beads of condensation slid off to print the neck of her dress, not so much a fat woman as a woman whose skin was deserting her in loose falling folds that pooled down the bones to collect around her wrists and chin. The room was dark and she occupied it like a piece of furniture, heavy and antique.

"She's gone," she said, and leaned back into the window light. "Back out the door and zipped right on her way. But you sit down."

Malcolm stood there and tried to blink away the darkness. "There was a boy with her," he said.

"Weren't no boy with her. Sit down for a minute."

He pulled out one of the ladder-back chairs but did not sit, close enough to the door to see the hall wallpaper was patterned with tiny starlike arabesques moving beneath the grainy vertical stripes like creatures beneath ice, symmetrical hints of some larger presence, life having bloomed on the seafloor and risen. He scratched one nail along the seam where the wallpaper had wilted.

"She come up here with that one all tattooed up but she come running out alone. Shit-Toe they call him. Got him a little witch from Russia or somewheres." She leaned back from the light. He thought she must be looking at him but couldn't discern her face. "As far as I can tell she don't speak a lick of English cept what of the Bible she's learned by rote."

"I need to go."

"You sit down," she said again, and this time he did. "You been out to walk my land yet?"

"No, ma'am."

"That land's been in my family for I don't know how many generations. Since they run the Cherokee off. Papaw had one hundred and ninety-seven acre all the way down to the river. The government took the river land." She tapped one nail on her glass. "But I don't care two shits for it. That probably shocks you, an old woman talking like that. I'd sell the house out from under my daughter if I thought I had a son-in-law that could afford another. You work as a boy?"

"A little."

"I didn't do nothing but. Down in them fields with old dad when I wasn't but a child. To you it ain't nothing but TV, some old black-and-white program. Bunch of poor rednecks hoeing and boiling sugar cane." She stopped, reached for her tea, but there were only ice cubes left. "I don't give a damn. It wasn't nothing but hard times for me."

They sat until the lights flared. The kitchen lit brilliantly and Malcolm looked up to see three women standing just inside the door, laughing and holding cans of beer. They were in their early twenties, dressed in cutoff jeans and T-shirts, hair mussed. One wore a man's tank top over a green sports bra.

"Oh, Miss Rose," she said, "Miss Rose, who is this young stud you got with you?"

The other two girls fell against each other and laughed. The old woman put her eyes back on her plate.

"Oh, Miss Rose," the girl said, and sat down across from Malcolm.

With the light on, he took the measure of the room, the orthopedic shoes, the bowls crusted with day-old oatmeal. The lithe tank-top girl, her pipe-cleaner arms strung with blue veins, her wide brown eyes and a right ear that appeared to have been crumpled, then pieced together again. It looked like tinfoil, balled and then made smooth beneath a passing hand. He drew back just before she swatted him.

"You like what you looking at?" she said. Malcolm was quiet and the girl broke into a smile. "He's been back there with Shit-Toe's girl. You been back there with Shit-Toe's girl, ain't you?"

"Oh, no," one of the girls said. "Oh, no he wasn't."

They were laughing again, leaned against the Formica counter, holding each other up. The tank-top girl turned and lobbed her empty into the sink. "He been back there with her, Miss Rose?"

"He back there fucking that midget thing?" said the other girl.

"Look at me, Miss Rose. Was he back there with her?" She looked at Malcolm. "You one of Leighton's people? You up here buying?"

He shook his head and she smiled. "Can you not talk or something?"

"I can talk."

"He can talk," said one of the girls at the counter. "He could talk the ears off a billy goat if the mood struck him."

"Shut up," said the tank-top girl. "And sit down a minute. Y'all making me nervous."

They fell into the chairs so that all five sat at the table, the image of a happy family twice removed, three generations of borrowed bliss. A heat rash ran up one of the girl's arms. She took a baggie from her pocket.

"Don't get that out, honey," the tank-top girl said. "Not right now."

"Maybe he wants some?" she said.

"He don't want none. He's not up here buying."

"Maybe he wants some still. I mean if he's been in the back with Shit-Toe's dwarf."

"I said to put it away."

The girl put her fingernails on Malcolm's forearm and scratched lightly. He could see the sparkles in her green eye shadow, her eyes glossed with crank. "Why would you go back there with that ugly thing, sugar?" she said. "Knowing somebody like me is out here all by my lonesome."

"Oh, fuck," the third girl said.

She kept her nails on his arm. "I think you must like that crazy shit," she whispered.

The tank-top girl stood. "Let's get out of here."

"Not me. It just might be I like that crazy shit, too." She scratched again, harder this time and Malcolm felt tears rise in the corners of his eyes. "We might just go in the back and see what happens."

"Get up, Sandy. Both of you."

"You go yourself."

"Get up. I mean it."

"Fuck you, Charlotte."

The tank-top girl cuffed the side of Sandy's face and her head knuckled forward, her dirty ponytail splayed onto the table. She whimpered but stood, three red fingers impressed clearly below her left ear. "You bitch. You just blew it for lover here." She winked at Malcolm. "The heavens'll be rent wide before he gets a shot at something this good."

"Both of you," the tank-top girl repeated. "Time to go."

She touched Malcolm's arm a last time, pouted. "Maybe later, lover."

The tank-top girl waited until the other two had disappeared into the house before she spoke again. "'For all the nations have drunk of the wine of the wrath of her fornication,'" she said solemnly, "'and the kings of the earth have committed fornication with her, and the merchants of the earth have grown rich from the power of her luxury.'"

"The Book of Revelation," Malcolm said.

"The third verse of the eighteenth chapter." She pushed the door open. "At least somebody up here ain't a heathen."

Rick Miles was on the porch when Dallas walked around front, his Mossberg shotgun propped against the railing. "Mr. Dallas Walker," Miles said. "Good evening, chief. Nice little meeting, wasn't it?"

Dallas rocked his weight onto his toes. He could feel his back beginning to tighten, a pain around his ribs, soreness in the costal spaces—he'd felt it years ago at Georgia—but he felt ready. "Shep Parsons know you're out here?"

"Shep," Miles said. "Shep is I-don't-know-what. Shep is preoccupied. But Shep's not my concern. What I'm wondering about is your partner back there, the good doctor. I'm wondering about Brother Leighton and you should be, too. There're things you need to know."

Dallas looked back at the trailer. The night was quiet, cicadas and whip-poorwills, occasional laughter. A light was on upstairs. He supposed Malcolm was still in the truck, asleep, he hoped.

Miles broke into a grin. "They ain't coming out here. They know you're my little bitch."

"Fuck off."

"I'm messing with you, tomcat. Seriously though." He leaned onto the rail. "Let's take a little walk."

"I need to go home."

"Whoa, cowboy." Miles stepped in front of him. "Home's where you hang your hat. Tell me what he's said about me first."

"I don't know what you're talking about."

"Leighton Clatter, asshole. I know he has issues regarding my—how shall I say it?—my continued presence." Miles took a step back and smiled. "How about you just tell me what he said."

"Just about what you'd expect."

"That being?"

"That being he's afraid you might lose your shit," Dallas said. "That you're not the type to break bread with."

"He said that?" Miles shook his head. "As if he's chairing the mess at the goddamn table of international goodwill and brotherhood. He really said that?"

"I need to get moving."

"What else did he say?"

"You're drunk." Dallas took a step around him. "And I'm done with this, all of it."

"Any of them know that?"

"You heard me. I told em I was out."

"I did hear you, and I dig what you're saying, brother, I do: you drop out, put a wrinkle in their game. I'm just saying that ain't how it plays. You're out, but they're still in. Shep." Miles put his hand on Dallas's arm. "God love him. Brother Shep is, as they say, ideologically pure. The last of the true believers. The man will respect your decision. But your partner's the one that should scare you. The man's a fucking opportunist. He'd hitch his wagon to whatever star he saw rising."

"What about you?"

"Me, I'm just jazzing along." Miles loosened his grip on Dallas's biceps. "Staving off the boredom. Boredom's the only thing we got going for us. Our chief export. Getting the outside as fucked up as the inside."

"What the hell's that supposed to mean?"

Miles shrugged. "All I'm saying is when the lights go out, be elsewhere. Unless, of course, you got that boredom rooted down deep. In that case you better cowboy up." He put one palm flat on his chest. "Understand, I'm not casting aspersions. Me, I'm fishing around for it, anything to shake me awake, you know? Jazzing around Sadr City like it's Disney on Ice. It whips you up bad. You get this meanness you can't quite quench. So I say bring the shit, bring all of it, deep down we all need it."

"I'm going home."

Miles put his forearms on the rail. "Cut the shit and walk with me."

Dallas followed him around the trailers and past the dog pens toward the rear of the house where Miles opened the screen door and waved Dallas inside.

"I don't know how much of this is Shep's fuckup," Miles said. "He's seemed off his game lately, but I've seen him play it that way before. False sense of security—and then he zaps you. Rattlesnakes do the same thing."

They walked into the basement and Miles pushed the door shut behind him, took a pen light from his pocket and clicked it on. The beam flashed on several empty propane tanks with their brass fittings removed, a commercial pressure cooker, a long tube of aluminum foil left on a folding table. Boxes of discarded VHS tapes, Polaroids pinned to a cork board, a wool overcoat hung from a rafter, fuzzy with mold.

"They had a grow room down here back in the day," Miles said. "I guess this is just the next evolution."

When he reached the deep freeze Dallas remembered Gresham Haley and his missing hiker.

"What's your level of commitment here?" he said to Dallas. "Every morning I wake up and ask that question and every day I answer it."

He unlocked the freezer and Dallas leaned into the cold as if into a solid thing. Boxes of frozen vegetables, beef patties, and dinner rolls sat along the shelves. The body waited on the bottom, ten pound bags of ice pushed against the bloated torso and broken neck, a blush of broken capillaries still visible beneath the skin. The head looked like bruised fruit with its mashed eye and fractured skull. Ice crystals had formed in the hair.

"This asshole just didn't know when to quit," Miles said. "Crossed the property line after we warned him, just kept coming right back toward the camp. Had a pair of binoculars and a fucking Audubon guide in his pocket."

"I don't want anything to do with this," Dallas said.

"Yeah, I dig. But I thought you might appreciate it. It's educational, if nothing else. For me, it's like staring at the transfiguration. Which is about two degrees away from staring straight into the sun."

"I need to go home," Dallas said.

Miles let the lid fall. "That's cool. I'll see you later."

"No you won't."

"Sure I will, cowboy," he said. "I'll see you in hell."

Through the thin gauze of his eyelids he watched her move about the room, a red shape in the pink half-light, blurry as a ghost and saying things, he felt certain, she did not understand. And surely didn't realize he understood. This last thing, she kept repeating. The child. The bear. The old man stared at the square of ceiling that had come to embody the totality of his world, the slow wheeling fan, a single hairline fissure in the sheetrock splintered across the plaster. This last thing. The child. The bear. He watched her raise the window sash, a spectral image, trailing herself across the room as if time had come not so much undone as loose.

"You keep your eye on that one, Elijah," his dead wife said.

The by God bear, he thought, and then bears began to inhabit that other world in which he resided, bears crawled down out of the wasted tree line, the torn fronds and burning vegetation, the crown of a palm that lifts like a green star; bears lumbered off the earthen dams and splashed in the rice paddy, crawled from bunkers to sniff the dead waiting for the medevac dust-off.

"You don't let that one outta your sight," his dead wife whispered.

And when he looked back for her, he looked back at the choppers offloading, a train of bears passing down the metal ammo boxes. The hot LZ. The smell of cordite and night flowers. A Phantom burned on the runway and he watched a bear run from the wreckage, its furry head lit with fire. Bears dropped charges into tunnels and burned like torches when a napalm run fell short. Bears everywhere, bears and—how had he missed her?—his dead wife. Evelyn in the brown water, crawling on all fours. How odd, how strange, and for a moment he was back in the bright cold room with its tiled walls and a brass drain centered in the floor and Evelyn was back on the metal gurney, a sheet lowered to her naked waist.

Jordan put something to his lips, a dropper. He sucked like a newborn.

And then Christ, the .30-caliber round eating His face. The paste of his brain chin-strapped to his limp body. That sorry-ass flak jacket that rotted in the heat. Carbines that jammed. Socks eaten with mold. The bear motioned around him and now the old man saw Evelyn again, plasticized, floral in her coffin. He saw Tillman—they were boys again—then Dallas toting the ball on an end-around against Auburn, Malcolm crucified along the altar rail.

"He can't ever know what's inside me," he heard her say, this woman named Jordan, or believed he heard her say. He thought his eyes were open—there was light, at least—grained and yellow. "Never, never, never," she said, and he heard her go out of the room.

Never, never, never. He heard it long after she was gone and then he heard nothing at all. But he was patient: something would come out of this silence if he waited long enough. If only the sound of dust settling on his face.

"Watch her," his dead wife said.

"We have to do something about Tillman," Dallas said when they were back in the truck. His hands were shaking and he spilled Copenhagen onto his pants, went to brush it away and only smeared it against the fabric. "That bitch wife cheating right there in front of him."

"That what the meeting was about?"

"I'm fucking serious. He's going to die in that chair if we don't do something. Daddy should at least see him one last time."

They were sitting in the driveway when Malcolm asked about Jordan.

"You said there was something you wanted to tell me."

"No."

"Last night on the phone."

Dallas wouldn't look at him. "Talk to Randi." He looked straight ahead. "Don't ask me about that. It should be pretty clear to you by now that at bottom I'm a coward. That's the one thing you should have detected."

When she heard Dallas's truck pull into the drive Jordan took her glass from the end table and swallowed what was left of the bourbon. She thought of it as her last stand, a final fortification against the onslaught; if nothing else, she wanted to be prepared. All evening and into the night she had sat and imagined the sort of life they might build together. It was very clear to her now: he would teach Sunday School and talk patiently with their child—she had not the slightest doubt it was Malcolm's child—work long hours and come home to cut grass by porch light. They would have a daughter and it would be hard for Jordan to see herself in the girl, harder still to understand her. She was already afraid of the child. We should be allies, she thought, the two of us aligned against the mean slant of the universe. But even in the dim flicker of the Ativan her imagined child was barely understood. Malcolm would do this to her, give her this life, a house and a family to populate it. But she wouldn't allow it. The bear wouldn't allow it. It was no more hers to keep than the child whose name she refused to speak. She knew herself. She would ruin things, the child she carried more condemnation than gift. She saw no way around it.

"I will ruin things," she whispered to the house.

She spat back the ice cubes when she heard the kitchen door. He clicked on the lamp, looked at her, clicked it off again. The power light on the baby monitor pulsed green. He wasn't like her. She knew that now, and sat in the recliner, the dropper bottle of Ativan on the floor by her bare feet.

"Where's your brother?" she asked.

"He went on." Malcolm made no move toward her. "What are you doing up?"

"How was your little powwow?"

"What's going on here, Jordan?" She thought he might come to her but he did not. "What are you doing up?"

"I'm asking about your visit."

"Daddy's asleep?"

She nodded toward the foam of white noise. "Haven't heard a thing."

When he asked what she was drinking she held the nearly empty bottle by the neck.

"I thought Dallas had taken all his good stuff," Malcolm said. "What's the occasion?"

"Do I need one?"

He sat in the recliner facing her and picked up the Ativan. "How much of this did you take?"

She smiled. "The thing about you right now, Malcolm," she said, "you glow."

He said nothing. He watched her—she felt him watching her—then touched the bourbon with the tip of one shoe. "Maybe I'll have some that," he said, but did not move. "Just a little hit."

"A little hit never hurts. But don't do it on my account."

Outside, a car went up the highway, its lights stretched across the far wall. She watched her shadow elongate and disappear, head and shoulders, the back of her chair. Malcolm took the bottle and walked over to the front window.

"I'd pretty much convinced myself," he said. "The logic being that we'd weathered this. We were weathering it."

"You had your doubts," she said. "You always had your doubts."

"Maybe."

"It's okay to say it. I forgive you before you even say it. I declare you innocent of everything."

He choked and she thought he might be laughing.

"That's good of you," he said. "That's very good." He swished what was left of the bottle and she knew he was holding it above him. "Maybe just a little," he said. But instead of drinking he walked back over and stood by her shoulder and for a moment she wished she might see their reflection together like that, framed in the window as if for a portrait. The family before it is not. The family before it is undone. Suddenly, the child within her moved. Except it did not move. It was impossible, it wasn't even a child yet.

Malcolm placed one finger on the part of her scalp and took it away.

"It's called the philtrum, by the way," she said.

"What is?"

"That little beautiful groove that runs from her lips to the bottom of her nose. That's what you called it. 'That beautiful little groove.'" She motioned for the bottle and he refilled her glass.

"So are we finished here? Is that what this is?" He walked back across the room. "I don't know what you want me to say if it is."

"You know, I've been thinking about that," she said. "All evening just sitting here thinking and thinking."

"And?"

"It has something to do with inertia, I think. Bodies in motion versus bodies at rest."

He stood by the window, the blue safety light reflected on his face.

"You know you never told me what you said to that boy about God," she said. "I was thinking today about all the petty bullshit that gets lugged around and it just occurred to me. You never said a word to me. This boy—"

"Will."

"Will. Will gets the God Talk. Me—"

"You want the talk?"

"I want something."

He didn't say anything, only moved closer again, one leg against the recliner. He was doing that: moving back and forth through the room as if changing his position they might somehow reorient their life. She could feel the heat coming off his leg.

"It's maybe not what you think," he said.

She reached up and rubbed the fabric of his sleeve between finger and thumb as if testing its quality. "But that's the thing. I don't think anything. I don't have any sense at all."

"The philtrum," he said. "With a 'p-h'?"

"I looked it up. I kept meaning to tell you."

"Maybe I'll have that drink."

"Maybe you should."

He took the bottle with him into the kitchen and came back with a water glass. "There's still plenty for you. The Ativan scares me, though."

"Don't be."

"Don't be what?"

"Scared," she said. "Don't ever be scared."

He crashed into the armchair facing her, an expanse of worn floorboards between them. She heard him pour and drink and lick his lips. The night was still, all the lights in the house off, the stars very near, silver and hanging.

"The room's going to lurch," he said. "I'm a lightweight."

"You're not a lightweight. You're a Christian."

"That's phase one: a lurching room."

"You're not a lightweight. You're born-again"

"Phase two," he said, "and the light goes blurry."

She listened to him drink, the tinkle of ice against his teeth like music from another room.

"This is killing me, Jordan." She heard him pour another glass and thought there couldn't be much left now. "I wish I could walk."

"I know you do."

"You'd see me on that highway," he said. "Like you say: one foot in front of the other. I could make a worldview out of that."

"You don't have to convince me, baby. People are always leaving me."

"You make it sound so sad."

"I don't mean to. But sometimes it is," she said. "Sometimes it's the saddest thing in the world. But I don't mean to make it sound that way."

They sat without speaking. The motion light over the garage had gone out and there were no shadows left. Around them the house settled, the roof tin contracted, the wind chimes sounded. She put one hand to her face. The baby monitor kept foaming white noise. She'd had nothing like that when she was a mother. You had to stay in the room. You had to listen with your ear. It was like you were God, except that they could take it all away from you.

"I asked you not to go over there," she said. "I told you this would destroy us. And now you've let some sort of virus in—"

"One evening—"

"Some sort of evil and now it's all lower vibration."

"One evening, Jordan. Nothing changes in one evening."

"You know it's not just that."

"And it's not me," he said. "Of course it's not me."

"Don't act like that, all sarcastic."

"How would you prefer me to act?" He sloshed another drink into his glass.

They sat for three or four minutes letting the night close over them. She thought she heard something skitter across the floor, but saw nothing and shut her eyes. What was coming was still out there, still waiting.

"Not like you're weightless," he said. "But it is a sort of glide." His voice had become thick and after a moment he said, "Phase two. We have liftoff."

She stared at him until he was a shape again. "I want the God Talk," she said. "The one you gave that boy."

"There's no such thing. No God Talk. No—"

His drink fell from the arm of the chair, banged on the floor, and rolled across the boards. She imagined the sound of watery bourbon sliding into slick shape, the ghostly cubes that slipped beneath the couch and out of sight, as insubstantial as sin.

"Leave it," she said. "Leave me the mess."

"Fuck you," he said softly and exhaled. He seemed to wheeze when he spoke. "Listen to me. You're turning me into a barbarian."

"Even without the God Talk."

She crossed the room, her face inches from the bay window that looked out onto the side yard, the window that might have framed them. It felt cool, so near her skin. "There're less lightning bugs," she said. "Ever notice that? You don't see as many any more. Is that like a sign of the times or something?"

"It's called the apocalypse," he said. "From here out we get the plagues."

VII.

The room smelled of Lysol and Malcolm raised windows and washed the bedsheets. The old man was down to the Ativan and a single can of Glucerna split between two feedings, that and a few squirts of Pedialyte taken from a sports bottle. He had diminished for weeks but now seemed arrested on the edge of dying, occupying some point just short of erasure. He slept mostly, hour after hour, but when he woke he was often alert. Women from El Shaddai brought casseroles and baskets of biscuits and a home health nurse came every other day to take his blood pressure and pulse. Dallas came about as often, usually when the old man was asleep, always careful to slip out before he woke.

One afternoon Malcolm read in an alumni magazine of the death of Jefferson Roddick. At the library he entered Roddick's name in a search engine and found an article in the *Roanoke Times*. Everything was there, his short life compacted to a few lines. The thirty-four years of living. The degrees and deployments. The breakdown and his final discharge. The cause of death was a self-inflicted gunshot wound to the head, exactly as Malcolm knew it would be. He had shot himself on the Fourth of July, and Malcolm thought for a moment of Haiti—it was only weeks away and he hadn't spoken of it to Jordan—then logged off and drove home.

In late July a thunderstorm settled over the mountain. Rain fell for two days and on the third day, a Sunday, two fly fishermen came across the prow of a canoe washed from its mud cocoon. By mid-week a team of archeologists from the state university were preparing an extraction. The evening news showed a giant aluminum frame, half stretcher and half flotation device that would be fitted beneath the canoe so that it could be carried out. The Cherokee dugout had already been dated to the early- to mid-eighteenth century and on Saturday volunteers and Forest Rangers would attempt to haul it the three-quarters of a mile from the river to the parking lot where a truck would carry it to a submersion tank.

"We should go watch," Malcolm said. "Maybe help if they need it."

"It's Saturday," Jordan said. "You know I can't on Saturday."

"Maybe just this once. This is kind of extraordinary."

"If you cared about me you wouldn't even ask."

She was leaving on Fridays now, had been since he had rode out with Dallas to The Settlement. The noise was unbearable, the voices, the screaming. All unending lower vibration. She understood the bear's message. She told him that, but nothing else, and they began to fight not over her absence but over his inability to hang a wet towel, the dirt carried in the tread of his boot up the back steps and into the kitchen. He was messy with the feeding tube, spilling the milky Glucerna on the bare stomach of his father. She brought home another bag of Ativan and smoked every evening until her lips cracked.

"You're looking for a way out," he told her one night in bed. He lay flat on his back and addressed the ceiling. She was still but he could tell from her breathing that she was awake. "You're just looking for an excuse to walk away."

"I told you before what was happening." She spoke without moving. "I told you there was this bad energy."

"You're being ridiculous. If you want to walk away just say so."

"You think—" She faltered and he sensed her start to rise, then ease back against the mattress. "I don't need to fabricate some reason to walk out that door, Malcolm. Do you really think I'm so deluded as to think I belong here?"

"I hope that you know you belong here."

"I've never belonged anywhere. And I told you not to leave in the first place."

"Where is it you're going every weekend? I haven't asked and I haven't asked."

"You're asking now."

"You have a home here."

"You're asking me now."

He couldn't take his eyes off the ceiling for fear that were he to turn from the lesser dark something worse would await him. The child. Malcolm knew he was near though he had yet to spot him. "You owe me that much at least," he said and felt her turn, saw her arms rise: she was dropping Visine into her eyes and he thought of his father. *If your eyes are sound, your whole body will be full of light.*

She blinked the beads from her lashes. "I told you not to walk out that door."

"Look at me," he said. "Jordan, look at me."

She would not. But Sunday afternoon she came home and they ate dinner quietly, peaceably, and when they went upstairs made love slowly and then slept, acting—if not quite becoming—people whose future had been returned.

It was later that night, or another night—if any sense lay in measuring such things—that the old man attempted to rise and walk. Malcolm heard the dull thud of his body against the floorboards and made it downstairs before the water glass on his father's nightstand could still itself.

"I'm all right." He was already trying to sit up. "Tell your mother leave me be."

After that, Malcolm kept waking, certain that his father was no longer breathing, creeping into his room to stand over him until he was reassured of life. When he did sleep, he dreamed of a woman, face down and freezing on a bare mattress. He made careful study of the long contour of her body, white sheet gray in the ambient light. She flexed one slim ankle and rolled onto her side. There was just enough light to see the silver Ankh in the hollow of her throat.

"What are you doing?" she asked.

"Standing here."

A narrow arm stretched above her. "Come back to bed."

She wore a silver toe ring that held and released the dull streetlight. But when he reached for her foot he found it wax and realized she was not a woman but a mannequin, naked and plastic, and he was alone again.

Finally, he gave up on sleep, dropped the attic stairs, and climbed to his war. Sometime later he looked to see Jordan standing by the trapdoor in her nightgown. He felt her eyes but said nothing as she entered the green oval of lamplight that spread over the desk and tinted the room.

"Scared me," he said.

Without a word she lifted his glasses and kissed him, guided her fingers down the gauzy phosphorescence of his chest and kissed him again.

"Do you still believe in God?" she asked.

"Why are you asking me that?"

"Maybe because I'm desperate. Maybe because I think you might take pity on me."

He could see the vacant shadows where her eyes should have been. "I want you to be happy," he said. "That's all I want. But I don't—"

Know— She made the motion with her lips but no sound escaped. He shook his head and turned from her, felt her hands float up. But instead of touching him they simply hung there, unable to alight.

"I think about you," she said. "Poor Malcolm sitting in his room."

"Drinking."

"Drinking and thinking about God." She stood and put her forehead against the top of his head. "You're just a conduit," she said. "But not *just* like in a bad way. I can feel it coming through your crown chakra." Her gown was printed with tiny blue cornflowers and she slipped it up and off in a single motion, planted her knees on his chair so that her delicate frame straddled him. "I came up here to tell you something," she said. "But I'm not sure now."

He was eye level with the smooth plane of skin that slipped to her small chest, the gentle upsweep of her ribs. A tear landed on one of her breasts, a tiny star-shaped splatter. The murmur of heat. Only her eyes were crying.

"We'll leave here if you want," he said. "We'll leave this house. Go anywhere in the world. Just tell me what you want."

"I wanted you to answer my question," she said. "But I've thought about it all weekend and now I think maybe don't answer. I think maybe it's too late."

When he opened his mouth she put a finger to his lips. "Maybe not another word," she said, and kissed him until they slid onto the floor and made love among the wounded, among the ones left bleeding on the field, the soldiers caught in their three-quarter-inch death throes. The dead refusing the grave.

A few days later, Malcolm came home from cutting brush to find Jordan on the living room floor, the old man asleep in the recliner beside her, an afghan over his legs and socked feet.

"I have to talk to you," Jordan said.

Malcolm leaned from the doorjamb. "What's going on?"

She shushed him and Malcolm walked over to touch the wisps of gray hair that traced his father's freckled skull.

"Come with me," she said. "Don't talk."

He followed her into the kitchen and stood in the door frame.

She turned to the refrigerator and removed a large metal bowl and they started shucking corn, tearing the silky husks and brushing away stray threads.

"I saw Dallas today," Malcolm said. "I tried to get him to come see Daddy and—"

Jordan broke a cob and tossed the two halves into the bowl. "I don't think you should be saying anything against Dallas. At least Dallas means what he says. At least Dallas stays."

"What are you talking about?"

"I'm talking," she said, "about how I warned you. I knew and I told you and you couldn't have cared less. And now look at where we are?" She took an opened envelope from the counter and handed it to him. "I'm talking about this. I'm talking about you leaving." She turned back to the corn. "I knew something awful was about to happen."

It was another letter from the All Servants Ministries in Haiti. An orientation letter. He was to arrive in just under three weeks.

"I knew this was out there," she said. "Something like this, something just waiting, and I asked you to stay here that one day—"

"I had forgotten about this—"

"Forgotten to tell me you're moving to a foreign country in a matter of weeks?"

"I was going to tell you—"

"Wait." She raised one finger; a thread of husk clung to the nail and fell away. "You forgot or you were going to tell me? Those seem like two entirely different things."

"Don't yell." He glanced toward the bedroom. "You'll wake him."

"I need to wake him."

"Jordan—"

"I need to fucking wake him. He might like to know what kind of son he has."

He tried to take her wrist but she pulled away.

"So you're what? Just waiting him out? Waiting me out? Waiting for him to die and me to move on, is that it? I came back to you."

"Listen to me."

"I came back to you Sunday. Did you even realize what was happening when I left? Did you even realize that was it? That night when you went with Dallas? I decided that night, and I was this close to not coming back."

"Please, Jordan."

"You know I've always been one of those people who could never figure out when something was over. Like it would just crumble beneath me and then I'd realize there was nothing there and hadn't been for I don't know how long." Her eyes glittered. "But at least I know this is over. At least I know this is done."

"Jordan—"

"I read it, Malcolm. I read the letter. There is no way you can explain this. No way." She moved around the kitchen to avoid him, the island between them. "And what kills me is the way you acted like this was so permanent, like this was something that mattered or was going to matter or whatever. 'You have a home here, Jordan.' You disgust me. I disgust myself. Even thinking such a thing was possible."

She moved through the living room and up the stairs where she stopped to face him. "I came back to you," she said. "I left here. Do you understand that? I left here and then I just thought: we don't have to be these two people screwed up by our families and our past. That doesn't have to be us."

"Jordan."

"I came back to you, goddamn it, I came back to you. I believed you."

"Believe me now."

"Haven't you saved enough black people already? Isn't one enough?"

"Please," he said. "Believe me now."

"I wish I could, but all I can think, Malcolm—and I wish to God I didn't, but all I can think is how you managed to wiggle down off this cross, too."

The second letter was signed THE COMMITTEE TO PROTECT WHAT IS SACRED AND WHAT IS OURS, though the text was essentially no different from the first in its promise of death. Still, certain expressions caught in the throat, a phrase or construction that teased at memory, as if Dallas had been reading the same letter every day of his life but only today had realized it. *What you are doing is an act of desecration and this land is not yours to desecrate . . .*

He folded it back into its envelope and sat for a moment at his desk. Randi was outside somewhere, doing whatever it was Randi did. He listened but heard only the false whisper of air-conditioning. When he got tired of listening he put the envelope in the drawer and locked it. He was still sitting there when Leighton called.

"I got another letter," Dallas said. "Same as before."

"Forget it," Leighton said. "We got bigger worries."

"The Committee to Protect What Is Sacred and What Is Ours. All caps."

"I said forget it. I just got a call from Gresham Haley."

Dallas took the phone from his ear.

"I want to know what the fuck you said to him, Dallas."

"Nothing he wanted to hear."

"Well, that right there might be the problem, partner, cause a judge just issued an order for another impact survey."

"It took the bastard long enough to find one."

"Dallas." Leighton sounded like a patient father nearing patience's edge. "Why don't you come see me, Dallas? Why don't the two of us have a little back-and-forth."

"We've had our back-and-forth."

"Well, fuck you then," he said and laughed.

"I'm serious, Leighton."

"You're serious? You're off your goddamn rocker is what you are."

Dallas parted the blinds and spotted Randi out in the yard dropping the bodies of small birds into a Ziploc bag. All summer, birds had swooped down in kamikaze runs against the glass doors that opened onto the veranda, and every morning there would be two or three, beaks open, bodies stiff but without a mark, lying there on the tiles or on the lawn. Crows. Catbirds. Mockingbirds. You could look out and see scratches of color in the grass.

"Dallas?" Leighton said.

"I'm here."

"Hang up the phone, Dallas. Hang up the phone and sleep whatever shit this is off, all right? Nobody's done with nothing till this is finished." There was a long silence over the line and then only Leighton's heavy breath. "If you're serious, you son of a bitch, I will nail your ass to the wall," he said finally. "You're serious, aren't you, you ungrateful pissant redneck hemorrhoid. You think about this, Dallas, because I promise you this: if—and that's a big if—if you stay out of prison you can look forward to spending the rest of your miserable fucking life tied up in litigation. I'm only this patient because we go so far back."

"Fuck you, Leighton."

"Yeah, fuck you. Fuck me. You sit on this a few days, Dallas, and then you call me back. We'll pretend this never happened."

He sat for a while after hanging up, watched the sun fall through the rectangular panes to pattern itself across the floor, a series of paling shapes stretched across the good heart-of-pine boards. Arrogance—that was Randi's diagnosis, and he thought for a moment of the good days, every day their net worth growing, appearing in their account as if out of nowhere, a string of ones and zeros transmitted over fiber-optic lines. It would be gone before they could count it. Just another bit of datum awash in a sea of green.

It was always theoretical anyway, he told himself.

But then again so was the future.

Eventually, he walked down to the basement, opened the gun safe, and took out the TEC-9 he'd bought in Anderson. So it had all run to this: a man with a gun, alone in his basement. He considered his options but none of them felt right. Only the gun. There was a mirror on the opposite wall, and he watched himself without really meaning to, feeling the gun, turning it one way and then another. He stood like that for a long time, measuring its weight in his hands. It felt exactly as the man had promised: like a brutal little motherfucker. It felt inevitable, too, and it occurred to him that this was exactly as it should be.

He looked to his left and that wasn't Jesus beside him in the bright green of the paddy, just a boy he'd known since boot, not even a friend really, just another grunt face down and wheeling beneath the rotorwash. The old man lying to himself all these years. Except it wasn't really a lie. God had ate that round as sure as anything. The stacked sound when it found flesh—that had been his Savior. Jesus in that sloppy gook mud. If that didn't sound too by God uppity, which of course it did.

In August there was no more rain and the fields turned the yellow of thirst. The sky bronzed with dust and within the air-conditioned front room the old man's skin began to dry and fall in tiny tricornered sails. Wisps of Elijah Walker dusting the floor while he slept twenty hours a day and Malcolm stood in the threshold and watched. He could see his father's skeleton now, papery skin stretched over delicate bones. His wattled throat corded with what appeared to be green yarn. They were down to four ounces of Glucerna forced once a day through the feeding tube, a few drops of Ativan, a sponge to wet his lips, a bit more to wash down the crushed painkillers. The dog days were hot and empty, and when Malcolm turned from his sleeping father it was to stand on the porch and stare out at the burning grasses. The garden had desiccated, vegetables rotting on the vine, and in its dryness the world appeared underwater, as if vision was little more than the angry trick of a perverse God.

He had not heard from Jordan and, in truth, wasn't sure what he would say were they to meet. He had dialed her cell a few times, but quit when he realized it was no longer in service. For days he had expected her to call from her grandparents and then, when she didn't, found himself cruising past her old house downtown. He had almost stopped once, spotting her cousin Archimedes on the front porch, a Chopin nocturne swelling through the open windows. But Jordan's car was never there and Malcolm didn't dare knock. Sundays he stayed away from church.

"You never told her about leaving?" the old man had asked that evening after she left.

"No. I never did."

And that was the last thing he said to Malcolm about the matter, a rightful benediction. Instead of arguing, he lay in his bed and closed the thin membranes of his eyelids while Malcolm stumbled through the house, everywhere tripping over reminders: strands of hair caught in the forest of a brush; the garden he watched wilt; the flowers he refused to water. He moved aimlessly about the bedroom, touching things, tracked by the patient eyes of Grunewald's crucified savior, the Simone Weil on the nightstand, the ornate clasp knife in the drawer. If you sat in a room long enough the room would forget you, settle, become itself again. It was a form of absent presence, this sitting, and he found himself taken with it for hours at a time, posing silent questions the child would not answer—*What did you think just before you touched the shiny thing? Did you think it a toy? Who sent you?*—watching the suck of the child's missing nose, the flipper of skin that was a such a poor excuse for a nostril.

A week after she left, Dallas came by in gym pants and an Adidas T-shirt and sat on the couch, sweating and drinking canned protein.

"You haven't heard from her?" he asked.

"No," Malcolm said. "You haven't by chance—"

"Nothing. I'm sorry."

"It came apart fast at the end. Before I even caught on to what was happening."

"It's always like that. It's like you're going along and then you just step off this cliff."

"And you haven't heard—"

"Nothing, bro. I'm sorry."

"I thought maybe Leighton might have heard something."

"I haven't seen Leighton. We had kind of a falling out."

"This about the new survey?"

"Honestly, I don't even know if there is any new survey. Sometimes I think Leighton just makes shit up. The survey, the indictment. I guess he figures the more scared I am the more I'll just shut up and take it."

The nurse came daily now, a compact woman with callused hands and silver bangs. "We're not far from systemic failure," she told Malcolm. "You need to be prepared for that."

They stood at the front door and he tried to will her down the steps.

"He's lived a good life," she said. "But it's normal to be sad."

After that, Malcolm started sleeping on the floor, a pallet of quilts and the foam egg crate off his bed. He could not be convinced of the old man's persistence and woke every couple of hours to listen for his ragged nasal breath. Other nights, he sat in a straight-back chair, but inevitably woke back on the floor, unaware of when he had crawled down.

He opened his eyes one morning to find Randi in the rocking chair.

"There's no need for you to do that," she said. "All you're going to do is wind up sore. But maybe that's what you want, I guess."

That day he drove to church for the first time since the healing service with Jordan. It was a Tuesday, but he knew the doors would be unlocked, Preacher Dell somewhere about, praying or mowing the grass. He entered the sanctuary and sat in the front pew, then felt something cold against his neck, as if floating in a summer lake he had suddenly drifted into a shaft of cool water. When he turned he saw Mildred Carter in the far corner, a pew cushion wedged behind her. She stared back at him like an owl, her round face and big eyes, the beak of her mouth clapped shut. Malcolm walked to the back.

"Hello, Mrs. Carter."

"Hello, Mr. Walker." A silver walking cane stood before her, its bottom splayed to four rubber-stopped feet. She wore old pantyhose and the same clunky orthopedic shoes he remembered from The Settlement, hands folded atop a Bible fat with old bulletins. "Well," she said. "You have something you want to say to me? Or was you just being neighborly to the old granny woman?"

"I didn't see Preacher Dell coming in."

"Was you looking for him?"

Malcolm shook his head so slowly he might have been testing it.

"He's done run off to town," she said. "I don't know for what."

Malcolm stood. "I should probably go myself."

"Your brother got my land now." She looked at him, makeup caked around her eyes and along her jaw. "Probably already setting to chopping it up. He tell you?"

"No, he didn't."

"I hope he enjoys the ruining of it. You tell him I said that."

He was at the door when she called to him.

"They don't talk about karma at the church house," she said, "but you an educated man. You know what karma is, don't you, Mr. Walker? Karma's just another function of the good Lord, really. It's the reaping of what we've sown. I've always thought that was the most interesting thing about life. Maybe the cruelest, too."

He walked outside into the blinding heat and realized summer had somehow escaped his notice. But it was palpable now, wine-ripe, the air shuddering with june bugs. He was still on the steps when Preacher Dell drove up and got out of his pickup with a paper sack marked ACE HARDWARE.

"I always feel guilty whenever I see you," Malcolm said. "Like I'm just slinking around, avoiding church."

"Ain't me nor the Lord keeping attendance," Dell said. "How's your daddy?"

"The same, or a little worse, maybe."

"You want to come in and sit a minute?"

"I better get back to him."

They shook hands and Malcolm was getting in his truck when Dell called to him. "You remember what I said about finding the beauty in life, Malcolm?" he asked. "About not getting lost just in the hurtfulness. You remember me saying that?"

"I do," Malcolm said. "And I almost had it there for a while."

When he got home the kitchen was full of food. Randi came in the back door carrying a picnic basket.

"Two women brought it all over," she said. "From the church, I guess."

"He sleep the whole time?"

"He was awake for a minute, but I'm not sure he knew where he was."

She unloaded casserole dishes and plates covered in plastic wrap and aluminum foil. "What do you want to do with this?"

"I don't know. Can you take some of it?"

"Let's just put up what you don't want. There'll be plenty of people here to feed pretty soon."

He reached for one of the baskets but instead found himself staring out at what had once been Jordan's garden.

Randi put her hand on his forearm. "She's an addict, Malcolm. This wasn't your fault."

That evening he left the baby monitor in the old man's room and climbed to the attic. Though his father slept soundly, Malcolm refused to turn down the volume. To listen to the rasp of his father's chest seemed a moral absolute. Like listening to one's child crying, refusing to shut out the sound so that the suffering of another was his suffering, too. He sat in his straight-back chair and ran through the things she had told him, whispers in the balm of night. *My holiness envelops everything I see. God's will for me is perfect happiness. There is no sin; it has no consequence.* He had gone looking for her book after she left, thinking she might have forgotten it, but it was nowhere to be found, only the jeweled knife in the nightstand.

He refused to touch it.

He had not touched his war either, not since the night he and Jordan had made love here—the last night, it occurred to him now, they had touched—but tonight he needed its nearness. Not to touch it, not even to consider it, simply to sit where his father had sat so many years prior when the world felt ordered and right.

Look in his eyes, son. If your eyes are sound, your whole body will be full of light.

She met Leighton at a bar in Greenville called the Fifth Column, top floor of the NationsBank building, the place all glass and steel, apple martinis and a giant aquarium of neon tetras. She waited by a window, two Maker's Marks on the table and a pair of three-hundred-dollar heels she had just bought with her MasterCard on her feet. He had told her on the phone he had a suite for her, empty and waiting, and if nothing else Jordan wanted out of the motel she'd been living in with its pea-green carpet and color TV. The remote bolted to the nightstand by an ashtray shaped like a tomahawk. The mattress broken with the slow curve of resignation, of all those years and bodies, a lifetime spent waiting for the next seedy affair.

She had called Leighton because there was nothing else to do. The bear had brought her here, to this place where she did nothing beyond sit in the motel armchair with its cigarette burns and touch her thickening middle. The sink full of ash and the carpet full of dead bugs. For the last week she had stumbled around the room, fish-eyed and distracted, sitting for hours rocking a child that did not yet exist. She would lean into the window screen and feel it shift within her, brush her ribs, the slow swim of its footless paddling.

Away.

But she knew now there was no going away just as there was no going back. She had given up on the God Talk, given up on salvation, on the reappearance of Rose's Pilgrim angel. Malcolm was as dead as Roosevelt and she felt just as before: the trees naked and raking a bone-colored sky while another man lay inside, inclined on his rented hospital bed, a Styrofoam cup untouched on the nightstand. Nothing had changed. It was just that she hadn't been able to see it.

Her failure to learn.

Now she felt unable to move past the day they had taken her child. For weeks, she had let the deodorant cake beneath her arms, flakes of white powder that snowed like dandruff so that she quit wearing it, simple as that, just walking through the house in panties, swollen breasts swinging and matted until she was a confusion of knotted hair and crusted nipples.

But the day they took the child she made herself clean and whole. She would be damned if she gave her nana the satisfaction of seeing her broken, and arranged herself in the mirror, showered, brushed out her hair and put on a little makeup. Then saw that one of her breasts had leaked a damp oval onto her shirtfront. When she heard her nana calling she raised the padded seat and finger-pumped colostrum into the toilet, sudden clear splashes that turned to murky rainbows as they spiraled down. It wasn't her fault. You needed to be so much stronger than she could ever be.

"Strange," she said when Leighton sat down. "Seeing you like this."

"You missed me."

"No."

"You called, darling."

"You shouldn't necessarily take that as a compliment," she said, but took his hand anyway. She had planned this, prepared for this, and touching him thought: this is what desperation feels like. There was her performative state, her theatrics, but this was something else entirely: this was desperation, and it came over her that she'd never really known it before. "I dreamed about the bear last night," she said.

He shook his head and she looked past him to the fish in the aquarium that sparkled like costume jewelry.

"I won't ask about your little prophet," he said.

"He's painting cannons right now. These tiny little plastic tubes he paints brass. He has all this model glue."

"Did he freak when you left?"

"No more than you'd expect."

Twenty minutes later they were in a room at the airport Hilton, Jordan on the edge of the bed in a silk kimono, a gift, while Leighton walked naked from the bathroom and left his watch on the nightstand.

"Let's talk about how we never talked," he said.

He stood over her and touched her shoulder, slid his hand up her neck. She let him. She kissed his hand and everything moved with a time delay, their actions, an absent pause, and then the slow reverberations as they slid up onto the bedspread. When she reclined against the headboard he pointed to the bathroom.

"Clean your filth," he said.

She turned the dial to HOT and emerged steaming, skin damp, hair a lacquered helmet. She had a bottle of baby oil and handed it to Leighton and lay flat on her stomach.

"What is this?" he said.

"Rub."

She had no idea why she did it. Or perhaps she did. It was a stay against her carefully tailored nana, hands moist with lotion; a caution against a papa reasonable and devoted and useless. She purred as he worked it onto her shoulders and arms, kneaded it into her back and over her butt and calves and feet, rubbing her until she shone like a polished stone.

When she rolled over he began with the tops of her feet and shins, moved up to her thighs and over her stomach and breasts where he rubbed slow wide circles. His hands glided down her body and when she felt his lips along the inside of one thigh she tilted her pelvis forward. It was the slightest of movements but felt like the most daring thing she'd done since Rose had passed. A moment later her arms were spread as if crucified, hands pulling at the sheets, little gurgles escaping her throat.

When she came it was in a small, perfectly controlled fit. She hated herself for it.

He slid inside her then, slowly, and then faster, and then faster still atop the oil slick of her body, a recklessness to the act, like driving a car on black ice, in control but only just, always a moment from losing everything.

Afterward, they lay half-clothed atop the sheets watching *Regis and Kelly*, Jordan's kimono loose over a pair of powder-blue panties, Leighton's shriveled groin beneath his boxers.

"I really am hurting right now," she said.

"Maybe I want that. Maybe I want you to hurt a little."

"It's bad, Leighton."

"How bad?" he said. "Tell me, why don't you? I want you to describe it in detail."

She couldn't meet his eyes. This is horrible, she thought. But it is not me.

Dallas stood on the ridge behind the silver Airstream for some time before he could bring himself to walk down the rutted track and knock on Uncle Tillman's door. Not that he was stalling. It was another beautiful day, hot, but beautiful, and the view of the valley spread beneath the faultless sky was enough to hold any man. He couldn't remember it being quite so lovely. He'd been up before Christmas, but had somehow let the year slide by without returning. Somehow nothing had moved him, not Malcolm's return, not his Daddy's accident. Shit, Dallas thought, I'm just standing here for a minute. It's not like I'm gonna get back in the truck and drive off before we can even talk. He just wanted to see the place.

When he had come up in December the puddles were skimmed with ice and patches of dirty snow lay beneath the scrub pines. Now the forest floor was lush with ferns and thickets of rhododendron and wilted azaleas. He looked for traces of the people Malcolm claimed to have seen, but saw no evidence beyond a few charred beer cans in a fire ring and what appeared to be the remnants of a tent farther down the tree line.

But he wasn't here to admire things. He was here on business.

He had explained this visit to Randi as a little tough love for a wayward uncle. She had warned him against this, and standing with one foot on the cinder block that served as a front step he felt his will melt. He raised his hand to knock but held it there long enough to look around. Tire tracks crossed the sandy yard and sitting in a folding chair was a plastic roach clip and a baggie of rolling papers ruined by the weather. Trash in the hedges. Paper bags of fast food and larger plastic bags of garbage. The place was a mess. He had missed all of it coming in.

When he turned again for the door he was angry enough to tear it from the hinges. Instead he shouldered it open, not bothering to knock. A chinchilla leapt from Tillman's lap while another stood in a pie tin of milk and yapped. Tillman's head snapped forward.

"Dallas," he said.

Even with the windows up the smell was rancid. Tillman sat naked with a bath towel over his genitals. Open sores covered him and he looked like a great oozing map, purple skin textured and seeping.

"Hey, brother," Tillman said.

"Jesus Christ, Tillman." Dallas plowed through the trash, the Pizza Hut boxes and beer cans tossed in the sink, and pushed open the door to the sleeping area.

"You all right, Dallas?" Tillman called.

Dallas came back with a flattened box of Trojan condoms and an empty pint bottle of Jim Beam.

"Am I all right?" He bounced the box off Tillman's chest. "You're asking me if I'm all right?"

"You come through the door all worked up." Tillman had lifted the chinchilla from the pie tin and stroked it. "I sure am glad to see you, but you just about got me on edge coming in like that."

"I came in like the whirlwind," Dallas said. "You remember the whirlwind, don't you? You remember Job?"

"You scaring me, brother."

"I came in to goddamn scare you."

"I wish you wouldn't cuss."

"I came in to wake your obese ass up. Do you have any idea what's going on here? I guess those are your condoms, aren't they? I guess that's your Jim Beam?"

"Some of Maia's friends—"

"That MySpace bitch is fucking her Navajo boyfriend in the other room, waiting for you to die so she can get your land. You realize that? They're out in the yard smoking pot and getting drunk. That even bother you? Them out there getting high while you sit here dying in a plastic goddamn chair?"

"Don't you take the Lord's name in vain."

Dallas kicked the pie tin. Milk splashed the wall and the chinchilla sprang beneath a sleeping bag.

"You think God's going to save you? You think you're going to be healed? You think you're Job sitting here? Tell me," Dallas said. "Honest to God, I want to know. You think He's going to fix this mess?"

"I've always fixed my eyes on Jesus."

"You've always fixed your eyes on bullshit is what you've fixed them on. You've shut your eyes is what you've done."

"Brother," Tillman said. He was starting to cry now, staring at Dallas with incomprehension. He had never quite understood their relationship, Dallas thought, brother, cousin, nephew. He had never quite understood anything.

"You think God is going to heal you?" Dallas said. "You think God is going to lift up your fat ass?"

"Dallas, I think maybe you ought to go."

"And these bullshit text messages you send. You think anyone reads that shit?"

"I only want to be an encouragement."

"An encouragement?" Dallas clutched his skull as if it might fly apart. "You're a pestilential open wound is what you are. Do you understand that?"

"Dallas." Tillman was crying now, head down and chin rolled against his chest. "Please just go."

"You think—" Dallas said, and then stopped.

"I know, I know," Tillman was saying. His sobs shook his body, heavy ripples like the shifting of seismic plates. "I know," he said. "I know what's happening. I know I'm alone."

"Oh, Jesus."

"I know."

Dallas sat on the edge of a lawn chair, put his face in his hands, and viewed his uncle through the cage of his fingers. Tillman's skin was pink, the sores wine-dark, his face a mess of snot and tears.

"Oh, God," Dallas said very quietly.

Tillman began to wail. "I know, I know, I know."

"I'm so sorry. I shouldn't have—"

"I know God's done turned His face from me."

"Tillman—"

"You think I don't know how disgusted He must be to look at me?"

"Tillman, I—" Then Dallas was crying, furious now, though his anger found no object outside of himself. "We're so screwed up. What's wrong with us?" he asked his uncle. "What's wrong with me?"

Tillman's body shook. "I don't know."

"I come into people's lives and I wreck them. I fuck everything up."

"I don't know. I don't understand."

"I say terrible things I don't mean."

"Yes."

"I think about how to hurt people."

"Yes."

He faced Tillman who sat shaking, a giant slab of uncooked beef. "I remember making you cry when I was maybe ten years old, teasing you about being fat. You were smiling and I just kept wanting to wipe that smile off your face—telling you how fat you were—and then you were just crying." He ran the back of one hand across his slick face. "The way I do people. It's like a sickness. Do you remember what you said to me?"

"Yes," Tillman wailed. "No."

"You said you'd rather be the fattest man alive than ever treat anyone the way I had just treated you. What is wrong with me?"

"Just go."

"Why do I do these things?"

"Please just go."

Dallas cleaned his face, nodded. "All right," he said. "I can do that. I can go."

Outside the trailer he listened to his uncle panting like a dying animal, the Airstream quaking on its cinder-block foundation. He started to go back inside but instead walked to his truck and started down the mountain.

He drove miles of blacktop before he realized he was headed toward Leighton's house. A wave of sadness had broken over him and he felt washed back into the world as it was, not as he desired it to be. The practicality of things felt forced on him. He knew it was time to talk.

He parked outside and climbed the back steps to the kitchen, called for Leighton but heard no response. On the counter beside several pills stood an open unlabeled bottle of bourbon and Dallas poured himself a glass. He knew the taste immediately: twenty-seven-year-old Pappy Van Winkle, the finest stuff Leighton owned. The pills were Viagra. Dallas refilled his glass and walked into the living room where Leighton's black-and-white feist slept on the couch.

"Leighton," he called. The dog cocked its head, but did not rise. "Leighton? Where are you, asshole? Come make me feel better."

He sat on the couch for a moment, petted the dog, and pressed the cool glass to his forehead.

"What the fuck?" he asked the dog, and downed the bourbon, left the glass on the table, and started up the spiral staircase. "Leighton," he called again, and noticed from the landing the bearskin was missing from the wall.

He started down the hall toward the bedroom, suddenly filled with dread, but knowing that he had to go forward. His only regret was not having had another glass of the Pappy.

At the end of the hall he pushed the door open.

"Jesus Christ," he said.

"Afraid He couldn't make it," Leighton said.

He stood naked but for the bearskin draped over his back, his body glossed and his erect penis red and tilting in front of him like a swollen, slightly crooked finger. Jordan Taylor was naked in the bed, eyes dull and spaced, hands bound to the headboard. Leighton put his hand on a pistol that rested on the nightstand beside a bottle of olive oil.

"I had some Pappy in the kitchen," Dallas said.

"Get your shit-kickers off my carpet, cowboy."

"You should never leave the good stuff out."

Leighton touched the pistol with a single finger and looked at Dallas.

"So the bear's out of hibernation," Dallas said.

"Get out of here, Dallas. This isn't for children."

"I just came up here to tell you we're finished."

"Is that right?"

"You're goddamn right it is. Finished doing business, finished doing everything."

"Oh, what joy I must feel."

He looked past Leighton at the angular shape of the woman in his bed. She looked like a starving child. "I thought maybe we could work something out," Dallas said, "then it just hit me on the way up."

"Just like that?"

"Just like fucking that."

Leighton smiled. "You should have brought Randi. You're no fun without Randi." He picked up the pistol. "Now get the hell out of here before I make some tree hugger cry tears of joy."

"Just so long as you know we're through."

It rained through the walls of his dream and they drove with the wipers streaking the windshield, heads bent forward so that they inhaled the defrost cancering the glass. The old man and his resurrected wife again in the yard of what had once been their home, this place he knew so well, the falling rain and dying light that folded over the house. Except there was no house now, only a space of dust where it should have stood, the ground loamy and churned, even the foundation removed. They walked through the rain, hand in hand like the lovers they never really were, and found everywhere the orange flags of surveyors.

"The Lord will leave us enough," Evelyn said. "We will suffice."

"He ain't left nothing."

"Then nothing," she said, "will suffice."

Elijah let go her hand and stared down to where the orchard had once been, the shed, the well house—all gone—and when he looked back it was not his wife in her Wishbook shoes but his old granny, her hair like broom straw, a feedbag of penny candy for all the younguns. He was ten years old and she examined his hands, front, back, nails, and fingers—Lord have mercy, what working them fields is done to your hands, child. They had subsisted on stubborn insistence, eating the air, the refusal not to go on as precious as the summer haul of vegetables, but he saw now the fruit had been anger and then resignation, and then, ultimately, despair. He had carried it across the ocean, seeded in the heart, that spore of desperation that rattled in the lungs.

He looked back at his wife, her mouth set, fists balled on her hips.

"He will provide," she said.

Then kinfolk began to rise from the dust, surrounding him like stalks of corn, pale and wizened and impossibly thin, and he traveled back across the ocean, the dry rot crumbling away from his heart as surely as the ports of call—San Diego and Pearl Harbor and Subic and Okinawa and finally the C-130 that had skimmed the green mountains—and remembered again how important it was to keep your feet dry, remembered the way you scratched in your sleep from the mosquitoes, a foxhole and an olive drab tarp, a little rain in the bottom like discarded self, nothing more. Remembered the paddy and the way she lay on the metal slab—the great purple impression that was her head, and then the coroner pointing and saying "Windshield"—and then he began to pray while around him his kinfolk went out like lamps, the yard unpeopled, empty as he knew it would remain. *He will provide.* But he would not, and now Elijah was running out of air. He prayed, failed, started over, and failed again.

"It's all going quick now," she said.

And then there was no air, nothing to breathe and he looked up—above him hung the Chinook, the wind pressing his fatigues against his body—tried to swallow the rotorwash. Shut his eyes to the noise. But nothing to fill the lungs because, ultimately, he had failed. He would not go on. He looked up again: another figure above him, hunched and stiff as a towel left too long on the line. The devil, perhaps, or God. He'd seen the devil once before, spitting into an open grave in the Ia Drang. *Had I breath to accuse,* he thought, *I would accuse You.* But it wasn't the devil he saw. And it wasn't God. It was Preacher Dell who stood over him as if in saddest parting because how could he have forgotten? How could he have deluded himself? He'd thought his war over, but there was this last fight to lose. And I have lost it.

The last enemy to be destroyed, he remembered, is Death.

He walked into the foyer and brushed rain from his sleeves and slung his head so that water sprayed the door and ran down the frame in narrow courses.

"Soaked to the damn bone," Dallas said.

Malcolm could hear him from where he sat in the front room with the old man. The hospice nurse had come and gone, and it was only a matter of time, though, she had made clear, not much time. She gave Malcolm her cell number and asked him to call when it was necessary. There were formalities to be attended to, a death certificate, the funeral home. But don't feel rushed, she told him. Allow yourself to experience the moment.

Dallas stood on the threshold and Malcolm saw Randi brush past him to the kitchen.

"You have any coffee?" Dallas asked.

"Nothing fresh."

"She'll put some on. What did the hospice lady say?"

It was around six in the evening. A late-afternoon thunderstorm had steamed the air so that vapor shimmered up to warp the blacktop. Malcolm had the air conditioner off and the windows up. He sat in the rocker, Dallas collapsed in the lawn chair facing him. Randi came back with two cups of coffee and asked who was hungry.

"Nobody," Dallas said.

"There's still all this food."

"We'll come get something if we need it. Sit down with us."

The sleeves of her shirt were pulled down to her fingertips. She looked like a woman preparing for her own disappearance. "I'll be in here," she said.

"Sit down with us," Dallas said again.

"I'll be in here. Just say something if you need me."

Thereafter followed the waiting, the only sound that of the old man's troubled lungs: a scrape of breath, a moment of nothing, then the exhalation. Then more waiting as his failing body climbed toward respiration, the moments between growing longer, or perhaps only seeming longer.

Around eight Randi brought them plates of food—fried chicken, green beans, creamed corn, mashed potatoes—and they ate mechanically and without comment. Outside the evening drew down, dusk, cicadas and tree frogs calling from the reaches of the pond, the occasional car that whirred past, slatting shadows down the far wall. Time slanting jaggedly.

"Tillman should be here." Dallas heaved out of the lawn chair. "I should have gotten Tillman here. Fuck." He sat back down, stood. "Doesn't matter now."

Malcolm was quiet. He had only realized that the child sat in the corner, one arm curled around his legs.

"Goddamn it." Dallas walked to the window and sat again in his chair. "Goddamn it," he said quieter. "Is this the best chair we've got?"

When it grew full dark Malcolm shut his eyes. There was nothing now excepting the sound of his father's breathing. It seemed some larger force, responsible for tides or the migration of birds, and Malcolm found himself breathing in time, inhaling and exhaling only when he heard the old man do as much, and in those growing seconds he lived lifetimes, his mind bent with the clarity of self-asphyxiation. He was counting five seconds between breaths, too long, and stood abruptly. The rocking chair lurched and Dallas's eyes snapped open.

"What?" he said.

Malcolm shook his head. The darkness was soft and he saw clearly the face of his brother. "Nothing. Bathroom."

"What time is it?"

"I don't know. Late. Go back to sleep."

"Give him some more Ativan."

"He's all right. Go back to sleep."

Dallas lowered his head back into his hand.

Randi was asleep on the couch when he passed through. In the kitchen he opened a can of Coke and drank it by the sink, ate a handful of peanuts, and stared out the back window into the ambient glow of the streetlight, the hard shapes rounded by darkness.

She was sitting up with a blanket over her knees when he walked back through.

"You all right?" she asked.

"Yeah."

"You should try to sleep a little."

"I need to call the nurse as soon as the sun comes up."

Just before first light something began to gurgle in the old man's chest; his lips began to move. Malcolm flicked on the bedside lamp and woke Dallas, who stood at the footboard. The old man was trying to speak but what issued forth was the soft babble of a child, the spitting of a constricted hose. His head rose slightly.

"Oh, Jesus," Dallas said. "I wish Tillman were here. Tillman would know what to do."

"Don't talk," Malcolm said.

The head lowered, turned. Randi stood in the door, wild-eyed.

Malcolm sat back down and held the old man's hand while Dallas paced. He was rasping again, long shallow draws of breath, and Malcolm tightened like a line, felt the old man pull air through his throat and lungs like a string. The child was awake now.

"We should call his nurse," Dallas said. He was crying. Outside it was almost light.

"Not yet."

"Jesus Christ, why didn't I get Tillman here? I could've gotten him here."

Randi stood in the door frame like a trapped animal.

"I remember the first time I realized he was old," Dallas said. "I was home from the Marines and he came out in the morning, just for breakfast or something, and I remember he had this god-awful comb-over."

"Please don't talk," Malcolm said.

"And he was just standing there in a white T-shirt like he always wore. Pajama pants. But it was his hair—his hair was like standing up on end and just sort of floating over his head. That comb-over coming undone, peeling back. And he just looked so damn disoriented standing there. I was twenty-four, I guess, and I'd just always thought of him as this rock of a man, this mountain. The war hero. And there he was, standing barefoot with his hair sticking up like that."

"Please be quiet."

"I wish Tillman was here," Dallas said. "Tillman would know what to do."

The spaces lengthened to impossibility.

"Please," Malcolm said.

"We should call." Dallas looked at Randi, her face mascara-streaked. "We should call. Get the phone, baby. Get the phone." But instead of getting it she held him and he wept. "Get the phone," he said into the hollow of her shoulder.

"Please," Malcolm said.

The old man inhaled and exhaled while outside the sun began to rise. The child in the corner had not moved, and Malcolm leaned forward, impatient, fingers laced, awaiting the next breath.

But the next breath would not come.

VIII.

Early on the Saturday of Labor Day weekend, Dallas pulled into the yard, his pontoon hitched to the truck and loaded with fishing tackle. In the bed of the Dodge was a forty-liter Igloo secured with two bungee cords. He had iced two cases of Coors and a carton of Ripped Fuel, and packed a bottle of Johnnie Walker Blue in the truck box. Malcolm carried his bag out to the cab. The old man was five days in the ground and they were headed to the far shore of Lake Keowee for the long weekend. That the impact survey was scheduled for Sunday morning seemed not to matter to Dallas. Fuck em, he'd told Malcolm on the phone. I haven't talked to Leighton in weeks. They can have it.

They headed down the mountain and on through Walhalla, the U of Dallas's right triceps visible when his sleeve rode up, both forearms rivered with fat veins. His neck was a stump, his eyes glossed and shivering. He looked at Malcolm and back at the road.

"What?"

"You been working out this week?"

"Kinda been on a little jag the past few days. Trying to get my head right."

"You take anything?"

"Don't worry about me," Dallas said. "I'm a champion. I am a professional-grade, world-class world beater."

In Seneca Dallas's Blackberry vibrated in the cup holder. He thumbed the keyboard and handed the phone to Malcolm. "That's from your uncle right there. The glorious fat bastard."

The message read:

AND WHEN JESUS CAME INTO THE RULER'S HOUSE, AND SAW THE MINSTRELS AND THE PEOPLE MAKING A NOISE, HE SAID UNTO THEM, GIVE PLACE: FOR THE MAID IS NOT DEAD, BUT SLEEPETH. AND THEY LAUGHED HIM TO SCORN.

"Write him back and tell him to go fuck himself," Dallas said.

"Just drive."

"You think I'm joking, but I'm completely serious."

Malcolm rested the phone back in the cup holder.

"You're no fun today," Dallas said. "Big goddamn surprise."

Near the lake, firework stands gave way to real estate offices and vacated strip malls, a flea market that was already filling with pickups and old Caprices and Town Cars. Muddy fields cleared of pine. Signs for lake communities. KEOWEE KEY. POINTS WEST. A new banner going up that read: BLUE WATER ACRES. They drove to a bait-and-tackle shop that served breakfast on folding tables. Bass arching off wall mounts. Old Tiger football posters on the block walls. Steve Fuller and Refrigerator Perry. Danny Ford's jaw packed with Red Man. Dallas moved through the room, slapping backs and shaking the hands of the local old-timers who sat in Dickies coveralls or Mossy Oak T-shirts.

"It's a new day," Dallas said when their breakfast arrived. "Don't mope on me."

"I'm not moping," Malcolm said. "I'm just waking up."

Dallas smiled. On the table sat a bottle of King's Syrup and a plastic bear filled with honey. He took one in each hand and spread them on his plates, swirled the mixture until the glittery black and gold was a single tar-like substance. "Remember how Daddy would mix this? Sit at the table every morning and gobble down a pan of biscuits. Told me once he had Tillman thinking it was a miracle cure, some old-time mountain potion. You want some?"

"I'm allergic to honey."

"You're shitting me. How did I not know that?" Dallas pointed with his fork. "See, that's the kind of thing I should know. I'm gonna learn that kind of shit."

"All right."

Dallas tore a feathery biscuit with his teeth, syrup stringing and pooling on the plate, thick as cake batter. "You're 'all righting' me, but I'm serious. I'm a new man. I started thinking about Tillman even. The guy can't help it—I need to remember that. And he's family, after all. My new belief is that all things are possible."

The lot where Dallas's lake house sat appeared neat and bare but for the high pines with their lower limbs trimmed to sap-blistered stubs. Past the trailer, the yard sloped to the red bank that dropped a foot or so into Lake Keowee.

"The sun is the cure," Dallas said, standing on the back deck. "We ride around the lake, drink a few tallboys. The good old boys will be shooting fireworks tonight, thinking it's the Fourth of July."

It was only eleven when they backed the pontoon down the ramp but the lake was already a chaos of boats and Jet Skis. Every lake house and trailer occupied, men and women out on blankets or tethered to docks on giant floats big enough to accommodate four. Kids bounced on inflatable trampolines. Radios played Bad Company and Aerosmith and Bob Seger. Everyone raising their bottles in salute as the pontoon motored through the desultory heat, Dallas hugging the shoreline and drinking beer, mirrored Ray-Bans hiding his eyes. His mood had sunk and Malcolm sat opposite him and nursed a bottle of water. Neither spoke. The clouds had blown over and the sky was perfectly blue and perfectly empty, only the white glare of the sun directly overhead.

They held to their course past dockside restaurants and a marina, weekend shacks, and monstrous glass houses pitched on steep banks cleared of trees, the only vegetation the browning ferns that lined the pea gravel walkways that led to the shore. Further out, the water was zippered with the plowlines of boats and skiers, the surface a wash of foam. The air smelled of gasoline and ozone, and in the stolid heat Malcolm sensed the absent presence of the old man, always a little past them, his bladed ghost just beyond the next bend, while the two brothers pressed on as if they might arrive at whatever place he now inhabited, slowly and patiently, as if they lacked for many things—comfort, relief—but never for time.

"Hungry," Dallas said finally.

He stood behind the console, one hand on the wheel, the other on the throttle. In the open cooler were six or seven empty Budweiser cans. "There's a little place near here. Burgers and fries." Dallas crushed his beer and popped another. "That breakfast didn't do a thing but upset my stomach."

They anchored on a sandbar and waded ashore. The restaurant was an old carnival food cart with barking seals and clowns faded from around a window marked ORDERS. Between the cart and the water were several picnic tables and a pit for horseshoes. A man in jeans and a greasy apron cooked their burgers on a charcoal brazier and they sat in the shade and listened to the meat spit grease.

"Randi thinks I might be bipolar," Dallas said. "She thinks I need grief counseling. I think I just need my dick sucked." He lifted his beer and held it just beyond his lips. He had taken his shirt off and sat massive and hulking, eyelids sagging so that he appeared sleepy and unkind, a lazy snap-turtle half-submerged in warm mud. "Shut up," he said. "I know I'm drunk."

He threw his can against a telephone pole and it spilled into the dust. "It wasn't like this losing Mamma. With Daddy—" His face was pink and the sallow skin around his eyes gave him a slightly goggled look. "I'm sorry about before," he said, "with Tillman and all."

"You don't have to apologize."

"He just wears me out sometimes. And I feel like I'm on edge as it is. This business with Leighton. One minute I think I'm headed to prison. The next I think it's all just a big joke. They do another impact survey in the morning."

"Maybe that'll be the end of it then."

Dallas smiled. "I've done a lot of stupid shit in my life. It's like there's this magnetic attraction or something. You know I haven't even told Marilynn about Daddy yet? Her grandfather's dead and as far as I know she doesn't have a clue." He put his arms on the table. "You want to head back? Rest up for tonight?"

"All right."

They pushed off and let the boat drift.

"I don't know, brother," Dallas said. "We might yet be worth saving."

Malcolm was asleep on the couch when Dallas came in the trailer door with several sacks of groceries and a can of Ripped Fuel.

"Don't get up," Dallas said. "This is all of em."

Malcolm followed him into the kitchen.

"I had a power nap and hit the Bi-Lo," Dallas said. "Now I'm going to shower and fix us a feast. Pork chops. Wild rice." He pulled off his collared shirt and threw it over the back of a chair. "I got stuffed peppers in the bag there. I got a watermelon in the cooler," he called, walking back to the bedroom.

He came out clean and buoyant, dressed in khaki shorts and a Chattooga Estates golf shirt. Malcolm sliced carrots and tomatoes for a salad while Dallas moved around the kitchen tending assorted pots and pans.

"The thing," Dallas said, "and this just hit me driving back—but the thing is that I'm happy to be here. I am. And I can mope around and act like a whiner or I can be glad to be alive. I can drink beer and have a good time with my baby bro or I can just sit here and act like a spoiled brat. I hated that old son of a bitch, but I loved him, too. Loved him more than I hated him. It just took me a while to figure that out."

They ate on the porch in the cool of the waning day. Around them minivans and trucks pulled into the surrounding driveways, the red brake lights blinkered down the narrow lane.

"You know people," Dallas said, "the great mystery of it all, whatever you want to call it, they always see sex sitting right at the center. Sex and fighting and Jesus, I guess—that southern cross. But all I want right now is to sit on this porch, sip a glass of tea. I'd be happy doing that for the rest of my life."

"Simple man."

"Southern man," he said, and sipped his drink. "I'm not the person you think I am, Malcolm. I'm a better person than this."

"I know who you are."

"It's just that the good gets stuffed down beneath so much ridiculous shit."

"I know exactly who you are."

It was after nine by the time they eased the boat out of the cove, still light though dusk was near so that they motored with their running lights on, the air warm and soft. Fireworks were already going up along the far shore, snowy streaks that burst red and white in the clear night. Dallas stood at the wheel and drank Johnnie Walker.

"Beautiful," he said. "Just smell that air."

Forty minutes later the lights of South Vegas appeared, giant neon letters reflected in the bleary water. PARTY TONIGHT! LIVE BAND! pulsing like a heart. Boats were tied up all along the dock and they could see the gravel parking lot full of cars and trucks, past it an ABC package store and a Phantom fireworks stand. They slowed by a NO WAKE buoy and tied up at the flotation dock. Dallas finished his drink, threw the ice in the water, and tossed his Nalgene bottle back into the boat.

"Wait a second." He took his Blackberry from his pocket. "You mind holding onto that for me?"

It was packed inside and past the bouncers men sat at the bar and leaned over drinks, while women in short-shorts held server trays and snaked between tables. Several TVs played a drag race, the NHRA logo levitating above the words SPEED CHANNEL.

"Here's my girl," Dallas said.

The bartender's name was Cheyenne or Dakota or something else Dallas couldn't remember, only her spiky blond hair and purple eye shadow that arched onto her temples like fairy wings.

"Dallas Walker," she said, "my, my," and smiled, wet light on the pearl of her tongue stud. "How long has it been?" She leaned both forearms on the bar and let her tank top fall open on a dark push-up bra, close enough that Malcolm could see the sparkles in her eye shadow. She put a silver fingernail on Dallas's chest. "Little brother here have a name?"

"This is Malcolm."

"Howdy, Malcolm."

"Let's get a tab going here." Dallas handed her a credit card. "Johnnie and Coke, for me."

"What about baby brother?"

"What about it, Malcolm?"

"Ginger ale."

"Ginger ale." The woman spray-gunned the drink into a glass. "Daring."

They sat in a booth against the far wall and watched a conga line wind past. A waitress kept bringing over drinks and Dallas kept sucking them down. "Shit," he said, and spread his arms. "Me and you, out like this. That makes me so happy I could almost cry. Let me see my phone back for a second. Take a look at this."

Dallas passed the Blackberry back as a video began to play, grainy enough for it to take Malcolm a moment to realize he was looking at a woman. Then it occurred to him the woman was—

"Please," he said, and slapped the phone back across the table. "That's—"

"Randi. I shot it the other night."

"Please, put that away."

"What's wrong?"

"For God's sake, please."

Dallas threw back his head and howled. "Jesus, what the hell is wrong with me?" He put the screen face down. "I'm sorry. God, I'm sorry. She doesn't even know I shot that."

"Just please—Let's forget it."

"The phone was just right there on the nightstand. She'd kill me if she knew. God, I'm a fuckup."

"Let's just forget it."

Dallas put his head in his hands. Behind him on the wall was a black-and-white photo of Merle Haggard. "Man, I am so sorry."

"Forget it."

"You know I have this feeling sometime," he said. "Like—you realize I was born perfectly between two wars: too young for Vietnam and too old for Iraq. I mean there've been all these other little wars but nothing like those." He stopped. "What the hell am I saying? I'm gonna hit the head."

"You wanna get some food?"

"All I want to do is take a piss."

Malcolm watched him stagger across the crowded dance floor. A few minutes later Randi called.

"Where's is he?" she wanted to know.

"The bathroom. We're at some club. Everything okay?"

"Yes," she said, "or no. Definitely no, everything's not all right. Tell him to call me the second you see him."

Malcolm put the phone in his pocket and walked to the bathroom. No sign of Dallas. The band was playing Junior Kimbrough and he waded toward the stage but couldn't find Dallas there either. He got another ginger ale and sat back down. The phone went off again, this time a text from Tillman.

SO HE SENT HIS BROTHERS AWAY, AND THEY DEPARTED:
AND HE SAID UNTO THEM, SEE THAT YE ARGUE NOT ALONG THE WAY.

The band finished their set with the Stones' "Far Away Eyes" and karaoke began, a woman lilting into a Loretta Lynn number before dissolving in laughter. Randi called again but Malcolm let it go to voice mail. A little while later he saw Dallas cross the room and followed him down a long hall and through a beaded curtain, reaching the back just as a woman in a yellow rain jacket and boots came on stage.

Dallas and another man were in a red leather banquette, surrounded by strippers and several bottles of Jameson whiskey. Wisps of thinning fog. Rap music.

"Malcolm," Dallas yelled. "Malcolm, come here. I lost you in there, bro." He pushed the girl off his lap. "Look here. You won't believe what the pussycat dragged in. This old son of a bitch here is Mitchell Conrad. Mitchell, this woe-is-me gentlemen is my baby brother, Malcolm. Sit down with us, Malcolm." Dallas tipped his chair back onto two legs. "Me and Mitch, we used to wolf-pack the ladies in Athens. Drove em like sheep."

"Delta Tau Delta," Conrad said.

"The Downtown Daddies. We'd love em and leave em. But we got a task before us tonight, Mitch. We've got to turn this boy's frown upside down."

Conrad looked at him as if appraising a used car. "What's wrong with you, Malcolm?"

"A girl just threw him out of her life."

"Well, you know what they say: sometimes the best way to get over one girl is to get on top of another."

"Man," said Dallas, "I needed you today. Where were you?"

"Told my wife I was cleaning out the basement but I just sat in the boat and drank beer." He looked at Malcolm. "Basement flooded back in the spring when we had all the rain. The water's out but I've got mud a foot deep. I get out of that shithole and all I want to do is smoke a fattie. Throw that Shop-Vac in the lake."

Dallas motioned at a chair. "Sit down, bro, and tell this young lovely what the name Herschel Walker means to you?"

"I swear I recognize you," the girl said. She looked nineteen with narrow little-boy hips and silicone breasts.

"TV, baby," Dallas said. "I'm practically famous." He pointed with his glass. "Come on, Malcolm, tell her about me going off tackle. Tell her about Dallas Walker."

Malcolm tossed Dallas's Blackberry into his brother's lap. "Randi called."

"What?"

"Your wife called."

Dallas smiled. "That's irrelevant. Tonight I'm rigged for speed, not comfort. Hear what I'm saying, doll?"

The girl put a finger on Dallas's chin, turned his head, and kissed him.

"Sit down here and have a good time with us," Dallas said. "He's trying to get over his lady friend," he told the woman.

"I'll get you over your lady friend," said a woman with a single teardrop inked by the corner of her left eye.

Dallas motioned around the table. "This is us getting over things," he said. "This is us living our lives."

"No, thanks."

"Seriously," Dallas said. "They got my card up front. This is all on me."

"I'm not interested."

"Come on, Malcolm. Take you a good sniff." Conrad shivered. "Damn if cocoa butter don't get my shit in locomotion."

"Don't mind him," Dallas said.

Conrad threw back his head and sang. "Can't you see? Lord, can't you see? What that woman—"

"He's just drunk is all."

"Shit, yes, I'm drunk." Conrad started laughing. "Don't call my wife."

Malcolm walked to a table at the back, the room a hangar-like expanse of risers and banquettes that led down to the stage. A waitress came toward him and he waved her off. Farther down, a woman in four-inch heels climbed onto a table and began to stomp. Past her he could just see the backs of Dallas's and Conrad's heads and the four or five girls that gravitated around them.

Sometime later Malcolm started for the bathroom but stopped at the sight of someone he thought he knew. Two men sat at a round-top table cluttered with seven or eight empty martini glasses and wads of shredded napkins, a green candle giving them the sickly pallor of plague survivors. One of the men waved him over.

"You look lost, amigo," the man said. His forearm read *JUIF ERRANT*. "Why don't you sit down and join us."

The second man put his face down and began to laugh.

"I was just heading to the bathroom," Malcolm said.

"Just sit down for minute and chat," the first man said. "I got some bad Saturday night fever."

Malcolm stood at the edge of their booth. The air was full of perfume and cigar smoke, but the room was cold—this suddenly occurred to him. Then something else did, too.

"Brother Rick," he said without thinking.

The man smiled. "My *nom de guerre*. But I prefer just plain Rick."

"I saw you before."

"I'm all over the place. Light and truth—that's my worldview. Let's not hide it under a bushel." He nodded at the booth. "So you ain't sitting, partner?"

The second man began to giggle and opened his fingers as if to reveal something. On his shirt was the silhouette of an M-16 above the words: THE BROTHERHOOD OF THE TREE OF LIBERTY.

"Boom," he said. "We're coming to get all of you."

Miles shook his head. "Don't listen to him."

"Most fun we'll ever have." He had curled onto the table, one cheek against the Formica and a glimmer of saliva trembling like oil in a skillet. "Got people in the parking lots. Got bats and shit."

"Shit-Toe here's just messing with you. Why don't you sit down and we'll order another round? I think you might be my flavor."

"No thanks."

"I promise I taste a lot better than I look."

"I don't think so."

Malcolm walked to the bathroom and was facing the urinal when the door opened behind him.

"How do you know, Brother Rick?" a voice asked. It was the second man, Shit-Toe, Miles had called him. Malcolm zipped himself up but did not turn.

"I don't know him."

"Well, he seems to know you." The man was very close, just off his right shoulder and edging closer. "He's a maniac, but smart as a whip. I wouldn't plan on fucking with him."

"I don't." Malcolm could smell him, a fog of aftershave and feral stink. The word *venereal* came to mind, a venereal stench. "How about backing off?"

"It's just that these are crazy times, is all. It's in the air, in the water." Shit-Toe rested a hand on Malcolm's elbow and Malcolm jerked away.

"Ain't no call to be rude."

"I said how about backing off?"

He crawled his fingers to the outside of Malcolm's thigh and Malcolm turned away, walked to the sink and put his hands beneath the automated faucet, Shit-Toe palms up and plaintive in the mirrors, eyes watering and blood-bright.

"I'm just saying, baby. The man's a machine," Shit-Toe said. "Eats nothing but raw food. Live and active cultures. Reads a book a day. I seen him pop the head off a rattler one day. Just—pop—and there it was. You best police your shit up before you mess with Brother Rick." He turned and stopped by the door. "You don't remember me, do you?" he asked. "Two years behind you in high school and you don't even know my fucking name." He looked genuinely hurt.

Malcolm dropped his head. "I'm sorry."

Shit-Toe waved him off. "Don't matter. Shit was years ago. I was on the fringes."

"I'm bad with names anyway."

"Shit don't mean a thing."

Malcolm stood at the sink until he was gone.

When he passed on his way back Miles and Shit-Toe had just tossed back shots and were waving over another round. Shit-Toe smiled with an olive clenched between his rotten teeth. Malcolm walked back to his table. Sometime later the teardrop girl came up and sat in his lap and began to twirl his hair around one finger.

"Honey," she said. "I'm so bored I could die."

She felt like a bird, slender to the point of emaciation, the tip of one pelvic bone against his stomach. He looked at the teardrop, heavy and perfectly formed, always on the cusp of falling.

"Let's go party," she said. "Come on, baby."

She stood and took his hand and he followed her down the risers, past Rick Miles—there was a third man with him now—past Dallas and Conrad, and back into the narrow hall past an ATM and cigarette machine. When she stepped into a side room he kept walking, on through the beaded curtain and across the dance floor where people were line-dancing in front of the stage, not stopping until he was at the pontoon. Across the water fireworks streaked up from the trees, flowered red and gold, and sank toward the water leaving spiders of smoke, gray and diffuse.

He sat down in the boat, suddenly happy beyond belief.

It had just come to him. There is a moment, he thought, when you realize what is possible, and that what is possible is everything. The Simone Weil he had read in the spring: *any human being . . . can penetrate the kingdom of truth . . . if only he longs for truth and perpetually concentrates all his attention upon its attainment.* The truth Jefferson had been unable to grasp, or perhaps had grasped too clearly. Still, there was no reason, really, not to call Jordan, to actually try to reach her. He would fix things, explain that it was all a mistake, a plan set in motion before he had ever met her. He wasn't going to Haiti; he was going wherever she was, or—and the idea burst in his mind—he wasn't going without her. He would go to her, explain things: a school for orphans; a place for people like us. We spend a year there, let things settle. Maybe we come back. Maybe not. Let's not worry about that now. Let's just go. He realized he was smiling. Everything was possible. Love. Salvation. A sliver of God revealed like the Cherokee canoe.

He watched couples stagger out toward their cars and sometime later walked back inside. There was no sign of Dallas and eventually he circled the building to the parking lot where he found him alone and collapsed by a

Porta-John. Malcolm rolled him onto his back and brushed sand from his face. The gravel had textured his skin to a crosshatching of bulges and his right eye had almost swollen shut so that he looked not unlike a larger, fuller version of the child.

"Fuck." Dallas spat, wiped the blood on one sleeve. "Fuck. Where's my wallet?"

It was in his pocket; so too was his Blackberry.

"Fuck," he said. "Help me up."

"What happened?"

"Help me up."

They staggered down toward the dock.

"That dumb fuck and two of his pervert buddies. I sent one to the hospital."

Fireworks burst above the water.

"Where's Conrad?" Malcolm asked.

"Fuck Conrad."

Dallas lay in the floor of the boat and began to laugh. "I took that nine iron right out of that asshole's hands. Fucking James Earl Ray on his arm, talking his faggot shit. He said you went back with him."

"What?"

"Let's just get out of here."

Malcolm untied them and started the engine.

Dallas put an opened beer can to his face. "I can't feel a goddamn thing," he said.

"Help me get back."

"I'm drunk."

"There're a thousand coves on this lake. Help me get back."

"I took that nine iron right out of his fucking hand."

"Dallas."

"I never had my war," he said, and started to cry. A moment later he was snoring.

After thirty minutes Malcolm began dipping into coves, slowing as he neared the docks, accelerating out when he failed to recognize anything. He couldn't wake Dallas and kept driving, the air growing chill as night wound toward morning. After almost an hour he cut the engine and rolled Dallas unto his stomach. He splashed ice water from the cooler onto Dallas's face and Dallas whimpered and stirred but didn't wake. The boat drifted toward another cove, the lake silent but for the tree frogs. He could smell the pines.

"Wake up." He dipped Dallas's face into the cooler, first just his forehead, then his entire head. "Wake up." He plunged in his head again and then over and over. "Wake up. Wake up." Dallas began to gasp, water up his nose, coughing and gagging though still not awake, and finally vomiting onto the carpet, and it came over Malcolm that this was a form of torture, and that he had become its instrument. His brother lay in his vomit and Malcolm started to cry, very softly, then looked up and realized they had drifted into the right cove after all.

They left the lake house around four, Malcolm at the wheel and Dallas leaned against the door, his damaged face cradled in one hand. Malcolm drank one of Dallas's Ripped Fuels and dropped two more in his bag. When they got to Walhalla, Dallas asked him to check his voice mail. Malcolm listened and sat the phone back in the cup holder.

"It was Randi. She said come home. It's an emergency."

"What kind of emergency?"

"That's all she said. 'Come home. It's an emergency.'"

"Just drop me off and take the truck. I'll get it tomorrow."

They were headed up the mountain when the blue lights appeared behind them. Malcolm pulled onto the shoulder and a deputy walked forward carrying what appeared to be the plastic lid off an ice chest. He asked for Malcolm's license and registration and studied them by flashlight.

"Are you aware that things have been blowing out of your truck for the last half-mile, sir?" he asked.

"Go fuck yourself," Dallas slurred. "We're just two good old boys."

The deputy put the light on Dallas's face. "Is he intoxicated? Are you intoxicated, sir?"

Dallas had begun to sing: "Straightening the curves, flattening the hills—"

"I'm taking him home," Malcolm say. "I'm sorry about the lid."

"I'm not drunk," Dallas said stoically.

The deputy put the light back on him. "Sir, I'm going to ask you to shut your mouth."

"I'm taking him home," Malcolm repeated. "We're going home."

The deputy hesitated, then returned Malcolm's license. "Both of you," he said. "It's late."

"Fuck you," Dallas said. "Do you know what's happened to my brother here?"

"Dallas," Malcolm said.

"Do you know what she did to him? Do you have any fucking idea?"

"I'm going to ask you just once more shut your mouth, sir." He turned to Malcolm. "I see either of you back out you're both going to jail."

"Do you have any idea where's she at?" Dallas yelled at the retreating figure.

The deputy cut his blue light and pulled onto the road past them. When he was gone Malcolm turned to his brother. "What are you talking about?"

Dallas sank into the seat and shielded his face. "I shouldn't have encouraged you like I did. This whole weekend, I mean. This whole summer. You know where's she at."

Malcolm looked at him. Dallas's right eye was pinched shut. With his hand up he appeared to be hiding.

"You want to find her you go to Leighton's," Dallas said. "She's been at Leighton's since she left. Since before then. He's pays her or something. Drugs, I guess." Dallas's head rolled back on the headrest. "And don't fucking look at me like that. We've all spent the last four months lying to ourselves."

Dawn had not yet broken when he pulled into Dallas's yard.

Dallas opened the door but did not get out. "Why don't you come in," he said after a moment. "Might as well stay the night."

"It's all right. Go see about Randi."

"It wasn't supposed to turn out like this."

"It never is."

Malcolm waited until his brother was in the front door and pulled back onto the highway and drove home. The sky was graying, but the moon was still up, a few stars pinpricked beyond it. It was warm, but he sensed some cold construction pulling him, the guylines tight against his skin. It was clear now why he had been spared the antifreeze, why the child had appeared, and Malcolm was all purpose, all cold articulation.

He passed through the house and out the kitchen door to the shed where he found a bottle of 3-in-One oil and a gas can. In his room he kneeled beneath Grunewald's Christ and took the walnut box from beneath the bed, removed the pistol, and unfurled the chamois. With a wire coat hanger he ran an oil-soaked rag through the barrel and cylinders. The bullets were in a small cardboard box marked Remington Mag Jacketed Hollow Point. He inserted them, spun the chamber, and stared up at Christ.

"I didn't understand anything before," he said. "I get that now."

He took his time showering and shaving, washing off the stench of the club, careful of every detail, the attentive suitor dressed in a blue suit he had not worn in a year. The pistol went in the back waistband of his pants, the jacket covering it. In the nightstand he found the knife—Jordan's knife—and slid it into his sock. Another of Dallas's Ripped Fuels went in a bag he slung over his shoulder. And all of it—the preparation—it was so much like that morning he'd left Mary Ann to wake Will, the way he'd whispered into her hair, the way he'd sweated beneath the wool hood. His self-crucifixion had left nothing pure—he saw that now. He had once imagined he possessed a savant's stutter of perception, and had looked at his congregation and thought he understood entire lives. A martyr who knew too well the ways of those who rushed to cut him down. But he had been wrong. He had thought himself separate.

He was not.

In the kitchen he drank a second Ripped Fuel, left the bottle in the sink, and carried the gas can to the attic where he bathed first the slopes of his war and then the surrounding books and walls. A trail ran to the trapdoor and there he lit the edge of a cardboard box and pushed it toward the dark fluid. The fire leapt up and began licking the box. He watched it until it found the brown felt of Fort Wagner and he knew, finally, their war was over, the Winter House smited. Then he got in Dallas's truck and left.

It was around five thirty in the morning when he pulled into Clyde Dell's yard. The preacher lived in a small farmhouse collapsed onto its cracked foundation, shutters off center and a wasp nest bulging beneath the eave. Brown Masonite siding. Tangled azaleas and several pecan trees. Past the house was a shed for the well pump, and past that a wooden cross erected in the dust of the backyard, slender as spirit.

Malcolm took Dallas's Blackberry from the cup holder, scrolled back to Tillman's last text and hit "Reply." IF THIS CUP MAY NOT PASS AWAY FROM ME, EXCEPT I DRINK IT, he typed. THY WILL BE DONE. When he hit "Send" he smelled the gas on his fingers.

He crossed the lawn and knocked at the door. Through the part in the curtain he could see Dell's hunched figure in the kitchen. When he opened the door Malcolm smelled bacon and wet carpet.

"Malcolm," Dell said. "It's good to see you this morning."

"Can I come in a minute, preacher? I know its early."

"Sure, sure." He stepped back from the door. "I was just fixing Annabelle some breakfast. How are you?"

Toward the back Malcolm saw Dell's wife, a misshapen bulk resting in a hospital bed behind a nightstand jumbled with Styrofoam cups and amber medicine phials.

"Could we talk for just a minute?" Malcolm asked.

"Of course. Come in the kitchen here."

The kitchen was full of baskets and cow-shaped knickknacks, a popsicle cross on the refrigerator. Old linoleum and a bird feeder knocking against the window.

"Let me get you some coffee," Dell said.

"That's all right."

"Sit down here and I'll have some bacon and eggs in just a minute."

"That's all right," Malcolm said, but sat anyway. "I really just wanted to ask something of you. I wanted to ask if you might pray for me."

"I pray for you every day, son."

"Right now, I mean."

Dell turned with a spatula in one hand.

"I think you might be the only decent man I know," Malcolm said. "I think you might be the only decent man I've ever met in my life."

Dell sat down across from him. He had big hands, and when he laid them on the table they looked like something one might dig out of a winter garden, some knotty gourd or tuber, the knuckles swollen and scratched. "Are you all right, Malcolm?"

"I don't know."

"Well, there ain't no burden in this world that don't get lighter when we take it to the Lord."

Malcolm nodded, the barrel of the .357 cold against his bare back.

"That ain't to say we won't suffer," Dell said. "But we won't never suffer alone when we call on Jesus' name."

"That's what I want you to do for me," Malcolm said. "I want you to call on Jesus' name for me."

Dell put his hands on Malcolm's wrists.

"Pray for me," Malcolm said. "I'm going to save a friend. I have to save her. No one else can save her."

Dell tilted back his head and stared into heaven. "Hear his prayer, Lord Jesus."

"I have to go to her," Malcolm said. "No one else can help her."

"'And Jesus came and spake unto them,'" Dell prayed, "'saying, All power is given unto me in heaven and in earth.'"

The barrel felt like another bone, a branch grown within him, stiffening. He could smell the eggs burning in the pan.

"'Go ye therefore, and teach all nations,'" said Dell, "'baptizing them in the name of the Father, and of the Son, and of the Holy Ghost: teaching them to observe all things whatsoever I have commanded you.'"

"Yes," said Malcolm.

"'And, lo, I am with you always, even unto the end of the world.'"

"Amen."

"Amen and amen." Dell let go of his hands and wiped his eyes. "I know right now your Daddy is looking down on you," he said. "I know how proud he must be." The look on Dell's face was joyous. His glasses seemed to catch all the light of morning. "'This is the day,'" he said, "'that the Lord hath made.'"

Randi was on the front porch holding closed the neck of her gown when Dallas came up the steps. She had showered, her hair matted against her neck, and looked, Dallas thought, years older than when he'd left. Beneath the motion light circled a cloud of moths and he stopped only long enough to look at Randi's hand, to watch it float in the space between them, thinking all the while what a pathetic thing the human hand really was, so utterly delicate, yet beautiful, too, somehow beautiful there in the soft glow. She said nothing, reached two fingers to Dallas's face, but did not touch him.

"Please don't ask," he said. "I know it's late—or early."

"I wasn't sleeping anyway."

He stood in the kitchen while she fixed coffee. The counters were empty, wiped clean and flashing spirals of silvered moisture. A plate and saucer were stacked in the sink and several glasses were cloudy with grainy solutions. Beneath the streetlight, he watched the leaves of a gingko tree tremble with the breeze, their undersides translucent and veined. One floated free to drift down, swirling for a moment before coming to rest in the yard, a quiet rustle he imagined but could not hear.

They walked into the living room and sat thigh to thigh on the couch.

"You came back," she said.

"Obviously."

"I didn't know. The way you tore out of here. Then I kept calling."

"Your emergency."

"But you never answered."

He kept his busted eye turned from her. "I told Malcolm about Jordan."

"What did he say?"

He waited for what seemed days. "He didn't say anything."

She picked up her coffee and put it down, walked into the kitchen and poured a glass of red wine, stood in the doorway with the bottle. "You want some of this? I mean if we're going to do this."

"What is it we're doing? I'd rather not do anything."

"Yes or no?"

"All right," Dallas said. "I guess."

She sat, and both of them looked down into their drinks, past their drinks at the graining of the polished floorboards. He could sense her waiting for him to speak and said finally: "Here's the thing, baby. I really don't want to get into this right now. I don't think I've got the energy."

She said nothing and Dallas thought of them together in another room. An apartment in Atlanta during that first year together. The windows up and the breeze blowing hot off the interstate. The bed was always unmade, the radio always on. He couldn't remember the address and that worried him, as if something irretrievable had been lost, the door shut on an entire epoch of their collective life. Somewhere west of here. That would have to do, he supposed. Somewhere west of where they now sat willfully ignoring their lives.

"I don't think I have what it takes," he said.

"That's fine," she said. "You should rest anyway."

He stood and walked to the window.

"What I wish right now," he said. "I wish I could take certain things back."

"Oh, baby."

"I really wish I could."

"Poor baby, you just can't take regret and make it a worldview. It doesn't work like that."

"Still."

He stared out at the sleeping yard. When he looked back she raised both hands and wine glass in a gesture of surrender, let them fall back to her knees.

"Let's go to bed," she said, and walked into the kitchen.

He heard her wine splash into the sink, nodded and walked past her to the bedroom where he lay on the side of the mattress, stared up at the ceiling with his feet on the floor. Randi stood in the doorway and tensed her hands.

"I'm scared of everything right now," she said.

"Let's sleep."

"What I called about, I was on the Stairmaster earlier and—"

"Let's sleep right now, baby. Let's rest."

He felt the bed shift with her weight and then she was beside him.

"I want settled, Dallas."

"That would be the word for it."

"These letters and texts. Running out at night to meet Leighton. I don't want that. I want it all like it was."

"I know you do."

Sometime later he heard her breath settle and then he was waking, no idea how much time had passed though light was beginning to pale the blinds. He slipped from the bed on down the stairs to the basement and his guns, stopped to see his reflection in the glass of the display case, his face beginning to discolor and swell. He looked at the antique rifles and turned and opened the safe.

It was empty.

It took him a moment to realize it. A moment longer to register what this might mean. Then a shadow crossed his body and he turned to find Randi standing in the door, crying with her right hand between her teeth.

"I didn't want to tell you," she said. "I thought if I didn't tell you—"

"Randi—"

"I called and then you didn't answer and I thought maybe—"

"Randi—"

"It was Leighton." She took her hand out of her mouth. "Leighton and another man. They came last night."

Malcolm parked at the foot of Leighton's drive to make the long walk up. Bison grazed the yellowed grass or lay like hulks of tattered carpet along the slope, but otherwise nothing moved, the morning still, the air weighted with the gamey tang of manure. He shifted the gun and readjusted his shirt. He was sweating, the dew having burned off the fields and the day just beginning to reek with heat.

When he reached the house, he walked onto the front porch and looked inside, saw no one, peered into the garage and saw Jordan's car. He circled to the back deck, past the hot tub where he had sat with the girl months ago, and climbed the stairs to the kitchen door. He smashed a pane with the pistol grip and reached in for the latch. Glass lay in shards on the tile, bright as the copper hood above the range, the silver Sub-Zero refrigerator. The kitchen vast and sleek and empty.

He crossed into the sunken living room and stood for a moment between two birds of paradise, ethereal torsioned stalks slim as a woman's wrist, walked to the foot of the spiral stairs he had watched her ascend. There was a sound from upstairs now, a dog barking. He held the pistol before him and started up. But the room was empty, the bed unmade, only the feist standing centered on the mattress.

It barked twice more and began to cry.

In the truck, Malcolm used Dallas's Blackberry to call his house. Randi answered on the first ring.

"Dallas?"

"It's Malcolm. Let me talk to him."

"You've got his phone?"

"He left it in the truck. Where is he?"

"God, I don't know where he is." She was breathless. "Do you know what's happening? Do you know what's going on? Oh God, I've got to calm down. I've got to calm down."

"Randi, listen to me."

"They're going to shoot those men, Malcolm. Those engineers doing the survey. It's why I kept calling last night."

"What are you talking about?"

"It's why I kept calling. Leighton and another man came by here yesterday looking for Dallas and wound up taking a bunch of guns out of his safe. I wasn't going to tell him but then—" She was gasping. "They're going to shoot those engineers when they get in the woods. He said they were going to ambush them. I told Dallas and he took off—"

"Where did he go?"

"He had this little machine gun I didn't know he had. God, I don't know where he is. I called the police—"

"What was he driving?"

"I told him and he just took off—"

"What was he driving, Randi?"

She started to cry and he took the phone from his ear while the pickup rattled over the Chauga River Bridge. Beneath the clanging he heard her repeating his name and hit END. It started ringing almost immediately, but before he could consider answering it he slung it into the brown slurry that foamed beneath him. No man who puts his hand to the plow and looks back is ready for the Kingdom of God.

When Malcolm turned onto the Forest Service road the sun that was just beginning to climb the horizon slipped into the upper boughs of the trees and diffused into an inky-green half-light. The canopy thickened and the gravel was patterned in shadow, time running back onto itself so that he slipped not toward day but back into the last hasp of night, as if the darkness refused absolution. He entered a clearing, passed the decrepit farmhouse, and reentered the forest gloom. The gate he remembered from his previous trip stood open and a little past it a police car sat on the shoulder, the right front tire in a ditch so that the cruiser canted forward like a toy. Malcolm pulled behind it and got out, the morning perfectly still. When the truck fan shut off he heard the gunfire—a series of shots, a pause, another series—and then the high wailing of dogs.

He walked behind the car and saw that the passenger door hung open, another step and he saw the man inside, crumpled behind the spidered windshield, his head tipped and his hands arranged neatly in his lap. The car was riddled with jagged holes, glass shattered and the manifold punctured. White puffs of stuffing spiraled out of the upholstery. Malcolm looked at the deputy in the driver's seat. A small entry wound like a stoma flowered at the base of his throat, dry now, but alive with dragonflies. But for the insects and blood that soaked his shirt he appeared to be sleeping.

Malcolm walked back to his truck. His hands trembled but he still managed to check the pistol's cylinder, shove it back into his waistband, and flip back the tail of his jacket. He slung his bag over one shoulder. The knife was still in his sock.

When he put the keys beneath the visor he saw the child in the passenger seat, his single eye bright with what appeared to be tears.

"You shouldn't ask these things of anybody," he told the child, though he knew the child had not. He said it again just to say it: "You shouldn't ask."

He walked along the shoulder until he spotted the dead dog, a pit bull that lay on its side as if exhausted, and was standing over it before he saw the crudely sutured gut fat with ball bearings. Wires ran from the slit to a cell phone half buried beneath leaves. He thought of the riddled police car and took a sudden step back just as someone pressed a gun barrel to the back of his head. He turned enough to see a tattooed forearm—*JUIF ERRANT*—turned a bit more to see the Walther PPK pushed against his temple.

"Stop right there," Rick Miles said. "Don't move a fucking muscle." He touched Malcolm's backpack. "What's in the bag?"

"Nothing. Some water."

"Give it here."

"It's just water."

"Well, you get thirsty you let me know."

Malcolm slipped it from his shoulder and felt the barrel move from his head. The man tapped one yellow fingernail on the handgrip and moved in front of him. Miles shirtless in a bed of glossy ferns, springs of black hair curled on his chest and what appeared to be a dead snake hung around his neck, its golden head smashed so that one eye had unpacked on a narrow red taper. A pit bull trotted out of the scrub to stand at his feet.

"You can't take a hint, can you?" Miles said. "What are you doing up here?"

"I need to see Leighton."

"You walk in?"

Malcolm nodded and Miles looked at some point past Malcolm and shook his head. "Fucking stupid," he said. "A goddamn police blockade and you just walk in, a half-step ahead of the cops."

The heat was intense, languid and wet. Malcolm hadn't felt it before but he felt it now, the way it sat on the face like oil. He'd drunk too much caffeine and sweat ran down his back.

"Leighton's expecting me," he managed to say.

"The hell he is."

"There's a woman with him."

"You know you're lucky I didn't IED your ass." The dog ground its head against his leg. "You done strayed, kitten. You done fucked up bad."

Malcolm looked around him. He was maybe a quarter-mile from the house, the road here a perfect plumb line cut through the oak and pine, the understory thick with stagger bush and scarlet sumac. Gnats were beginning to gravitate to his face but he kept his hands by his side. It felt as if he were deciding, but knew he had decided a long time ago.

"I'm not going back," Malcolm said.

"Well, you ain't going forward either."

"Then shoot me."

"After last night." Miles took a peanut from his pocket and threw it at the dog. "That's the wrong shit to say."

"Then let me see him. I just need to talk to him."

"Really?" He reached around Malcolm and took the .357 from his pants. "Cause that's a lot of firepower for a social call."

Malcolm started to move and Miles shifted the barrel between his eyes. Smoke was beginning to drift through the pines.

"Somebody's gonna come out here any minute," Malcolm said.

"Ain't nobody coming out, chief. Shep went after the Feds and the rest of em packed up and went home."

"The police—"

"Ain't no police coming. They're all sitting down there waiting for the helicopters. It's just you and me."

"Take me to Clatter then."

"Fuck Clatter and fuck you, too. I was just about to skip on out and here you go and complicate things."

"Then go. You don't have the power anyway."

Miles looked at him.

"I have the power," Malcolm said. "I carry with me the power of God."

"You got shit is what you got."

"'Contend, O Lord, with those who contend with me; fight against those who fight against me. I take up shield and buckler, brandish spear and javelin.'"

"You got a goddamn death wish."

"Take me to see Leighton then," Malcolm said. "Let him grant it."

They had reentered the forest when they came upon the second deputy. He had flattened a stand of mountain laurel and sat with his back to a tree, wilted petals and brass casings scattered around his legs. Crawl marks led past an abandoned pyramid of crossties soft with rot on back to the road. The air full of smoke and the howling of dogs.

"Please," the deputy whimpered.

One hand covered his eyes and the other held an empty pistol. Miles slapped the gun out of his hand and kicked him.

"Stop crying," Miles said.

A milky fluid ran from between his fingers and one ear was slashed, the lobe dangling, adorned with a ruby stud of dried blood. Three empty magazines lay in the dust.

"I said to stop fucking crying," Miles said.

"Please don't shoot me," the deputy said. He reached with his free hand up to Miles who knocked it away. "Please. I'm blind."

"Get up." Miles waved Malcolm forward. "Help him up. You are fucking up my war," he told the man. "Do you understand that? This is embarrassing."

Malcolm pulled him onto his feet and for a moment the deputy clung to him. He had wet his pants and dirt fell from the damp fabric. What was left of his eyes leaked between his fingers.

"Face him toward the road," Miles said. "Now get out of here, asshole."

"I can't see."

"Well, that right there's the voodoo of the human heart, now ain't it? Walk straight and somebody'll find you."

"Please don't shoot me."

"I said to fucking go."

"Please—"

"Goddamn it," Miles said, and kicked the man's rear. "This is a war zone. Would you please act like it?" He prodded him with the shotgun and the man stumbled. "Go."

He stumbled out toward the road, crying.

When he was gone, Miles put the gun back on Malcolm. "Onward, Christian soldier."

The house appeared through a cloud of butterflies, smoke boiling around a Confederate flag that hung limp in the dusty stillness, thicker as they walked down the muddy slope and passed from the relative cool of the shade into a fetid heat, Malcolm smelling the pens before he saw them, twelve-by-twelve chain-link kennels built on concrete and topped with heavy gauge vinyl. The dogs were pit bulls and most appeared to be unconscious with smoke inhalation, one placidly lapping water from a plastic container marked KOOL WHIP, languid despite the fire that crawled toward it.

They passed the pens and were headed behind the house toward the basement door when Malcolm saw Leighton Clatter's Navigator parked tight against the last trailer. So, he thought, he would find Jordan after all. It would happen, and he placed a finger in one wet palm to remember what he was about. He remembered his Bloy: *You do not enter paradise tomorrow, or the day after, or in ten years, you enter it today when you are poor and crucified.*

"Get on, Elvis," Miles said to the pit bull at his feet. He tossed it the dead snake, opened the screen door, and motioned Malcolm forward.

It was cool inside and he blinked against the darkness. Shapes. A large deep freeze that hummed like an incubator. Two grainy blurs it took Malcolm a moment to recognize as people. The man slept face down at a folding table covered with Barbie dolls in various states of undress, their bodies colored purple with a Sharpie. A sign hung around his neck and his face was streaked with pomade and sweat.

The woman slumped in a metal chair marked WALHALLA ASSEMBLY OF GOD. She had removed her leg braces and they rested in a puddle of urine, the glass pipe still between her fingers.

Miles slapped several Sudafed boxes. Outside a dog began to bark.

"Shit-Toe and his Chechnyan bitch," he said. "Fucking tweakers too ripped to skin out with the rest of the cowards."

Miles stepped toward him, lifted the sign that read DO NOT SHIT IN MY MOUTH, and cracked the back of his skull with the butt of the pistol. The head slumped forward onto the desk, a dark flower of blood blossoming between the follicles.

"I'm sick of him fucking up," Miles said.

"They're not dead," Malcolm said.

"It'd be a mercy if they were." He motioned toward the stairs. "Now get your ass up there."

Dallas headed down Whetstone and had hardly turned south on Rock Crusher Road toward The Settlement when two state police cars screamed past. A moment later came the sheriff and a moment after that a panel van marked SWAT. He was near the Westminster Speedway's abandoned dirt track when the helicopter skirted the treetops and rose toward the mountain's green spine, tail up and nose down, like an animal in hunt.

He swallowed the warm air that poured through the open window. Here was his war, assembling around him. Here was everything he'd ever wanted. He took a pull of Johnnie Walker from his Nalgene bottle and pressed the accelerator to the floor, past the racetrack's muddy oval and half-circle of metal bleachers, past the horse farms and ranch houses, the trailers with martin houses hung from clotheslines and satellite dishes mounted on fence posts.

He topped the rise doing ninety and had to jam the brakes when he saw the roadblock ahead. It appeared as a sudden panicked whole: police cruisers flashing their blue lights behind sawhorses and orange traffic barrels. Four, maybe five cars amid a scattering of guys in Smokey the Bear hats toting shotguns. An ambulance beside a news truck in the broad shade of a tulip poplar. Dallas slid off the shoulder onto the loose gravel, hopped back onto the asphalt, and finally came to a rest just in front of the barricade, a long peel of rubber smeared behind him.

A local cop came forward shaking his head and smiling. Everyone everywhere appeared to be smiling. Dallas lowered his window.

"You wanna shit and get, you better find another road," the cop said.

"What's going on here?"

"Is that a XJ?"

"Are you letting anybody through?"

"You were flying there, buddy. You got your license and registration on you?"

"What's happening up there?"

"You ain't turned a TV on? What's happening is the doom of man. Got us a regular war up there." He put one sunburned hand on the door panel. "I'll most certainly take that license about now."

Dallas leaned forward and when he did saw the cop's eyes shift to the Tec-9 resting on the passenger seat. His hand flew back toward his holster and Dallas flung open the door and jumped out of the car. The cop scrambled, reached for him, but Dallas stiff-armed him and ran for the sawhorses, thinking: *It's happening. It's happening right now.* A state trooper came forward and Dallas shoved him aside as well, untangled himself from a spindly cop, and holy shit, it was just like a punt return. He was running, back on the field, back in the game. He could hear the yelling and the distant gunfire and knew he had waited all his life for this. There was chaos but he sensed it as a happy chaos, the clarity of action, men jumping up only to be knocked aside by Dallas.

He thought he could run forever but went down just past the barricade. A beefy sheriff's deputy who planted his crew-cut head in the bend of Dallas's left leg. The old trick knee. A repaired medial collateral ligament repaired no more. The snap no more than a rubber band. Jesus, he thought in that moment of falling, I'll walk the rest of my life. And then the asphalt, the macadam glittery as glass. He went down like a dead bear and a moment later they were all over him, his face shoved against the ground and his wrists zip-tied behind his back. When they pulled him to his feet he saw the wake of his carnage: cops picking themselves up and readjusting radio belts, a state trooper walking up from Randi's Jag carrying the Tec-9 and the Nalgene bottle out from his body like contaminants. All of them giddy with disaster, thrilled to have blood on their faces. Several people were screaming but it was the big grain-fed deputy who had him. A defensive end, probably. Six foot three and maybe two fifty-five; four-seven wheels if they caught him on a good day.

"Get the fuck over there." The deputy shoved him forward and Dallas limped over to the ambulance, stood on one knee while someone wearing captain's bars walked over and held up Dallas's gun.

"This yours?"

"He was headed to the big show for sure." The deputy was panting but happy, acne scars flushed with blood.

"What's his name?"

Someone had his wallet out: "Dallas Graham Walker."

"This your firearm, Mr. Walker?"

Bloody spittle strung from Dallas's mouth and he spat at the man's feet. That distant gunfire. It had just occurred to him that his brother was up there somewhere.

The deputy shoved him in the back. "He asked you a question, asshole."

The captain shrugged. "Just keep him locked down till the Feds get here."

"The A-T-F," the deputy said. "You are fucked royally, my friend."

Dallas was leaned against the back tire of the ambulance, hands still tied behind him, legs spread slack before him. The chaos died and he sat feeling the tremor of pain that ran from his knee up his thigh and on to his jaw. It was a hard, stonelike pain, bone on bone, a grating that climbed him like a vine. But it was a good pain. If he could do nothing else he could at least hurt. He spat blood and listened to the squawk of radios. Out on the highway, cars were beginning to back up and turn around. Sirens blared. The helicopter he'd seen earlier circled, a little wasp of a machine tacked against the blue like a green star. A K-9 unit was just ahead and he could hear a bluetick howling in the back of a Ford Explorer, nails scraping the windows. Dallas shut his eyes. He couldn't feel his hands. Here was his war, all around him, and he couldn't feel his goddamn hands.

When he opened his eyes a man sat across from him, one arm in a sling, the other zip-tied to his ankle. His head floated above a yellow neck brace, one eye purple and swollen shut, so that it took Dallas a moment to recognize him as Shepherd Parsons and not an ugly inversion of his own face.

Parsons bent forward and his single good eye rolled in its socket. He had a small twig gripped in the hand bound to his ankle and he managed to cut two intersecting furrows in the dirt.

"Walker. You made it. Now look here," he whispered, his voice slurred and sliding off toward failure. "Pay attention. We don't have much time."

"What happened up there?"

"Shut up and listen to me," Parsons said.

"Is my brother up there?"

"Shut up and look here. This is the main runway. Over here is the terminal."

Parsons managed to put a rock at the intersection of the lines. Dallas looked at the rock, then over at the cops who were eating sandwiches, roast beefs out of an Arby's bag someone had delivered. Behind them grazed Herefords, a wide green pasture he'd somehow failed to notice.

"You met him before," Dallas said. "Malcolm Walker."

"Pay attention to the terminal."

"What terminal?"

Parsons pointed at the rock. "First Battalion is all along this line. The snipers are in the minarets."

"Parsons—"

"Those fucking hajjis."

Dallas leaned back, understanding, just as one of the cops started walking over.

"Here's an aid station," Parsons whispered. "Over here, a few civilians have been hit. Things get ugly but we drop a JDAM here."

"Hey," the cop called. "No talking."

"This is a war," Parsons slurred.

"I don't give a shit if it's halftime of the Super Bowl. Captain said for y'all not to be talking." The cop had the Arby's bag cradled in one arm. "Look here. Y'all hungry?"

"We need to put those minarets downrange," Parsons said.

"He got hit in the head too damn hard," the man told Dallas. "Sunday," he said turning to Parsons. "You boys couldn't keep just one day holy?"

"Tell your captain to put fire on the minarets."

The cop shook his head and turned to Dallas. "Captain said to offer you something. Looks like the rest of your boys turned chickenshit and ran, but it might be a while yet."

"Tell your captain to put those hajjis downrange."

"You want something or not?" the cop asked Dallas.

Dallas looked down at his feet and the man left them. When he looked again at Parsons he saw that one side of his face had collapsed, his single eye clouded and unseeing. He had a scar Dallas had never noticed, barely visible through the neck brace, a waxy sandbar that paralleled his jugular like a waking dream. He looked very old and very broken and all at once Dallas knew this was coming for him as well, not war but old age, not glory but decrepitude, his life a bright stone that had smoldered but would ultimately fail. A bad marriage, a daughter he would never know. Me, he thought. Dallas Graham Walker. Athlete, land developer, failed ascetic. Like his father: a defeated man.

Miles tied him to a chair in the front room. It was the same room where Malcolm had seen Mildred Carter and little seemed to have changed, the wool couch, the splintered paneling. The Confederate flag was gone but the Japanese sword still hung above the table of skulls. He heard muffled gunfire and the insistent wailing of dogs being burned alive and knew he needed to focus. He tried to breathe but his heart spiraled and he found himself surprised by the motion. He hadn't thought it could do that, turning so, revolving, a new little trick. Or maybe a last trick. He was crashing and looked around for the child. He didn't want the child watching.

"Sit still," Miles said, and disappeared through the interior door.

He came back with Leighton Clatter, a pump shotgun in one of the doctor's arms, Malcolm's bag in the other. The good doctor shirtless and fat, his gut snowy with curls of white hair, his legs bound in red running tights.

"Well, look at you," Leighton said, and touched the lapel of Malcolm's jacket, "all dressed for success."

"Exactly what I told you," Miles said.

Leighton reached into the backpack, took out the last bottle of Ripped Fuel and studied the label. "These are terrible for you, probably banned too."

"Dallas must still have a case or two."

"Well, Dallas of all people should know better." Leighton tightened the cap and returned the bottle, zippered shut the bag. "Malcolm, Malcolm, Malcolm," he said. "You're of a certain age, my friend. A hair too old to be walking round all jacked up on ephedrine, gun in your pants."

"Bring her out, Leighton." Malcolm kept his voice level.

Leighton's stomach lurched over the tights like a bundle of sewn flesh, white skin crossed with capillaries and purple veins. He rubbed his matted chest and smiled. He had dyed his hair to an oily black sheen and seemed greatly pleased. "Making demands and shit," he said. "I like that. All cool as the other side of the pillow. But do try to be serious."

"Bring her out here and we'll go."

"Go where?" Leighton said. "Did Richard here not tell you the *federales* have us surrounded? I suppose the sensible ones left last night—they should be in Guadalajara by now—but not us, we're the true believers, aren't we, Malcolm?"

"Just bring her out."

Leighton turned contemplative. "You know, I guess I have been waiting on you. I suppose on some level I've known all along we'd wind up here."

"Jordan?" Malcolm called. "Jordan?"

Leighton turned toward the door, cupped his ear, and smiled. "Jordan," he mocked. "Jordan." He turned to Miles. "Cut him loose, Rick."

"I don't think so."

"Cut him loose and get the fuck out of here. I thought you were itching to shimmy south."

"You better get Shep on the two-way first," Miles said.

"Shep'll be up soon enough," Leighton said. "I'll give your regards."

"I don't think you got that kind of time, partner."

"Get out of here, Rick."

"Trust me, brother. I'm just about to."

"And yet you're standing there," Leighton said, "fucking up my view. Cut him loose."

Miles moved his eyes from Malcolm to Leighton, removed a clasp knife from his pocket and cut the bungee from Malcolm's wrists and ankles. He took the sword mounted on the wall and tucked it beneath his arm. "You dumb hick," he said, "they'll have a SWAT team here in half an hour, every last one of them gunning to cap your ass. You're getting the apocalypse you wanted."

Leighton shook his head. "No, no apocalypse, baby. Just a fucked-up planet. Another billion years of it."

Miles seemed to concede this with a shrug. "Either way," he said.

"And here," Leighton said, "I thought you were on your way out."

Miles put his hand on the door. "Yeah," he said. "Still, it's shittier than I remembered. It's supposed to sparkle."

"Never. That's just the way they sell it on TV."

He opened the door so that a triangle of light flooded the room. In the distance was gunfire and—Malcolm was almost certain—the low whir of a helicopter. "You hear that?" Miles said. "They won't take Shep alive."

"Shut the door, Rick."

"Gladly," Miles said. "*Vive la Muerte,* motherfucker."

They listened to his footsteps and then the sudden growl and thump of a four-wheeler starting. Malcolm sat in the chair and rubbed his wrists. Leighton had the shotgun pointed at his chest.

"Bring her out here," Malcolm said.

"Stay in the chair," Leighton said, and backpedaled to swing open the interior door.

Malcolm stood and Leighton raised the shotgun.

"Whoa, now, what did I just say? You need to sit down, player."

"Malcolm?" Jordan was in the door now, hair dyed the same black as Leighton's.

"Sit," Leighton said, "down."

Malcolm looked at her and eased into the chair. Across the room the child bent forward, touched his right sock, and nodded. Malcolm understood, and let his own hands dangle. The boy's destroyed face attempted a smile. Then he began to speak. Leighton turned and Malcolm had the knife out before he could notice.

"Malcolm," Jordan said.

Leighton flinched, took a half-step back, and put the shotgun's stock against his shoulder. "Put it down," he said.

Malcolm raised the blade. "This is all over."

"Fucking put the knife down," Leighton said, "before I have to call someone to fix the drywall."

"Get your things together," Malcolm said.

Jordan stood there while Leighton wagged the gun in Malcolm's face.

"Malcolm," she said, "please."

"Put the fucking knife down," Leighton said. Malcolm could see sweat bead his forehead. "Put it down, Malcolm. I promise you: I will shoot your ass dead. Are you fucking listening?"

And he was, but it was not to Leighton Clatter. What he heard was softer, the voice of the child, inarticulate but beautiful, the child speaking at last, and when Malcolm came forward with the knife he felt the child's words fit to his shape like river stones worn smooth by the current. He had been waiting all his life to hear them and wanted only to tell her, because she had been waiting, too. They were the same—he knew it now. If they walked out—*when* they walked out—they would change. There was so much beauty in the world, so much terror, too, but it was the beauty that was incomprehensible, the beauty that he had missed. But he was free now, they were free, and he would tell her and they would walk out the door beneath the dome of heaven and start over, love each other, cling. That was the child's message: *you're free.* Dear Jordan, we're—but before he could finish the thought she screamed and then her scream was obliterated by the explosion of the shotgun, and Malcolm staggered, awash in warm heat and the erasure of that heat, the erasure of all sound.

This is over, he wanted to tell her. You're free. We're free.

And though he was falling, he fixed his eyes on her so that she might see and so that she might understand, so that they all might understand: his father and brother and uncle, his dear dead mother. Will and Mary Ann. For they were all suspended before him, as bodiless as he was broken, and he stared back as the light paled and exhausted so that only his eyes held life. But that was all right. He knew his eyes would be enough. If your eyes are sound, your whole body will be full of light.

ACKNOWLEDGMENTS

Heartfelt thanks to: Gene Adair, Amy Blackmarr, Alex Boldizar, Rand Brandes and the visiting writer program at Lenoir-Rhyne College, Craig Brandhorst, George Brosi and everyone at *Appalachian Heritage*, Casey Clabough, Beverly Coyle, Johnny Damm, Spencer Deck, Chris Doucot, Pete Duval, the Reverend Dr. Art Farlowe, Tom Farrell, Larry Friedes, Silas House, Tracy Haisley, Bill Koon, Denton Loving, Donna McClanahan, Mike Mullins, Donald Ray Pollock, Ron Rash, Jon Sealy, Lindsey Satterfield, Simmons, George Singleton, Dave Shull, Jon Sternfeld, Kerry Webb, Charles Dodd White, Randall Wilhelm, Dave Winfrey, Terri Witek; and all the good people at the Appalachian Writers' Workshop, the Collegeville Center for Ecumenical Research, Stetson University, and the University of Tennessee Press.

Thanks to my patient and tolerant family. I'm glad we all choose to live on porch time.

And, of course, Denise: best friend and first reader.

The book Malcolm cannot recall is Ian McEwan's *Atonement*.